"A taut, ori[...]own."

[...]or of *Below*

PRAISE FOR OTHER NOVELS
BY ROBERT J. MRAZEK

"Great writing . . . great history."
—Nelson DeMille, #1 *New York Times*
bestselling author of *The Quest*

"A priceless novel . . . a must-read book . . . a great
tale." —*The Washington Times*

"A novel of suspense and intrigue woven into the fabric
of . . . history." —*The Atlanta Journal-Constitution*

"A superb piece of literature, rich in texture and of sur-
passing literary merit."
—Robert K. Krick, author of
Stonewall Jackson at Cedar Mountain and *Lee's Colonels*

"A rattling good adventure story."
—James M. McPherson, Pulitzer Prize–winning
author of *War on the Waters*

"A simple tale almost magically rendered."
—*The Denver Post*

"A rare find: a book that successfully combines mystery,
historical drama, and impressive wartime verisimilitude . . .
stark, graphic, bloody, and exciting."
—*Publishers Weekly*

"A fast-paced thriller laced with violence and filled with
unexpected twists that keep the reader guessing to the
last page." —Rennie Airth, author of *River of Darkness*

continued . . .

"A first-rate World War II adventure."
—Susan Isaacs, *New York Times* bestselling
author of *Goldberg Variations*

"Tautly gripping, with vividly malevolent characters and some excellent historical color." —*Kirkus Reviews*

"[An] exciting thriller." —Historical Novel Society

"Full of dark twists and turns, this brooding drama underscores the brutal nature of both the physical and the psychological casualties associated with war." —*Booklist*

PRAISE FOR
ROBERT J. MRAZEK'S
MILITARY NONFICTION

TO KINGDOM COME

"Riveting." —*Library Journal*

"A great book with 'hold on to your seat' suspense."
—Donald Miller, author of *Masters of the
Air: America's Bombers Who Fought the
Air War Against Nazi Germany*

"Rendered . . . in vivid clarity."
—Hugh Ambrose, *New York Times* bestselling
author of *The Pacific*

"[A] work of cinematic sweep and pace."
—Richard B. Frank,
author of *Downfall* and *Guadalcanal*

"Superb historical research and powerful narrative writing."
   —Tami Biddle, professor, U.S. Army War College, and
            author of *Rhetoric and Reality in Air Warfare*

A DAWN LIKE THUNDER

"Strap yourself in as Robert Mrazek takes you on a heroic flight into history."
                        —James Bradley,
            author of *Flyboys* and *Flags of Our Fathers*

"A spectacular achievement."
            —Hon. Charles Wilson of *Charlie Wilson's War*

"A remarkably vivid tale . . . [an] epic story."
                  —Rick Atkinson, author of *The Guns
                     at Last Light* and *The Day of Battle*

"Destined to become a classic."
                  —Alex Kershaw, author of *The Liberator*
                        and *The Longest Winter*

"Fast-paced. . . . [Mrazek] melds a good story with solid and skeptical research."   —*The Washington Post*

"A must read . . . gripping."
                        —Curled Up with a Good Book

"Robert Mrazek has, with a raw, unsparing telling, given grace and life to so many who died so young . . . so gallantly."   —Frank Deford, author of *Over Time*

"Compelling."   —*The Columbus Dispatch*

Also by Robert J. Mrazek

Valhalla

THE
BONE
HUNTERS

ROBERT J.
MRAZEK

A SIGNET BOOK

SIGNET
Published by New American Library,
an imprint of Penguin Random House LLC
375 Hudson Street, New York, New York 10014

This book is an original publication of New American Library.

First Printing, December 2015

For more information about Penguin Random House, visit penguin.com.

ISBN 978-0-451-46873-4

Printed in the United States of America
10   9   8   7   6   5   4   3   2

Penguin
Random
House

To Susannah, James, and Ilse Rose

AUTHOR'S NOTE

In 1928, an archaeological expedition led by Austrian paleontologist Otto Zdansky unearthed a human fossil specimen at an excavation in Zhoukoudian, China, a prehistoric cave system thirty miles southwest of Peking. Paleontologists later estimated that the fossil had lain buried and undiscovered there for about 780,000 years.

The Peking Man, as the fossil was called, was generally viewed to be the earliest living example of *Homo erectus*, the first man to stand erect and use primitive tools. It was and is considered to be one of the most important fossil discoveries in the history of human evolution.

Concern for the protection and preservation of Peking Man began to mount after the Japanese invaded China in 1937. The fossil was moved from the site of its discovery in Zhoukoudian to the Peking Union Medical College, which had been founded by the American Rockefeller Foundation. At that time, the Japanese army was still respecting the assets of foreign interests in the country.

In late 1941, a request was made to the American ambassador, Nelson T. Johnson, for Peking Man to be sent to the United States until its security could be guaranteed inside China.

After some delay, the request was approved. A few days

before the Japanese army entered Peking, the Peking Man fossils were sealed inside airtight glass containers and carefully packed in two wooden crates.

On December 8, 1941 (Chinese time), Japanese officials arrived at the medical college and demanded the turnover of the Peking Man fossils. The Japanese then ordered medical staff members to open the locked safe in the anatomy building in which the fossils had been stored.

The Peking Man was not there. He remains missing to this day.

Monday, 8 December 1941
Chinwangtao Trunk Road
Quipao, China

It was one of the two darkest nights Corporal Sean Patrick Morrissey could ever remember.

The other one had been during that long winter in the Upper Michigan Peninsula after his stepfather had gotten the job as a watchman for the lumber company and the family had lived in a one-room shack near the Two Hearted River. Sean had been a skinny twelve-year-old back then. Now he was almost eighteen, tall, strapping, and a China marine, riding shotgun in the first truck in the military convoy. Beside him, Gunnery Sergeant James Donald "J.D." Bradshaw was driving.

"It's going to be a long night, kid," J.D. said, taking off his felt campaign hat, with its pinched Montana crease, and laying it carefully on the bench seat next to him.

Reaching under the seat, he pulled out a dimpled bottle of Haig & Haig and handed it to Sean. The youngster took a healthy swig and felt it race like fire down his throat.

J.D. was one of the old breed. Three tours in China since 1928 and he spoke Chinese fluently. At thirty-six, he was old enough to be Sean's father, and his crew cut had faded to pure white.

Over the previous year, he had played that role better than Sean's real father, not to mention the two stepfathers who came after him. J.D.'s homely, acne-scarred face always seemed to be smiling, at least when he was around Sean.

It was J.D.'s example that had made Sean proud to be a China marine, proud of its traditions in this faraway place and proud of the way the marines were respected by just about everyone in the Far East—except the Japanese.

Back at Parris Island, the drill instructors had described the Japanese as little men with buckteeth and Coke bottle eyeglasses whom you could knock over with a soupspoon. J.D. told Sean not to bet on it, not after the way they had whaled on the Chinese army in one battle after another for the past three years. Now the Japanese army was on the move, and everybody else seemed to be on the move too, trying to get away from the Japanese. No one knew where they would strike next.

Sean felt better having the Colt 1911A1 .45-caliber pistol in his hip holster and the Thompson M1928A1 .45-caliber submachine gun sitting snug on his lap. Three spare twenty-shot magazines lay next to him along with a satchel of fragmentation grenades.

A few days earlier, the dependents of the American military officers, diplomatic officials, businessmen, and correspondents had embarked on a train for Shanghai.

Only the embassy guards and a small detachment of marines remained behind in the legation compound.

Captain Theo Allen commanded the marine detachment. With pale blue eyes behind wire-rimmed glasses, he reminded Sean of his mild-looking high school English teacher, but according to J.D., Captain Allen was one of the toughest men in the outfit and an expert in hand-to-hand combat.

That morning the captain had received a cable from Fourth Marine headquarters up north at Camp Holcomb to assemble a small truck convoy and stand by for further orders. Two recently repaired Studebaker trucks were brought to the compound from the depleted motor pool. Captain Allen would lead them in his staff car.

All three vehicles were painted the same flat green with the letters USMC stenciled on the doors in black paint. Canvas roofs lashed to metal struts covered the freight beds of the one-and-a-half-ton trucks.

Late in the afternoon, Captain Allen received his orders and the convoy departed from the legation compound with nine marines aboard. One rode with Captain Allen in the staff car, and the other eight were divided into each truck.

As always, Sean was entranced by the crazy mix of sounds and smells that filled the ancient city. The streets were choked with people and animals, and the air was alive with the chants and clappers of the street musicians, the aroma of spicy foods wafting from street stalls, and the stench of the open sewers that carried along rotting fish and animal dung. Radios blared in Chinese from the open doorways of the shops and eating places.

The convoy made a long, slow, circuitous route across

the city before the captain's staff car swung left off a crowded thoroughfare and passed through a pair of towering stone gates that flanked the high stone walls of a large compound. Sean saw the words PEKING UNION MEDICAL COLLEGE engraved over the entranceway.

The street noise receded as soon as they were inside. Up ahead of them, an elderly white man was standing outside the main building in a brick-paved courtyard. He was surrounded by a dozen Chinese coolies. It was obvious he had been waiting for them.

Before Captain Allen's car rolled to a stop, the old man began limping toward it with the aid of a long walking stick. He was wearing an old-fashioned tweed suit with a white shirt and a bow tie. Spectacles were perched on the long nose of his horsey face.

When Captain Allen emerged from the Studebaker, the old man began speaking English to him in a singsong voice, as if he was more used to speaking Chinese than English.

"We are ready," he said. "You must hurry."

Sean heard a boom of what sounded like distant thunder.

"Long-range Jap artillery," said J.D. as the noise became a low constant rumble.

That was when Sean saw the two big wooden crates sitting on the brick courtyard behind the first row of coolies. Each was the size of a large refrigerator. One was painted bright Chinese red, and the second was raw teak.

Speaking Chinese, Captain Allen directed the coolies to put one crate in the back of each truck. There were Chinese symbols painted in black on the red one they put in Sean and J.D.'s truck.

Captain Allen gathered the detachment around him.

"I can't tell you what is in those crates, because I don't know," he said. "Whatever is in there is important and our orders are to see they arrive at Chinwangtao, the seaport next to Camp Holcomb. When we get there, the S.S. *President Harrison* will be waiting for them. It's the last American liner still in China."

Sean felt a surge of excitement. At seventeen, he had never felt true fear.

"It's about two hundred miles to get there," the captain added. "We'll drive all night and make just one stop to refuel. Gas cans are lashed in the back of the trucks. You should know that Japanese troops might already have cut the road in several places, so be vigilant at all times."

When he dismissed them, J.D. taped strips of white surgical tape over the headlights on all three vehicles to reduce their visibility. Captain Allen inspected the two marines in the back of each truck and made sure they were armed with .30-06 Browning Automatic Rifles and a supply of twenty-round magazines.

When they started the engines and prepared to move out, the old man in the tweed suit called out to Captain Allen from the edge of the courtyard. Tears were running down his cheeks.

"Guard them with your lives," he shouted in his singsong voice.

"Easy for him to say," said J.D., spitting tobacco juice through the open window as they rolled through the entrance and back onto the main road.

"What do you think is in the crates?" asked Sean.

"Not heavy enough for gold," said J.D. as he focused on maintaining the fifteen-foot distance between each vehicle ordered by Captain Allen, "but the red box is the important one."

"How do you know?" asked Sean.

"The Chinese lettering," said J.D., and Sean remembered he was fluent in the language.

The darkening sky to the west was still tinted with a reddish glow when they passed through the last gate on the edge of Peking and proceeded east along the trunk highway. The rumble of artillery fire slowly faded as they left the city farther behind.

At first the trunk road had a lightly macadamized surface, with two lanes running in both directions. After twenty miles, the roadway shrank to two lanes and went from macadam to rutted hardpan. The convoy was forced to slow down to thirty miles an hour.

Along the route, they passed thousands of Chinese refugees heading away from Peking in the freezing darkness. A few lucky ones were driving old charcoal-powered trucks and cars. Others rode in oxcarts, their personal goods and furniture piled around them. Sean even saw a rickshaw coolie trudging along in his long padded gown, hauling a family of four behind him.

Most of the refugees were on foot, straggling along in the middle of the road, oblivious of the blaring horns. More than a few lay along the sides, their dead bodies stripped naked.

A bitter Siberian wind began blowing from the north, and the surface of the road became a swirling mass of gray dust. It sent little tornadoes of fine powder through the cracks in the windows and filled their mouths with grit. J.D. passed Sean the bottle of Haig & Haig again.

The refugee traffic began to thin out as they headed

farther east. At one point, they saw a Rolls-Royce stopped along the side of the road, its engine pouring black smoke. A slender and pretty young woman in a blue silk dress was standing next to it, waving frantically for the convoy to stop, her face contorted with fear.

"Maybe we should stop," said Sean.

"Might as well stop for everyone," said J.D.

Sean pulled out his wallet with the dog-eared photograph of Cathy. She was standing in her father's backyard in Pontiac looking back at him with a shy smile. Cathy had written in November about how proud she was of his promotion to corporal. Her father was a foreman at the Chevy plant and didn't think Sean was worthy of her. He would think differently when Sean got back with his new stripes.

Rain began to fall when they were better than halfway to Camp Holcomb, the heavy downpour turning the dusty hardpan into a rutted mess. Glancing out the rain-streaked window into the darkness, Sean saw a few lights in the distance. They turned out to be a deserted train station along the Peking-Mugden Railway.

They had been driving more than five hours when the staff car slowed down and pulled over to the side of the road. It was nearly midnight. Captain Allen emerged from the passenger side and walked back toward them through the rain.

Sean lowered his window.

"Replenish your canteens while we gas up," he said, "and turn off your lights."

J.D. grinned as the captain went past, took another quick swig of the Haig & Haig, and passed the bottle to Sean. Sean heard the two marines behind them on the freight bed unleashing the gas cans to refill the tank.

A deserted rural village straddled both sides of the road around them in the shadowy darkness. Fenced animal pens rimmed the open spaces between a dozen clay-walled huts. There were no lights in the buildings. The animal pens were empty.

J.D. opened a large paper sack and pulled out a handful of Chinese raisins. Stuffing them in his mouth, he began chewing the fruit. Juice trickled down from the corners of his mouth to his chin.

"You take a leak first," he said, scanning the buildings, "and check the tires."

Leaving the satchel of fragmentation grenades on the seat, Sean took the Thompson and stepped down from the cab onto the muddy apron. After circling the truck to make sure the tire pressures were holding, he stopped by the front fender to relieve himself. While one of the two marines in the back poured gas into the tank, the other trained his BAR toward the closest line of huts.

Another marine moved between the trucks, refilling the men's canteens from a five-gallon GI can. Sean watched raindrops dripping off the edge of the brim of his campaign hat.

A dog began to bark. Its cries seemed to be coming from behind one of the buildings on the far side of the road. The dog stopped barking for a few seconds and then began again, more excited now.

Then the dog's cries stopped.

Sean pulled back the bolt on the Thompson and inserted a bullet into the magazine. A few moments later, a shadowy figure of a man emerged from one of the darkened buildings. The man was swaying a little as he headed toward the captain's staff car. Sean wondered for a moment if he was drunk. He saw that the man was carrying something in his hands. It appeared to be trailing smoke.

"A Jap mine," shouted J.D. "Hose him down."

Resting the butt of the Thompson against his arm, Sean pulled the trigger and fired a short burst. The bullets hammered into the man's chest, throwing him backward. Two seconds later, a huge explosion engulfed him and lit up the night.

Sean felt fragments of road gravel peppering his face like hard rain, and the air was filled with the reek of cordite. The driver's-side door of the staff car swung open and the marine driver climbed out, taking cover behind it.

"They're coming," he shouted, firing at one of the doorways with his .45-caliber pistol.

A Nambu machine gun opened up on them from the roof of one of the buildings. Tracer rounds flashed through the rain and hammered into the staff car and the windshield of their truck.

This is what it's all about, thought Sean Morrissey. It was really happening to him. Not what he had imagined from comic books or war movies. This was the real thing.

He heard the marines at the back of their truck begin to return fire with their BARs, momentarily silencing the enemy machine gun as more figures emerged from the dark buildings and began moving toward the convoy.

The driver of the captain's staff car started running back toward Sean's truck, ducking and weaving as he came. Muzzle flashes erupted from the ragged line of Japanese soldiers, and the marine went sprawling face forward. He didn't move again.

Using the hood of the truck for cover, Sean aimed the Thompson and pulled the trigger, this time firing a full magazine. Four enemy soldiers crumpled to the ground.

Replacing the magazine, he began firing in short bursts, three or four rounds at a time, as their return fire smashed the headlight next to his elbow and shattered the cab's windshield.

Another shadowy wave of soldiers emerged from the darkness of the houses. They came on together, running flat-footed with their legs spread wide. Sean saw one of them raise his arm and smack something loudly against his helmet.

Sean remembered that to arm Japanese grenades they had to be hit against a hard surface. He fired at the soldier as he prepared to hurl the grenade. The explosion dropped him and two others. One kept coming.

"Banzai . . . Banzai," he yelled.

He was the tallest Japanese Sean had ever seen, over six feet, and was waving a sword as he closed to within five feet of the truck. When Sean fired a longer burst, he stayed suspended for a few moments, dancing grotesquely as the bullets tore into his chest before he fell away.

Sean could now hear the BARs firing from the direction of the roadway behind the convoy. The Japanese were obviously trying to encircle them, attacking from both directions along the road.

He heard a loud moan from inside the cab of the truck. It had to be J.D. As Sean dove through the open passenger door, he felt a sharp stab of pain in his right arm. Glancing at the sleeve, he saw that a bullet had passed through the fleshy part of his shoulder.

J.D. was still sitting upright in the driver's seat behind

the shattered windshield. A shot from the Nambu machine gun had torn away his right eye. He was barely conscious and blood was puddling on the seat around him from another wound in his side. Sean dragged him out of the line of fire and laid him on the floor of the passenger-side. J.D.'s good eye briefly regained its focus.

"I'll be back," said Sean.

He dropped through the open passenger door and found a new firing position in the shallow drainage ditch that ran along the edge of the roadway. The wound in his arm was starting to throb as he reloaded another magazine.

The staff car was now on fire and the blaze from its gas tank illuminated the roadway ahead of the convoy. Dead Japanese lay all the way back to the darkened buildings. There were no more attackers, at least for the moment.

The firing was constant at the other end of the convoy. Out of the corner of his eye, Sean saw someone crawling toward him from that direction along the ditch. It was Captain Allen. There was a tourniquet around his thigh, and blood was flowing from a wound above his scalp.

"They've got us surrounded," he said through clenched teeth.

A Japanese soldier who had been lying beyond the staff car suddenly got to his feet and began charging toward them. His head was lowered to the ground as if he didn't want to know what was waiting for him. Sean cut him down with a single burst.

"Can you drive this truck?" said Captain Allen.

"Yessir," said Sean.

"Get the red crate to the port at Chinwangtao," he said. "The *President Harrison*."

"Yessir," said Sean.

Captain Allen took the Thompson from him and aimed it toward the nearest buildings.

"Go," he said.

Bullets from the Nambu machine gun thudded into the dirt in front of him as Sean rose from the ditch. A moment later, he was through the open passenger door and behind the wheel as Captain Allen returned suppressing fire at the machine gun position on the roof.

Ramming the gearshift into first, Sean engaged the clutch and the truck lurched forward. As it gained speed, machine gun bullets raked its side and the engine compartment. The truck kept going.

They had gone several miles when Sean slowed down and stopped again. They were in open country. He gently lifted J.D. back onto the seat and examined his wounds. The right eye was gone, but the bullet had only creased his skull. Sean placed a gauze bandage around the empty cavity. The bleeding from his chest wound had slowed to a trickle. Sean removed an ampoule of morphine from the truck's medical kit as J.D. grimaced at him through the pain.

"Don't want it," he said.

"I need to get you to a corpsman," said Sean.

J.D.'s left eye squeezed shut.

"Get to the port," he said. "We can't be more than a couple hours away."

If the road ahead is clear of Japs, thought Sean. He picked up the half-full bottle of Haig & Haig and tipped it toward J.D.'s mouth. The sergeant took several deep swallows before Sean poured another inch onto his wound.

"Let's go," J.D. growled.

Sean drove through the night repeating the same silent prayer. *Save him, Lord. Save him, Lord. Save him, Lord.* J.D.'s breathing got increasingly ragged. Each time they hit a mud-clogged rut in the roadway, the cab would shudder violently and J.D.'s hand would tighten convulsively on Sean's wounded right arm.

It was after three in the morning when Sean saw the lights of Chinwangtao in the distance. The always bustling city was nearly empty. As they drove through the streets, the quiet was unearthly. Sean didn't stop until they reached the piers where the big oceangoing ships had to dock.

When he was heading across the concrete jetty that led to the outlying piers, J.D. regained consciousness. Sean pointed out to him a small detachment of Chinese soldiers hauling bales of cotton toward the walls of two large warehouses.

"They're setting fire to the port," said J.D. "The Japs must be close."

Sean drove down the length of the last pier. All the ship's berths were empty until he reached the end of the wharf. A darkened ship slowly materialized out of the gloom. Sean could see Chinese coolies rolling oil drums up the gangway to the forward deck. Far above them on the bridge, an officer was yelling down to the men on the dock and waving his arms in a circular motion.

"They're pulling out," said J.D. "I can't see the name of the ship."

Sean got out of the truck and ran to the edge of the gangway.

"Is this the *President Harrison*?" he yelled up to the officer on the bridge.

The man looked down at him and laughed.

"I hear she vas sunk by de Japs," he said in a thick European accent. "This the *Prins Willem*."

The *Prins Willem* was obviously an old coast runner. It stank of leaking fuel, and reddish stains streaked the once-white paint on the superstructure. The hull plates were covered with huge patches of rust. Sean didn't know much about ships, but this one didn't look as if it could make it out of the harbor.

"Ve leaf now . . . Jap here anytime," the officer called out.

His crewmen began hauling in the mooring lines.

"There is something real important in that truck," yelled Sean as the ship slowly began to edge away from the pier. "Can you take us with you?"

"Vat is it?" demanded the officer.

"I don't know, but they don't want the Japs to get it," he called out.

The officer stared at him for several seconds. Then he waved to the half dozen coolies who were still standing on the dock. When he called out something in Chinese, they ran to the truck, dropped the rear gate, and swarmed aboard.

Sean watched as the red crate was hauled across the dock to the gangway and then up to the deck of the ship. He could see it was punctured with bullet holes and he wondered if what was inside had been destroyed.

"Are you coming?" asked the officer.

Sean ran back to the cab of the truck and opened the passenger door. J.D. was sitting there in the same upright position. For a moment Sean wondered if he was still alive.

Suddenly, he heard the sound of gunfire from farther down the pier. In the garish light from the burning warehouses, a Japanese motorized detachment was heading swiftly across the concrete jetty. He watched it turn onto the pier and accelerate toward them. Behind him, he heard the lines being cast off. The gangway was still attached to the pier as the ship began to pull away from the dock.

"We have to go, J.D.," he said, reaching to move him out of the seat. "The Japs are here."

"I ain't goin'," said J.D.

Sean looked down and saw the pile of fragmentation grenades sitting on his lap. J.D. had removed them all from the canvas sack. Sean glanced back toward the departing ship. Its metal gangway was trailing along behind it, the end still barely attached to the dock.

"Go," yelled J.D.

Sean ran toward the gangway, which was already separated by two feet of black water. He leaped for it and managed to land on the bottom rung. As he began climbing toward the deck, he looked back to see the first Japanese armored car in the motorized detachment pull to a stop next to J.D.'s truck.

Behind it came a light tank. Blocked by the truck, the tank's gun turret swung smoothly toward the retreating cargo ship and opened fire. The first round from its 37 mm gun slammed into the stern of the *Prins Willem*, opening a four-foot jagged hole in the hull plates.

His fingers working in their familiar rhythm, J.D. Bradshaw began pulling the pins from the grenades on his lap. As he finished the task, the passenger door swung open and a squat Japanese officer with gold teeth pointed a pistol at him.

"Welcome to hell," said Bradshaw before the massive detonation erased the end of the pier.

ONE

5 May
Bellamy Annex
The Long Wharf
Boston, Massachusetts

It had turned out all right after all, thought Dr. Barnaby Finchem.

Astrud was originally from Norway, but after coming to Boston as a doctoral exchange student, she had become a devoted citizen of the Red Sox nation. One of her cherished fantasies was to sit in the first row of seats next to the Pesky Pole in right field. Barnaby had acquired tickets from a Harvard colleague who owed him his tenure.

Barnaby had then endured four innings of the actual game, his six-and-a-half-foot and three-hundred-pound slab crammed into a plastic seat designed for Tom Thumb. Their seats faced the Green Monster across the outfield, and the only way Barnaby could see the batter's box was to lean forward over the railing and crane his neck around the person one seat closer to home plate.

Of course, everyone near the Pesky Pole was leaning forward and craning their necks as well. In the second inning an inebriated fan in the row behind him started harassing him over his free-flowing mane of snow-white hair.

"Hey, Medusa, you're blockin' the whole goddamn outfield," the fan called out, generating laughter from the morons around him. Barnaby turned around. The man was as bald as a cue ball.

"Jealousy is no excuse for stupidity," he retorted.

From there the man's comments had become increasingly obscene.

It had all mercifully ended when the Red Sox pitcher gave up a fly ball that sailed wide toward the Pesky Pole and straight toward Barnaby. An obese woman in the seat behind him rammed him forward over the railing in her zeal to catch the ball. After a stern warning about lifetime banishment from Red Sox security, he and Astrud were escorted to the nearest exit gate. Thankfully, she hadn't blamed him for the fiasco.

In the cab going back to Cambridge, she had become increasingly solicitous, at first stroking his sore knee before her supple fingers slowly moved up his thigh. When they hit a traffic logjam near the Longfellow Bridge, Barnaby decided on the spur of the moment to bring her to his secret lair on the Long Wharf, which was only a few blocks away.

Now, as he was approaching seventy, Barnaby's past two heart attacks had forced him to severely curb his libido. He now took pride in a strict regimen of never attempting to seduce one of his doctoral students. Only if one of them seduced him, and she was unbearably desirable, would he allow his defenses to be breached.

Astrud met the standard.

He had met her at an academic competition for Norse scholars organized by one of his colleagues in the archaeology department. Barnaby now taught only one course, the Origins of Civilization lecture series, and it was harder to get into his course than the seats by the Pesky Pole.

Nine doctoral candidates were in the academic competition. As the star of the archaeology faculty, Barnaby had been chosen to chair the jury. His life achievements were legend.

After achieving first-class honors at Cambridge, the expatriate Englishman had spent forty years becoming the foremost expert on Norse culture and language in the world. There had been other candidates for that honor, but they were now dead, including a man he was forced to kill a year earlier.

Each student in the academic competition had been charged with the task of creating an original depiction of ancient Norse life. Three of them were triumphs of vision and inspiration, magnificently rendered, deeply felt, and intuitively recreated, projects that resonated within Barnaby's own carefully nurtured imagination. Five of the remaining projects were less than brilliant. And then there was Astrud's.

In her primitive oil painting, she had imagined a fifth-century Norse funeral scene in which a young woman lay in a wooden bier, her white-clad body covered with wildflowers. Historically, he knew it had absolutely no connection to Norse life, but the face was indelibly lovely surrounded by its helmet of blond hair. Looking at it, he realized it was a self-portrait of the doctoral student standing beside him, the artist herself.

"How did you research the context for this funeral scene?" he found himself asking her. "We have no evidence of how a Norse funeral was conducted in the fifth century."

"I imagined it, Dr. Finchem," she said, gazing up at him with those exquisite blue eyes.

By all that was holy, he knew he could not vote for her project, but when the competition was over, she expressed no disappointment at all when she came up to him at the reception.

"Just meeting you, Dr. Finchem, has been the greatest thrill of my life," she said.

He felt his resistance melting away.

Twenty minutes after leaving the Red Sox game, he was unlocking the great steel door that led into his lair on the Long Wharf. He turned on the overhead lights in the single massive chamber.

About fifty feet by fifty feet, it had twenty-foot-high ceilings and rough-hewn oak beams that braced the whole expanse. The windows overlooking the harbor were clad with iron shutters.

The first section of the chamber included a fully equipped laboratory with all the assets necessary for both an archaeologist and a pathologist, including a computer lab, printers, cameras, recorders, and flat-screen television monitors.

Astrud was nearly overcome with emotion in the second area of the chamber. It was Barnaby's Norse library, with documents, diaries, old vellum manuscripts and rune tablets going back twelve centuries. On the wall she saw a hint of his vast collection of Viking swords, tools, shields, and knives.

The final section was his living area, which included an expansive kitchen. Copper pots and pans hung from an iron rack above commercial appliances and granite countertops.

"I like to cook," he said.

Her eyes wandered away from the kitchen to the nearby elevated sleeping loft, which was constructed from raw timbers and covered with animal pelts and sheepskin rugs.

"A tenth-century Viking sleeping pallet," said Astrud observantly. "I've always wondered if they would have been comfortable while sleeping in the nude. . . . How would you research that, Dr. Finchem?"

They came together on the pallet. Barnaby no longer cared whether his students bedded him for his brains, his fame, his marking pen, or his ability to further their career. At sixty-nine, he still loved the feel and touch of a beautiful woman without having to pay her alimony. He had been down that road more than once.

The only impediment to his anticipated pleasure was buried inside his upper chest. It was an implanted cardioverter defibrillator, or ICD, which he had been assured by his doctors would correct most life-threatening cardiac arrhythmias after the last heart attack.

The ICD had never met Astrud.

When they had finished, he turned wearily onto his back and stretched out his six-and-a-half-foot frame. It had been good, very good. He was falling into a deep sleep when the cell phone he had left on the kitchen counter began to ring.

It was a new phone, and he had set the ring tone to the cries of a flock of seagulls, the least obnoxious tone on the list. He had not bothered to set a ring limit before it went to an answering message, and the cawing went on and on. After two minutes of the shrieking cries, the gulls sounded as if they were coming to eat him alive.

No one except Astrud knew the new number, and she was lying insensate next to him in the Viking pallet. But what if she had shared it with someone else? That was the likeliest possibility. What had seemed like such a good decision in the cab was probably going to be a grave mistake, he decided. If she was that indiscreet, he needed to gently but firmly disengage.

When the gulls finally stopped, he realized he was desperately hungry. He had avoided the "Green Monster dog" in the concession stand at the baseball park, and the lovemaking had added to his appetite. In his mind's eye, he contemplated the array of superb meals he had prepared and were now frozen in the big Viking refrigerator.

One of them was a classic Norse wine stew, savory chunks of venison and imported wild boar slow-cooked in a tureen of Swedish truffles, carrots, and onions. He had found the recipe in a rune parchment from the eleventh century. Heading down to the kitchen, he brought it out to defrost.

When the delicious aroma began to permeate the living area, Astrud descended from the pallet wearing one of his Abercrombie & Fitch flaming red flannel shirts. It ended becomingly at her thighs and set off her naturally flaxen hair. He decided to hold off confronting her about giving out his cell phone number.

After pouring her a glass of Castello Banfi's 2010 Centine, he removed a loaf of shard bread from the oven and they sat down to enjoy the feast. They were finishing the second bottle of wine when Barnaby broached the noble idea that it might be a good decision for her to find a worthy man no older than her father. A moment later she was clinging to him again like a limpet mine, her sweet mouth on his.

After another session on the sleeping pallet, he knew how a sled dog felt approaching the finish line at the Iditarod. He was finally falling asleep again when the carnivorous seagulls began to shriek again.

"Aren't you going to answer it?" she asked with that remaining echo of her native Norwegian accent.

"No one aside from you has the number, Astrud," he said in a less than fatherly baritone.

"I haven't given it to another soul," she said, her eyes going liquid.

The ringing stopped again and he waited in the silence for it to resume. Instead, someone began knocking on the steel entrance door. The pounding echoed through the chamber.

"For the love of Thor," Barnaby growled.

Planning to verbally lash whoever it was standing in the hallway, he climbed off the sleeping pallet and stalked naked to the door. Putting his nose against the glass peephole, he looked out into the shadowy passageway and frowned.

TWO

A man with the torso of a sumo wrestler gone to seed was standing in the brick-lined corridor sweating as if he had just run a marathon. His face was drenched, along with the collar of his blue oxford shirt.

The last time Barnaby had seen him was in a hospital room in Rockland, Maine. It was the day after his protégée Alexandra Vaughan had discovered the burial tomb of Leif Eriksson on an island off the coast of Maine. And it was after enough murder and mayhem to last Barnaby for ten lifetimes. Back then, the man in the corridor had been the deputy national security adviser to the president of the United States.

"I know you're in there, Dr. Finchem," called out Ira Dusenberry. "Let me in. It's very important."

Time had not been kind to him since. He had put on

at least thirty pounds, and his blunt, jowly face had the patina of painter's putty. His brown suit was stretched across his torso like a gigantic sausage casing.

Barnaby suddenly realized that his new cell phone number hadn't been given out by Astrud. It had been hacked by one of the intelligence minions of the all-knowing Big Brother called Washington. They could find out everything about any American they targeted. It made him angry to be on their radar again.

Barnaby unlocked the door and swung it open. Ira Dusenberry took in the full spectacle of his nakedness and immediately averted his eyes.

"I don't need to ask how you found this place," said Barnaby bitterly. "With your untrammeled domestic spying network, you know all our secrets these days, the guilty and the innocent."

"Not all of them," said Dusenberry, "and it wasn't easy. We had to use extraordinary measures."

He still could not force himself to look at Barnaby.

"Is that really necessary?" he finally demanded, stepping past him into the chamber. Barnaby closed the door and locked it again.

"Only if it irritates a dishonest excuse for a public servant like you," said Barnaby.

"I am not dishonest," Dusenberry said indignantly.

"Really . . . ? Last year we made the greatest archaeological discovery since Howard Carter blundered into Tut's tomb in the Valley of the Kings," said Barnaby. "We proved that Leif Eriksson got to these shores five hundred years before Columbus and you decided to sit on it in the name of national security."

"It *was* a matter of national security," said Dusenberry, still refusing to look at him.

Walking to the ornately carved oak hall tree next to the steel entrance door, Barnaby grabbed the Moroccan *jeleba* from his Sahara expedition and wrapped it around himself.

"National security as defined by the Italian-American vote in the last election," said Barnaby.

Dusenberry didn't respond.

"Now that the president has won reelection, you should have no concerns about our announcing the discovery."

"Perhaps that could be arranged," said Dusenberry with a curt smile, "if you can provide assistance to us on a far more important matter."

He glanced around the vast expanse of the chamber.

"Are we alone?" he asked.

"You should know," Barnaby responded, walking back toward the living area.

Astrud emerged from the sleeping loft and came downstairs. She was fully dressed in her Red Sox jersey, shorts, and sneakers, looking even younger than her thirty-one years.

"I think I've seen you on television," she said to Dusenberry.

His eyes betrayed a hint of satisfaction at her recognition of his important role in the White House.

"You're one of the contestants on that reality fat show, correct?" she said, smiling. "The one about how much weight you can lose without killing yourself?"

Dusenberry didn't know if she was serious. "If you leave now, young lady, you will probably not be indicted

THE BONE HUNTERS 27

as a threat to the national security of the United States of America."

"I was leaving anyway," she said.

She turned and looked up at Barnaby.

"I'll see you later," she said, taking her purse and closing the steel door behind her.

"In addition to all your other sins," said Barnaby, "you may have ruptured one of the great romantic relationships of this century."

"I need your help," said Dusenberry. "The president needs your help."

"I don't do mental counseling," said Barnaby.

Dusenberry ignored the barb and said, "Look, I'm sorry about this. I was planning to meet you at Fenway Park, but you were thrown out of the game before I could get there."

Barnaby had already noticed the brown mustard stains on his shirt and tie.

"How many monster dogs did you eat?" he asked.

Dusenberry's face revealed the accuracy of his guess. In fact, he had consumed three of the eighteen-inchers with sauerkraut and mustard, flushing them down with drafts of ice-cold lager. Gluttony was his only sin, he kept assuring himself.

"Can we sit down?" he asked, turning away from Barnaby to loosen his trousers while he headed for the nearest club chair in Barnaby's library next to the open kitchen.

Barnaby sank into the leather couch across from him.

"Have you ever heard of Peking Man?" said Dusenberry.

"He was once the most valuable man on earth," said Barnaby.

"Was?" asked Dusenberry.

"He disappeared."

"Precisely. You already know about him."

"Every archaeologist knows about him," said Barnaby. "His disappearance was probably the biggest disaster in the history of the fossil record of human evolution."

"We need to find it . . . him," said Dusenberry. "It's a matter of the highest national security."

"It always is to you," said Barnaby.

"He isn't just a priceless fossil," said Dusenberry. "Have you ever heard of Falun Gong?"

"There are few things I haven't heard of in this world, but that is one of them."

"Falun Gong is a contemporary Chinese moral philosophy in the qigong tradition. It is based on truth, compassion, and tolerance."

"The Tibetans tried that and look where it got them," said Barnaby. "Good luck in China."

"Actually, Falun Gong was founded by a Chinese trumpet player named Li Hongzhi in 1992, and the religion took off like a comet. His followers call him the living Buddha. He now lives in Arizona."

"A trumpet player," repeated Barnaby.

"Yes, from humble origins, we might say, as was the carpenter from Galilee," said Dusenberry. "Of course, he has to live here now or he would be rotting in a Chinese prison. Their government is bent on eradicating it. They have used every means to crush it. We have reports of thousands of atrocities, including the torture, murder, and even organ harvesting of its followers. A million of the followers have been forced into reeducation camps like the ones set up under Mao during the great purge."

"How does Peking Man fit into it?"

"There is a new offshoot of the movement and it has spread like wildfire. It is predicated on the belief of its holy men that Peking Man, the first known human being to stand erect and use tools, was in truth the original man, the anointed deity who started the human race."

"God himself," said Barnaby.

"Precisely," said Dusenberry. "And as with Falun Gong, the Chinese government is stamping this sect out wherever it gathers traction."

Dusenberry removed a creased photograph from his breast pocket and handed it to Barnaby. The edges were moist with sweat.

"Meet the Chinese oligarch Zhou Shen Wui," said Dusenberry.

A benevolent Oriental face beamed up at Barnaby from the photograph, cherubic in its wholesome roundness. He was bald except for a fringe of hair and had thick eyebrows below his broad forehead. The man's eyes were large and knowing, his lips curled into a beatific smile.

"Zhou was chosen by the Chinese politburo to stop the spread of this new branch of the movement. Over the years, he has built an impressive record of chicanery, even on Chinese standards," said Dusenberry. "When he isn't hacking into our top secret military programs or stealing intellectual property from American corporations, he rides around the remote hinterlands of China in a fortified train with a palace guard of two hundred trained ninja warriors. I'm talking executioners and torturers. Wherever they find the faith beginning to flourish, and it is mostly in the rural hinterlands, they go there to wipe them out."

"They were Japanese," said Barnaby.

"Who?"

"The ninja warriors or *shinobi* were in feudal Japan, not in China."

Dusenberry ignored him. "The Chinese government is now searching for the Peking Man. Their worst fear is that if he is found and introduced to the Chinese masses as a deity, the religious conversions among the lower economic classes will be uncontrollable. If the movement is embraced by the masses, especially the rural peasant class, it would only take a small percentage of them rebelling to completely overrun the Chinese military. In spite of the size of their army, the peasant population vastly outnumbers it."

"And what does your crack team of advisers believe?"

"We believe it would be good to find Peking Man and present him to his followers."

"And give the ruling clique in China something to focus on besides destroying us."

"Precisely," repeated Dusenberry. "We have had an informant in Zhou's entourage. His malevolent son, Li, is in charge of a paramilitary team that is dedicated to finding him."

"This informant should give you whatever you need to know."

"He disappeared from sight a month ago. Presumably he is dead."

"So why me?" asked Barnaby as Dusenberry continued massaging his bloated stomach.

"A number of leads about the disappearance of Peking Man have surfaced over the years," said Dusenberry. "We set up a Washington interagency task force to explore them three years ago, but as usual, they can't even agree on how to cooperate. We're dead in the water."

"My field is Norse archaeology. I wouldn't know where to begin."

"You have extensive contacts and good relationships among the leading archaeologists in every field. You also proved your ability to decipher an ancient mystery in the unfortunate Valhalla saga."

Without confirming it, Barnaby was intrigued. He felt the hairs rising on the back of his neck. Forgetting for a moment about the bloodletting in China, Peking Man was the greatest archaeological discovery in history concerning the evolution of man.

"I might add that the president has authorized me to say that if you are successful in this, he is prepared to remove the security restrictions on the Leif Eriksson discovery."

"I would need help," said Barnaby.

"Anything you need," said Dusenberry. "The whole task force is available to you."

"It doesn't sound like they know how to get out of their own way."

"A little leadership would go a long way," cooed Dusenberry. "What about Dr. Vaughan and General Macaulay? The last time I saw them with you, they seemed bound together like Siamese twins. They could be very helpful again."

"They are no longer conjoined," said Barnaby. "Leave them to me."

"Then we have a deal," said Dusenberry, raising the lid on the tureen of Norse wine stew that was still sitting on the granite countertop. "This smells delicious. Do you mind if I help myself?"

THREE

"It is not here," said Jurgen Ritter, his eyes squinting from the snow-brilliant late-afternoon sun streaming through the big plate-glass picture windows of the Führer's conference room. Another foot of snow had fallen during the last hours, and the piercing light glancing off the summit of the Sonntagshorn forced Jurgen to look away from the windows.

"On what basis do you state this?" asked the Swedish archaeologist Sven Nordgren, tapping his iPad Mini to retrieve his latest text messages.

"I vud feel it inside me if it vas here," said the German Jurgen, the expedition team's expert on pulse induction metal detection.

"How very scientific," said Nordgren with a facetious grin.

Even though it was early spring, the raw afternoon wind on the Kehlstein was gusting at forty miles an hour and the loud shrieks echoed through the dimly lit passageways like a succession of anguished moans.

Nordgren had built a raging fire in the fireplace that dominated one wall of the conference room. It was still rimmed with the red marble and bronze tiles that had been a gift to Hitler from Mussolini. The flames barely warmed the room.

"I alvays feel dese things inside me," insisted Jurgen in his fractured English. "You haff no head in your brain."

The expedition leader, Dr. Alexandra "Lexy" Vaughan, moved to head off the confrontation between two key members of her six-person team.

"Let's go back over the tunnel data one more time," said Lexy, gazing down at the snow-covered valley of Berchtesgaden below Hitler's mountain redoubt before moving to the fireplace to warm herself.

Roy Boulting, the Oxford-trained archaeologist who specialized in pre-Flatejarbok Norse manuscripts, brought over the five-foot-square architectural diagrams from the engineering company that had supervised construction of the Eagle's Nest in 1937. Unrolling the design plan for the tunnel system that had been bored into the granite mountain, he spread it out across the end of the conference table.

The first tunnel led from the roadway at the base of the mountain to the ornate elevator that had carried the Führer and his guests to the summit. Four hundred eighteen feet long, the tunnel was large enough for a man to stand erect for the long walk to the elevator.

"I haff scanned every centimeter of the tunnel floor,

side valls, and ceiling," said Jurgen, "and dere is no air pocket or thing metallic."

"Maybe your pulsating detector doesn't feel it inside," said Nordgren.

"You are clot," said Jurgen.

For the next three hours, they again examined the detailed construction plans, placing special emphasis on sections of the tunnel that housed electrical wiring, ventilation pipes, and exhaust filters, and then comparing them to Jurgen's readings from his PI detector. Taking only an hour to eat a cold supper, the team worked until nearly midnight before Lexy decided they needed to rest for the night.

They were three days into the search for a fourteenth-century calfskin parchment that had been stolen along with dozens of other rare Norse artifacts from the national museum in Trondheim after the Germans invaded Norway in 1940. Many in the Nazi hierarchy had admired all things Norse and held their race in reverential awe.

The parchment contained firsthand accounts of the sagas of two Norse expeditions across Canada in 1362 and 1374. Lexy was convinced that the accounts would finally prove her thesis that the Norsemen had established settlements in Minnesota more than a hundred years before Columbus sighted Hispaniola in the Bahamas.

Although she would never have revealed it to her expedition team, she actually agreed with Jurgen about the value of following one's instincts in the discovery of new archaeological finds. She had used her own instinctual gift on numerous occasions, including the discovery of Leif Eriksson's burial tomb off the coast of Maine.

Unlike with Jurgen, her own inner light was telling her that the ancient Norse manuscript was in fact very close, buried with other archaeological treasures deep inside Hitler's aerie.

Time was running out to prove it. Six months earlier, the charitable trust that operated the Eagle's Nest as a tour site had considered her request to search for the missing historical trove, reviewed her supporting evidence, and granted permission for the search during the same four-day window when other repair and maintenance requirements were already scheduled.

It had been a long, circuitous journey that had brought her to the windswept Kehlsteinhaus. She had found the initial clues to the possible resting place of the Norse treasures in the postwar trial documents of a German Gestapo officer who had commanded the police unit that had stolen them in Trondheim. Upon receiving the death sentence after the war for murdering a hundred French hostages in 1944, he attempted to save his life by writing a letter to the trial judge offering to provide details to the location of important art treasures that had been secreted in the "Bavarian Redoubt," the birthplace of Nazism and the place where Allied war commanders believed Hitler would make a last stand. He was hanged without revealing the information.

Lexy's search had eventually led her to a war diary she found in the Schutzstaffel (SS) archives captured by the U.S. Army in 1945. To her knowledge, the diary had never been cataloged by the National Archives in College Park, Maryland, and no one else had ever seen or reviewed it.

The diary had been kept by a Waffen SS officer named

Kurt von Seitzler. In late 1944, he had commanded the security guard battalion at the Berghof, Adolph Hitler's Bavarian retreat in Berchtesgaden. A number of entries in the diary had led her here.

"We have only tomorrow to find our answer, if there is one," said Lexy to the others as they broke up to go to their rooms. "Let's gather back here first thing in the morning."

"May I join you?" whispered Jurgen as she picked up her transcript of the von Seitzler diary and headed back to her cot in the Eva Braun Room.

"I need to study this," she said as she went past. "And I must ask you to review your detection readings again before we meet in the morning."

When she realized he was following her, she turned to face him.

"I vership you, Alexandra," he whispered. "I drim of you. You are so beautiful."

Jurgen resembled a young Maximilian Schell, strikingly handsome and well aware of it. In her years in the field, Lexy had learned how to fend off unwanted advances from other archaeologists sharing her tent. It was something she had had to deal with since she was fifteen and had somehow been transformed from a skinny tomboy with close-cropped hair into a creature that caused the boys in school to stop in the hallways and stare slackjawed at her when she passed by.

The only two words below her photograph in the senior yearbook read THE TEN. One of her girlfriends had to explain to her what it meant. At Harvard, all her energy went into her course work and field trips.

There had been only two serious romantic affairs in

her life. The first had ended badly when the man she thought she loved stole her doctoral thesis. The second had been forged in a traumatic and dangerous set of events they had shared. She had fallen in love with him by the end, but even that relationship had given way to her dedication to her work. She still wasn't sure she had handled it well. There were times she missed him terribly.

After the team had assembled at the Eagle's Nest, Jurgen had followed her around like a smitten puppy, waiting for the few chances to be alone with her and declare his undying love. If he hadn't been the best interpreter of metal detection and side-scan radar in Europe, Lexy would have fired him after the second or third pass.

"I vership you," he repeated.

"I don't have time for this," she said, brushing past him again.

Back in her room and burrowed into her sleeping bag, Lexy reviewed the diary entries one last time. Turning off the light, she fell asleep as the howling wind outside her window brought a flood of surrealistic images to her brain.

In her tortured dreams, she saw the Braun sisters, Eva and Gretl, young and alive as they were before the war, seemingly carefree and happy as they cavorted in these same rooms, oblivious of the evil being perpetrated by the monster that was Hitler.

She was up before dawn and sitting at the conference table when the others gathered with their coffee and strudel. Another raging fire barely staved off the bone-chilling cold.

"We know that, according to von Seitzler's diary, a pioneer regiment of combat engineers arrived in Berchtesgaden on October 6, 1944," said Lexy, her breath condensing in the air, "and immediately began hauling drilling equipment up the Kehlstein road toward the Eagle's Nest."

"What if they came to shore up the tunnels against bombing attacks?" asked Jurgen. "We know that Hitler hated the Eagle's Nest. Why vud he vant to create the treasure vault here?"

Lexy ignored his pleading look.

"Von Seitzler personally witnessed the pioneer battalion removing several tons of crushed bedrock from inside the tunnel and removing it to their waiting trucks," she said. "I know from his shorthand style that he believed they were creating a space to store something. And no, it probably wasn't a decision made by Hitler. Martin Bormann supervised the construction of the Eagle's Nest. He probably ordered construction of this hiding place as the end of the war drew nearer."

"And von Seitzler refers in one entry to a pallet of metal boxes that he observed near the entrance to the tunnel," added Roy Boulter.

"They could have held food rations," insisted Jurgen.

Looking down at the unfurled architectural design plan, Lexy pointed at the four-hundred-foot vertical elevator shaft that led from the base of the first tunnel to the Eagle's Nest perched on top. "It's possible that they crafted the hiding place in the vertical elevator shaft, not the tunnel leading to it."

"Another goose chase," protested Jurgen. "Let's return to Salzburg."

"It's worth considering," said Lexy, getting up from the conference table and leading the team through the Eva Braun Room to the elevator passage.

The elevator car had not been altered since Hitler was a passenger. The machinery to operate it was original as well. All the appointments were intact, including its polished brass fittings and the Venetian mirrors mounted on the walls above the green leather seats.

"Hitler was claustrophobic," said Lexy. "Supposedly the mirrors gave him the illusion of more space."

"How are we going to get access to the shaft?" demanded Jurgen. "The steel walls of the car will interfere with my signals."

"I hate to agree with Jurgen," said Nordgren, "but it would have been impossible to drill into the granite walls from the elevator without creating a huge mess. Look at the elevator car. It is original and still in pristine condition."

"In one of the construction files, I read something about a freight elevator," said Lexy. "They could have bored into the granite wall from there."

"You're right," said Roy Boulting with mounting excitement in his voice. "I read last night that an open-walled freight elevator was originally attached underneath the Führer's elevator. It was removed some time after the war."

"Can we rig a platform on the original mountings?" Lexy asked Tom Luciani, the logistics specialist for the expedition.

"Shouldn't be a problem," he said.

Two hours later, a freight bed made of heavy oak planks had been cut to the needed dimensions and bolted to the original mountings of the freight elevator. Jurgen's pulse induction detector had been mounted into position with clean access to the solid granite walls in the shaft. It weighed less than ten pounds and took up very little space, but there was still only room for him and Lexy.

Tom Luciani had rigged a governor on the submarine motor that powered the elevator. It allowed a smooth, controlled descent at less than five feet per second. They planned to make four trips, two descents and two ascents, with Jurgen focusing his detector on a different wall each time. Lexy gave the go-ahead to Hurd in the elevator above and the freight bed began to slowly descend.

Jurgen stayed too busy adjusting the discrimination settings on the monitor to pay unwanted attention to her. During the first descent, the LED indicators reflected no change in ground mineralization, meaning the area behind the wall was solid granite for a distance of at least one hundred feet. The detector was equipped with an external speaker so that both of them would hear any changes in the signal volume.

"No change in signal strength," he said with frustration at one point.

When they reached the base of the shaft with no positive reading at any point, Jurgen adjusted his equipment to scan the second wall.

"Begin your ascent," called out Lexy to Luciani.

They reached the top of the shaft about two minutes later with no pulsating alarm emitted from the detector.

"I told you," said Jurgen as he adjusted the detector to face the third wall.

They were halfway to the bottom on the second descent when the detector began pinging out like a telephone busy signal before fading out again a few seconds later.

"Stop and then slowly begin climbing again," Lexy called out to Luciani.

They had risen back about ten feet when the detector began pinging again. Luciani stopped the elevator when it reached its strongest setting. Lexy stepped close to the wall and began to closely examine it. Almost immediately she saw faint striations in the rock surface. They appeared to be straight lines.

"We found something," she called out to the rest of her team waiting in the elevator.

Removing her Case bone-handled pocketknife from her coveralls, she opened the blade and inserted it into one of the striated edges. It sank in an inch. As she twisted it to one side, a small eruption of powdery shavings crumbled away from the edge. She caught some of them in her hand.

"Concrete," she said, grinning at Jurgen.

Using a marking pen, she outlined the circumference of the striations and then had them return to the Eagle's Nest. Tom Luciani assembled some basic digging tools and they were soon on their way back down, this time with Jurgen replaced on the freight bed by Luciani and Roy Boulting.

Two sharp blows from a small pickax caved in a small section of concrete. Lexy saw that the concrete wall patch had a thickness of about four inches. Dampness had softened the concrete and Luciani expanded the opening to a hole about three feet in diameter using an iron bar. Beyond the opening, there was only blackness.

"I'm going in," said Lexy, turning on a high-intensity flashlight and positioning herself to climb through.

Crawling inside, she tipped the flashlight upward to confirm there was enough space for her to stand up and then played the beam in a midlevel arc. The cache looked to be the size of a railroad car. It resembled her grand-mother's basement, cluttered, chaotic, and smelling of mold and mildew.

One reason for it was only a few feet away. What at first appeared to be a small herd of woolly animals lying dead on the floor turned out to be a pile of fur coats, seemingly thrown in at the last minute before the cache was sealed.

Beyond the furs were stacks of unframed canvases piled on crates of labeled medical supplies. She turned over one of the canvases and bathed it in light. It was an oil painting, a mother and child standing in a sun-splashed garden. She gently scraped away the light patina of dust in the bottom corner, revealing the painter's signature. A. Renoir.

She slowly worked her way through a six-foot-high corridor of hastily piled wooden crates that were labeled DEUTSCHE BANK. One of them had split open, revealing what looked like a bar of gold.

There was no way for her to know yet if the Norse documents stolen from the Trondheim Museum were part of the treasure lode that had been hastily secreted in the stone cavern, but she felt confident they were.

She was unable to escape a feeling of failure, a letdown she couldn't explain at first. It was a feeling that she had uncovered a place of plunder, that she had exposed some-thing morally corrupt, a reminder of the evil that was Nazism, and perhaps something that should have re-mained buried.

Crawling back through the hole, she regained her place on the freight bed.

"As soon as we are back on top, please call Dieter in the German Department of Interior," she said. "It's a looter's paradise in there."

Exhausted, she made her way back to the Eva Braun Room. Closing the door, she began to remove her soiled clothes, desperate for a long, hot bath and a full glass of Calvados.

"I vership you, Alexandra," came Jurgen's voice from the shadows near the closet.

He came up behind her, making a low noise like a barking seal. His hands began groping her breasts as he shoved her forward, using his strength to force her over the edge of Eva Braun's dressing table.

"Get off me," she demanded.

His face craned around to kiss her, his eyes looking crazed.

She raised her right leg and stomped down on his instep with her boot heel. He let out a yelp of pain and released his grip.

"Du Schlampe," he hissed in German.

"Yes, she's a bitch," came a deep, resonant voice behind them. *"And du bist gefeuert."*

Lexy turned to see the massive figure filling the doorway. He was smiling at her in a paternal way.

"Barnaby," she said.

FOUR

11 May
Qiao Jia Bao Village
Sichuan Basin, China

Yu Wei watched from the kitchen window of her cottage as a lone mallard circled twice over the lake and slowly descended to the shallow, fetid water at the edge of the bank. As soon as it landed, the bird tried to clean itself from the polluted lake water before attempting to climb up to the grassy shoreline. That was when she saw it could not stand up on both legs.

Seeing the bird was in distress, she slowly approached it, noticing immediately that one of its legs was either broken or badly sprained. Kneeling next to it, she began to sing the first verse to the Buddhist chant her mother had taught her as a little girl. Somehow it seemed to ease the bird's fear and agitation. When it was completely relaxed, she picked it up and carried it back to her cottage.

After creating a splint by shaving two small wooden stems from a block of soft wood, she carefully set the leg and fastened the stems in place with silk thread. She then entrusted the bird to Me Lei, the ten-year-old daughter of her closest neighbor, showing the girl where the mallard could rest its broken leg in the small spring behind her cottage.

Wei returned to the job she had been doing, which was cleaning the sweet potatoes she had picked earlier that day from the acreage shared by all the farmers in the village. Her yams should have been plump and mature by now but instead were stunted and soft. The fibrous skin sloughed off as she tried to rinse them in the enamel tub.

Wei spent the rest of the afternoon preparing the message on note cards for the evening prayer service she would be leading that night at the village meeting hall. Remembering how the mallard had recoiled at the putrid condition of the lake, Wei recalled her early childhood years when the water had been pure, a welcome resting place for migrating ducks, geese, and other waterbirds. She silently vowed that she would help restore those days again.

Wei had left the village at the age of seven to enroll in the classical Chinese dancing academy in Chengdu. A prodigy, she had become its leading dancer at fifteen. Twenty years later, she had been forced at thirty-five to retire like the other dancers to make way for younger artists.

Wei decided to return home to her small farming village in Sichuan. By then, her parents had died, their ashes spread on the lake they had once cherished. She moved back into the thatched hut where she had been born and set to work farming their family's share of the community-owned acreage.

At forty-seven, she still maintained her proud and lithe dancer's figure. Her skin was taut and unblemished, her large brown eyes stunning against her polished ivory complexion. Her only concession to vanity lay in keeping her face covered with a broad-brimmed hat when working in the fields.

Unlike Wei, many of the villagers had recently been beset with a range of serious health problems. The village's "barefoot doctor" had told Wei that some of the medical conditions, including an alarming number of cases of bone cancer, were probably caused by the fact that many villagers drew their drinking water supply from the lake.

Wei thought she knew what was happening. Five years earlier, the Dong Tao Chemical Corporation had begun buying up farmland in the area around the lake to the north of the village. Those farmers who refused to accept the company's purchase offer had had their land confiscated by the local municipal court.

A few months after moving back to the village, Wei walked the two miles north along the edge of the lake to the site of the factory. As she approached the chain-link fence that surrounded it, the noxious air made her eyes water and her nose run. In the distance, she could see a man wearing a mask in a bulldozer moving material from the factory to a twenty-foot-high pile of waste deposited nearby.

Examining the terrain, she could see that each time it rained, the waste pile would leach down the hill toward the lake. The trees below it were brown and dying, the bark looking as if it had been burned by fire.

Wei returned home determined to try to make the

factory stop its actions. Nearly everyone in the village was able to contribute at least a small amount of money to the effort each month. When she felt she had enough, Wei traveled to Meishan and retained a young lawyer to represent them.

The lawyer quickly learned that the factory manufactured chlorate, which was used in bleach and disinfectant. Its waste products included chromium 6, which was known to cause cancer and respiratory problems. Wei engaged him to bring a suit against the chemical company, alleging that it was polluting the land and water around it.

Before the action could be brought to the regional court, however, the lawyer suddenly disappeared, and no other lawyer in Meishan would take the case. Wei remained undeterred. By then, she had acquired an inner strength to see her through any and every trial. It came down to one simple word.

Faith.

The holy man had arrived one night at her door in the midst of a fierce rainstorm.

"I seek shelter, Shou Yu," he said when she opened the door.

"How do you know my real name?" she asked. "Wei is my stage name."

"I know all about you, Little Jewel," he replied. "I have journeyed far to come to this place."

In manner and dress, he looked like nothing more than a common beggar, wrinkled with age and dressed in a simple wool robe drawn at the waist by a sheep's wool strap and black cotton slippers. His smiling face reminded her of an ancient monkey. Moved by his plight, she invited him to stay for the night, making him comfortable on her spare sleeping pallet in front of the fire. In the morning she asked if he had eaten recently, and he responded, "Not for a few days."

He ate like a ravenous bird, consuming four poached eggs with steamed corn bread and peanut milk. The holy man remained with her for a month, slowly rebuilding his strength. Each evening he would talk to her about his own life journey from the westernmost province of China, where he once fought alongside Mao Tse Tung against the Japanese invaders, but now devoted his life to sharing the word of the Ancient One.

"I can see that you are eager to learn, Little Jewel," he said, "and I will do my best to teach you."

He had come with a message, he said, and he wanted to share it with her. It was a message of hope along with the promise of eternal life and inner peace. The Son of the Universe had descended from heaven to save the entire Chinese race, he said. He had come to her because she had been chosen to play a special role in leading her people. She was set aside to serve.

During the days and nights he stayed with her, he told her about the discovery of the bones of the Ancient One in 1926. He was the original man, he assured her, the Son of the Universe who taught the earliest Chinese people to live in accordance with the highest qualities of the universe—truthfulness, compassion, forbearance, labor, and love. Through the Ancient One, there was a chance for every man and woman to join in that spiritual journey.

It all suddenly made sense to her. The meaning of life itself and her place in the great firmament, simply but magically told. A week later, Wei asked the elders to introduce the holy man to the entire village.

When he spoke to them that night bathed in the gentle glow of the oil lamps, the holy man's words about the Ancient One's power to heal the sick and finding a path to eternal life seemed to resonate with them all. What other hope did they have to survive the disaster looming in front of them, their drinking water poisoned, their babies dying, their crops withering in the sun? By the time the holy man had moved on a few weeks later, all but a handful of the villagers had embraced his truth.

They would need allies, Wei decided, and she began trying to rally the farmers in the nearby villages to their cause. By then she had taken to wearing the same simple garb as the holy man. Her proselytizing of the faith began to find converts around the countryside. Many came to meet her and listen to the message of truth. A roving reporter at the provincial newspaper even wrote a story about her.

Zhou Shen Wui gazed out at the sun-splashed provincial countryside as it flashed past the bulletproof windows of the pressurized railroad car. With the train traveling at more than two hundred fifty miles an hour, the distant panorama sped past in lush copper brushstrokes. Whenever his eyes would lock on something closer to the train, the fleeting image of a horse or a tractor would disappear a millisecond later.

Li Shen Wui bowed at the entrance to the dining compartment and waited to be summoned.

"Enter," said Zhou, a benign smile on his pink, rotund face.

At his age of fifty-eight, his bald head retained a fringe of the rare ginger hair color that had once been lacquered into a luxuriant pompadour. Only his butterscotch eye-brows remained thick and bristly above his gold-flecked brown eyes.

"Thank you, my lord," said his oldest son.

Li came and stood by the inlaid mahogany dining table that had once graced the palace of the Yellow Emperor in Xinm. He formally bowed to his father again before sitting down across from him.

Zhou speared a chilled jumbo prawn from a filigreed silver platter and placed the crustacean in his mouth. He chewed the tender meat with pleasure before taking a sip of well-chilled sauvignon blanc.

"We will be arriving in thirty-five minutes, my lord," said Li.

There were no longer any royal titles in the Chinese ruling class, but one of the women in Zhou's personal entourage assured him that based on genealogical research, Zhou was a direct descendant of Liu Bang, the founder of the Han dynasty. Liu Bang had assumed the formal title of Huangdi, or Yellow Emperor.

In a rare moment of self-perceived humility, Zhou had announced that even though he was entitled to be called emperor, in the future he was to be addressed by all as simply Lord Zhou. This included his family.

Li favored his mother's looks, his face almost simian in caste with a bulging lower lip and close-set black eyes. Also in contrast to his corpulent father's, his sinewy body was muscular and strong, and he worked hard to keep it so as an example to the men. His only physical weakness lay in his severely myopic eyes. In public he masked the affliction with contact lenses, but in private he wore thick spectacles.

"These people need to be taught a lesson," said Zhou. "An object lesson to show the others."

"It will be done, my lord," said Li as the train's speed began to perceptibly slow down.

Zhou had his own set of the train's gauges and instruments in his personal car. He had been fascinated by trains from the time he was a little boy, back when the steam locomotives barely exceeded forty miles an hour on the old narrow-gauge tracks.

Now he could afford to indulge his passions. This fifteen-car train had cost Zhou three hundred million dollars, but it was proving to be a sound investment. It housed and fed his paramilitary team of two hundred Special Forces troops along with their weapons and attack vehicles.

Alone among the oligarchs, he had foreseen the rapid development of high-speed rail in China, a network that had grown exponentially since 2007. More than twenty thousand miles of track now connected every part of China except the western provinces.

Zhou hadn't been born at the time of the Chinese revolution, but his father, Xi Shen Wui, had become a senior bureaucrat in the party and he had paved the way for his son's rise to the politburo. Zhou had come to power during the capitalist reform period in the late 1990s.

One of the first oligarchs, he had built partnerships with other members of the politburo before outmaneuvering them and stripping them of their holdings. His fortune was now estimated at eighteen billion dollars.

Much of his wealth was situated in Sichuan Province, historically called the "Province of Abundance." His holdings included millions of acres of oranges, peaches, grapes, and sugarcane. His pig farms produced nearly ten percent of the pork output in the country. In recent years, he had acquired a major interest in the companies producing vanadium, cobalt, titanium, and lithium, along with a string of newly constructed chemical companies.

"Did your legionnaires enjoy their feast?" he asked.

He inserted a gold-tipped oval Turkish cigarette in his ivory holder, lit it, and took a deep, contented puff.

"To a man, my lord."

Zhou had arranged for three Bengal tigers that had been captured in Nepal to be delivered to a smuggler of rare animals in Guangdong. There they had been tranquilized and delivered to the train by truck. The freshly butchered animals were then roasted for the men on the way to their current mission.

"I abhor the taste of tiger meat, but your legionnaires apparently believe it bestows one with bravery and strength," said Zhou.

"My men have great bravery and strength," agreed Li.

Zhou looked at him skeptically. "On the other hand, tiger eyeballs are considered an excellent tonic for impotence."

"I do not have that problem, my lord," said Li humbly.

"And reportedly good for improving eyesight too," he said, glancing at his son's thick spectacles.

Li said nothing. Removing them, he cleaned the lenses with a white silk handkerchief.

"Are they ready for their mission?" said Zhou, his chin hardening.

"Like tigers," said Li.

"Tigers are not meant to be caged," said his father.

"No, my lord," said Li.

"A tiger never shows mercy," said Zhou.

"None will be shown."

"These people have become a security threat. I am told by Colonel Wong that there is a woman in the village who is particularly troublesome. You will make sure that she no longer makes trouble."

"Yes, my lord."

"You are humorless, my son," said Zhou. "You must find something in your life that gives you pleasure."

"I have already found it, my lord."

Leaving his father, Li walked back to the fourth car in the train, which included the fitness facility and swimming pool. Stripping off his clothes, he dove into the lap pool that ran half the length of the car.

He churned through the water with long, powerful strokes until he reached the end of the pool and did a racing turn to make his return, his arms reaching forward and the muscles of his shoulders sliding and meshing in flawless harmony.

Wǒ hèn tā . . . I hate him, his brain silently screamed in perfect cadence to each stroke. *Wǒ hèn tā, Wǒ hèn tā, Wǒ hèn tā.*

Twenty minutes later the train came to a stop along the length of a broad steel passenger platform. It was an hour before dawn. Although a factory city was planned in the future, nothing had been built yet in the countryside surrounding it. They were only ten miles from their objective.

The aerodynamically designed titanium metal doors of the last four railroad cars slid open simultaneously. Li's tactical assault force emerged from each car in columns of four, marching in lockstep as they formed up in ranks on the platform for inspection.

Li had inserted his contact lenses and looked every inch the commander in his starched mission uniform. Aside from the gold stars on the collars, it was identical to the uniforms worn by the men standing before him.

Dark khaki, the uniforms were formfitted to each man and employed a powered exoskeleton to carry weapons, ammunition, equipment, liquid body armor, and built-in helmet computers with night vision.

"At least the men look ready," said Li to his deputy commander, Colonel Wong.

"They are—to perfection, General," he responded. "They have been briefed on every aspect of the mission."

Behind them, a hydraulic platform slowly slid free from the side of the last railroad car. It held Li's command helicopter, a jet-powered gunship with stepped tandem cockpits protected by armor plate, one 30 mm cannon, air-to-air missiles, and a new antitank rocket.

"Prepare to move out," ordered Colonel Wong to the closest unit on the platform.

It was the first time their new "cavalry" unit would be used on a mission. Zhou's engineers had developed a hybrid "stealth" motorcycle that used jet fuel to reach a speed of one hundred twenty miles an hour but could also operate in an electric mode with no sound at all. It allowed for both speed and stealth, and two men were assigned to each machine, one to drive, the second to dismount and fight when confronting the enemy. The motorcycles could handle virtually any type of terrain.

"Are the men prepared to employ their swords?" asked Li.

It was the only part of the unit's equipment that had been originally conceived by Li. A childhood fan of the actor John Wayne, Li had seen the famous "bowie knife" employed by Richard Widmark against the Mexicans in the film *The Alamo*. He had designed his own version, which was more like a short broadsword, with both edges razor sharp. The wooden grips were engraved with his initials.

"The men are very fond of your gift to each of them," said Colonel Wong. "They will be put to good use."

Li watched as his cavalry unit mounted their machines.

"How many believers are there in the village?" he asked.

"Including the children?"

"All of them," said Liu.

"Approximately two hundred," said Colonel Wong. "However, my intelligence officer does not believe we will encounter serious resistance. Most of them will just be waking up."

"There is always resistance," said Li.

"I meant organized resistance," said Wong.

Li turned slowly and stared at him for several seconds. When he wore the contact lenses, Li discovered that he rarely blinked. The phenomenon had led to his nickname within the ranks of his men.

Tā bù zhǎyǎn. He does not blink.

"You are a good leader of men, Wong. Leave the thinking to me."

"Yes, sir," said Wong, a bead of sweat rolling down his cheek.

"Commence the operation immediately," declared Li.

*   *   *

Arising from her bed, Wei began heating her tea water while she gazed through the kitchen window across the lake to the distant mountains. It had rained during the night, and the chrysanthemums and plum blossoms in her garden glistened cleanly in the sun.

After performing her ablutions, she began her preparations for the ceremonial service in honor of the Ancient One that would be held that evening at the meeting hall. Every family in the village was bringing something for the feast.

She was kneeling in front of the dried herbs shelf in the stone-lined root cellar under the cottage when she heard a shout followed by the ringing of the alarm bell in the square. Her first thought was that there might be a fire in one of the thatch-roofed buildings.

Climbing out of the root cellar through the opening in the kitchen floor, she looked out the window to see a phalanx of machines coming swiftly toward the village. They were closing fast, the machines about twenty feet apart from one another. The line stretched in both directions as far as she could see.

As the machines drew closer, she saw that they were actually large motorcycles with two figures dressed like spacemen riding on each one. One of the motorcycles came straight through the alfalfa field on the outskirts of the village and headed toward her neighbor Chen Wa, who was standing in the field watering his plants.

He stopped to look up at the men riding toward him and lifted his hand in a formal greeting. The figure on the back of the motorcycle extended his arm as the motorcycle flashed past. A moment later Chen Wa's head bounced to the ground, his body crumpling next to it a second later.

Watching the machines racing toward the village, Wei ran to the front room windows that faced out toward the square, reaching them in time to hear the agonized scream of a woman standing in front of the health clinic next to the body of her husband.

More motorcycles arrived in the square, most of them driving people ahead of them who had been on the streets. It all seemed so unearthly. None of the motorcycles was making the slightest sound. For a moment she wondered if she might have gone deaf. Then more screaming broke out on the other side of the village followed by the staccato rhythm of a machine gun.

As if in a choreographed ballet, the men on the back of the motorcycles dismounted and began running to surround the village square, herding the people they met into the village meeting hall.

Other men armed with machine guns began storming into every building, cottage, and hut, quickly reemerging with the occupants. Small groups of sobbing women and children followed the first wave of people into the meeting hall.

One of the invaders turned from the crowd and began running toward the front door of her cottage. Racing back into the kitchen, Wei dropped through the hole in the floor and covered the opening with the removable wooden floor panel.

Moments later, she heard the soldier storming through the cottage, slamming doors and searching each room. She heard glass smashing in the kitchen above her and then silence.

Crawling to the end of the root cellar, she looked through the small opening at the edge of the crawl space beneath the house. It gave her a view of the center of the square, the village school, health clinic, and meeting hall. She could see more villagers being beaten and shoved toward the meeting hall.

One of the invaders shouted out that the search was complete. As a cordon of them stood silently guarding the square, four of the men wearing the space suits walked slowly toward the meeting hall. Each appeared to have a short metallic hose in his hand connected to a gleaming silver canister on his back.

The first one remained at the front entrance and the others disappeared around the sides of the building. As Wei watched in horror, the man aimed his hose at the front wall of the building and it was suddenly engulfed in fire.

She could hear the people inside the hall beginning to shriek in terror. The man with the metallic hose continued to spread raging fire everywhere he pointed it. Within seconds the whole wall of the building was aflame. The agonized screams grew even louder.

As she watched, a window was smashed open from inside the hall and something dropped through the opening to the ground. Wei saw that it was a child wearing a white cotton dress. She stood still for a moment as the flames consumed the wall behind her. Then she started running away from the fire toward the line of men.

It was Me Lei, the little girl Wei had entrusted to mend the leg of the injured mallard. As she drew closer to the ranks of the invaders, she stopped and began to cry. One of them smiled and beckoned her forward. Timidly, she walked toward him. Laughing, he waved his sword and lopped off her head. He stared down at it for a moment and then kicked it like a football across the square.

The continuing screams from the meeting hall were drowned out by the rumbling of a powerful engine. The noise became a deafening roar. Through the opening in the crawl space, Lei watched four earthmovers rolling toward the square on their massive treads, leveling every house and building in their path and driving the smashed debris into a huge pile.

When one of them swerved to flatten the village health clinic, she recognized the blue crest on its yellow driver's cab. It was the emblem of the Dong Hao Chemical Corporation.

Beyond the bulldozers nothing was left standing. It was as if the thousand-year-old village had never been. Now she could hear other machines grinding loudly from the area behind her own cottage. As she watched the men with the hoses set fire to the huge mounds of debris, she called out, "God save me, Ancient One. Please spare me to bear witness."

Her voice was lost in the din of the machines. Moments later, she heard a crashing roar as the walls of her cottage disintegrated above her. Lying next to the ancient stone walls of the root cellar, she felt a searing pain in her back and legs and then total darkness.

"I wish they would fight back just once," said Colonel Wong as he and General Li boarded the command helicopter.

"Why do you say that?" demanded Li.

"It would seem more honorable . . . less like . . ."

"Less like what?" shouted Li. "Like butchering a herd of pigs?"

"Forgive me, General . . . I just meant—"

"You are not cut out for this task," interrupted Li. "I will so inform my father."

FIVE

Steven Macaulay came up out of the dream to the moaning wail of a rising wind. It rattled the shutters and drove fine particles of sand through the open bedroom window to gently prickle his face and upper body. The air was hot and humid.

Without opening his eyes, he contemplated his latest hangover. It was a thing of beauty. His head felt like a bowling bowl rolling down a wooden staircase. But it hadn't blotted out the dream. Rum only went so far.

It was always the same one. The Lexy dream. Alexandra Vaughan. Her face invaded his hangover with astonishing clarity, moving right past his defenses, the only woman who mattered, the woman who had left him. After nearly a year, it was still too close, too raw. It was the finality of it all.

Opening his eyes, he sat up slowly in the bed and

glanced through the window. The fronds on the royal palms along the beach were thrashing wildly back and forth in the wind. Macaulay figured the gusts to be about twenty miles an hour, and that was in the sheltered part of the harbor.

He remembered it was his day off and that he wouldn't be flying today. Frank Jessup had the duty. Macaulay was on standby. It didn't matter anyway. With a wind like this one, the old Grumman Goose couldn't be trusted to get passengers in the air, much less land safely on the water. The wealthy tourists who had flown into Dangriga that morning would have to wait for their rides out to the resorts on the emerald belt of offshore islands.

Trudging into the bathroom, he stood under the shower a full ten minutes, letting the cold water massage his scalp and body. Toweling off, he put on his khaki cargo shorts and faded tennis sneakers. It was his regular uniform in the tropical heat along the Belize coast.

Knowing what would cure the hangover, he headed straight over to Lana's Retreat. Set back from the beach and protected by a dense stand of Caribbean pines, it was a thatch-covered chikee hut built on a foundation of coquina rock.

Lana's was a favorite drinking spot of locals and tourists, many of whom just came to ogle her. Under the cascade of naturally blond hair, she had the face of a Texas angel and her skin was a rich golden brown. Barefoot, she was wearing a cream-colored shift that came down to her thighs and accentuated her breasts, thin waist, and dancer's hips.

"Morning special," said Macaulay with a pained grin.

It was her signature hangover cure, a sixteen-ounce

tumbler filled with vodka and juice she blended from root vegetables, spinach, fresh parsley, horseradish, and tomatoes. The good earth.

"You sure you don't want coffee?" she said in her slow drawl.

Lana had arrived in Dangriga on a vacation visit ten years earlier and fallen in love with the coastal scene. She had paid cash for the chikee bar and never gone back to the States. Frank Jessup had once told Macaulay that she had been one of the highest-priced call girls in Manhattan and was now frigid when it came to men. Of course, she might just have been frigid toward Frank, who portrayed himself as a dedicated family man while continuing to sample the local talent.

While she put together his drink, Lana glanced at the network of pencil-thin scars on Macaulay's forehead and neck that remained livid against his deeply tanned body. There were deep weather wrinkles around his sad blue eyes. She wondered when he had last eaten.

"I'm taking a break in a little while, Steve," she said. "Want to join me for lunch?"

"Can't," he said. "Have a lot to do today."

His plan was to drink himself back into a semistupor and sleep the rest of the day. She looked at him wistfully and walked down the bar to serve the other customers. In truth, she didn't understand why she was so drawn to him. New York had nearly cured her of men.

There was something different about him. The fact that he had the same tall, rugged good looks of a young Gregory Peck was only part of it. There was an air of nobility about him, as if he had once been somebody or done something important. He had those sad blue eyes.

And there was the dangerous side. One night at the bar, a hulking Russian tourist tried to force one of the local girls to go with him. Macaulay had put him in the hospital.

A week after he took over the job as backup pilot for the Hurdnut Air Charter Services, she made her play. He had gotten so drunk that night that he needed help getting back to his tiny beach cottage. After removing his clothes and putting him to bed, she had taken off her dress and joined him under the covers.

It hadn't worked out as she had planned. When she felt him stirring in the morning, she slid in close and kissed him, at the same time gently exploring his lower body with her skillful fingers. Giving physical pleasure had been her greatest talent and she felt him immediately rise to the occasion.

"Wake up, Sleeping Beauty," she whispered.

Opening his eyes, he grinned up at her.

"Thanks," he said almost shyly, "but this probably isn't a good idea."

When she kissed him again, he slowly pulled away from her and sat up.

"It would be better if you pitched in," she said.

"I'm sorry," he said, his back to her.

"About what?"

"I'm just not looking for this right now," he said.

It might have been awkward except for the fact that she had slept with hundreds of men and had seen it all. He certainly wasn't gay. It was more probable he hadn't gotten over something. Or someone.

"See you later, amigo," she had said.

From then on they were just good friends.

Macaulay was on his third hangover cure before the pain began to recede from behind his eyes. By then, the wind was clocking a solid thirty miles an hour and all flights had been canceled at Dangriga Airport. The bar began to fill up.

He was feeling the warmth of the alcohol in his stomach when the image of Lexy's face came roaring back into his mind. He could even hear the cadence of her voice. He wondered how she might have changed in the last year, if she was with another man. The bleak emptiness of his own life stretched into the future. He closed his eyes and pounded his fist down on the bar. When he opened them again, Carlos was standing there.

"Why you be mad, Steef?" he said.

"I'm not mad."

Carlos was their airplane mechanic on the Grumman Goose. He was illiterate when it came to words, but when it came to engines, he was a modern Shakespeare. Sparrow-chested with a gaunt, handsome face, Carlos was probably in his early forties, although he didn't know for sure.

"You sure be look mad," said Carlos. "You not be happy, that's for sure, Steef."

"Happiness is overrated," said Macaulay before ordering a glass of straight rum.

Carlos had grown up in the interior to a mother who was descended from the ancient Mayans. His father had been a Puerto Rican named Carlos who had arrived in Belize with a hotel construction crew. By the time the resort was finished, the girl was pregnant and Carlos was gone. She had named the boy after him.

Carlos took in the new barmaid. She was deeply endowed.

"He be something, no, Steef?" he said, his voice raspy from his constant smoking.

In addition to his fractured English, Carlos always got his pronouns wrong.

"You be right about that," answered Macaulay, "he be something all right."

Two hours later, Macaulay was stumbling back along the lane to his cottage, his face peppered by the wind-driven beach sand. Before passing out on his bed, he had one final thought. Sooner or later a man hit bottom, he realized. He might have finally made it.

"Wake up, Boss. You gotta wake up."

The voice finally penetrated. He opened his eyes to see Carlos hovering over the bed and shaking his shoulder. It was dark outside and he could smell rain coming.

"Tom she be need to see you at the office, Boss," said Carlos. "It be important."

Tom Hurdnut was the owner of the air charter service.

"What time is it?" asked Macaulay.

"Jess pass four."

So the sky was only storm dark. He had slept most of the day.

Macaulay climbed off the bed, ran water in the basin, and quickly washed his face. He glanced in the mirror long enough to see that he was a mess, his thick salt-and-pepper hair matted on one side, his dull eyes completely bloodshot. He smelled of stale rum.

Together they walked over to the corporate headquarters of Hurdnut Air Charter Services, which consisted of two second-story rooms over a large wooden boathouse at the edge of the harbor.

The rain began coming as they arrived. Climbing the stairs, Macaulay looked across at the mooring of their Grumman Goose seaplane. Even in the most sheltered part of the harbor, the plane was bobbing back and forth like a hobby horse.

Tom Hurdnut was on the phone at his desk when they stepped into the office. Across the room, Frank Jessup stood nervously in his starched white pilot's uniform in front of the windows facing the beach. Macaulay could hear voices on the radio transceiver in the other room. There was a stammer of scrambled static noise and someone at sea began sending a mayday signal.

Hurdnut shook his head and hung up the phone.

"So here it is," he said, running his hand through his thinning gray hair. "Two tourists . . . a young American couple . . . went camping last week on one of the uninhabited islands out past Columbus Cay. Frank flew them out there. Two days ago, the wife was bitten by a yellow-jaw tommygoff."

"A what?" asked Macaulay as he poured himself coffee from the chipped enamel pot.

"Crazy name," said Hurdnut. "It's the most dangerous snake down here . . . also called the fer-de-lance . . . and unlike most snakes, it's aggressive and its venom is deadly. The husband couldn't get his handheld radio to work until about an hour ago. He said his wife has gone into a coma. I just got off with the doctor at the clinic. He said she needs a dose of antidote soon or she won't make it."

"What about the Belize Coast Guard and their vaunted

search-and-rescue boats?" said Jessup, his tone angry. "We can't fly the Goose in this."

"I called their forward operating base at Calabash Cay. They're clocking fifteen-foot seas in the Atlantic, and the island is twenty miles out," said Hurdnut. "All they have available is one of their Boston Whalers. It wouldn't make it in time."

Macaulay listened to the growing intensity of the rain drumming on the roof. Through the rear window, he watched a huge palm frond separate itself from one of the trees along the beach and sail across the lagoon.

"Well, Frank, you're right," said Macaulay. "It's fair to say that the flight would be a bit hairy."

"Hairy?" shouted Jessup. "You can't make me fly in this . . . it's a suicide run . . . the Goose can't even take off in these seas. I have a family. I won't do it."

Apart from the sound of the rain and wind, there was silence.

"Hell, I'll go," said Macaulay.

Jessup took in his physical condition.

"Look at him, Tom," he said. "He's drunk."

"Just hungover, Frank," said Macaulay. "You ought to try rum more often. Maybe it would give you some guts."

"Are you all right to fly, Steve?" asked Hurdnut.

Macaulay thought about it. Yes, he could fly. Whether he was hungover or sober, it was the one thing he could still do well. The Goose might not have been his old F-16, but those days were gone long ago along with the intoxicating thrill of leading his men in battle.

"You'll never get her in the air," said Jessup.

"You be shut the fuck up," said Carlos with a menacing glare.

Jessup turned and walked slowly to the door. Shoving it open, he went out without another word. The wind slammed the door shut behind him

"You won't have to land out there," said Hurdnut. "We're in radio contact with the husband. We have his GPS coordinates. It'll be dark by the time you get there and he'll signal you his exact position with a Maglite. All you have to do is drop the package."

"Yeah," said Macaulay as the lights in the office fluttered for a few seconds and went out.

The outer door swung open and a heavyset, dark-skinned man wearing a white lab jacket came into the room. He was carrying what looked like a plastic DVD case.

"Is that it, Doctor?" asked Tom Hurdnut.

The man nodded and handed him the case.

"There are two doses in there in case there is a problem with the first injection," said the doctor.

Hurdnut weighed it in his hand.

"Needs to be heavier," he said. "We'll insulate it with plastic and strap it to a brick with orange reflective tape. Steve, you'll just need to come in low and drop it as close as you can to the base of the Maglite beam."

"Yeah," repeated Macaulay, looking out at the billowing wind sock on the pole outside the boathouse.

"It's bad luck about the wheel strut," said Hurdnut, and Macaulay nodded.

A week earlier, the strut on the Goose's right wheel well had been compromised after a rough landing. They were still waiting for parts. Otherwise, Macaulay could simply have run the bird up the launching ramp and then taxi over to the dirt landing strip for his takeoff and the landing when he came back. Now they were confined to the sea.

"Where you planning to lift off?" asked Hurdnut with a forced smile.

"The only place is the sheltered side of the inner lagoon."

"That would be awful tight, Steve. You sure you have enough room?"

"It's the only choice," said Macaulay. "There are already six-foot seas in the harbor."

Ten minutes later, Carlos was rowing him out to the mooring in the big company skiff. Looking up at the darkening sky, Macaulay watched as a swarm of brown pelicans and cormorants headed inland. *Smart move,* he thought as the wind-whipped rain stung his eyes.

"You be crazy to go, Steef," said Carlos.

Macaulay held on to the gunwales as the skiff rode crazily down a deep swell.

"I go with you, man," said Carlos as they reached the Goose's mooring ball.

"Not this time, compadre," said Macaulay. "You be too heavy to get us off."

Carlos stared at him morosely for a few seconds, the rain pouring off the brim of his Yankees hat.

"I be buy you a Goombay Smash at Lana's when you be get back."

"A deal."

The green water was roiling violently under the Goose's hull as Macaulay stepped across the stern of the skiff to pry open the cabin door. Timing his jump to the wave action, he leaped inside. Seawater surged in behind him and covered the carpeted floor of the compartment.

He shut the cabin door and moved forward to the cockpit.

The Grumman Goose was tired. In 1944, it had been shiny and new, and its original motors had carried it across the Pacific in the naval war against Japan. Now the eight-passenger cabin was permeated with decades of cigarette smoke, spill stains, and body odor. The latest coat of white paint was flaking off the frame, and red rust was showing through. The cockpit windshield was cracked in two places.

The plane had absorbed thousands of takeoffs and landings, and the metal itself was nearing the end of its operational life. Macaulay wondered if she had one more important charge in her.

He sat down in the leather pilot's seat and automatically turned on the switches for the flight instruments and gauges. The fuel gauge showed he had about an hour's worth of flying time, which was plenty. Once he was airborne, it would take less than fifteen minutes to reach the island.

He fed the GPS coordinates Tom Hurdnut had given him for the offshore island into the navigation system and tuned the VHF radio to its emergency frequency. He heard several distress calls as he started the first of the two Pratt & Whitney 985 radial engines mounted on the leading edges of the wings.

The first engine caught immediately and he revved it a couple of times before starting the second one. It turned over for ten seconds before bursting into life with a loud backfire. When they were both running smoothly, he motioned for Carlos to unhook the plane from its mooring lines.

The Goose had a forgiving design for a seaplane, which was why there were still many of them in service after eighty years. The deep fuselage served as a hull and the plane was seaworthy in even moderately rough ocean conditions. It wasn't designed for the conditions where Macaulay was heading.

Pushing the throttles forward, he crossed the harbor toward the entrance to the lagoon, the Goose wallowing sluggishly through the water, barely making headway. Each new wave slammed into the windshield and coursed past along the hull. The wipers couldn't keep up. At times it felt as if he were underwater.

The wave action and swells subsided to eight feet once he was inside the lagoon, four feet up and four feet down. The far end of the lagoon was home to several exclusive resorts and a boat marina. Dotted across the water were sailboats and motor craft, all pitching wildly at their moorings. He spent a few minutes determining the longest clear path for his takeoff.

From end to end, it was less than two hundred yards long fringed at one end by a two-story hotel and at the other by the stone footbridge that connected the lagoon resorts to the harbor. The bridge towered about twenty-five feet above the surface of the water.

For Macaulay, flying a seaplane was the easy part. The biggest challenges were the variables of wind, speed of current, roughness of the sea, obstacles in the water, and other things over which he had no control. Wind was the worst. The Goose was like a weather vane, and its wind gauge was now clocking gusts of thirty miles an hour from the west. At least he wouldn't be bucking a headwind.

At maximum power the Goose would need about two thousand feet of sheltered water to clear a fifty-foot obstacle. Macaulay estimated he had less than a third of that distance to work with. At least the plane wasn't carrying a payload.

With the eight-foot swells, he figured he would probably need twenty seconds to become airborne and another five to ten seconds to gain enough height to clear the roof of the hotel or the crown of the stone bridge. Even though the bridge was higher, there were people in the hotel. He would take off from that end. With all the variables, he estimated his chances at around one in five.

Above him, the sky was purplish gray and growing darker as he taxied past a moored catamaran and two channel markers. As he neared the hotel dock, he swung the bird around in the opposite direction and gunned the throttles forward to maximum power.

The Goose staggered forward through the turbid water as it slowly picked up speed. After trimming the plane, Macaulay glanced toward the beach. A dozen tourists had braved the wind to come down from their resort villa to gaze out at the storm. One of them pointed at him.

He set the wing flaps at twenty degrees. Even though it put additional drag on the wings, he needed to gain as much uplift as possible to lift the bird out of the water. As the stone bridge loomed closer at the end of the flight path, he realized it was at least ten feet higher than he first estimated. The Goose began to yaw to the left and he counteracted it with the rudder pedals.

He could feel a small surge of speed as the Goose began to climb out of the swells and fully separate from the

THE BONE HUNTERS   75

sea. The unsettled and turbulent water brought up a rank smell of decay that filled the cockpit.

The bridge quickly began to fill the windshield. There was no turning back now. Macaulay was beyond the point of no return. Either he would clear the bridge or the plane would bury itself in the rock pilings.

They were free of the water now, climbing slowly but steadily toward the crown of the bridge. He pulled back on the wheel as far as he could without stalling her. Then they were there.

"Come on, baby," he shouted as the roar of the engines filled his ears.

Macaulay felt and heard a shuddering crunch beneath his legs. When he looked down, there was a newly rent section of the cabin floor, and he could see the base of the hull. It had been breached at the wheel wells. The top of the bridge had torn off a six-foot-square section of the air frame.

He knew the plane would still be airworthy. He just wasn't sure how he was going to land it and walk away.

The sky had turned a menacing purple. Clusters of thunderheads marked the approaching squall line as Macaulay leveled off at two thousand feet. There was no point in trying to get above the storm. By the time he had gained enough altitude, he would be at his destination. He checked the GPS coordinates he had fed into the navigation system. The island was about twenty miles away, due east. Maybe fifteen minutes of flying time.

He thought again of the all-too-brief weeks he had spent with Lexy after getting out of the hospital in Maine. He had never known what love could be until then, the hope and promise of every new day, the intensity of it all. Then she was gone.

He was into the squall line now, the Goose cruising at one hundred forty miles an hour. A lurid flash of lightning lit up the purple sky. He would have to descend when he approached the island, close enough to the ground to see the Maglite beam. He thought about the possibility of a sudden downdraft and what it would do.

The Goose shuddered in the wind. It was as rugged as they came, a big lumbering workhorse, but even a workhorse came to the end of the line. There was no margin for error. He would need plenty of luck.

Macaulay glanced down at the Norse medallion that he had hung from the altimeter knob. He had never thought of himself as sentimental. Lexy had been wearing it when he hauled her ten miles across the Greenland Ice Cap in the middle of another hellacious storm. She had given it to him in the hospital.

He checked the GPS coordinates again and began a slow descent. Rain was drumming hard against the windshield, and visibility was only a few feet as he took her down through the dense clouds.

He was still flying blind when the plane began to buck and tumble in the violent air. The altimeter read a thousand feet, but when he looked down there was only more ink. He wondered if there would be any break in the cloud cover at all.

He handled the controls with calm disinterest. Over his twenty years as an air force pilot, he had flown just about everything in the arsenal, from Apache helicopters to F-15 Eagles and C-5A transports. He flew on instinct and experience.

The altimeter read four hundred feet when the clouds finally broke apart in the night sky and he could see the whitecaps of mountainous seas raging beneath him. According to the coordinates displayed on the navigation system, he would be over the island in less than a minute.

He fought the controls to stay on the exact course heading as the Goose was buffeted on both sides by vicious gusts. An updraft suddenly took him up a hundred feet before he brought the plane under control and dropped back down toward the deck.

Then the island was there ahead of him. It was no more than a quarter mile wide and maybe a half mile long. Unlike most of the offshore islands it had a belt of Caribbean pines dotting much of its surface. In the heavy downpour of rain and darkness, it looked lifeless and deserted.

He slowed the air speed to seventy-five. Anything less and the Goose could stall. He could see shadowy waves crashing into a sand beach as he came in just above treetop height. He looked for the Maglite beam, but there was nothing to be seen in the dark stillness below him.

He was already past the island when he glanced back and saw it.

It was little more than a flicker, but enough for Macaulay to get a sense of its general location in the trees. He swung the Goose around and headed back. Opening the side window, he grabbed the package from the copilot's seat and extended it from the cockpit in his left hand.

The Maglite beam was now clearly visible ahead of him and tracking toward the Goose. Macaulay roughly estimated the distance and then dropped the package. A moment later, the light beam went horizontal as the man ran to retrieve it.

Macaulay was headed home. He climbed to two thousand feet, shut the window against the howling wind, and punched the reverse GPS coordinates in the navigation system. Another fifteen minutes or so and he would be arriving back at Dangria. He looked down through the torn cockpit floor at the massive rent in the fuselage and remembered that his landing options were limited.

Actually, the options were practically nonexistent. He couldn't land the plane on the retractable wheels because they were no longer there. He couldn't land in the water without the sea engulfing the plane through the hole in the fuselage.

The wheel began vibrating and shaking in his hands. He was again flying blind. The sky around him was an impenetrable black. It didn't matter. The navigation system would take him exactly where he needed to go.

A minute or so later the electrical system failed and the instrument lights went dead. Macaulay threw the switch to engage the backup power system. The gauges and instruments remained unlit. He remembered that the batteries for the backup system were located in the hull below the cockpit. The wind-driven rain blasting through the open cavity had probably killed them.

His best chance was to fly on a westerly heading toward the coast while descending low enough to find the lights of Dangria. He checked the floating compass on the flight console to get a rough westerly heading and stayed on it while he began to descend through the storm.

The wind was beginning to diminish now, but without a functioning altimeter, he had no idea how close he was to the water. If the ceiling went all the way to the deck, he would crash into the sea.

As in all his air combat missions in the Persian Gulf, Macaulay felt no physical fear. He didn't believe in a benevolent God. He did believe in fate. If he were to die now, it would be with a profound sense of regret that things with Lexy had not turned out as he had hoped.

The Goose broke through the solid black cloud layer. He was no more than a hundred feet above the sea. In the near distance he could see the lights of Dangria. After turning to head toward them, he saw something even better.

There were two sets of green beacon lights running parallel to each other in the pitch-black sea. He realized that Tom Hurdnut must have set them up to designate a safe landing path for him.

As he drew closer, Macaulay saw that the flight path ran parallel to the beach, about twenty yards out in shallow water. Hurdnut had erected light stanchions along the beach to illuminate the water. It was still very rough with five- or six-foot seas. If the Goose hadn't lost its belly, he could probably have landed her safely.

There was no point in delaying the inevitable. Dropping down toward the lit flight path, he saw that a crowd had gathered on the nearest section of beach. A few of them began pointing at him as they took in the gaping hole in the hull.

He engaged full wing flaps and pulled the nose higher to try to put it down on the part of the air frame that still had integrity. The engines suddenly lost power and began spluttering as sea spray clogged the intakes.

The nose dropped down and an instant later the damaged forward section of the plane hit the water. There was a shriek of tortured metal and the Goose stopped dead as if hitting a brick wall.

Macaulay was thrust forward in the safety harness, his head hitting the wheel and momentarily stunning him. A cresting wave slammed into the nose of the plane. He watched the already cracked windshield disintegrate in front of him.

Throwing up his arms to protect his eyes, he felt a jolt of sharp pain in his hands and right arm as the glass exploded through the cockpit. Then the cold sea was around him. Macaulay took a deep breath before seawater covered his head and filled the compartment.

Moments later, he felt a jarring bump as the nose of the plane rammed into the sandy bottom of the harbor. He was sure the depth of the water couldn't be more than eight feet. He simply needed to unbuckle his safety harness and swim through the opening where the windshield had been.

His lungs strained against his locked throat as he reached down to unbuckle the separate harnesses around his chest and midsection. There was no quick-release mechanism in these old belts. Both had buckles that were joined in the right lower corner of the pilot's seat.

It was when he tried to raise his right arm to release the buckles that he realized it had been broken by the exploding windshield. It hung inert and seemingly paralyzed by his side. He twisted to the right to attempt to reach the buckles with his left hand. He was able to reach the chest buckle and tear it loose. The waist buckle was too far down to reach.

In the still swirling maelstrom of cold water, a section of loose debris slashed his face and dislodged his tightly shut jaw. He swallowed seawater. Planting his feet on the cabin floor, he drove himself upward. The second safety harness remained tight around his waist and he sagged back down in the seat.

As his brain began to shut down, he momentarily considered the absurdity of having survived the flight only to die because of a belt buckle in eight feet of water. If his lungs had not been filling with seawater, he might have laughed. Something large rocked into him from the direction of the empty windshield.

In his last semiconscious moments, he felt he was now somehow free and floating weightlessly in the dark sea toward a brilliant light in the far distance. Maybe there was a heaven after all, he thought as his mind finally shut down.

A voice intruded on his eternal rest. It was an angel's voice.

"Breathe, baby."

He slowly came back up out of the darkness to the same voice.

"Breathe, baby."

He felt someone's mouth on his own, breathing air into his lungs.

"Breathe, baby," the voice repeated.

He thought he knew the voice. Macaulay opened his eyes.

The face materialized above him, wet with the rain.

It couldn't be. But it was.

Lexy.

SIX

He came awake to the gaunt, beaming face of Carlos leaning over his hospital bed. Macaulay only wished it had been the face he had seen when he was regaining consciousness on the beach. Had Lexy been there or had it been delirium?

Macaulay's head was throbbing, but it wasn't from a hangover. He reached up with his left hand and felt the bandage on his forehead. He remembered slamming into the steering wheel when the Goose hit the water. His right arm was immobile and wrapped in a soft cast. There were bandages on both his hands from the shattered windshield.

"You made it, Steef," said Carlos. "I no believe it. The lady he dive on the wreck and he bring you back."

A mammoth figure appeared in the doorway and approached the other side of the bed. Carlos glanced up and took him in. He had never seen the man before and he sure didn't look like any tourist. He was wearing overalls and was nearly seven feet tall, with a huge chest and a head of white hair that ran halfway down his back. His slanted nose was as red as a kumquat.

"It would appear that every time I see you, General Macaulay, you are lying in a hospital bed," said Barnaby Finchem. "You should be ashamed of yourself for slacking like this."

"Genral?" repeated Carlos. "You be a genral, Steef?"

"Once be upon a time," said Macaulay. "How did you find me?"

"It only took a simple people search on my computer. I just typed in the words *lovesick former general* and your name popped right up."

"Thanks," said Macaulay, turning away from him.

"All right," said Barnaby. "I enlisted the help of a small agency called the U.S. State Department. They tracked your passport."

"Where is she?" asked Macaulay.

"Waiting in the visitors' lounge," said Barnaby. "I wanted to see you alone for a few minutes before you two meet again."

Carlos had no idea what the big old circus freak wanted, but he didn't trust him. "I be right outside if you need me, Steef."

Barnaby pulled a side chair over to the bed. "At my age it's a little late to begin a career in relationship counseling."

"I've seen you use your relationship skills with your female students at Harvard."

"Try not to be too judgmental," said Barnaby. "I've

also been married three times and learned one or two other things along the way."

"Go ahead," said Macaulay.

"You and Alexandra shared something special . . . lest I minimize the import, you and Alexandra shared love."

"You should have your own reality show . . . Dr. Barnaby."

"It would probably be a ratings bonanza. May I continue?"

Macaulay nodded.

"You also shared some of the most harrowing experiences within the last year that any two people have possibly ever endured," said Barnaby. "They include the slaughter of your expedition team in Greenland, your narrow escape across the ice cap, surviving the assassination attempt in Maine, the running gun battle at Leif Eriksson's tomb, the burying of men alive. One might well describe those experiences as highly traumatic."

"Yeah . . . agreed."

"People react to emotional trauma in different ways as they attempt to deal with it," said Barnaby. "Some turn inward or simply run away. For you it became an idealization and adoration of Alexandra . . . for her it was total immersion in her work. The two approaches were irreconcilable."

"I'd like to see her now," said Macaulay.

Barnaby walked to the door. Stopping, he turned and said, "When we arrived last night, you had already embarked on your flight. Alexandra and I were waiting with the rubberneckers on the beach when you came back. After your plane hit the water, everyone else stood around taking cell phone pictures while watching the rescue boat coming in the distance. Alexandra swam out there and pulled you from the wreckage before the boat got there. I gather it was a close thing. It would seem to suggest that she still harbors some affection for you."

"Why did you come down here?" asked Macaulay.

"Let's leave that for later," he said. "I have a Defense Department plane waiting for us . . . if you're in shape to fly again."

Macaulay nodded.

When Barnaby had gone, Macaulay lay there waiting with almost boyish anticipation as he stared at the closed door. It was as if he were a kid again and waiting for his parents to call him down on Christmas morning.

The door opened and she walked into the room. Her face was in shadows as she approached the bed. Without a word, she leaned down and kissed him lightly on the mouth. She smelled of soap and shampoo. Honeysuckle.

The big violet eyes gazed down at him. Her still-damp auburn hair was parted in the natural crown above her face. There were glints of gold in it. She took his hand in hers. It was warm and soft.

"Another feat of derring-do," said Lexy with the hint of a smile. "You can't seem to stay away from them."

"It seemed like a good idea at the time."

"Whatever failings you have, Steve, courage isn't one of them," she said.

She was dressed in an oversize men's cargo shirt and shorts. He wondered what had happened to her clothes.

"I didn't stop to think about the danger."

"You never do," she said. "The woman who was bitten by the snake received the antidote in time. You saved her life."

"Thanks for my life," he said.

"I was just returning the favors from Greenland and Maine," she said. "I'm still two or three behind."

"How did you . . . why did you . . . ?"

"We had just gotten to the beach when we heard your plane coming back," she said. "I saw that the lit flight path would bring you down close to shore. As soon as we saw that gaping hole in the hull, I got rid of my shoes and stripped down to my bra and panties."

"That must have caused a scene," he said, grinning.

"No one was looking at me," she said. "I started running down the beach to the point where I thought you might hit the water. When you did, I leaped in and swam out. The depth where you went in was less than ten feet. I dove down toward the cockpit and found that the windshield was missing. The plane's running lights were still on and I could make you out in the pilot's seat. You weren't moving but appeared to be trapped in your safety harness. I had to go back up for air, but on my second dive I found the safety belt was still buckled. It was easy from there."

"Yeah, piece of cake."

She leaned down and kissed him again. This time she let her mouth linger on his before pulling away again.

"I've missed you," she said.

"Wish I could say the same," he said. "Just too busy down here."

"You aren't a good liar, Steve," she said. "About us . . . I had to do what I did . . . leaving."

He didn't say anything.

Barnaby loomed above them like a behemoth.

"Forgive me for intruding on this tender reconciliation scene, but there is a plane waiting for us," he said. "To answer your question, General Macaulay, what happens now is that we spring you from this pest-ridden hole and make you comfortable on the plane. The game is afoot, my boy."

The white Learjet 45 was waiting on the tarmac when they arrived, its engines whining and the cabin door open. The words *United States of America* were painted along the fuselage in bright blue.

When Macaulay was settled in the passenger compartment, Barnaby came back to check on him. He was holding a full, long-stemmed wineglass.

"Do you prefer white or red with your prime rib?" he said. "Our galley steward aims to please."

"I'd prefer Sam Adams," said Macaulay with a wan grin, "as cold as Valley Forge."

Barnaby sat down next to him.

"What do you know about the Peking Man?" he asked.

Macaulay thought about the question.

"I remember now," he said. "It used to be a good Chinese restaurant in Arlington when I was stationed at the Pentagon."

"Excellent," replied Barnaby. "You're fully up to speed then on what we're doing."

SEVEN

17 May
American Museum of Natural History
Central Park West
New York City

"This could be a good starting point," said Barnaby Finchem as he led Lexy and Macaulay through the high-columned stone entranceway to the museum. "One of my Harvard colleagues told me this man Sebastian Choate knows more about the disappearance of Peking Man than anyone alive."

"With no success in finding him, I gather," said Macaulay.

"He might be able to give us some promising leads," said Barnaby, ignoring the gibe. "Incidentally, I'm told he is exceedingly eccentric"

"Then you two should get along like blood brothers," said Lexy with a grin.

Since leaving Belize, Macaulay had begun to heal after an overnight stay at Bethesda Naval Hospital. The dressing on his forehead had been replaced by a small butterfly bandage and he no longer needed the cast for his dislocated shoulder.

"Choate is a substantial patron of the museum and the grandson of one of the original founders," said Barnaby as they joined a crowd of tourists and schoolchildren milling about in the vestibule.

A slender Chinese woman in a green pantsuit approached them through the crush. She looked up at Barnaby with a tentative smile of recognition.

"I am Dongmei, Dr. Finchem," she said in slightly accented English, "Professor Choate's assistant. He sent me to bring you to him."

In her sixties, she had a delicate oval face, a helmet of shiny black hair, and radiant brown eyes.

"How did you know who I am?" he asked.

She colored and said, "Your physical description left little room for doubt."

"I will take that as a compliment."

Barnaby had made a serious attempt to look presentable. His thick white mane was harnessed into a long ponytail and he had put on a clean red gabardine jumpsuit. The tourists waiting in line for the exhibitions gawked at him as he passed by.

While making their way across the Milstein Hall of Ocean Life, Lexy heard a chorus of excited shouts and looked over to see a throng of elementary schoolchildren gazing up in awe at the hundred-foot-long model of a blue whale suspended from the ceiling. She remembered her own sense of wonder when she had visited the museum's Hall of Human Origins as a child. It was one of her inspirations to become an archaeologist.

It took ten minutes to navigate through the rabbit warren of corridors and stairways that led from the principal exhibition halls to the hundreds of offices and research labs in the twenty-seven interconnected buildings that made up the museum.

Arriving at the first floor of the oldest museum building in the complex, Macaulay noted the date 1869 in the cornerstone. The Chinese woman led them up several flights to the top floor and then down a dark passageway. The Victorian-era ceilings were fifteen feet high. The flickering lighting came from old gaslight sconces embedded along the plaster walls.

"Maybe they never heard about the invention of electricity up here," whispered Macaulay to Lexy.

Lexy smelled the aroma of exotic incense as the Chinese woman came to the last office along the corridor. A brass nameplate next to the massive oak door read SEBASTIAN CHOATE, HUMAN ORIGINS. Dongmei removed a key from her purse and unlocked a dead bolt before leading them inside.

As Macaulay gazed around the walnut-paneled walls inside, he heard the door being locked again behind them and wondered why the security was so tight. There were two tall windows in the room, but they were both shuttered against the daylight. A single Tiffany-shaded desk lamp provided the only illumination. Through an open doorway into another, larger room, she could see a wood fire burning in the grate of a marble fireplace.

Before ushering them into the next room, Dongmei gestured toward a silver tray that held several pairs of open-heeled brocade slippers.

"If you would, please," she said politely.

"I regret the need for you to remove your shoes," came a thin, chirping voice from the next room.

After putting on the slippers, Lexy stepped inside and saw a man perched on a cushioned Victorian armchair near the fireplace. He pointed down at the rug on the floor and said, "It is the second oldest documented Chinese rug in the world, a cousin to the Pazyryk. At least two thousand years old."

Looking down at him, Macaulay thought he might be about the same age.

"Please forgive me if I don't stand to greet you," said the man. "I am Sebastian Choate."

No more than five feet tall, he was dressed in a red silk robe emblazoned with golden tigers. His little legs extended onto an ottoman set closer to the fire and were covered with a red afghan.

The room was incredibly warm, maybe ninety degrees or more, thought Macaulay. The smell of incense was overpowering as the man motioned for them to sit down across from him.

"Dongmei," he chirped again, "please bring some tea for my guests."

She bowed and left the room.

"I am afraid that, like cold-blooded insects, I exist principally on heat," said Sebastian Choate. "Steam heat."

"Thank you for taking the time to see us," said Barnaby. "We have traveled a long way to seek your advice."

"I'm afraid I am the last person you should seek for advice," said the tiny man.

It was hard to estimate his age. A dollop of white hair covered the pinnacle of his slightly pointed head. His body was skeletal and the skin on his hands was like wrinkled parchment. There was a simian caste to his face, and the unnatural grin that remained fixed at his mouth indicated a past stroke.

"We were hoping to learn more about the disappearance of the Peking Man fossils," said Barnaby, "and perhaps some new information that will help us locate them."

Choate studied Barnaby's face for several seconds before responding.

"When I was young, Dr. Finchem, it was my dream to become a scientist," he said, "and to make a serious contribution to the field of anthropology. I wanted to have the chance to help interpret each new discovery that would define the origins of man. I was a young man of some ability, but in the course of my life, I discovered that ability is only an artifice. Without dedication, ability is worth nothing. Instead of becoming a scientist, I merely became a man who studies science . . . not inconsequentially, mind you."

Lexy glanced around the huge room at the collections adorning the walls and filling the glass and mahogany display cases. They were all in homage to ancient man, plaster cast molds of skulls, ancient stone tools and weapons, shards of bone, early black-and-white photographs of archaeologists at various digs.

"Some years ago, I contributed several monographs to the fifteen-volume history of science edited by Professor Charles Gillispie of Princeton," he went on. "But in truth, Dr. Finchem, I am a complete failure. I failed at marriage. I failed as a father. I failed in the most important quest I have ever undertaken. And now the end awaits me."

Macaulay started to sweat. Taking off his jacket, he

wondered if the end would ever come as far as the man's ruminations on his past life. Sitting close to Lexy, he focused his mind on the fine texture of her hair where it joined the back of her neck.

"In the course of my ninety-eight years, I look at what we have achieved after a million years of human progress. The world has become an insidious place, sir, grotesquely violent, with warring religious factions fighting in every part of a world abetted by poverty and famine," said Choate. "Not that it wasn't always a cesspool, but it has gotten progressively worse."

The Chinese woman came back into the room wheeling a trolley that held a silver tea service. With practiced ceremony, Professor Choate poured them each tea in thimble-size china cups. There was no interruption in his monologue.

"As you can imagine, I belong to no organized religion. At one time, I fancied myself a transcendentalist in the mold of Emerson and Whitman, but even that small step into the spiritual pond collapsed under the weight of what can only be termed a divinely inspired hell on earth."

Macaulay glanced at his watch again. If the man continued at his present pace, they would reach the next millennium before the old man got to the subject they were there to discuss.

"You referred at one point to your great quest," Barnaby gently interrupted.

"Of course, forgive my perambulations. At my age, the truths seem to pour out like a mighty river. In fact, I have spent millions of my family inheritance and seventy years of my life hunting for the *Homo erectus pekinensis*," he said, shaking his tiny head sadly, "dedicating myself to restoring him to history. Sadly, it was not to be."

"We know there are many theories about what happened to him," said Barnaby.

"Yes, and I know them all," answered Choate, "all the many promising leads, all the initially auspicious paths, all leading me to a dead end."

The unnatural grin was supplanted by a short giggle.

"My goodness . . . I believe I made a joke."

Barnaby gave him a forced smile and said, "What about hard facts?"

"The one fact we know for certain is that the last time Peking Man was seen on this earth was on the afternoon of December 8, 1941, Chinese time, when the fossils were sealed inside glass cases and rolls of waterproofed oilcloth in two teak crates at the Peking Union Medical College. Panic had broken out in the streets of the city amid the chaos of the Japanese advance. Everything after that is pure conjecture."

"I gather there was a concern that the Japanese wanted the fossils," said Barnaby.

Choate sat up in the chair, the permanent grin not hiding his agitation.

"It wasn't just a concern . . . the Japanese were fossil raiders," he said, "when they were not indulging their lust for slaughtering Chinese women and children. On the same day the invaders arrived in the city, a delegation of Japanese archaeologists went immediately to the college and demanded to open the locked safe in the department of anatomy, which until the day before had held the fossils of Peking Man. They knew it was there and they wanted it. When the Japanese did not find Peking Man, the Chinese archaeologists at the college were interrogated and tortured. Two were executed."

"Why did they want the fossils so badly?" asked Lexy.

Choate stared at her for a few moments. From the intense expression in his eyes, Macaulay thought he might be about to reveal something important. A moment later, he shrugged and said, "They were beasts."

"What are the most promising theories about what happened to the fossils?" asked Lexy.

"Over the years there have been many, Dr. Vaughan," said Choate. "And may I say that I am a great admirer of your monographs on the Norse expeditions to Minnesota in the fourteenth century? You make a very convincing case."

"Not to everyone," she replied.

"You are young . . . your future is bright."

"What is your own theory?" asked Barnaby.

"It has changed over time. Some of them seemed ludicrous upon first consideration and yet gained credibility after further research. Others appeared very logical but turned out to be false. For example, there were supposedly definitive accounts of the crates being sent by train to Tientsin in the north and there were other supposedly definitive accounts of the fossils being buried for safekeeping at the American embassy."

Choate pointed to what looked like a large, polished black wall cabinet across the room. Macaulay saw that it was a state-of-the-art steel safe, as close to impregnable as any made. The two combination locks did not actually open the steel door. They released the mechanisms that sent out 50 mm steel bolts in all directions to protect every edge of the steel door. The steel-plate walls were probably three or four inches thick.

"All the data I have compiled over the past seventy years is in there," said Choate. "Among the four thousand pages, you will find transcripts of every interview conducted during my quest, the names of everyone I have collaborated with along the way, the results of dozens of fruitless searches, and the manifests and schedules of every train, ship, or aircraft we were able to track that was operating between Peking and the north during that week in 1941. You are welcome to review it all at your leisure."

If they had to review it in this hot house, Macaulay was sure he would die of heat prostration in the process. Choate's energy suddenly seemed to flag and his head dropped toward his chest. Dongmei took the teacup from his hand. Stirring, he revived again.

"You were about to tell us your own theory, Professor Choate," said Barnaby.

"Yes, well, right after the war ended, I posted a fifty-thousand-dollar reward for information leading to the return of the Peking Man fossils," he went on. "That led to three Chinese students who were at the medical college in 1941. I interviewed them individually. Although they differed on details, all three said they witnessed the crates being put aboard two green trucks and taken away by a small detachment of U.S. Marines. The marines were led by a single officer. The students were unfamiliar with our military ranking system but stated he was young.

"After seventy years, my own conclusion is that there was in fact a marine truck convoy that picked up the fossils and that it headed for Camp Holcomb, the only remaining U.S. Marine base to the north at the port city of Chinwangtao," said Choate. "The question is, did it ever get there? One of my agents interviewed a retired marine in San Diego who was stationed at the Chinwangtao docks in 1941 and who claimed that the two crates were delivered to a Swiss warehouse and buried there. I myself visited Chinwangtao in early 1949, shortly before the Chinese communists took over. By then, I had interviewed another marine who claimed to have been at Camp Holcomb when the truck convoy arrived and he told me that the crates were buried under a barracks in the old marine compound. He even provided me with a map. I immediately hired a construction company to carefully excavate the whole area. They found nothing. I next ordered them to start excavating at the former site of the Swiss warehouse near the docks, but I was forced to give up when the so-called Peoples Liberation Army arrived. It cost me a small fortune and most of my hair to escape from the country."

"Under the assumption that there was a marine convoy," said Lexy, "one assumes it was going to the port city because there was a ship waiting for it."

"Very astute, Dr. Vaughan," said Choate. "In fact, the last American ship in China at that moment was en route from Manilla and heading for Chinwangtao. It was the S.S. *President Harrison.* Unfortunately, it was attacked by Japanese warships and never made it past the Yangtze River. If the marine convoy did reach Chinwangtao and saw there was no ship there, it stands to reason that they hid the crates. That dock area is now a Chinese manufacturing complex. Ten years ago, I acquired an interest in one of the companies solely because its paved parking lot stands in the same place as the original Swiss warehouse. We have been surreptitiously digging there ever since to no avail."

"What about the possibility of another ship having been at the port when they got there?" asked Lexy.

"According to all the records, there were no other ships in Chinwangtao by that time," said Choate. "Every shipping line reported that they had already put their ships out to sea rather than have them confiscated by the Japanese."

"Military after-action reports should have been filed by the marine officer commanding the detachment on December eighth," said Macaulay. "Have you checked the marine records from that time?"

Choate turned to see the sweat dripping down Macaulay's face. "Are you ill, sir? Should I call for medical assistance?"

"It's called the water cure," said Macaulay. "I'm fine."

"As you can imagine, those few days at the beginning of the war were incredibly chaotic," said Choate. "The Japanese were on the move throughout the Pacific. The Americans would soon surrender in the Philippines and the British at Singapore. The remaining marines in China were trapped and had no place to escape. Most were forced to surrender and they disappeared into the Japanese death camps."

"There must be personnel records of the marines who were there at the time," insisted Macaulay.

"I retained a retired three-star marine general to try to track down the existing military records along with the names of the marines in that convoy so I could interview any who might still be alive. He sent people to the National Archives in St. Louis and at College Park and the Marine Corps Records Center in Quantico, Virginia. They found no record of any marine convoy leaving Peking on December 8, 1941, and no record of a truck convoy arriving at Camp Holcomb before the base was evacuated. He did provide one interesting note. He said that many of the activities of our military personnel in China at that time are still classified as top secret."

"Why would that be?" asked Barnaby.

"He suggested there may have been back channels between the State Department and the Communist Chinese that could have been embarrassing to our government in the 'who lost China' fiasco," said Choate.

"That was a long time ago," said Barnaby.

"Yes," agreed Choate.

"I noted the security precautions you are taking here," said Macaulay. "Is there a specific reason?"

"In the last three weeks, there have been two break-ins at my home in Riverdale while I was away. Nothing of value was taken, but my home office and library were both targeted and searched."

"As you have said, we live in violent times," said Macaulay. "Perhaps it's only a sign of them."

The sally nearly brought the little man out of his chair.

"I may be diminutive in stature, sir, but I can assure you I have had many adventures in my time. I have lived on the run in Communist China and other dangerous places. One develops an extra sense about these things. I don't expect you to believe me."

"Actually, I do believe you," said Macaulay. "I would strongly urge you to continue your security precautions."

Barnaby stood up and said, "We would be grateful to have a chance to review those records in the safe."

"There is a secure room next to my office here," said Choate. "You can schedule a time with Dongmei. I will have to be here to unlock it."

They were at the door when the little man chirped once more.

"Please come back for a moment, Dr. Finchem," he said, "and close the door."

Barnaby returned to his chair.

"You have probably heard of the new religious cult in China that has come to deify the Peking Man. Millions of peasants now worship him as a god," said Choate. "I believe there are new forces at work in this drama."

"You may be right, Professor," said Barnaby.

"Are you familiar with the paleontological research of Davidson Black?" asked Choate.

"He was the Canadian anatomist who conceived the Asian Hypothesis," said Barnaby.

"Very good," said Choate. "Yes, he believed that Asia and not Africa was the cradle of humankind."

"One of the few," said Barnaby.

"In 1927, a molar tooth was found at the Peking Man site on Dragon Bone Hill. Black placed the tooth in a small copper case lined with velvet that was attached to his belt. He carried it with him until the day he died suddenly from heart failure in 1934. The tooth was then restored to the Peking Man collection."

He paused for nearly a minute, as if wrestling with a decision of vital importance. "You are a scientist of the highest repute. I will tell you something I have never shared with another living soul. At the age of ninety-eight, I suppose it is finally time to reveal it to someone. After the initial discovery of the molar, Dr. Finchem, Davidson Black thought it belonged to a new human species. Over the years, he conducted a series of tests on it as the technology slowly improved for dating methods and other scientific tools. He also discovered that a number of the other bone fossils in the Peking Man collection were also different from the rest. Uniquely different."

"Are you suggesting . . . ?"

"I am suggesting nothing more than the fact that an acclaimed scientist came to certain conclusions shortly before his death . . . one conclusion being that based on the bone matter itself along with the physiology of the thorax, Peking Man did not conform to the train of human evolution as we know it."

"Why has his research never been made public?"

"The tests he performed on the tooth and the findings he made as a result of them were recorded in his private journal. The journal was among the things later given to his widow after his untimely heart attack. It came into my hands at great expense in 1945. It is the sole reason I began my lifelong quest to solve the mystery. Call it ego or hubris or whatever you like. I wanted it to be my discovery."

"Where is Black's journal now?" asked Barnaby.

Choate turned to glance over at his safe.

"Will you allow me to see it?" asked Barnaby.

Choate nodded and said, "It is time."

"Thank you," said Barnaby.

"I'm beginning to wonder if this new religious sect in China has somehow independently confirmed Black's conclusions," said Choate, his wrinkled monkey face wreathed in a grotesque smile. "I have noted that they do not refer to him as the Son of God, but rather as the son of the universe."

"I share your skepticism about all organized religion," said Barnaby, getting up to leave.

When they were gone, Dongmei locked the dead bolt and returned to Choate's inner office to retrieve the tea trolley. The old man was already asleep when she wheeled it across the room and into the small utility kitchen that adjoined it.

After washing and drying the tea service in the slop sink, she reached under the lower shelf of the lacquered walnut tea trolley and removed the voice-activated digital recorder from its magnetized slot near the front wheel.

EIGHT

17 May
Harvard Club
27 West Forty-fourth Street
New York City

"Conclusions?" asked Barnaby, as he, Lexy, and Macaulay sat down at a corner table in the main dining room. It was shortly past two in the afternoon and all but three of the tables were empty. From the wainscoted wall above their heads, a long-dead alumnus gazed down at them with a dyspeptic grimace from a life-size oil painting.

On their way downtown in the chauffeured Lincoln limousine provided to Barnaby by Ira Dusenberry, Barnaby had briefed them on the startling revelations about Davidson Black delivered privately by Sebastian Choate.

"Black was a brilliant paleoanthropologist," said Lexy. "I've read much of his published work. He was no charlatan, but when he died in 1934, there was no carbon dating technology for him to rely on, much less the ability we have today to test a fossil's DNA. I only wonder what kind of tests he could have conducted that would have led to those conclusions."

"I assume they were outlined in his journal," said Barnaby, "along with his notes on the strange composition of the Peking Man's bone matter and the physiology of the fossil's thorax."

Lexy looked up to see a waitress standing nervously near their table as if uncertain whether to approach.

Macaulay spoke next.

"I would completely ignore the 'not of this earth' angle," he said. "Even if there is a semblance of truth to it, there will be no proof unless the fossils are recovered. The best chance we have to find them begins with that small marine convoy. I don't care what Choate's hired three-star general told him. If the convoy existed, there will be a record of it somewhere."

"I'm glad you are so confident about that," said Barnaby. "That will be your first task. Where will you start?"

"I have a friend at the Marine Corps Records Center in Quantico," said Macaulay. "I'll call him to say I'm coming and you can have Dusenberry alert him to the fact that it's top priority. There's an afternoon courier flight from La Guardia to Quantico. I'll be on it."

"Good," said Barnaby. "Alexandra and I will focus on what is inside that safe. I'll call Choate after lunch and arrange a time for this afternoon if possible."

Lexy excused herself to go the ladies' room. As she was crossing the dining room, Macaulay glanced over at the last two remaining diners. They were two middle-aged men in their forties wearing business suits. One of them had fiery red hair. He said something to her as she went by. If Lexy heard him, she ignored it.

The waitress was still standing near Barnaby's table.

"I will have my usual," he said without looking at the menu. "A crimson cocktail and the native Jonah crabs bonbons." Turning to Macaulay, he said, "Knowing of your fondness for red meat, General, I would strongly recommend the grilled Thai beef or the liver and bacon en compote. For Alexandra I'll order the pan-seared scallops."

"I'm sorry," said the waitress, "but the steward is coming."

"Excellent," said Barnaby. "I always have new ideas for the menu."

As Macaulay watched, the redheaded man stood up from his table and followed Lexy out of the dining room. He was built like a former football player, a defensive tackle or linebacker.

A short, slender man passed by him at the entrance and strode straight toward Barnaby's table. He looked to be in his thirties and wore a double-breasted charcoal suit, white oxford shirt, and maroon club tie. His tawny blond hair was artfully tousled above his head like a recumbent lion's. He had tried to mask his receding chin with a short goatee.

"My name is Tor Hinchcliff, Dr. Finchem," he said, arriving at the table. "I am the assistant club steward."

"I was just telling my guests that I have some excellent ideas for improving the menu," said Barnaby.

"Thank you, but I must ask you to leave the dining room," said Hinchcliff. "Other members have complained, sir."

"What other members?" he demanded, looking around the empty dining room.

"I'm not at liberty to tell you, sir," said Hinchcliff. "We encourage all our members to do their duty and personally enforce the rules of decorum."

"How have I failed to meet my moral obligations?" asked Barnaby.

"Business attire is always required in the main dining room," he said, with a churlish smile. "A plumber's boiler suit is not considered business attire. Again, I have to ask you to leave."

"This is not a boiler suit," said Barnaby. "It was designed by Churchill during the Second World War. He wore one just like it to the White House."

"Mr. Churchill—whoever he is—would not be allowed as a guest in this dining room wearing such outlandish attire," said Hinchcliff. "If you do not leave voluntarily, I will call the police and have you removed as a public nuisance."

Macaulay glanced at his watch and wondered what had happened to Lexy.

"May I ask where you went to college?" asked Barnaby, barely holding his temper.

"Harvard, sir . . . class of 2004."

"And your concentration?"

"Women, gender, and sexuality," said Hinchcliff. "I was also captain of the diving team."

"And your birth name is Tor Hinchcliff?" asked Barnaby with a smile.

Macaulay stood up and headed for the restrooms. A sign near the entrance led him down a paneled hallway past the men's room and around a corner. Up ahead, the redheaded man was standing in the corridor near the ladies' room with his arms extended to the wall. He appeared to be talking to it.

As Macaulay drew closer, he saw that a phone booth was recessed into the wall, the kind with a single seat and a glass-paneled door. The door was in the open position. He could see Lexy's knees extending a few inches out from the opening.

"Please let me leave," he heard her say from the booth.

The redheaded man laughed and said, "I still need your number."

"I've got her number," said Macaulay with unreasoned anger. "It's unlisted."

The man kept his arms positioned against the wall but turned his head to look at Macaulay. He might have been called ruggedly handsome if his eyes weren't set so close together. There was a raw abrasion over his left cheekbone and Steve wondered who might have had the pleasure of putting it there.

"I can handle this, Steve," said Lexy, standing up and trying to force her way past the man out of the booth.

The redheaded man kept his long arms in place, boxing her in.

"I would leave now, asshole," said the man.

"Please, Steve," said Lexy.

"Please, Steve," mimicked the man in a girlish voice.

Macaulay grabbed his left wrist and pulled it away from the wall. The man outweighed him by thirty pounds and was fast. He stepped toward Macaulay and swung a long right hand at his face. Macaulay ducked the punch and came up hard with his knee into the man's crotch. When he bent over in pain, Macaulay grabbed the seat of his pants and drove his head into the opposite wall. He slid down the side onto his knees and was still.

"If you're finished, General, I know a place named Mulligan's on Ninth Avenue that makes the best lamb stew in New York," said Barnaby from the end of the corridor.

NINE

A green Lincoln Town Car was parked on the apron at the edge of the runway when Macaulay emerged from the Marine Corps courier plane at five that evening. A fresh-faced young lieutenant in fatigues stepped forward to greet him.

"Welcome to Quantico, General," he said. "I am pleased to escort you to Colonel Alexander."

It had been twenty years since Macaulay last visited the sprawling base. Back then, he had just gotten out of the air force and was attending a charity tournament at the Medal of Honor Golf Course.

He and his close friend, the billionaire John Lee Hancock, had gotten drunk on tequila and never finished the round. Life was crazy, Macaulay decided. They had both survived plane crashes and serious air combat in the First

Gulf War, only to see John Lee murdered by a Norse religious cult on the Greenland Ice Cap. In his mind's eye, Macaulay could see him standing inside the cave containing the ten Vikings from Leif Eriksson's expedition in 1015. His eyes alive with excitement, seemingly indestructible.

The Quantico base was booming with construction activity. Dust clouds swirled outside the windows as the car moved slowly past earthmovers, bulldozers, and construction trailers. Macaulay watched as a steel girder was lifted into position atop one of the new buildings by a gigantic crane and thought about Lexy.

"No derring-do while you're gone, Mr. Quixote," she had said just before he got in the car that took him to La Guardia. "Your armor is too banged up . . . too many dents, too many patches. Your lance won't pierce the windmills anymore."

"There's nothing wrong with my lance," said Macaulay.

As he continued to gaze down at her, she had given him a light kiss on the mouth.

"I hope there's more where that came from," said Macaulay.

"Be a good boy and one never knows," she said.

On the courier plane from New York, he read the latest reports from Ira Dusenberry's national security task force about the recent activities of the Chinese oligarch, Zhou Shen Wui, and his son, Li. One report alluded to reports of a massacre that had recently taken place in Sichuan Province. Zhou had possibly orchestrated the attack to blunt the surge in religious fervor sweeping the rural provinces.

The Marine Corps Archival and Records Center was one of several modern office buildings near the base university complex. Colonel Joe Alexander was waiting for him in the reception foyer when he stepped inside.

His blue eyes were clear and alert below the gray crew cut and the weather-beaten face. His grin was warm and genuine as he reached out to shake hands. Alexander had been a lifer in the corps and a decorated battalion commander in Vietnam. After retiring from the corps as a full colonel, he had become a leading military historian on the World War Two Pacific amphibious campaigns at Tarawa, Peleliu, and Iwo Jima. Now he was a senior military archivist in the records center.

His office on the third floor was windowless and bare aside from the photographs on the walls of the Corps elite, including Lewis "Chesty" Puller, Smedley Butler, Merritt Edson, and the former commandant, Thomas Holcomb. Macaulay pointed to the photograph of Holcomb.

"The reason I'm here starts with a marine base in China that was named after him," said Steve. "It involves something that could have happened there the day after the Japanese attacked Pearl Harbor."

"Sounds pretty intriguing," said Alexander.

"It is," said Macaulay.

He slowly went through the details they knew surrounding the possible truck convoy that had departed from Peking on December 8, 1941, and could have been headed for Camp Holcomb when it disappeared.

When he was finished, Joe Alexander said, "Chaos reigned at that point in the war. No one was sure what to do. Most of the marines still there surrendered to the

Japanese before they knew what was happening, including more than a couple hundred at Camp Holcomb and Chinwangtao. Most of them ended up at the Woosung prison camp near Shanghai. You can imagine what happened to them. It's possible the men in your truck convoy ended up in that group."

"How can we find out one way or another?" asked Macaulay.

"I'll try to track down any after-action report or written orders or possibly eyewitness testimony from marines who might have known one of the men at Camp Holcomb or at the prison camp," he said. "Thanks to the magic of our new computer system, we have cross-referenced the reports and orders by unit as well as date. If the detachment was based in Peking in 1941, that will provide one reference. If the action took place on December eighth, that will give us another reference. Once we know the unit involved, we can identify the names of the men who served in it and pull their personnel records from the archives at College Park and St. Louis."

"How long will it all take?" asked Steve.

"There was a time not so long ago when I would have had to search for the original flimsies and three-by-five cards in ten-foot-high stacks of file boxes in a warehouse the size of Fort Knox," said Alexander. "It might have taken me a month. These days . . . give me an hour and I should be able to come up with something preliminary."

"Look . . . I haven't eaten all day," said Macaulay. "Could we meet at the officers' club?"

"Sure," said Joe.

A little more than an hour later, Macaulay was finishing his rare sirloin with garlic mashed potatoes and green salad when Joe Alexander joined him. He was empty-handed when he sat down at the table.

"Very odd," said Joe after ordering a Sam Adams lager.

"What is?"

"Your little military action apparently did take place. At least it was ordered."

"You found the record? It actually happened?"

"I found a copy of a two-line written order from marine headquarters at Camp Holcomb, dated December 7, 1941. It directs a captain named Theodore Allen, who was stationed at the legation compound in Peking, to organize a small truck convoy to escort someone or something of importance from the Peking Union Medical College to Camp Holcomb."

"What is odd about it?"

"It happened more than seventy years ago," Joe said, "and it's still classified top secret."

"What happened to Theodore Allen?"

"His personnel record is classified top secret along with the records of the men in his detachment and whatever details might exist of what happened to their convoy during the mission."

"Why the hell . . . ?"

"I've run into this before," said Joe. "It probably means that the mission was embarrassing to either the Marine Corps or the State Department or the White House. It gets stamped top secret. Then it gets forgotten. Of course, there might be more to it."

"Who has the authority to remove the blanket?" asked Macaulay.

"Hard to say these days," said Alexander. "It depends on the purview of the original request. I can try to find out, but it might take a while. No guarantees."

"We don't have that luxury," said Macaulay.

"I just don't have the horsepower, Steve," Joe said, his eyes conveying the frustration.

"What about Dusenberry, the president's national security adviser?" asked Macaulay.

"I would ordinarily say yes, but he's in trouble with Congress as well as the CIA for that last fiasco in North Korea," said Alexander. "In these times, I doubt he could do it. And if he tries and fails, they'll lock it down even tighter. You know anybody at the agency?"

Macaulay thought for a few moments. "Do you have a secure line here I can use?"

Barnaby Finchem stood in front of the ornate mahogany desk once owned by Theodore Roosevelt Sr., which was now occupied by Horace Starling, the deputy director for security at the museum. Starling was in his mid-fifties, with a melancholy face, a fleshy, red-veined nose, and receding brown hair. He wore a rumpled brown suit with a yellow polka-dotted tie.

"There is no one at Professor Choate's office, and the person answering the phone at his home on Riverside Drive says he is not at liberty to tell us anything," said Barnaby.

After leaving Mulligan's, Barnaby and Lexy had gone straight back to Choate's office. No one had answered their knock. They had waited for thirty minutes and then sought out the head of security at the museum.

"Professor Choate maintains his own schedule," he

said. "I must confess that he is somewhat eccentric in his activities and methods."

"Eccentric?" said Barnaby. "There are Victorian-era gas lamps in his office suite."

"His grandfather was a cofounder of this museum. Those were originally his offices. I might add that Professor Choate continues to be a significant patron for us. . . . We indulge his idiosyncrasies."

"I need to reach him right now. He has promised us access to some very important papers in his safe."

"I can't help you," insisted the deputy director, his nose becoming redder. "Professor Choate has already made clear his personal estimation of my own abilities. You'll just have to wait for him to return and then schedule an appointment."

"I know this is an overused refrain, but it's a matter of national security," said Barnaby, remembering his own skepticism when the same words were said to him at his lair on the Long Wharf.

"You'll have to prove it," said the deputy director with a tired smile.

Barnaby turned to Lexy. "Contact Dusenberry right away . . . have him authorize an immediate search for Choate, tell him to check any other possibilities too, hospitals, accident reports . . ."

Barnaby felt a sudden tightening in his chest. It felt as if someone were clenching a giant fist around his heart. A moment later the excruciating pain radiated to his teeth and jaw. He had never experienced anything like it. Dizziness crowded his brain and he felt himself falling.

"Call an ambulance," he heard Lexy cry as if she were shouting from a long distance.

Barnaby's last conscious thought was that if this was the end of the long, winding road of life, he wished he could have gone out in the proverbial saddle like Nelson Rockefeller instead of lying facedown on this green carpet.

TEN

Lieutenant Colonel Thomas Everett "Tommy" Somervell IV (retired) sat in the cracked leather easy chair in his cramped, windowless office and pondered for maybe the tenth time that day if it was time to finally turn in his papers and resign.

Tommy had been put out to the proverbial pasture again three months earlier by the new director and his senior staff. First they had given him another "golden ager" award and then relegated him to the basement again.

Until a few minutes earlier, the blue phone on his desk hadn't rung all week. Then came the call from Steve Macaulay. After hanging up, Tommy called the guard post security team to put General Steven Macaulay on the admittance list and provided his office number in the basement library annex.

The last time he had heard from Steve was right before the bottom dropped out of the Valhalla mess. It was the last good work Tommy had done. Now the only reminders of his colorful career were on his desk, not that anyone saw them except the cleaning staff. A handful of photographs documented his journey from Exeter to Yale to his years as an air force fighter pilot, the stint in the Pentagon, and then the agency.

Over the years he had arm-wrestled the "reformed" KGB in the Baltics and later on the Islamic fundamentalists in Beirut. Along the way he had earned his share of honorable wounds, including the shards of shrapnel that still ached in his left knee.

Steve Macaulay. There had been a time during the buildup to the First Gulf War when Tommy lusted after his boyish squadron commander. His one attempt at seduction had been artfully deflected without judgment or contempt. In those days, Tommy had largely sublimated his sexual passions for the survival of his military career. Later on, the agency used them to good advantage.

He was tired of trying to find a stimulating Internet chat room in Dubai or Caracas. He no longer slept more than an hour or two at a time, dozing fitfully after lunch and during the lonely nights at his home near Leesburg.

"Tommy?" came a voice after a light knock on the fiberboard door.

"Come in, dear boy," said Tommy, climbing heavily out of his chair to greet him.

Macaulay looked more handsome than ever, kind of a rangy and seasoned Gregory Peck in *On the Beach*. Macaulay accepted his brief hug.

"Good to see you, Tommy," he said. "I never had a

chance to thank you for pulling my chestnuts out of the fire after the Greenland massacre."

"A bit of an exaggeration to be sure but welcome in these times," said Tommy. "You made me temporarily relevant again."

As Steve watched him carefully lower himself into his easy chair, his face registered the serious physical decline. Tommy was only a few years older than him and had once looked like a more rugged version of Tennessee Williams. Now his hair was the color of old snow, and liver spots mottled his cheeks. As always, he was wearing a rumpled seersucker suit.

"You have quite an office here," said Macaulay. "It reminds me of a horse stall I once cleaned at the academy."

"Don't mock, dear boy. I'm just waiting for the Somervell spring."

"You had better hope that winter doesn't last too much longer," said Macaulay.

"On the phone you said you might have something interesting for me," said Tommy.

"I need your help again," said Macaulay. "It's not as dire as when I was on the run for the two murders. This involves a search we're undertaking for an ancient fossil called the Peking Man."

"I once wrote a paper about its disappearance at Yale."

"Then you know the general background. The Chinese government is trying to find it too. I gather a lot is at stake and time is of the essence. We have one pretty good lead going back to 1941 except it's classified top secret."

"After more than seventy years?"

Macaulay told him what he had learned from Joe Alexander about the marine truck convoy that had left Peking on December 8, 1941, and was heading to Camp Holcomb at Chinwangtao.

"We believe they were carrying the Peking Man fossils, but that's where the trail ends. All we have is a two-line order from the headquarters at Holcomb to a marine captain named Theo Allen. Allen was apparently stationed at the legation compound and was ordered to organize the convoy. That's all we have."

Tommy Somervell winced and rubbed his left knee.

"Would classified material this old still exist after all this time?" asked Macaulay.

"Hard to say without doing some digging."

"Where would records like this be stored?"

"Probably with all the UFO material," said Tommy without betraying a grin.

"We need the records as quickly as possible," said Macaulay. "I'm hoping we don't have to go through all the standard protocols with the intelligence review board to remove the veil. That could take weeks."

"First we have to find out if it's there," said Tommy. "No need to put more chips on the table until we confirm it. I'll put June Corcoran on it. She's the best paper hauler in the agency, a living legend among those few of us who have an institutional memory. If it's there, she'll find a record of it."

"I don't have to tell you this has to be kept confidential."

"June is totally loyal to me. Give me twenty-four hours, dear boy. That should be enough for us to at least gather some preliminary information."

"You're amazing," said Macaulay.

"I know," agreed Tommy. "I only wish that view was more widely held."

"If she comes up with anything that proves UFOs exist, I want to know."

"That's above your pay grade, dear boy," said Tommy.

"It's a complete mystery to me," said Dr. Nancy Nealon as she looked down at Barnaby and then glanced again at the test results on her clipboard.

The senior cardiologist in the hospital's intensive care unit was an attractive, compact woman in her fifties with intelligent blue eyes, short reddish brown hair, and a low, sultry voice.

"How are you feeling now?" she asked.

"If anyone tries to inject me with another needle, they will find out," said Barnaby, his face a burgeoning storm cloud.

His massive frame completely overwhelmed the hospital bed and he had been forced to lie in it from corner to corner. His bare feet extended past the footboard.

"Our initial tests confirm that you did not suffer a heart attack," she said, "yet you clearly experienced all the obvious symptoms—dizziness, chest pain, shortness of breath, plus your history."

"He turned pasty white before he collapsed," said Lexy. "It was frightening."

"I would have leaned toward the possibility of pacemaker syndrome," said Dr. Nealon. "It sometimes occurs when the timing between the two chambers loses synchronization and less blood is delivered with each heartbeat. However, your implanted ICD is designed to orchestrate cardioversion, defibrillation, and the pacing of the heart. It's programmed to sense an abnormal heart rhythm and respond automatically to address the tachy-cardia. Your device appears to be functioning perfectly."

"Fine," said Barnaby. "I did not have a heart attack. Have someone bring me my clothes."

"I'm afraid not," said Dr. Nealon firmly. "This may have been a fortunate precursor, an episode that gives us the opportunity to perform additional tests to find out what is happening inside you."

"What is happening inside me is that I'm ready to sign a release form stating that I decline to be experimented on any longer," said Barnaby. "I can only assume that your tender concern stems from the fact that like all hospitals you are besieged by contingency lawyers. I pledge that I won't add to your burden."

"That is absolutely untrue," said Dr. Nealon with heat in her voice. "Based on your history, your life is genuinely at risk until we have the opportunity to find out why this arrhythmic anomaly occurred."

"Just how would you do that?" he asked.

"Like Sherlock Holmes," said Dr. Nealon with a grim smile. "Eliminate all other factors and the one that remains must be the truth."

"Please, Barnaby," said Lexy. "Give her a chance."

"Fine. Question away," said Barnaby.

"Have you recently played any contact sports?"

He stared back up at her with such a look of sheer incredulity that Lexy burst out laughing.

"I know it is unlikely," said the doctor. "What about any activities that might have involved an intense magnetic field such as arc welding . . . or possibly a new set of head-phones to listen to music? They can also cause an arrhythmic irregularity or loss of the atrial input to the ventricle."

"Arc welding," repeated Barnaby with another level of astonishment. "I'm leaving."

Lexy put her hand on his shoulder to restrain him.

"What about a malfunctioning battery in his ICD?" she asked the doctor.

"They typically last at least six years," said Dr. Nealon. "We already checked. His battery is functioning normally, as is the computer chip, the capacitor, and the electrode wire to the right ventricle. We have to perform more tests before we can rule out other possibilities."

Barnaby removed the sheet from his naked chest and began climbing out of the bed.

"You can't be released until—"

"I'm releasing myself," said Barnaby, his half-naked form attracting the stares of the patients in the adjoining beds as two more nurses arrived. "If you don't bring me my clothes, I'm walking out of here in my birthday suit."

Finally surrendering, Dr. Nealon directed one nurse to bring his clothes and another to get his signature on a release form. Barnaby's only concession was to allow them to deliver him to the hospital entrance in a wheelchair, and that was only after Dr. Nealon threatened to call the security guards to put him in restraints.

Ten minutes later, he was dressed and rolling toward the hospital's emergency room entrance in a wheelchair pushed by one of the nurses. Lexy had called ahead, and the car assigned to them by Ira Dusenberry was waiting outside.

"Thank you for your kind ministrations," Barnaby said to the nurse as he climbed out of the chair and began walking toward the car.

He walked briskly through the door with Lexy following close behind. As they drew nearer to the curb, she saw the driver step out of the car and open the rear passenger door for them.

She heard Barnaby issue a loud sigh and his step faltered. A moment later, he collapsed to the pavement. He was barely conscious as Lexy and the driver lifted him back into the wheelchair.

Dr. Nealon was standing with her arms crossed by the automatic doors of the intensive care unit with a smug and superior smile on her face when Barnaby was wheeled back inside a few minutes later.

ELEVEN

Macaulay awoke in his room on the seventh floor to traffic noise below as the morning logjam of cars and taxis inched its way toward the K Street lobbying towers. He had always slept well at the club ever since his academy days. The phone next to his bed began to ring and he picked it up.

"I have something important to discuss with you, dear boy," said Tommy Somervell. "Are you free for breakfast?"

"Fifteen minutes," said Steve.

"I'm bringing June Corcoran with me," said Tommy. "She loves the Eisenhower special with shirred eggs."

Macaulay happened to be looking at a wall-mounted photograph of Eisenhower addressing the men of the 101st Airborne as they were about to take off for the D-day invasion. He recalled that June Corcoran was one of the people in Tommy's team when they exposed the mole in the White House. The phone rang again. It was Lexy.

"He's resting," said Lexy, "but not very comfortably."

"The doctors would have had to use an elephant tranquilizer on him for that," said Macaulay.

They had talked on the phone the night before when Lexy was leaving the hospital for her hotel after making sure Barnaby's condition was stable. She had told Macaulay about his first seizure at the museum as well as the second one as they were leaving the hospital the first time. Odd timing, Macaulay had thought.

"The FBI and the police are still searching for Professor Choate," she said. "We may have been the last people to see him."

"He seems to have a pretty good instinct for self-preservation," said Steve. "He may have gone into hiding if something triggered a warning."

"I think you should get back here," said Lexy. "We have to plan our next steps if Barnaby isn't physically capable of continuing."

"I'm meeting with Tommy Somervell in a few minutes," he said. "I'll take a flight from Andrews as soon as we're done."

"I'm amazed that man is still around," said Lexy. "He is so . . . gaudy."

"Gaudy is the right word," said Macaulay. "But he's still going strong. Let's meet at the Homeland Security Building on 125th Street. If Tommy learns something important, we may need to receive encrypted material."

Tommy was waiting for him downstairs in the lobby under the painting of Admiral David Farragut.

"This is June Corcoran," said Tommy, introducing the

rail-thin woman who was standing next to him. "She tracked down the mole in the White House for us."

Looking down at her, Steve was reminded of the Willie Stargell model first baseman's glove he had once had in Little League. His brother had left it in the backyard and it had been lying outside all winter when Steve found it in the spring.

She might have been attractive once, but now her perceptive gray eyes gazed up at him from a mass of tiny cracks and fissures in the elfin face. Well into her sixties, she had dead-looking, brownish gray hair and was wearing a red pantsuit with a frayed collar. She smelled of cigarette smoke.

They entered the elegant main dining room together. Tommy looked up at the familiar murals and the soaring ceiling as the waiter escorted them to their table. Like Macaulay, he had enjoyed many celebrations in this room over the years. He was glad that there were no other diners in the nearby tables.

After they ordered, Tommy confided in a low tone, "June has already confirmed that the top secret documents related to that truck convoy to Camp Holcomb still exist in a top secret archive. The papers aren't itemized, so there is no way to know how much there is without getting access to the folder."

"Its official designation is Support Facility Twelve," said June Corcoran, finishing her first cup of coffee. Her voice was as gritty as sand.

A white-jacketed waiter rushed over to refill it a few moments later from a sterling silver pot. She waited until he moved on to another table.

"It was one of the first true intelligence repositories

and is located in the Catoctin Mountains near the presidential retreat at Camp David," she said. "World War Two was coming when it was built, and there were German spies all over the country. The War Department used it initially to protect material from their counterintelligence investigations and it was expanded during the Cold War with Russia. It's very secure."

"How secure?" asked Macaulay.

"I was there once. It's built into a mountain and equipped with the latest intrusion-detection systems, permanent guard patrols, closed-circuit video monitoring, and steel-lined vaults," said June.

Macaulay's face reflected his obvious disappointment.

"Don't worry, General . . . I think I have a workable plan," she said, polishing off another cup of coffee.

When the waiter left again, she said, "The documents are stored in an unsealed file box with other contemporary material from the beginning of the war that was classified top secret at the time. Some of those documents have since been declassified, but never removed from the box. I found the reference numbers for all of them, including yours. I needed to find one of the declassified folders that has enough seeming relevance for Tommy to request access to it now."

Tommy grinned.

"Give," said Macaulay.

"The folder we have chosen is relevant to understanding how high-ranking political officials place themselves in jeopardy of blackmail through indiscreet sexual alliances. I've informed my betters that I am planning to do a paper on it."

"Well, you're definitely the man to write a paper on that subject," said Macaulay.

"Entirely true, dear boy," said Tommy. "Once we are into the file box, the challenge will be to divert our archivist long enough for me to copy what is in your folder."

"Why would you need to go there personally?" asked Macaulay. "Why wouldn't you just send for it?"

"Enhanced security, dear boy," he said. "These days it's all about enhanced security . . . going the extra mile or two to protect the source."

"Do you remember Sumner Welles?" June asked Macaulay while removing an unfiltered cigarette from a silver case.

"You can't—" began Macaulay.

"I know," she interrupted. "We're just getting acquainted."

"The name is familiar," said Macaulay.

"Franklin Roosevelt made him undersecretary of state under Cordell Hull during the Second World War," said June. "Welles and FDR both went to Groton. Someone once wrote that Welles had enough dignity to be the viceroy of India. . . . Anyway, he was running the State Department at the time and Hull didn't like it."

"Very noble looking," agreed Tommy. "In September 1940, Welles accompanied FDR to the funeral of an important congressman from Alabama. On the way back to Washington, Welles paid for sex with two black car porters on the train. Word somehow got back to Cordell Hull, who was looking for a way to get rid of him. That's what started the paper chain in the file box I asked to see. We're heading out there after breakfast."

"Was it true?" asked Macaulay.

"The car porters were questioned by the FBI and the information slowly went up the food chain. The same week that our truck convoy was making its way to Camp Holcomb in China, the information about Welles was leaked to a Republican senator from Maine who opposed Roosevelt. Interestingly, J. Edgar Hoover refused to release the FBI file and Welles hung on at state with FDR's support until 1943, when he was forced to resign."

"I'm going out for a smoke," said June.

Macaulay saw that she hadn't taken a bite of the omelet on her plate.

"Is she all right?" asked Macaulay.

"Hardly," said Tommy. "She's dying of lung cancer . . . maybe six months."

Macaulay nodded.

"She's had a good run," said Tommy. "Up until a few years ago, she was doing the only thing that she said made her life worth living. Now she's with me out in the pasture."

Steve told Tommy to call him on his secure phone if they were able to penetrate the intelligence repository and gain access to the top secret folder. He watched as Tommy went out through the front entrance and joined June Corcoran on the sidewalk facing Farragut Square. She took a last deep pull on her cigarette and placed it in one of the sand-filled urns near the entrance. Together, they began walking toward the parking lot across the street.

TWELVE

18 May
Support Facility Twelve
Catoctin Mountains
Maryland

The distant peaks of the Blue Ridge Range loomed high above the windshield as Tommy pulled the car off the road so they could consult the map again. The new Toyota was equipped with a global positioning system, but their destination was not recognized by the satellite.

The tree-lined country highway in the Maryland countryside displayed no markers at any of the turnoffs. June was working from a set of directions sent to her secure data phone by an archivist at the repository.

"It's right up ahead," she said, a dense plume of cigarette smoke passing out the half-open passenger window.

They turned off the highway and drove four miles along a two-lane macadam road. There was no break in the dense forest that bordered both sides of the road. Tommy noted the pleasant blend of white oak, maple, and birch trees. The leaves above them shimmered in the midday sun and at one point joined completely together above them in an enchanting canopy.

"Very beautiful spot," said June. "You can sprinkle some of my ashes along here when the leaves are turning this fall."

"I'll add it to the list," said Tommy. "That makes at least ten resting places."

"What else will you have to do by then?" she said.

"True," he agreed.

"Don't feel sorry for me," she said. "I'm old enough to remember when a man delivered milk and eggs to our door every other morning. I was lucky enough to have had two great loves in my life, believe it or not, and I buried both of them."

"I know, June," said Tommy. "Listen, we're going to need a diversion when we get into the stacks. I have one planned, although it will certainly draw attention."

"What is it?" asked June skeptically.

He slid his right index finger inside his belt and re-moved a thin sliver of plastic. It was about the size of a stick of chewing gum inside an airtight seal. "It's a smoke device. Once I tear the seal and drop it on the floor, it takes exactly seven minutes to activate and is designed to expend itself without leaving a trace. The trick is timing it so that we will have reached and opened the file box in time for the diversion to work."

"I don't like it," said June.

A ten-foot-high chain-link fence topped with barbed wire suddenly appeared along the right side of the road. It continued on for at least a half mile until they arrived at a white-painted steel gate. Tommy turned off onto the gravel road leading up to it. The gate was fifteen feet wide and anchored by two concrete stanchions.

"This is it," said June as Tommy slipped the piece of plastic back into the slit pouch in his belt.

There were no signs indicating a federal government installation. Tommy could see a video camera and another small electronic unit of some kind mounted on top of the left gatepost. The fence along the road beyond the gate extended as far as he could see. June thrust her identification card out the window and held the back side of it up to the electronic unit.

"They're reading the encrypted information on the card," she said, "and matching it to the visitors' schedule."

The gate slowly swung open. Two security guards approached them. One was carrying what looked like a mine detector. He used it to scan the underside of the car while the second one came to the driver's-side door.

"Please open your trunk," he said, "and stand away from the car."

When Tommy saw they were satisfied there were no bombs in the car, the second guard waved them into the car and told them to drive to the reception area. It turned out to be a nondescript one-story brick building with casement windows about a hundred yards farther along the gravel road.

A short, plump Chinese-American woman in a navy business suit was waiting for them just inside the entrance to the building. She introduced herself as Alice Chen and shook their hands. She was in her early thirties and had lustrous black hair pinned back in a bun. Tommy could see she was nervous. He wondered if word had come down from on high at Langley that they were to be denied access to even the declassified material.

It was a different reason.

"I just wanted you to know that you are my hero, Mrs. Corcoran," she said. "The reason I am here at all is entirely due to the example you set so long ago for us as career women in the agency."

"Thank you, my child," said June. "I have lived for the work. I don't recommend you do the same. Savor the days. There may not be as many as you—"

June suddenly turned her face away and was racked by a fit of coughing that lasted thirty seconds.

"I'm so sorry," said Alice Chen, her eyes going liquid.

Two more uniformed security guards were waiting for them in the area beyond the front desk. They flanked two metal detector units, one for people and the other for their personal items. Beyond those was a full-body scanner.

"Please remove all metal objects from your clothing and place them in the tray," said the first guard politely.

"I have none on my person," said June Corcoran.

"Go on through the scanners," he said.

Tommy removed everything from pockets, including car keys, lip balm, spare change, fountain pen, cell phone, and wallet. After looking over the cache, the guard returned the glasses, lip balm, and wallet and said, "We'll keep the rest secure here until you're ready to leave."

The second guard noticed the ribbon on Tommy's right lapel.

"Distinguished Flying Cross?" he asked.

Tommy nodded.

"Thanks for your service, sir," said the civilian guard.

"Long time ago," said Tommy, passing through the scanner, "but I'm proud of it."

Carrying a small flashlight, Alice Chen led them into a modern elevator and pressed the button for subbasement C. When the door opened, she took them down a brightly lit corridor with a polished linoleum floor. Tommy saw more video cameras mounted along the walls. Fifty feet farther along, she stopped at a red-painted metal door. Unlocking it, she stepped inside and they followed her in.

They were standing on an iron catwalk that over-looked a vast darkened area below them. As his eyes adjusted to the dim light, Tommy could see distant library stacks that had to be a hundred yards away. He was reminded of the ending to *Raiders of the Lost Ark*, when the crate holding the ark was being trundled through a warehouse of artifacts that seemed to reach infinity.

"It's actually the size of three football fields laid end to end," said Alice Chen, seeing their reaction. "We have approximately ten million documents in this repository. Although many of them have been declassified, the originals will always remain here."

Until they turn to dust, thought Tommy.

They descended an iron staircase to the first set of stacks. When they reached floor level, a set of lights automatically came on, illuminating the passageway directly ahead of them. Alice Chen consulted her tablet screen and began walking down one of the parallel passageways.

"If you need to reproduce any of the material in the folder, we can bring it back with us to the copying office," she said. "It can be recorded on paper or as an electronic file."

The stacks were eight feet high and about fifty feet

long. Each one had a set of four metal shelves filled with cardboard, tin, and accordion file boxes and holders. The upper shelves could be accessed by rolling metal ladders that were attached to runners along the length of each stack.

Even with the constant breeze of the air circulation system, it was impossible to mask the musty smell of decomposing paper. Tommy imagined the millions of yellowing documents that were stored there and wondered how many of them deserved to be classified. Probably no more than ten percent, he decided, based on his own experience. Better safe than sorry had always been the mantra.

Alice Chen checked her tablet screen again before proceeding down one of the perpendicular passageways. The lights from fluorescent bulbs above continued to come on automatically. Behind them, the lights dimmed a few seconds after they had left the previous stack.

"I believe we're about there," said Alice Chen.

As they headed into the next cone of light, Tommy lingered for a few moments, leaning on his cane. He was about to pull the smoke device out of his belt when June turned around and came back to him.

"Don't . . . Just pay attention," she whispered.

A few minutes later, Alice Chen stopped and pointed to the top shelf of the last passageway they had entered.

"The accordion file should be up there," she said.

She retrieved the rolling ladder and slid it into position. Climbing nimbly to the top shelf, she used her flashlight to read the small numbers on the folders and removed one from the shelf. After descending, she led them to the end of the passageway.

At the foot of each stack was a small alcove with an oak

office desk recessed into the opening and illuminated by a hanging brass lamp fixture. Putting the file box down on the desk, she removed the cover and began to finger through the nonacidic archival folders inside. Tommy saw there were about ten files, some bulging with pages and others slender enough to hold only a few.

"Here is the file on Sumner Welles," she said, pulling it from the folder and laying it on the desk.

She stepped back to allow Tommy access to the folder. It contained about an inch of documents. He began to scan the first page. It was a summary of the rest of the material in the folder, including Hoover's FBI report on the train incident, original copies of the subsequent reports, interview transcripts, and correspondence.

"This is going to be very valuable," said Tommy. "I'll need to have copies made of some of it."

Her back was to Tommy as he quickly scanned the reference numbers of the other files in the folder. He saw the one they had come for. It was very slim. He hoped it was worth all the risk.

"I hope you will meet me for tea the next time you are in Washington," said June.

"I would be honored," said Alice Chen.

Tommy removed the slim file from the accordion file and spread it on the table over the Welles file. There were only two pages. He separated them faceup. Both pages were covered with names and numerals.

"We can bring the entire file back to the copying room if you like," said Alice Chen, turning to face Tommy again.

At that moment June erupted in another fit of uncontrollable coughing and sank slowly to her knees. Alice Chen stooped to help her.

Removing the Distinguished Flying Cross pin from his lapel, Tommy aimed its microcamera lens at the first document.

"Thank you, my child," said June, clutching the Chinese woman's arm as she slowly regained her feet. Alice Chen patted her arm reassuringly as Tommy aimed the camera at the second page.

When she turned to face him a few seconds later, the file was back in the accordion folder and Tommy was leaning on his cane.

"That's a good idea," agreed Tommy. "Let's review it in the copying room."

He and June were trailing behind Alice Chen on their way back across the stacks when Tommy leaned down and whispered to her, "Bette Davis in *Dark Victory* . . . nominated for best actress . . . lost to Vivien Leigh."

THIRTEEN

19 May
New York/Presbyterian Hospital
East Sixty-eighth Street
New York City

Barnaby came awake in a private room inside the intensive-care unit. A computer monitor was hanging near the head of the bed and registering his vital signs. Lexy was sitting on a chair near the window looking down at her tablet. A blue-uniformed security guard stood in the open doorway.

"Are we under siege?" he growled.

"To the contrary," she said. "I asked Ira Dusenberry to have someone assigned here to make sure you did not leave the hospital until you were medically cleared."

"I can always count on you to do the right thing," he said.

Lowering her voice, she said, "I have to meet Steve at Homeland Security. It sounds like something might have broken on what happened to that marine truck convoy."

He shook his massive head in frustration.

"In the immortal words of Tony Curtis after nine months on the set of *Spartacus* with Stanley Kubrick," he said, "who do I have to screw to get off this picture?"

Lexy laughed.

"Go ahead and laugh," he said, watching the continual drip of sedative from a plastic IV bag into the vein of his left arm. "These people are obviously incompetent. I'm perfectly fine. All their tests have confirmed it."

"Dr. Nealon said you'll be cleared for release after they get back the final test results tomorrow," she said as an orderly came in bearing a plastic food tray. She saw the plate contained what looked like oatmeal or pablum topped by three prunes.

"Just sit back and enjoy the cuisine," she added, heading for the door. "You might want to guide them on the future menu."

The epithet he unleashed caused her to stop and turn around.

"That is anatomically impossible," she said.

Thirty minutes later she was at the Homeland Security Office Building on 125th Street. Macaulay was waiting for her in one of the small, secure communications rooms on the eleventh floor. The telephone call came in from Langley ten minutes later. Macaulay put Tommy on the speakerphone.

"I have something for you, dear boy," he said. "It consists of two sheets of paper that June is sending to you now at the encrypted data address you gave her. The first page is a document dated December 9, 1941. It was typed by someone serving in the Fourth Marines Headquarters Company at Camp Holcomb shortly before the detachment surrendered to the Japanese. The document includes a brief account of the convoy mission from Peking by a corporal named Fabbricatore, who claimed to be the only survivor after they were ambushed by a Japanese patrol on the night of December eighth. He states that Captain Allen was killed in the firefight after sending one of the trucks on in an attempt to break out. He didn't know what happened to the truck or to the two marines driving it. Aside from the typed account, there is a list of nine marines who were in the convoy aside from Fabbricatore, who died of his wounds. Seven are listed as killed in action. Two others, Sergeant James Donald Bradshaw, and Corporal Sean Patrick Morrissey, are listed as missing in action, presumed dead."

"And the second document?" asked Lexy.

"That's where it gets very strange indeed," said Tommy. "The second one is the summary of a hospital record for one Marine Corporal Sean Patrick Morrissey. It states that Morrissey was admitted to the U.S. Naval Hospital in Key West, Florida, on March 2, 1942, suffering from second-degree burns, head trauma, hypothermia, malnutrition, and a vertebral compression fracture, which I would translate as a broken back."

"Wait," said Lexy. "The first document says he was presumed dead. The second is his hospital record. How is that?"

"As I said, it's very strange."

"What is the last thing in the hospital record?" asked Macaulay.

"It states that he was released as fit for active duty on October 12, 1942."

"More than seven months later," said Lexy.

"I have something else for you. June has found an

obituary notice for a Sean Patrick Morrissey who died in 2011 in Detroit, Michigan. The birth date comports with that of our Morrissey, who had just turned eighteen years old at the time he was admitted to the hospital in Key West. According to the obituary notice, he left one family survivor, a younger brother named Daniel Morrissey, described as retired from General Motors. According to June, it would appear he is still alive and living in Detroit. I'll send you his address with the other documents."

"Thanks, Tommy," said Macaulay. "We'll follow up from here."

Lexy leaned toward the speakerphone. "Please consider it a top priority to locate any other information you can on Sean Morrissey."

"Of course, dear girl," said Tommy. "We wouldn't be deprived of the fun."

"I'm heading for Detroit," said Macaulay after briefly reviewing the documents and passing them to Lexy. "The brother is our only lead."

"I'm going with you," said Lexy.

"I thought you had to babysit the little prince."

"Little Big Man is in stir until tomorrow morning at the earliest," she said, grabbing her purse. "Call for our plane, General."

The Detroit neighborhood they drove through was an industrial city nightmare, a seemingly endless succession of abandoned freight yards, boarded factories, and empty, burned-out storefronts. The few businesses still operating were liquor stores, pizza parlors, and Chinese restaurants.

After leaving the airport, they had exited the Jefferies Freeway, driving along Wyoming Street and turning onto

Orangelawn. At one point, they passed a small group of homeless people who were clustered around a pup tent in one of the vacant lots. Lexy was gazing down at her smartphone.

"According to Neighborhood Watch, this is one of the three most violent and dangerous neighborhoods in America," she said.

"You can't call it a neighborhood anymore," said Macaulay. "They should tear it down and start over."

"Tell that to the people who live here."

One of the side streets off Orangelawn led to the address they were looking for. The house stood intact among the abandoned homes along the street. The afternoon light was beginning to fade when Macaulay stopped behind one of the derelict cars and they got out. In the distance he could hear the whine of a truck's air brakes as its driver downshifted to exit the Jefferies Freeway.

There was an acrid stench in the air. One of the cars farther down the block was on fire. Macaulay saw children playing in a weed-strewn yard across the street from it. No one seemed to notice the flames.

The house of Daniel Morrissey was constructed of redbrick and was three stories high with a wide front porch and large bay windows facing the street. At one time, it had probably been quite impressive. Now its bay windows were sealed with plywood and painted dark green.

As they approached the porch, Macaulay saw that every ground-floor and basement window had been sealed with plywood as well. Looking up, he saw that the second- and third-floor windows were still intact and framed with white curtains.

The house next door to the Morrissey home was identical to it, but the place had been gutted by fire. Through the charred downstairs window frames, Macaulay could see piles of ceiling debris rising from the living room floor. A small sign had been planted in the front yard. It read FOR SALE $2200.00. Someone had crossed out the original number with a Magic Marker and written $500.00.

"Fort Apache," said Macaulay as they climbed the steps to the porch.

Lexy saw that the front door had been reinforced with a big slab of two-inch-thick oak planking. There was no knob or handle on it. A tiny peephole was notched in the middle of the door at Lexy's eye level. From somewhere behind the door, she could hear the sound of laughter and applause from a television game show.

Macaulay knocked on the door. They waited. Thirty seconds went by. He knocked again more loudly. Lexy could no longer hear the television. Nothing stirred inside the house.

"Someone is in there," said Lexy, "and probably thinks we're from the City Tax Department or bill collectors."

"You definitely do not look like a bill collector," he said, glancing up and seeing a small surveillance camera mounted on one of the porch roof rafters.

Facing up at it, he said, "Mr. Morrissey, my name is Steven Macaulay and we are here to ask you about your late brother, Sean. It's very important and it will only take a few minutes."

Ten seconds later, he heard a dead bolt being unlocked followed immediately by a second one. The massive door swung slowly inward, revealing an unshaven old man in a wheelchair. He was wearing jeans and a raggedy Detroit

Lions sweatshirt. Behind him stretched a long, dark hallway. Macaulay could see a broad staircase leading up to the second floor.

"Daniel Morrissey?" asked Lexy.

The old man nodded. Motioning them inside, he rolled his chair away to allow them past. He rolled back and shut the door again, relocking the two heavy dead bolts before leading them down the hallway and into a brightly lit room.

It had once been an elegant front parlor with ten-foot ceilings, crown molding, and oak wainscoting covering the white plaster walls. With the windows now sealed both inside and out with green-painted plywood, it seemed more like a modern burial chamber.

The room was brightly lit with wall-mounted lighting fixtures. Two couches, several easy chairs, and a walnut coffee table were spread around the room. A massive old television stood on a walnut credenza along one wall. Macaulay wasn't sure what he had expected, but the room was clean and neat, everything in its place.

"Sit down," said the old man, waving them toward the couch. "Sorry I can't offer you anything. I'm on short rations at the moment. Not used to having guests."

The old man had been strong in his youth, decided Macaulay, glancing at the thickness of the wrists extending from the cuffs of the sweatshirt. The once-powerful slabs of his shoulder muscles had shrunk to sinew and bone. Weather wrinkles creased his face, which was pasty white aside from ancient scars on his neck and his large hands. The brown eyes were sharp with intelligence.

"I'll tell you why we're here," said Lexy. "We're trying to find out any information we can on your brother's early service as a marine during the Second World War. We know that he was stationed in China at the beginning. Did he ever talk to you about it?"

"What do you know about my brother?" asked Daniel Morrissey.

"Very little," she said, "just the fact that he was in China on December 8, 1941, and later was admitted to a military hospital in March 1942 after having incurred serious wounds or injuries. We know he was released to active duty that following October."

"I'll be honest with you, ma'am," said the old man. "We weren't close. When he came back from the war, he was a lot different than when he left. . . . He didn't want to work . . . didn't want to do anything. The only thing he did do was drink scotch whiskey. He was damn good at that. After a few months of it, my mother threw him out and he rode the rails out to the Northwest. We heard he went logging for a while and then he disappeared. He wasted his life."

Morrissey cleared his phlegmy throat and spat with perfect precision into the Mason jar that was nestled between his legs.

"My mother died in 2001," he went on. "Sean came back here around six years after that. He was a broken man, the worse for being an alcoholic. He was trying desperately to stay sober and to find work. My wife was dead from cancer by then. I took pity on him. We lived here together until he died in 2011. It was on the tenth anniversary of that Trade Center attack. He's buried next to our mother."

"You're retired from General Motors?"

He nodded.

"Thirty-five years as a shop foreman on the assembly

line with the pension to prove it," he said with a taut grin. "At least until the Republicans take it away from us."

"Did Sean ever talk to you about his experiences in the war?" asked Macaulay.

"You look ex-military," said Morrissey, giving him a hard once-over. "Am I right?"

Macaulay nodded.

"Thought so," he said. "I had a lot of veterans working for me at the plant in Pontiac. It's all gone now . . . the plant, my wife, my daughter down in Alabama, all the old neighbors . . . even the stores downtown where we used to shop."

"Why didn't you leave too?" asked Lexy.

"Good question . . . pure orneriness maybe. That and Sean was failing. He wanted to ride it out here."

"Can you tell us about his time in China?"

"He was in China and a lot of other places," said Daniel Morrissey. "He enlisted when he was only sixteen . . . lied about his age like a lot of them that had problems at home. Our mother made bad choices in men. They all had one thing in common. They didn't like kids. I was fifteen when the war ended and I was big enough to run the last one off."

He paused to clear his throat again and hock another wad of spit into the jar.

"At the beginning, he was in China like you said. He was in the hospital after that. Later on he fought at Iwo Jima and was badly wounded. They gave him the Silver Star. He got out when the war ended in 1945. His girl didn't wait for him. She had a husband and two kids by the time he got back."

"We're only interested in what happened to him in

China and how he ended up at the marine hospital in Key West three months later," said Macaulay.

"I don't know anything about that," said Morrissey. "He didn't talk about it, at least as I remember. I only know what he said it was like at Iwo Jima. He never got over that one."

"Is there anyone else we might contact who Sean might have confided more about China to, maybe a fellow marine veteran?" asked Lexy.

"I don't think he stayed in touch with anybody, at least as far as I know," said Morrissey. "It was like he was trying to put it all behind him."

Lexy looked at Steve and shook her head.

"I've got his Silver Star upstairs if you want to see it."

"That's all right," said Lexy. "Thank you for giving us your time."

"It's getting dark," said Morrissey. "You might want to be out of this neighborhood as soon as possible."

They were back in the car and four blocks away when Lexy said, "Stop."

Macaulay immediately pulled to the side.

"Did you notice those scars on his hands?" she asked.

"Yes," said Macaulay. "He was a plant worker for thirty or forty years."

"What about the ones on his neck?"

Steve shook his head.

"Those are burn scars. In the hospital record, it said that when Sean Morrissey was admitted, he was suffering from second-degree burns."

"You're right . . . and he also knew I was military . . . and he used the term *short rations*."

As he was about to turn the car around, Lexy's cell

phone began to ring. She put it next to her ear and then jerked it away.

"It was in my shoes," bellowed Barnaby.

For a moment she wondered if he was hallucinating after another seizure.

"The Chinese woman in Choate's office," he went on. "She put microchip transmitters in our shoes. That's what triggered the arrhythmic seizures. When all the tests came back negative, they decided to scan my clothes to make sure I hadn't been exposed to something bacterial or biological."

Lexy looked down at her feet. She had changed her shoes at the hotel from pumps to walking shoes. Macaulay was wearing his familiar chukka boots.

"Get rid of your shoes," she said. "They might have a transmitter in them."

Macaulay slipped them off and stepped out of the car. A pickup truck was going by and slowing down for the stop sign. He dropped them in the open freight bed and watched the truck head off into the night.

Driving back to Morrissey's, Macaulay hoped they had eliminated the threat. Still on the phone, Lexy told Barnaby about their suspicions of Morrissey and that she would check back as soon as they knew anything.

The street was still deserted when they walked back up to the front porch. Macaulay didn't bother to knock. He looked up at the surveillance camera and said, "Sorry to bother you again, Mr. Morrissey, but we had one last question for you. It won't take a minute."

They heard the dead bolts being unlocked again and the door swung open.

"What is it now?" he asked gruffly from the wheelchair.

"Why are you impersonating your brother?" asked Lexy.

She saw a quick dart of movement in the sharp brown eyes before they went slack again.

"If you're Daniel Morrissey, it'll be easy to prove one way or another," said Macaulay, "after we come back with the police and take your fingerprints."

"We would prefer not to do that," said Lexy. "All we want is information."

The old man looked past them into the street. Nothing was moving.

"I'm Sean Morrissey," he said.

FOURTEEN

"What I told you before is true, all of it, including the Silver Star at Iwo," said Morrissey. "I was a good marine. When I came back home, the girl I loved had gotten married. I went out to Oregon and later to Mexico. When I finally came back here, Dan took me in . . . nursed me back. He was already a hermit. The gangs tried to drive us off like the other older neighbors, but we knew how to defend ourselves."

He looked down at Macaulay's feet.

"What happened to your shoes?" asked Morrissey.

"They're on their way to Chicago," said Macaulay, confusing the old man for a moment.

"Why did you assume Daniel's identity?" asked Lexy gently, pulling out her notebook and a pen.

When he stood up from the wheelchair, Sean Morrissey seemed to momentarily dissolve into another man, tall, younger, distinguished. She could see the good bone structure in his face, a fragment of what he might have looked like as a strapping marine at the beginning of the war.

"I didn't plan any of it," he said. "I came downstairs one morning and found Dan lying there on the floor. He must have been dead for three or four hours. Rigor was already setting in. I called the police and told them my address and that my brother had died during the night. The dispatcher was too distracted to take my name and said she would send a sector car as soon as possible. It got here a couple hours later."

He gave them a grim smile.

"By then I had given some thought to his pension and the comforts it provided to survive here in this city. After Dan and I got old, we looked a lot alike. His wife was dead and his daughter hadn't visited in years. When the police officer asked me for his full name, I gave him my own. No one bothered to check. A week later he was cremated."

"Can you remember those two wooden crates in Peking?" asked Macaulay, cutting to the chase.

"I remember the one in our truck was painted bright red," said Morrissey. "It had Chinese lettering on it."

"Why didn't you ever tell anyone about them after you got to Key West?"

"I was out of it for months in the hospital. At first I couldn't even remember my name. By the time I started to get my memory back, it seemed . . . It just didn't seem important. Anyway, the crate was gone. . . . It went down with the ship I was on."

"Another marine was reported missing in action with you . . . Sergeant James Donald Bradshaw," said Lexy. "Do you know what happened to him?"

Morrissey was quiet. His jaw began to tremble and he turned away. When he regained his composure, he said, "Ol' J.D. . . . him I can see very clearly in my mind. I see him every day. He gave his life for me."

He described the scene on the docks at Chinwangtao when J. D. Bradshaw had ordered Sean to board the ship as the Japanese advance guard arrived. And what Bradshaw had done with the grenades as the ship pulled out.

"Did either of you know what was in the red crate?"

"When J.D. saw the coolies carrying them, he said they were too light to be gold. After he died, I didn't care. What did they matter? What did any of it matter? By the time my memory came back, I knew the red one was at the bottom of the sea."

"Do you have any idea where the ship went down?" asked Lexy.

"None," said Morrissey. "All I remember with any certainty is waking up in the hospital in Key West with a bandage about as big as a hornet's nest around my head."

"Someone had to have rescued you," said Macaulay. "You have no recollection of it?"

"To this day it's all a blur. Over the years, bits and pieces have come back. I remember the ship I left China on stopped somewhere for a long time. I think it might have been the engine. It was an old tramp. At that point, I was really sick from malaria."

Lexy continued jotting his statement down in shorthand as he sat down in one of the easy chairs opposite the couch.

"I remember it was night and the sky was full of stars. It was very warm with a soft breeze on my face and then there was a brilliant flash of light. I remember being slammed into a steel bulkhead. . . . Later I was floating on a piece of wreckage. I was alone. Then there was a strange voice around me. I was very thirsty. Then I woke up in the hospital."

"Don't worry about it," said Lexy, again very gently. "There are therapeutic ways to help you regain your memory. None of them are painful or harmful."

"I don't like hospitals and I don't like doctors."

"Who does?" said Macaulay with a grin. "Look, you won a Silver Star at Iwo. You've put your life on the line for this country. I want you to trust us that this is a matter of great importance."

Morrissey thought about it for a few moments and nodded. "I haven't done anything worth a damn ever since."

"Do you remember the name of the ship that was waiting at Chinwangtao?"

He shook his head. "I would tell you if I could. . . . It was some kind of foreign name."

He suddenly stared up at the ceiling.

"Did you hear that?" he asked them.

They shook their heads. Macaulay waited for a sound. Aside from the distant hum of traffic on the Mikeries Freeway, the silence held. Morrissey sat there with his ear still cocked toward the ceiling.

"Someone's gotten into the house," he said, going to the door that led into the hallway and barring it with an iron shaft. He did the same with a second door on the opposite side of the room.

"Check the monitor," he said.

Macaulay went to the small television monitor mounted near the front door that was connected to the surveillance camera. The screen was blank.

"It's down," said Macaulay.

"There are three cameras and they are all wireless," said Morrissey. "Someone has disabled them."

Lexy had punched Barnaby's number into her cell phone.

"There is no cell phone signal," she said.

"They're jamming it," said Macaulay, looking through the peephole in the front door. The street was dark. He thought he saw a shadow move across the lawn. A shudder went through him, an atavistic warning.

"This is a secure room," said Morrissey. "Dan and I built it over the years. The doors are bullet-resistant and the windows are backed with reinforced concrete. There are steel plates behind those back cushions on the couches."

Morrissey was standing at the third and last door off the room. When he opened it, Macaulay saw what looked like a small arsenal, including two rifles, a sawed-off shotgun, several handguns on pegs, and stacks of ammunition on the shelves. A set of stairs led down from the weapons cache into the darkness.

"The basement is secure too," said Morrissey. "The outside entrance to it is lined with a bed of concrete."

Picking up the sawed-off shotgun, he handed it to Macaulay along with a box of shells.

"Ten-gauge rifled slugs," he said.

It was a Browning pump action. The slugs looked big enough to stop a horse as Macaulay fed them into the magazine. Morrissey removed an M1 carbine from the wall rack and began loading it with .30-caliber hollow-point bullets. "I carried one of these at Iwo . . . good for close work."

Lexy heard a soft thump somewhere above them.

"They could be just gangbangers," said Morrissey. "We've had plenty of those over the years."

"I don't think so," said Macaulay. "I'm sorry we led you into this, but they're probably a Chinese paramilitary force. If I'm right, they're going to try to take you alive to find out what you know about those crates. She and I are disposable."

"Don't be sorry, man," said Morrissey, grinning back. "There are a few surprises for anyone who tries this place. One is waiting on the other side of that door leading into the kitchen, and there are more upstairs."

He turned to Lexy and said, "Ma'am, you better stay right there behind the couch."

"Hand me that .45 on the right shelf," she said. "I assume you keep it loaded."

He laughed and tossed it over to her.

"Semper fi," he said as she charged the first round in the chamber.

The lights went out.

Morrissey threw a switch and two small recessed spots came on, the cones of light aimed at the door into the hallway and a second one on the opposite side of the room.

"That one leads into the kitchen. I'll kill the lights when we know which way they're coming. These will help too," he said, passing Macaulay a pair of infrared night-vision goggles. "If these guys are using body armor, be sure to aim for the hands, legs, and face."

"You've spent your brother's pension wisely," said Macaulay.

They heard a sudden cry of raw agony from behind the door leading to the kitchen. It stopped a few seconds later and was followed by a loud thumping on the floor above them until it finally ended too.

"Dan imported and raised baby Indian cobras," said Morrissey with a short laugh. "After he died, I let them stay on. They have most of the house to themselves."

There was a sharp detonation and the bolts blew off the hallway door, the half below the iron bar bursting wide-open. As Morrissey killed the spotlights, a man in a black body suit darted through and dove to his right, his light machine gun extended forward and firing at the couch where Macaulay and Lexy were positioned. His rifle was equipped with a suppressor and the slugs thudding into the quarter-inch steel plates sounded like a high-powered nail gun.

Through his infrared goggles, Macaulay watched as a single shot from Morrissey's carbine drove the man's head back at an odd angle to his body. He hit the floor and didn't move again.

"Liquid body armor," Morrissey said calmly.

A small device was tossed through the door opening. A cloud of gaseous smoke billowed up from it as a second explosive charge shattered the door to the kitchen. The iron bar remained in place and the next attacker ran into it, stopping in his tracks. Macaulay fired from behind the second couch, the ten-gauge rifled slug shattering his helmet and eviscerating his brain.

The odor of the gas reached Macaulay. A few seconds after smelling it, he knew it was some kind of immobilizing agent. He felt himself getting light-headed and knew the others would quickly suffer the same consequences.

"We have to get out," he said before holding his breath.

He heard a half dozen words barked out in guttural Chinese.

"The basement door," said Morrissey as a third attacker came through the hallway door in a low crouch, his infrared goggles swerving quickly back and forth to survey the room. He was bigger than the first two and carrying what looked like a heavy machine gun.

As Lexy dove toward the basement door, he fired at the couch where Macaulay was still hiding, ripping the couch apart and dislodging the steel plates. Macaulay fired back at the man's helmet before dropping prone to the floor.

The rifled slug hit the attacker in the chest of his body armor, driving him back against the wall as Lexy turned to fire a full clip from her .45. One round must have hit his right hand, because he dropped the machine gun. Morrissey did not miss his head with his next shot from the M1 carbine.

Morrissey covered for them as Macaulay headed for the basement stairs behind Lexy. They were into the darkness when a fluorescent light came on automatically below, lighting up the stone foundation walls.

As two more attackers came through the shattered doorways, Morrissey reached the door to the basement stairs and swung it shut behind him.

The diminishing shaft of fluorescent light attracted one of the attackers and he began firing, spraying the small opening with machine gun bullets. Morrissey dropped the iron security bar into position before tumbling head-first down the stairs.

Macaulay caught him in his arms as he reached the concrete floor. The old man was bleeding from three wounds stitched across his upper back.

"Behind the bookcase," he said, his voice hoarse, "a passage between this house and the one built by my uncle."

Macaulay remembered the identical house next door that had been gutted by fire. There was only one bookcase in the basement. He stepped toward it and pulled at the left side. It didn't move. When he tried the right side, it swung open on the steel rollers hidden beneath its base.

Lexy knelt next to the old man, his head cradled in her arms. Above them, another small explosion signaled the destruction of the reinforced basement door.

"Good luck," he said as blood swelled from the corner of his lips. "Semper fi."

FIFTEEN

Macaulay smelled the putrid water coating the base of the dank, moldy passageway. It squished through his socks as he emerged into the pale darkness of the basement in the house next door. In the subdued, ambient light from his cell phone, he carefully picked his way across the low-ceilinged chamber.

Behind him, Lexy attempted to call Barnaby again on her own phone.

"Still no signal," she whispered.

The basement exit door was blocked by fire-blackened wreckage that had congealed into a single mass. The staircase to the first floor was undamaged but covered with more fire debris.

He climbed slowly up the stairs in the darkness, trying to avoid making the slightest sound, feeling his way along with Lexy right behind him. Like in the Morrissey house, the staircase led to a door off the front parlor. The room was configured exactly the same, except that the bay windows facing the front yard were missing.

He could hear muffled voices across the yard from the Morrissey house. They were angry and excited. Through one of the empty windows, he saw the shadowy outlines of two men standing at each end of Morrissey's porch and two more near the sidewalk where Macaulay had parked his car.

Otherwise the neighborhood was quiet. In the wasteland of abandoned homes, the sounds of the explosions and gunfire had apparently not led anyone to call the metropolitan police.

Steve remembered seeing a tall stockade fence that stretched across the backyards of the two identical houses and was divided by a redbrick garage. The garage faced onto a rear alley that ran parallel to the street. That was their only avenue of escape.

He led Lexy down the darkened main hallway. The back door of the house opened onto a rear portico from the kitchen, which had been stripped of anything having value, including the stove, sink, and refrigerator.

Only the lower half of the back door was still connected to its hinges. Stepping past, Macaulay slowly descended the portico steps and stopped. In the dull reflected light of a car passing on one of the cross streets, he saw that another commando was deployed in the backyard of the Morrissey house.

The man's back was to him. He was wearing an infrared scope on his helmet, and his light machine gun was trained toward the rear of the house. Every ten or fifteen seconds, he swung his head around to scan the area behind him.

There wouldn't be time to make it all the way across the backyard. The man had to be taken out. While Lexy waited by the portico, Macaulay crept back inside the kitchen to find a weapon. Crossing the room, he tripped over something. Picking it up, he saw it was a rolling pin. He momentarily imagined all the piecrusts it might have rolled in more innocent times. He had a better use for it now.

Outside, he whispered his plan to Lexy and took off his soggy socks. He waited until the commando had scanned in both directions and then sprinted toward him while Lexy ran for the redbrick garage.

In full flight, Macaulay's right foot landed on a broken bottle, and he felt a searing pain shoot up his leg. Making no sound, he fell to the ground. At that moment, someone began shouting from the bowels of the house they had just left. They had apparently found the passageway behind the bookcase.

The commando turned his head toward the voice, which was clearly barking out a command in Chinese. He began running toward the house, at one point passing within ten feet of Macaulay's prone body.

Pausing at the back portico, the commando scanned the interior with his infrared scope and then disappeared inside. Macaulay was up and running again, the pain in his foot excruciating as it came down heavily on rocks and weeds. Lexy had already reached the garage. He hoped that the door leading into the alley wasn't jammed with junk.

Racing inside, he saw Lexy searching the back of it with her cell phone flashlight. The garage doors had been nailed shut to prevent intruders from coming through the alley. There was another brief staccato shout. They were out in the yard and coming closer.

A side door of the garage led past the stockade fence. It was their only chance. The door was swollen with mildew, but together they wrenched it open and stepped through. A distant streetlamp cast a faint shadow down the alley. Macaulay pointed in the direction away from the streetlamp and they began to run.

He Does Not Blink stood in the hangar office at the Coleman Young Regional Airport nine miles northeast of central Detroit and fixed a stony gaze on his second-in-command. Colonel Mu stood at attention in front of him, his eyes staring straight ahead at the gold stars on Li Shen Wui's uniform collar.

Mu was twenty-seven and shaped like a miniature Arnold Schwarzenegger. Although he had never been tested in combat like his predecessor Colonel Wong, Mu had proven to be merciless in Li's cleansing missions and he followed Li's every order without question.

Mu had just returned from the attack on the old marine's house and had given his report. The mission had been a complete disaster. It was impossible for Mu to mask the shame in his eyes.

Li again briefly contemplated the reasons he had decided not to lead it himself. It came down to his fear of failure. Now he would be held accountable anyway. He stepped away from Mu and paced around the decrepit office.

He had rented the airport hangar as a staging area for the assault team and to shelter their two transport jets from prying eyes. The whole complex was a decaying mess like everything else in the ruined city. When his jet had landed, he thought he was in Cuba.

While the assault team was carrying out its mission, Li had ordered his supply officer to organize a party for them to celebrate their returning with the old man who held the secret of finding Peking Man.

"When will the replacements arrive?" Li demanded.

"Their plane has departed San Francisco," said Mu. "They will be here in three hours."

"Assemble the men for me to address them in the hangar," said Li, dismissing him.

There was a light knock on the office door thirty seconds later. It was warped from age and misuse and wouldn't close properly.

"Come," said Li.

The door opened to reveal Sergeant Shi. He marched forward three paces, stopped, and saluted.

"It is Lord Zhou, Your Excellency," he said, "calling on the secure line."

Li pretended a look of supreme satisfaction.

"You may go," he said, picking up the secure phone.

"Tell me the thrilling news," said Zhou Shen Wui.

The clarity of his father's voice made it seem as if he were in the next room, his fat ass settled into his favorite throne chair. Li had to assume that one of his father's spies had already reported the debacle to him.

"I am writing the report now," said Li neutrally.

"How did your stealth cavalry do on American soil?"

Li tasted the hint of mockery in his voice.

"There is much work that remains to be done, my lord," he said.

"Did you lead the mission yourself?" Zhou asked.

Li wondered where his father was calling from, maybe aboard his high-speed train somewhere in the highlands or possibly in the bed of his favorite concubine, Chunwa, the girl who had once been engaged to Li.

"I thought it better to coordinate the mission from our base here at the airport so that I would be able to follow up immediately on the valuable information I expected to learn from the old marine," said Li. "My orders to Mu were to eliminate Macaulay and Vaughan and to capture the old marine and bring him to me."

"And has he talked yet?"

Li's rage and humiliation swept through his intestines like liquid fire, although the only physical indication of his true feelings was the further bulging of his protruding lower lip.

"Unfortunately, the old marine died in the attack," he said in a measured voice. "Macaulay and Vaughan have temporarily eluded us. We did find a blood trail that indicates that one of them was badly wounded by my force."

The silence lasted so long that Li wondered if the connection had been broken.

"Your force," Zhou repeated finally, "your stealth cavalry."

His voice was soaked in ridicule.

"Were there casualties?" asked Zhou.

"Yes, my lord," answered Li.

"Well?" demanded Zhou.

Li knew the gross pig wouldn't relent until every detail was extracted.

"Four men were killed in the attack, three by gunfire and one by a poisonous snake. One man is wounded. He is paralyzed from snakebite."

"Of course . . . the famous snakes of Detroit," said Zhou. "Did your men at least bring back the snake?"

"I do not know, my lord," said Li, his lower lip bulging even farther.

Wǒ hèn tā . . . Wǒ hèn tā . . . Wǒ hèn tā, he silently mouthed into the phone.

"Your men did no reconnaissance?"

"The old man's house was set up like a fortress, my lord," said Li. "The old man looked harmless. He was observed in a wheelchair. There was no way to know what was inside."

"Of course," agreed Zhou. "The outcome was inevitable."

Li was about to respond that he had developed a new plan to trace the movements of Macaulay and Vaughan, but by then his father had hung up and a tonal beep kept repeating itself in his ear.

He stalked out of the office to find that Colonel Mu had assembled the remaining members of the assault team in two ranks. They came to attention with clicking heels as he crossed the hangar to address them.

Smiling, he told them how proud he was of their first military engagement on American soil and that glory and reward awaited them at home in China after the assured success of their mission.

After dismissing them, Li told Mu to bring the man who had shot and killed the old marine to his hangar office. When they arrived, Mu vainly tried to shut the warped door behind him. The young man stood at attention and saluted.

No more than twenty, he was as comely as a girl, thought Li, with long eyelashes and a mouth shaped like a Cupid's bow. Li remembered him from the mission at the small village they had wiped out near the chemical factory. He had been the one assigned to shoot the surviving children. He had appeared to relish the task. Now he was sweating profusely, the moisture staining the collar of his uniform.

"Why did you fire against my express orders?" Li asked politely.

"We were told that the man to be taken alive was confined to a wheelchair," said the boy. "I saw a man escaping through the door. He was outlined against the light and standing up. I thought it was the target Colonel Mu approved for elimination."

"You disobeyed my orders," said Li as if he hadn't heard the explanation.

"It won't happen again, General," said the boy.

"Another mistake will not be tolerated."

"There will not be another."

"You can go," said Li.

After the boy saluted and left, Li gazed at the expressionless face of Colonel Mu.

"Make an example of him like you did the old man in the basement," said Li. "And make sure the replacements are aware of the penalty for mistakes. Did you leave my calling card with the body at the house?"

Colonel Mu nodded. "As you ordered, Excellency."

"If you need me I will be in the pool," said Li, heading into the adjoining office where he had ordered them to set up his ten-meter portable lap pool.

They had run ten blocks before the range of the jamming signal had been breached and she was able to call Barnaby.

They had stopped to rest in front of a well-lit liquor and convenience store. Steel mesh covered the front windows and entrance door.

While she briefed Barnaby on what had happened, Macaulay went into the store and bought a pint of Jack Daniel's, a roll of duct tape, and paper towels.

"I do no like my customer bleed on the floor," said the Asian proprietor.

Sitting on the curb outside, Steve took a deep hit of the whiskey and then poured two inches of it over the gash in his heel. Wrapping the foot in paper towels, he bound it with duct tape while Lexy told him that an FBI team was on its way to the Morrissey house along with the metropolitan police and that a squad car would pick them up within a few minutes.

The Morrissey house was lit up like a movie stage set when they returned fifteen minutes later. Police cruisers flanked both ends of the block, and the yard was brightly lit with truck-mounted flood lights. A small swarm of police officers with Maglites was already combing the weed-strewn yard in front and back.

An FBI agent waited for them on the front porch. Through the open doorway, Lexy could see members of a forensic team working inside the hallway and up the staircase to the second floor.

"My name is McAdams," said the agent.

To Macaulay he looked like Abraham Lincoln without a beard. Tall and spare, his gaunt, furrowed face and forlorn eyes were crowned by a mass of unruly gray hair. His voice was soft and husky.

"I've been told that I'm not allowed to ask you any

questions about what went on here," he said. "It would be nice to get a better understanding of why."

"We are not at liberty to discuss it," said Macaulay.

"Beyond my measly pay grade—I know," he said. "Just thought I'd ask."

They followed McAdams through the hallway and into the front parlor. A sharp metallic odor permeated the air mixed with the smell of cordite. Someone had set up halogen lights that garishly lit up the carnage.

"Some kind of gas residue here," said one of the forensic technicians. "We'll check it out in the lab."

"There is only one body left inside the house," said McAdams, "but enough spilled blood to indicate plenty more. Someone did a pretty good job of cleaning up the mess before they left."

Bullet holes laced the white plaster walls and the green plywood covering the bay windows. The couch where Macaulay and Lexy had hidden lay collapsed on the floor, its stuffing strewn everywhere and the steel plates indented with bullets.

"The body in the basement has been tentatively identified as Daniel Morrissey, the owner of the house, but I guess you knew that," said McAdams.

Lexy nodded.

McAdams glanced down at Macaulay's paper-towel-covered foot.

"I know better than to ask," he said as they headed down the basement steps.

Sean Patrick Morrissey was no longer lying on the basement floor where Lexy had cradled his head in her arms. He was standing and facing them, his wrists nailed in the crucifixion position to two of the pine studs. His head was strapped to the wall with a leather dog leash. He was naked.

Someone had carved the skin off his body from his neck to his waist. A knife had been driven through his heart and was embedded in the wall behind him. Lexy refused to turn her eyes away, letting the visual evidence of what they had done to him register forever in her brain.

"I've come to think that wolves are farther up the food chain than human beings," said McAdams. "They are cleaner, more honest and hardworking creatures, and they protect their young."

"He never felt anything," said one of the forensic technicians as he examined the hilt of the knife. "He was already dead when they did this."

"Why would they have taken the time?" asked Lexy.

The forensic man looked back at her with weary, cynical eyes. He was in his fifties, with rabbit teeth and metal-rimmed glasses.

"You should see the artistry of some of the gang killings in this city," he said, "the ones where they want to send a message. At least this poor guy still has his eyes and his genitals between his legs."

He motioned McAdams over to examine the knife in Morrissey's chest.

"Looks to me like a short broadsword," he said.

"More like a bowie knife," said McAdams, "except sharpened along both edges."

"It's hard to see because of the dried blood, but this appears to be an inscription of some kind," said the technician, pointing to the hilt.

"Maybe initials?" said McAdams, looking at it closely.

"They're probably Chinese," said Macaulay.

McAdams turned to look at him appraisingly.

"Any other important insights to provide?" he asked.

Macaulay shook his head.

Hard rain was spattering the windows, and Sebastian Choate's inner office was inexplicably cold. Someone had apparently turned off the steam vents to the radiators. Otherwise the room was exactly as Barnaby had remembered it. Choate's tiny silk slippers rested on the ottoman in front of his favorite easy chair.

The room was now crowded with the museum's deputy security director, three federal agents from Dusenberry's task force, two New York police detectives, a forensic team, and an officer from the precinct K-9 squad accompanied by his salivating German shepherd. Barnaby wondered what Choate would have said if he had seen them all in their muddy shoes tracking up the oldest-known carpet in the world.

"We really don't have anything to go on at this point," said Horace Starling, the deputy museum security director. "Professor Choate is very quirky in his habits. For all we know, he could be in Chile or Zanzibar."

"That's fine," said Barnaby. "All I want at this point is to gain access to his safe, and you now have the federal warrant allowing us to do so."

"That ain't so easy," said the little red-haired man who the local police commander had brought with him to "consult" on the problem of opening the state-of-the-art steel safe in which Choate had protected his seventy years of research into the Peking Man.

"I thought I made it clear to you that opening this safe was a matter of national urgency," said Barnaby to the police commander.

The portly senior officer was in his sixties and probably close to retirement. Barnaby assumed the little man was some kind of longtime crony. The commander was obviously uncomfortable with the situation.

"I believe Mr. Doyle gives us the best chance to do that," he insisted.

Doyle stared up at Barnaby with the same look of incredulity that Barnaby was feeling as he gazed down at him. Pushing seventy at least, Doyle looked like an extra in *Darby O'Gill and the Little People*. Almost as diminutive as a leprechaun, he had flaming red hair that was clearly a dye job. To say that he had a ruddy complexion was an understatement. His face matched his hair.

"You look like you're right out of central casting," said Barnaby.

"I'm right out of Leavenworth," said Doyle, "although I have had many years since to appreciate the error of my past ways."

"He's the best safecracker in New York," said the police commander.

"One of the last," said Doyle, sadly. "It's a dying art, you see. In my own case, it was a family business, handed down from generation to generation since the Doyles arrived here in 1847. My great-grandfather broke the safe of J. Pierpont Morgan when he lived on Madison Avenue during the Panic of 1907."

"Really?" said Barnaby. "And what did he find?"

"An Episcopal Bible," said Doyle, "along with some

letters written by Morgan to his son's governess that were indiscreet, you might say."

"I hope he put them to good use," said Barnaby. "Right now we have bigger fish to fry as the Irish are fond of saying. How the hell do you plan on opening this safe?"

It looked like nothing more than a polished black wall cabinet across one wall of the room, but the police had told Barnaby it was almost impregnable. Doyle walked over to it, opened the outer door, and knelt down.

"A double combination lock," he said. "If it was a key lock I could pick it in an hour. This little girl offers more of a challenge."

"What are our options?" asked the police commander.

Doyle slowly twirled the combination key and cocked his ear as if listening for voices. "The so-called modern experts would probably recommend a magnetic limpet drill with bits that can penetrate the hard plates. I'm told they now use a fiber-optic scope to read the position of the wheels. Unfortunately, there's soft steel back there to inhibit the drill."

Barnaby had no idea what he was talking about.

"How long will it take?" he asked.

"Those fifty-millimeter bolts extend in every direction," said Doyle. "You could burn the hinges off with acetylene and the door would still hold."

"How long?" repeated Barnaby.

"You could blow it, of course," said Doyle, "but there is no guarantee that anything inside it would survive the blast. Anyway, blasting ain't my line."

"What is your line?" asked Barnaby.

"He feels it," said the police commander.

"Please go ahead and feel it," said Barnaby.

"Here is what I do," said Doyle. "There is no click when the tumblers reach the right position, but I can usually hear when the lever descends into the slot for each number in the combination. I can feel it after getting to know her ways . . . at least most of the time."

"How long will all the feeling take?" asked Barnaby.

"Maybe four days," said Doyle. "Could be sooner, depending on her."

Barnaby looked around at the rest of the group. None of them would meet his eye except the German shepherd.

"You have my cell phone number," Barnaby said to the police commander.

An hour later, Barnaby had consumed two glasses of Orfevi Frascati to clear his palate and was about to sample the first of two dozen bluepoint oysters at La Grenouille when his phone began to ring. He picked it up.

"He's in," said the police commander.

When Barnaby returned to Choate's office, the door to the safe was cracked open a few inches.

"You have to see this," said the commander.

Barnaby swung the steel door open.

There were no papers or file folders such as the ones Choate had described. There was nothing in the safe at all. Except Choate. He was lying in the fetal position, facing the door. He looked as if he had gone to sleep.

SIXTEEN

Ira Dusenberry surveyed the sterling silver tray stacked with warm, freshly baked scones, donuts, and cookies that had been sent down a few minutes earlier from the White House Mess. Their fragrance filled the conference room along with the aroma of his favorite blend of dark Colombian coffee.

He was tempted to fill his plate with a full medley of pastries but saw that the others were already at the conference table and waiting for him to begin the meeting. Selecting a French cruller and an Irish cream chocolate tart, he took his place at the head of the table.

As the national security adviser to the president, he now used the largest of the three soundproof situation rooms in the intelligence management center deep beneath the West Wing of the White House. Today, it seemed a bit like overkill. There were twenty-eight chairs around the table and only six were occupied at his end.

Dusenberry glanced down at the president's morning book containing the latest update of pending matters of national security importance. It was opened to the Peking Man folder. He took a few moments to scan the summary page while ingesting the cruller.

His personal assistant, Darlene Choy, set a mug of the black coffee down on the coaster next to the morning book and took a seat in one of the staff chairs along the wall along with Dusenberry's deputy security adviser and two senior aides.

He took a first sip and glanced at the members of Barnaby Finchem's so-called team. Its makeup was not reassuring. Not for the first time, he wondered if he had made a serious mistake in enlisting Finchem's help.

To Dusenberry's left was the degenerate old CIA operative Somervell in his stained seersucker suit, and next to him the prune-faced crone June Corcoran, who was rolling an unlit cigarette back and forth between her nicotine-stained fingers like Captain Queeg juggling his steel ball bearings.

Alexandra Vaughan was as lovely as he remembered, although the retired air force brigadier general Macaulay looked as played out as he had been when Dusenberry last saw him at the hospital in Maine after the Valhalla matter. He had walked into the situation room with a distinct limp.

To his right, Barnaby Finchem was looking back at him with a sardonic and almost insulting grin, his tangled mass of white hair flowing down the back of his disreputable jumpsuit. Dusenberry hoped that none of his senior White House colleagues had witnessed their arrival at the situation room.

"I gather your team has made some progress, Professor Finchem," he said, deciding to keep it formal in front of his aides.

"We have indeed," began Barnaby. "In the last four days, we have accomplished more than your intra-agency task force has accomplished in three years."

"Really?" said Dusenberry with a skeptical smirk. "Let's hear it."

Barnaby glanced over at the four NSC staff members sitting along the wall.

"It's for your ears only," he said.

Dusenberry gave him a supercilious smile and said, "I can assure you that everyone on my staff can be trusted with the most sensitive information you have gathered."

"Like Jessica Birdwell, Ira?" asked Barnaby innocently.

Dusenberry flushed. She had been a member of the national security staff during the Valhalla matter and had turned out to be an enemy mole. Lovely woman, Dusenberry recalled, great legs and very bright. He wondered for a moment if she was still at Guantanamo.

Turning to his aides, he said, "I will handle it from here."

As they got up to leave, Darlene Choy looked at her watch and said curtly, "The NSC meeting on the Yemen crisis begins in fifteen minutes."

Dusenberry waited until they left the room.

"Now that you have insulted my staff, please tell me where we are in this thing," he said.

"Actually, we have a pretty good idea where the Peking Man can be found," said Barnaby, "at least within a hundred square miles."

Dusenberry's initially buoyant expression disappeared.

"We believe Peking Man is at rest under the Bahamian sea," said Barnaby. "We are in the process of narrowing the parameters of exactly where."

"On what basis can you make that assurance?"

Barnaby began with their visit to meet Sebastian Choate at the Museum of Natural History. He briefly summarized the conclusions drawn by Choate after seventy years of searching for the fossil, and concluded with the startling assertion that Choate had confided to him after reading the diary of the famed archaeologist Davidson Black.

"You're saying that Choate believes that the Peking Man was some form of alien being?"

"Believed is a more appropriate word," said Barnaby. "Choate was murdered shortly after our visit. His exact words to me were that Davidson Black concluded in his test findings in 1934 that Peking Man did not conform to the train of human evolution as we know it. We'll have to find it to prove that one way or another."

"And Choate had the journal or diary containing these test findings?"

"That's what he claimed. When I had your security experts crack his office safe three days ago, we discovered that his entire collection of Peking Man records and documents had been stolen. The only thing we found in the safe was Choate. According to the medical examiner, he was still alive when they locked him inside. The FBI is still searching for his Chinese research assistant."

Dusenberry got up from the table and replenished his plate with two cannoli and a hefty wedge of apple strudel topped with whipped cream.

"What makes you think the fossil is in the Bahamas and that you'll be able to pinpoint its location?" he asked.

"A good deal of pertinent research," said Barnaby. "I'll let Dr. Vaughan take it from here."

"You already have our report on Sean Patrick Morrissey, who was the only survivor of the marine truck convoy," she began. "Before he was killed four days ago by the Chinese paramilitary team, I took down his recollections in shorthand. His memories were often fragmentary, but together they formed a consistent pattern. The key elements were that after the ship sailed from Chinwangtao on December eighth, he remembered being on it a long time. Later, he thought it broke down somewhere from engine failure. He was suffering an attack of malaria at the time. We have concluded that the ship was actually stopped while waiting to go through the Panama Canal. The only other way the ship could have reached the Atlantic coast would have been by steaming around Cape Horn, and it could not have reached the Caribbean in the necessary timeline."

"How do you know the ship reached the Caribbean?"

"It's in the report you have there," she said, pointing to the president's morning book. "Morrissey was dropped off by an unknown rescue vessel at Key West, Florida, on March 2, 1942. You'll remember that the ship he was on departed from Chinwangtao, China on December 8, 1941. The distance by sea from Chinwangtao to the Panama Canal is approximately nine thousand miles. Morrissey referred to the ship as a tramp. Assuming it had a maximum speed of ten knots, it would have taken the ship at least thirty-eight full days and nights of steaming to reach the canal. At that time in the war, hundreds of merchant ships were desperately trying to escape Japanese waters and a logjam developed when they reached Panama. We believe one of them was Morrissey's ship. For our theoretical matrix, we also assumed that the ship was unregistered, since Sebastian Choate told us that he reviewed the records of all the shipping lines operating in China in December 1941, and none of them were in Chinwangtao on December eighth."

"I will concede it sounds theoretically possible, at least so far," said Dusenberry, surreptitiously unbuttoning the vest of his brown suit.

Dusenberry had recently taken to wearing three-piece suits after one of the White House social advisers suggested they were coming back in style. He had ordered them in three seasonal sizes from his Indian tailor in Trinidad. The smallest size was for baseball season, when he got out more and tended to lose some weight. The football season suit was one size larger, since he tended to binge-eat while watching the Redskins find a way to lose nearly every week. The basketball suit was the largest. He rarely had any physical exercise during the winter. Although the baseball season was already a month old, his body was now threatening to burst out of the basketball suit.

"June can speak to the next phase of our report," said Lexy.

"I flew down to Panama City four days ago at the request of Dr. Finchem," she began, "and requested access to the record vaults that the canal authority has maintained of all ships that passed through it since 1914. The records from World War Two were of course classified for security purposes, but thanks to the intercession of your office, I was permitted to review them."

Dusenberry saw that the cigarette she had been rolling in her fingers was slowly coming apart. The others appeared to take no notice of it.

"I began my review of the records by searching for ships that arrived at the canal in mid-January 1942, the earliest date our ship could have reached there from Chinwangtao. We know it must also have passed through the canal no later than the third week in January, since the ship had to travel another thousand miles to reach a point close enough to the coast of Florida to put Corporal Morrissey ashore at Key West on March second. I learned that in January 1942 the approximate wait time to go through the canal for merchant vessels was five days. Top priority was granted to warships. A tramp freighter would have been at the bottom of the priority list."

"This is all very interesting, but is there any way you could expedite your presentation, Ms. Corcoran?" said Dusenberry. "I admire your diligence to detail, but there are other pressing matters on my agenda for today."

She crushed the unfiltered cigarette in her right hand and dropped the loose tobacco on the table. Scooping a small portion with her thumb and forefinger, she placed it in her mouth and silently chewed for a few seconds.

"I found the record of a single merchant vessel that met all of our principal criteria," she went on. "The freighter's name was the *Prins Willem*. It arrived at the Panama Canal on January twenty-first and was carrying marine engines, tractors, and other agricultural equipment. Its port of origin was stated as Yingkou, China. Yingkou is slightly north of Chinwangtao on the Gulf of Chihli. Although the ship's captain had a Dutch passport, he could not provide the ship's official registration papers. He claimed that his ship was licensed to operate within Chinese waters, but that its papers had been left behind in Yingkou during the chaotic conditions after the Japanese advance. The *Prins Willem* was allowed to pass through the canal five days later."

"You said that this marine corporal Morrissey was aboard the ship when it reached Panama," said Dusenberry. "Why wouldn't the captain have let him off the ship there?"

"You may recall he said he was suffering from an attack of malaria at that point," said Lexy. "Putting ashore an ill marine corporal from an unregistered tramp steamer would only have raised unwanted questions."

"And by then the Dutch captain knew there was something of exceptional value in the crate," added Macaulay before relating to Dusenberry the circumstances under which it was loaded aboard the ship while under attack from the Japanese advance guard.

"So what happened to the *Prins Willem*?" asked Dusenberry, his curiosity now aroused.

"Captain DeVries declared his next port of destination as Martinique in the Lesser Antilles, with the ship's final destination being New York," said June Corcoran, after chewing and swallowing the last shreds of her cigarette. "The *Prins Willem* arrived at Fort-de-France in Martinique on February twenty-third. It departed after refueling on February twenty-fifth bound for New York. Then it disappeared."

"So how the hell would you know where to find it after all these years?" asked Dusenberry.

"One of the things Corporal Morrissey remembered was being on the deck of the ship on a warm night with a gentle breeze when there was a brilliant light," said Macaulay, "which was followed by his head being slammed into a steel bulkhead."

"A torpedo?" said Dusenberry.

Macaulay nodded and said, "By early 1942, allied merchant ships were being sunk every day from the Gulf of Mexico to the Bahamas. The navy called it torpedo alley. Tommy and I found the next key to the puzzle in the German Kriegsmarine records captured in Flensburg by the American army in 1945. They are all on microfilm in the military archives at College Park. Tommy felt that for security reasons we should do it ourselves. We personally went through the claims of every U-boat that was operating in Caribbean waters in early 1942."

"Aren't those records in German?" asked Dusenberry.

"I read and speak German fluently, Ira," said Tommy Somervell, as if speaking to a mentally challenged child. "So does June."

Dusenberry's smartphone began to chirp. He picked it up, listened for a few moments, and said, "I will be there shortly. It's only goddamn Yemen."

"We found more than three dozen claims by U-boat commanders of definite sinkings of merchant ships in those waters within the timeline we were looking for. We then cross-referenced those claims to the lists of vessels acknowledged to have been lost in the same period by allied maritime authorities and shipping companies. There were only three ships for which there was no corollary information . . . all of them freighters, all three apparently unregistered and without any survivors who reported the sinkings."

"Isn't it possible that the freighters claimed by the U-boat commanders weren't actually lost?" asked Dusenberry. "A lot of claims were exaggerated on both sides."

"Good point, Ira," said Tommy, "but in these three cases, the U-boat captains witnessed the ships going down. In one case there was a blurry photograph of its last moments. In any event, the one sunk off the Turks and Caicos went down in broad daylight. Another was attacked at night, but it was sunk near the Caymans southwest of Cuba. Whoever rescued Corporal Morrissey would not have taken him all the way to Key West from there."

Dusenberry had forgotten about Yemen.

"And the third one?" he asked.

"According to the after-action report, the third freighter was sunk a few miles north of a place called Dunmore Town on Harbour Island off North Eleuthera," said Macaulay.

"I've heard of Dunmore Town," said Dusenberry. "A lot of American Tories who sided with the British during the Revolutionary War ended up there when they thought they might get hanged."

"Unfortunately, the U-boat captain logged no specific longitude or latitude coordinates to mark the location," said Tommy. "In his after-action report, he noted that the ocean depth at the sinking was forty-two meters. There was one other reference to its location. In the margin, he wrote the words *Teufels Rückgrat.*"

He gave Dusenberry a lingering smile.

"All right, I give up," said Dusenberry.

"The Devil's Backbone," said Tommy. "It's a reef that runs east along the coast of North Eleuthera from the old pirate stronghold of Spanish Wells. One odd thing . . . the Germans were very meticulous about record-keeping. We found the captains' logs from every other U-boat except this one."

"Is it important?" asked Dusenberry.

"No way to know," said Tommy. "It's possible the submarine might have picked up a survivor or two who could shed more light on what happened to the crate, or maybe even the crate itself if they were told by a survivor it was valuable."

"I have asked Mr. Somervell and Ms. Corcoran to try to track it down," said Barnaby.

"What else will you need?" asked Dusenberry. "How can I help?"

"At this point, we should probably do an informal recon after creating a plausible cover story," said Macaulay. "If you send a military team down there now, it will only arouse questions and interest from the locals. Word would spread fast. I'm putting together a list of things we'll need to start the search . . . a boat, diving equipment . . ."

Dusenberry's phone began to chirp again. "Just keep me abreast," he said, trying to rebutton his vest. "Anything you need I'll make sure you get."

He was at the door when he turned and said, "One final question . . . wouldn't the fossils have dissolved or disintegrated in the sea by now along with the bones of the ship's crew?"

"According to the records at the Peking Union Medical College, they were carefully packed in airtight glass containers surrounded by oilcloth and straw," said Barnaby. "Knowing they were of significant value, we can assume Captain DeVries would have made sure the red one was stowed securely. We can only hope the crate didn't take a direct hit."

SEVENTEEN

Dawn found Steve and Lexy arriving at the end of the first pattern in the search grid along the reefs north of Harbour Island. Sipping coffee from a white ceramic mug, he sat at the steering console and watched as a garish orange sun climbed out of a calm sapphire sea. With its sudden intense glare, Macaulay had to squint to read the monitors on the backlit LCD display of the ultrasonic ocean depth meter and the side-scan sonar rig.

Completing the projected run, he steered north for one hundred meters and then punched the reverse westerly heading into the navigation system of the Regal Commodore thirty-two-foot cruiser. *Island Time* settled onto the reciprocal course at a speed of twelve knots.

Lexy emerged from the cabin galley with a turkey and

bacon sandwich and more coffee. Both of them had shed the clothing of official Washington. Macaulay wore only khaki cargo shorts. Lexy's white string bikini offset her quickly developing tan.

He glanced off to starboard. To the south, he could see white surf breaking onto a deserted white sand beach on North Eleuthera. Closer to shore, he saw patches of dark green where the jagged coral reef lay just underneath the surface.

The search grid covered a distance along the reef of almost seven miles. The width of the same grid was a fraction of that. A half mile offshore, the depth dropped well beyond the forty-two meters charted by the U-boat captain in March 1942. Close in, the depth was too shallow, less than a hundred feet.

It made their search for the final resting place of the *Prins Willem* a little easier. Scores of ships had come to grief on the Devil's Backbone from the times of the Spanish conquests. It would have been impossible to find the *Prins Willem* in that graveyard if she had ground herself to death on the reef itself. But if the U-boat captain had been correct in his report that she was lying at about one hundred thirty feet, her grave would almost certainly be a lonely one.

Used in conjunction with the boat's side-scan sonar, the depth meter's transceiver sensors were accurate to within a half percentage point and recorded the data transmissions as soon as they were received off the bottom. Coordinated with the GPS data that was being fed simultaneously into the laptop computer monitored by Lexy in the galley below, they would review the findings after completing the grid and come back to begin a sophisticated search of the bottom in every section that had the proper depth.

For further protective coloring from watchers on-shore, Macaulay had set up two trolling lines on the boat's outriggers and released them astern with side-winder lures from the rods and PENN Fathom Lever Drag reels that came with the boat.

It had been a busy four days for Macaulay since their meeting at the situation room in the White House. He had quickly sketched out a plan for how to undertake the search without attracting attention. Barnaby had given his approval and Macaulay had flown down to Fort Lauderdale that same day. He went straight to the boat brokerage owned by his old friend Chris Kimball.

Among the pilots in the F-16 squadron once commanded by Macaulay, Chris had been known as the King-fish, largely from his prowess with women but also for his love of boats and fishing. After his retirement, he had indulged his second passion by starting a charter boat company. Most important, Macaulay knew he could trust him with his life.

Chris had changed little since their days together in the squadron. He had stayed in great shape, and his thick tousled hair had yet to turn gray. In his paneled office overlooking the harbor, Macaulay confided to him that he was organizing an effort to find a sunken ship in the Bahamas, not for treasure purposes, but because it was important to the country. It needed to be done as quickly and inconspicuously as possible, he added.

Macaulay said he needed two boats, a smaller one to conduct the preliminary search and a bigger one for their team to live aboard in order to reduce informal contact with the local population.

"What is the budget?" asked Kimball.

"Whatever we need," said Macaulay. "But it's taxpayer's money . . . fair margins."

For the mother ship, Chris recommended a seventy-two-foot Hatteras Sports Fisherman called *Trader's Bluff* that was owned by a second-tier hedge fund millionaire from Philadelphia and immediately available for charter.

"It will confirm the idea that you're in the Bahamas to fish and it won't stand out against the grandiose yachts that usually cruise there. We can moor it right in the harbor at Dunmore Town."

"We?" asked Macaulay.

"I'm coming with you, skipper," said Chris with the same tone of admiration he had always displayed toward Macaulay. "Sounds like it could be fun."

"It could really be dangerous, Chris," said Macaulay. "Three of us are already being hunted and I can't even tell you why it's important."

"If you're doing it, I know it's important. Besides, I'm known there as a serious fisherman," said Kimball. "I can get any supplies you need without raising suspicion."

For the smaller search boat, he recommended a thirty-two-foot 1989 Regal Commodore called *Island Time* that was powered by twin MerCruiser four-hundred-and-fifty-four-horsepower engines with Bravo outdrives.

"It cruises at twenty-four knots and can top thirty-five," said Chris. "The boat is seaworthy and equipped with the latest electronics. The guy who owns it has been all over the Bahamas for the last twenty years, so the boat's familiar there."

Macaulay gave him a list of things to install in it, including an ultrasonic depth meter, side-scan sonar, a set of marine salvage airbags, and a portable high-pressure compressor for recharging scuba tanks.

"We'll need enough diving gear for at least four."

"I'll have the Commodore and the Hatteras waiting for you in Nassau," said Chris Kimball. "From there it's only fifty miles to the harbor at Dunmore Town. I'll stock the Hatteras and arrange all the permits and mooring reservations."

Macaulay handed him the credit card supplied by Dusenberry's office.

"Who is Ross Lockridge?" asked Kimball.

"You're looking at him," said Macaulay, "at least until this thing is over. My team will be arriving in Nassau in two days. There are three of us right now, another man and a woman. Aside from you, we won't need anyone else to crew for us. I've also got an engine man and diver I want to bring in on this, the best guy with motors I've ever seen."

From Kimball's office, Macaulay put in a call to Tom Hurdnut's Flying Service in Belize. After reaching him, he asked if there was any chance Carlos might be available to help him with a project he was working on.

"I had to lay him off, Steve," said Hurdnut. "After you left, he began spending most of his time drinking at Lana's. I couldn't rely on him. I'm not sure you can anymore either."

Macaulay tracked Carlos down at the bar.

"He's right here, Steve," said Lana. "Are you coming back?"

"Not any time soon," said Macaulay. "Can you put him on?"

"Where you be, Steef?" Carlos said in his fractured English.

"I might have a job for you," he said, "Keeping engines maintained, doing some diving."

"You be think of me?"

"Yeah," said Macaulay, "I be think of you."

Chris Kimball was watching him across his desk with a confused grin on his face.

"You no be getting drunk," Macaulay added.

"I stay sober, Steef," said Carlos. "There any clean pussy where we be going?"

Macaulay asked him to put Lana back on the line.

"Can you get him on the next flight to Miami?" he asked. "I'll wire the money right away."

"May I come too, Steve?" she asked, her voice as husky as he remembered.

He chuckled and said, "Not this time, Lana. Trust me, you wouldn't like this one."

As the first day of the preliminary search wound down off the Devil's Backbone, Macaulay figured they had already covered nearly a fifth of the grid. There were several target areas north of the reef that fit the depth requirements and looked promising.

"Let's do one more run before the light goes," he called down to Lexy. "We have to get through the reef passage and back to Dunmore Town before dark."

An hour later, Lexy was the first to see the fast-approaching thunderheads. She shouted to him over the engine noise. Macaulay turned from the steering console to look back. The storm front looked like a gigantic mass of greasy black smoke. It almost filled the sky to the west. Inside it, he saw pale blue flashes of lightning.

Hoping to outrace the squall, he gunned the engines and headed for the narrow gap in the reef a mile farther on that they needed to clear in order to get back to Dunmore Town. Off to port, he saw the small group of uninhabited islets that extended out from the edge of Hawk Point at the tip of North Eleuthera.

Lexy stood in the stern, watching as the front gained on them, darkening the surface of the sea as it came. The first rush of wind hit them as Macaulay was turning south. The gust was at least forty miles an hour and the boat heeled over sickeningly in its face, almost launching Lexy over the side. She could hear the clatter and crash of loose pots and pans in the galley as she regained her feet and held on.

A heavy curtain of slashing rain followed just behind the wind, blotting out Macaulay's visibility. Through the rain-streaked windshield, he could no longer see the narrow gap in the reef a half mile ahead of them. He couldn't see more than ten feet off the bow. It would be suicidal to try to make it through as long as the storm lasted.

He turned on his running lights as the boat lurched and reeled through the tossing sea. Remembering the small islets to the north, he turned north away from the route along the Devil's Backbone. Slowing the engine to fifteen knots, he continued on a northerly course.

He looked down to scan the 3-D display on the Furuno radar monitor. With each sweep of the antenna, he saw the islets grow larger directly ahead of him, no more than a quarter mile away. There were four of them, and one appeared to have a tiny cove or inlet on its eastern edge that could provide additional protection from the wind. He estimated it was now gusting fifty.

The cruiser was pitching and rolling wildly as he navigated through the gap between the first two islets. It was the next one that had the small inlet or cove. Flying blind with only the radar monitor as a guide, he turned into it and slowed the throttle until the boat was barely making headway in the roiling waves.

According to the depth meter, there was still four feet of water under the hull as he continued to inch forward. In a brief flash of lightning, he saw that instead of sandy beach, the land mass ahead of them was covered with a thicket of mangroves. They appeared to grow right down to the water's edge.

The mangroves had been there a long time and were tall enough to provide a small measure of protection from the wind. He ran forward along the upper deck and carefully set the Danforth anchor off the bow before tying it off. There was a twenty-pound mushroom anchor in the stern locker, and he set it off the stern.

Night descended with total blackness.

EIGHTEEN

28 May
Aboard *Island Time*
Devil's Backbone
North Eleuthera
Bahamas

Macaulay secured the mahogany hatch cover and lowered himself into the cruiser's tiny cabin. The height of the compartment was only six feet and he had to walk bent over before slipping into one of the seats at the galley table. Drenched from the cold rain, he gave an involuntary shudder.

"I called Barnaby," said Lexy at the stove as she poured a mug of hot coffee for him, "and told him we would resume the preliminary search in the morning and get back to Dunmore Town before dark tomorrow."

She had lit the cabin with two lanterns and Macaulay felt good to be down there. He reached for the bottle of Jack Daniel's in one of the secured shelves above the galley table and laced his coffee with a good pour.

"Hey, don't waste that," she said. "I need it to season my fish chowder."

"I'm not exactly wasting it," he said.

During one of the afternoon search patterns, a four-pound pompano had struck at one of the side winder lures and Lexy had reeled in the fish, cleaned and filleted it, and put it in the refrigerated locker.

"Your friend Chris Kimball certainly knows how to provision a boat," she said. "Incidentally, he's a very good-looking man."

The revelation only made Macaulay more moody.

He watched as she sliced the pompano fillets into thick chunks and added them to a cast-iron stewpot already containing diced potatoes, carrots, garlic, an onion, celery, and a pound of frozen scallops. She sprinkled in some Old Bay and other seasonings, added a pint of chicken stock, and a third of the bottle of Jack Daniel's.

As he watched her prepare their meal, he thought again of how much he had missed her after she went away. Standing there at the galley stove in the lantern light, she had never looked more beautiful to him. Her slender body had tanned easily, and the newly golden skin and thick auburn hair set off the white bikini to perfection. Stirring the pot, she looked back at him.

"You're looking pretty morose considering we had such a good first day," she said.

He sipped his coffee silently and listened to the rain hammering the deck above them.

"I haven't been very good to you lately, have I?" she said, searching his eyes.

"Not for one year and sixteen days," he said with a wry smile.

"I'll make it up to you with this chowder," she said, glancing at the bottle of Jack Daniel's. "Can I share some of that?"

He poured her a healthy shot and recharged his own empty mug.

A few minutes later, the wind shifted to the northeast and began dragging hard at the mooring lines. He went back on deck to make sure they were holding. The rain showed no signs of abating, and the severity of the wind gusts remained unchanged. Back in the cabin, he reviewed the data from the first day's search and began noting all the potential locations that warranted a refined search.

By the time she was finally ready to ladle the chowder out, its superb aroma had filled the cabin and made him ravenous. She served it with a small loaf of French bread she had found in the freezer and toasted with butter in the broiler oven. Macaulay opened a bottle of cabernet sauvignon.

"It's fun riding out a storm with you, Steve," she said after they ended the meal with two Almond Joy bars.

"Not just the storms, I hope," he said.

"You're a stalwart," she said, her violet eyes gazing into his across the table. "Old school, a classic . . . a throwback."

"You already threw me back once," he said.

"You know the reason I went away," she said. "At least I thought you understood."

"The words didn't matter," said Macaulay. "The only reality was that you were gone."

"I felt like I was becoming an extension of you instead of my own person. Of all people, you know how import-

198 ROBERT J. MRAZEK

ant my work is to me. There are so many things I want to accomplish. . . . Actually, it's a need. I'm not sure where it came from. My mother dying young was part of it. All I knew was that I couldn't give up my work, even for you."

"I didn't ask you to," he said.

"It wasn't what you said or didn't say," she said. "It was how you acted after we got back from Maine . . . as if I was a bird with a broken wing that needed your daily support to survive."

"I never thought I would see you again."

"Well, here I am."

"Yeah," he said, turning away so she wouldn't see the need in his eyes. "We should probably get to bed early. There's a lot to do tomorrow."

When he stood up from the galley table, it suddenly occurred to him there was only one comfortable berth in the forward cabin. He would have to convert the galley table into a dog bed. He looked back to see her staring up at him.

"I feel like I'm still coated in salt from today," she said, getting up too.

Stripping off the bikini, she picked up a plastic bottle of dish soap from the small steel sink and headed up the steps to the hatchway.

"You're welcome to join me," she called back to him.

He thought about the invitation for several seconds. As he turned to follow her, he bumped his head on the cabin ceiling. Slipping off his cargo shorts, he followed her up. She was standing by the railing near the stern and washing her hair. The shrill wind still showed no signs of abating. The rain was coming like a deluge. He felt little needles of sensation pricking the skin of his face and up-per body.

She held out the dish soap toward him. When he reached for it, she took him in her arms. A moment later, her mouth found his. Her fingers began roaming his body and he came alive to every touch. The next seconds became a confusing blur. Then they were lying together naked on the double berth in the forward cabin.

They made love quickly the first time, their mutual hunger overwhelming individual control. Afterward, they lay in each other's arms, the warmth of their body heat blending with the afterglow of pure sensation.

The second time was more intense. They chose to make it last, moving close to the edge of the abyss and then back away again. He wanted very much for it to be for her alone, to release the sweet intricacies of her body. She appeared to revel in the sure caress of his lips, tongue, and fingers. Lexy's eyes were slit partially open, seemingly drunk with desire as he stroked and caressed her. At the end, she kissed him with a raw hunger, as if his lips were a wonderful feast to be devoured before she finally sur-rendered to a last torrent of sensation.

They slept.

He awoke to a soft hissing of wind, a pale reminder of the tempest the night before. Waves gently lapped along the sides of the hull. They lay entwined together. Macau-lay watched a trembling beam of sunlight as it stabbed through the porthole above them and lit up the glints of gold in her hair.

Her beautiful, complicated face lay in calm repose. He had again sampled the deep well of physical yearning that was submerged inside her dedication to her work. She had seemed almost embarrassed at the intensity of her pleasure. He sensed that it was very hard for her to allow herself to let go, to feel safe enough with a man to indulge her passionate desires.

At some point during the night he thought he had figured it all out, everything that mattered going forward, but it was like one of those vivid dreams that one couldn't fully remember after waking up. He wondered what her own reaction might be.

When her eyes opened and took him in, he smiled down at her.

"I'm ready to perform an ancient massage technique that was handed down to me by a holy man in the Himalayas many years ago," he said softly. "To my knowledge it's only known to four human beings on this planet."

"I'll allow you to perform it," she said, "after my first cup of coffee."

Macaulay put the coffeepot on the stove and they went up on deck. The sun was still low above the sea, and the air was fresh and clean smelling, tinged from the islet with the scent of hibiscus and wild frangipani. The water beneath them was clear enough to see the bottom. Tiny fish darted in and out of small coral heads.

As he had seen in the brief flash of lightning the night before, thick mangrove trees on the islet grew right down to the edge of the water. There was no beach. To the east the ocean was a vivid bluish green under a cloudless sky.

They had gone back down to the galley and were sipping their coffee when Lexy heard the cawing screams of a flock of seagulls above the boat. Moments later, the loud explosion of a gunshot split the air.

Lexy quickly glanced out the edge of the starboard

galley window as Macaulay grabbed the .45 from the shelf above the galley table and charged a round into the magazine. He stepped toward the hatchway.

"I'm not sure you'll need it," she said. "It's a man and a bird."

Macaulay went up on deck, holding the .45 behind his right hip.

An old white man in a faded shirt and jeans stood by the wooden mast of an old lapstrake sailing skiff. Its multipatched canvas sail was flapping loose in the light breeze as he glared up at Macaulay.

"You leave now, mon," he said menacingly as Lexy joined Steve on deck.

It was hard to guess his age. Short and wiry, with skin tanned a deep leathery brown and clear blue eyes. Barefoot, he was wearing a sweat-stained straw planter's hat and ragged jeans. He was holding an old rifle loosely in his right hand. It looked like a Lee-Enfield bolt-action .303, the kind used by the British army a hundred years earlier.

"Don't you people come back," he said.

To Lexy his accent had the same Bajan cadence she had heard from local people on Harbour Island over the previous few days, both black and white. It was a harmonic combination of standard English and African.

A male frigate bird was perched in the stern of the sailing skiff, the biggest one she had ever seen. He had the familiar red pouch on the throat skin below the lower mandible of his beak. He sat quietly gazing at them from a faded plastic cushion, apparently unperturbed by the loud gunshot.

"Do you own this island?" she asked.

"Ah'm finished talking," said the man, putting his

other hand on the rifle stock and lifting it up again. "You go or you find out sure."

"This island looked uninhabited. . . . We just ducked in here during the storm last night," said Macaulay, slowly pulling the hammer back on the .45 behind his right hip.

"I habit it, mon," he said. "Just me."

Lexy caught Macaulay's eye and they silently agreed on what to do next. Neither wanted an incident reported that would attract the attention of the local constabulary or whatever passed for the local press.

"We're leaving right now," she said. "Sorry to bother you."

Macaulay turned and placed the .45 on the steering console and started the engines. He watched as the old man laid the rifle down on the thwarts as if he was too tired to hold it up any longer. While Lexy raised the stern anchor, Macaulay went forward to pull the Danforth.

The old man and the bird watched them silently as Macaulay shoved the throttles forward and they slowly made their way out of the inlet.

"The frigate bird looked friendlier than the hermit," said Lexy.

NINETEEN

28 May
Casa Grande Brugg
Harbour Island
North Eleuthera
Bahamas

Juwan Brugg arose groggily out of his Lunesta-induced stupor to the incessant chattering of a thin, shrill voice. It was coming from somewhere beyond the open French doors to the third-floor balcony.

He lay on his back and waited for it to stop. It didn't. The voice would pause briefly after a long prattling burst and then resume louder than ever. Feeling a growing sense of outrage, he rolled over onto his side and expelled a loud belch, waking up the young man sleeping beside him.

"Go back to sleep, my darling," Juwan said to him gently before heaving himself off the ultra-king bed and stalking to the bathroom to relieve himself. When he returned to the bedroom, the shrill cries were unabated.

Walking to the open French doors, Juwan passed by

the life-size cover of *Sports Illustrated* that he had once adorned after graduating from St. Paul's Academy in Nassau. The words below his sixth-form photograph read *At 7'2", Juwan Brugg: The Next Kareem Abdul Jabbar.*

He stared at himself in the photograph for a moment. He decided there was a regal dignity to his close-shaven head and his sensitive brown eyes. Juwan had once thought of himself as a little man in a big man's body, particularly after he passed the seven-foot mark.

Although his magnificent body was muscled like a gigantic steer's and he had always attracted attention wherever he went in the islands, he would have preferred to be anonymous, to observe others without being stared at like some carnival freak.

He stepped out onto the fourth-floor balcony and looked across the three-acre stone-walled compound. Beyond the ten-foot walls, the Bahamian sea was a dark Prussian blue beneath a bright sunny sky.

His ears were drawn to the half dozen eucalyptus trees that fringed the two-story brick barracks and sleeping quarters of the guard detail along the northern edge of the compound. His eyes quickly found the source of the shrill caterwauling on an upper branch of the largest eucalyptus, about twenty feet above the spiky grass lawn.

An off-duty guard was trying to coax it to come down with a banana.

It was the red howler monkey owned by Major Subito, the deputy commander of his guard unit. At twenty pounds, the animal was fully grown. Over the years Subito had trained it to be a crowd pleaser by blowing kisses and playing peekaboo by covering its eyes.

Juwan went to the archery rack in the nearby sitting room and returned with his longbow and a four-foot arrow with a carbon shaft and pink-barred feathers. Standing at the edge of the balcony, he watched as the monkey began waving and blowing kisses to the growing group of guards that had gathered below him to watch.

Juwan loved the longbow, much preferring it to the combination bows and crossbows he had used as a boy to kill wild pigs in the Exumas. When he drew it back against living prey, he felt like Mel Gibson in *Braveheart*.

Using the Mongolian thumb clasp, he slowly extended the leather cord back toward his ear and took careful aim. Holding the seven-foot longbow steady was a test of strength and his biceps bulged with the effort. He estimated the distance as approximately thirty-five yards. He raised the aim eight inches higher than the target.

The guards on the lawn were all chuckling at the howler's antics when they heard the loud thunk as the body of the monkey was hurled backward and impaled through its chest to the trunk of the tree. Not daring to look back at the third-floor balcony of the mansion house, the guards dispersed in every direction. The monkey let out one last woozy bleat as its arms sagged to its sides.

When Juwan returned to the bedroom, Varna was lying naked on his left side, his delicately chiseled, heart-shaped face in calm repose. Juwan kissed him on the right hip before tenderly pulling the covers back up over his chest to his neck.

Lately, his desire for him had become almost insatiable. Unlike with his many other conquests, Juwan had been faithful to Varna for almost two months, the longest romantic relationship he had ever enjoyed.

Of mixed racial extraction, Varna was Panamanian born, but his smooth mahogany skin hinted at mestizo. A superb athlete like Juwan, he had made the Panamanian Olympian team as a gymnast with a specialty in the still rings.

Unlike the grotesque bodybuilders that Juwan had found intoxicating as a young man, Varna had a taut body, with finely toned chest and shoulder muscles. Juwan had once watched him suspend himself in an inverted Maltese cross that had lasted a full minute without the slightest movement.

Juwan returned to the balcony and again surveyed his domain. The silence was now languid except for the distant cries of seabirds flying majestically over the harbor. Beneath the soaring birds, a dozen superyachts, each more than two hundred feet long and bearing the flags of many nations, rode gently at anchor.

While he was taking stock of the new day, it occurred to Juwan that he was proud of Varna in other ways too. Varna now ran the one legitimate undertaking owned by Juwan in the islands. They had begun the Academy of Spiritual and Self-Healing together.

Now the academy students were housed on the southern side of his mansion compound. As Juwan watched, they emerged in pairs from their sleeping quarters. There were exactly twenty of them in each class, marching in perfect order.

Each one had signed a contract agreeing to total lifestyle transformation, including Varna's vigorous daily fitness regimen as well as nutritional and behavioral guidance. There were hundreds of applications for each coveted spot in the class and they received final acceptance only after undergoing mental stress tests and a full body examination.

Among the tenets of Varna's teachings were that each man refrain from alcohol, smoking, and masturbation. Tattoos and body piercing were forbidden. There was group corporal punishment if any student was caught defiling his body. A second infraction led to humiliating public dismissal. Every man was body-waxed and oiled twice a week before the morning circle meeting, and their daily pledges were recited aloud during the subsequent promenade around the compound.

Graduates were then sent out into the world to recruit more self-healing spiritualists at an annual stipend of fifty thousand dollars, paid for by Juwan's other successful business activities. Hundreds of acolytes were already abroad in the islands and spreading the word. The thought of it made Juwan almost swell with pride.

Closing the curtains to the balcony doors, Juwan returned to bed. Although he wanted nothing more than to take Varna in his arms and make slow, passionate love to him, he turned away and closed his eyes, willing himself to sleep.

He was well aware of the image that he and Varna projected together to the men who worked in Juwan's various business enterprises. It was definitely an odd physical combination. Juwan remained on the lookout for anyone who had a hint of mockery in his face at the sight of a seven-foot-two man dancing with another man only five-four. The last one who had seemingly smirked had been dragged over the outer reef of the Devil's Backbone behind a shallow-draft Jet Ski and then served as chum to the striking sharks.

He could hear the academy students reciting their oath under the window as he fell back into a tortured sleep. The nightmare returned almost immediately, the same one that always destroyed his sleep, except that it was real.

It had happened to him at the NBA All-Star game in Phoenix in the waning seconds of the final quarter. They had been hacking him all through the second half and the referees hadn't called a single foul.

When Juwan clotheslined the Knicks power forward, two of the referees had stepped in his face and called the flagrant foul on him. When he tried to demonstrate his innocence, they called two technical fouls on him.

In his mind's eye, he could see it all happening again as if it had taken place in slow motion. He had lifted the two referees into the air, each one of their scrawny necks encased in his massive hands. The eyes were bulging out of one of the faces as he pounded their two heads together like coconuts.

He had never meant for it to happen. Truly. As he was looking down at them lying there unconscious, the first thought that entered his mind was what were they doing there on the polished floor in the middle of the All-Star game?

He had narrowly escaped a long prison term for deadly assault. One of the referees had been in a coma for a week, but he survived. The other one had only suffered a serious concussion. Juwan had had plenty of those.

His deliverance had come with no help from the NBA owners, all of whom had joined ranks to write a condemnation letter labeling him a murderous thug and imposing a lifetime ban. It was only through the multimillion-dollar settlements lavished on each referee that he was able to leave the country and return home to the Bahamas.

In Nassau, he had been welcomed back as a national hero after Juwan's publicity agent uncovered evidence from unnamed sources that both referees were skinheads and harbored hatred for all black people. The Reverend Al Sharpton had joined him at a prayer service to celebrate his redemption at Harbour Island.

His last thought before descending back into the oblivion of the sleeping pills was that he would someday return to the NBA, to his teammates, to the finals championship, to the roaring screams of the adoring fans shouting, *"Juwan . . . Juwan . . . Juwan."*

TWENTY

Barnaby surveyed the colorfully painted clay pots on the granite tabletop in the dining salon with obvious distaste. The pots were filled with granola, fresh fruit, yogurt, and a variety of grains suitable for a gerbil. One large plate held what looked like steamed fish. He looked in vain for the bacon, ham, bagels, or scrambled eggs.

"Chris Kimball and I worked out the daily menu," said Lexy, emerging from her stateroom in a white linen pants outfit and going straight to the pitcher holding the pineapple juice.

After briefly admiring her golden tan, Barnaby went back to his stateroom and fortified his coffee with the bottle of Courvoisier he kept under his bathroom sink.

His liquor supply was dwindling and he hoped they would make a breakthrough in the search soon.

Returning to the dining salon, he watched the others consume their animal fodder.

"If you follow this diet, you'll feel like a new man in a week," said Lexy.

"I already feel like a new man," said Barnaby, "and he is bored stiff."

In truth, he was bored in every way. Barnaby craved joining the pursuit of the greatest archaeological loss in the history of evolution, yet there was nothing he could do for the time being except stay cooped up on the boat, reduced to reviewing the depth readings and side-scan sonar results after each day's search.

The day they arrived, Macaulay had reminded him that the Chinese were probably combing the world for them.

"We know that Zhou Shen Wui and his minions now have all the records and documents compiled by Sebastian Choate," Macaulay said. "They're probably putting enough manpower into this to eventually find the shipping records of the Dutch tramp and to conclude that the ship went down somewhere in the Caribbean."

With Lexy nodding in agreement, Macaulay gently suggested that with Barnaby's "substantial girth, height, and arresting features," he would immediately draw attention in Dunmore Town.

Barnaby had to reluctantly agree.

At least the seventy-two-foot Hatteras was comfortable, with its eight-foot ceilings that didn't make him feel claustrophobic, five spacious staterooms, two lounges filled with overstuffed chairs and couches, and a state-of-the-art satellite communications system that allowed him to do his research.

Chris Kimball became the public face of the boat, fending off visitors from other yachts moored in the harbor and going ashore every day in their sixteen-foot Zodiac to pick up supplies and scout for potential threats.

He came back late on the third afternoon with a recommendation that Barnaby check out a local man in Dunmore Town named Mike McGandy. Kimball said that he was an American expat who had worked for ten years as an agent for the U.S.–Bahamian Drug Task Force. A former navy officer, he had fallen in love with a Bahamian woman and decided to stay. He was now the dive master at a local yacht marina and took groups out for snorkeling and scuba dives on the backbone. His wife operated a medical clinic.

"If he checks out, he could help us after we find the wreck," said Kimball.

Barnaby sent an encrypted message to Ira Dusenberry to have McGandy checked out. The result came back a positive and Kimball had approached him with their agreed-upon cover story. He had enthusiastically agreed to help.

Kimball brought him out to the Hatteras in the Zodiac and they joined Barnaby, Lexy, Macaulay, and Carlos in the dining salon. Macaulay liked what he saw right away. McGandy was an African-American, all military, trim, intelligent-looking, and no-nonsense. Sitting down with his coffee in the dining salon, he surveyed the others with an open, clean-cut face.

"By now you know the sensitivity of what we're doing," began Barnaby, "so you'll understand the need for tight security."

"I understand," said McGandy. "I had top secret clearance in the navy."

The cover story Kimball had given McGandy was that they were searching for the cargo of a Russian ship that had jettisoned the contents of its hold after being intercepted by an American destroyer off North Eleuthera during the Cuban Missile Crisis. The implication was that the ship was carrying nuclear weapon components. McGandy did not probe for specifics.

"We've already begun the search in a way that hopefully hasn't attracted attention," said Macaulay. "We did run into one man on a small islet off Hawk Point who ran us off with an old Enfield."

McGandy laughed and said, "That sounds like old Dieter. Those little islets are owned by the Bahamian government. He's a squatter and lives in a shack that he made himself from coquina rock and driftwood. Hurricane Andrew went right over it in 1992. The island was completely underwater. He somehow survived and rebuilt."

When Lexy got up for more yogurt, Barnaby saw her fingers gently brush Macaulay's tanned shoulders. He knew they were sleeping together again. He could see it in their faces, in the looks that crossed between them when they thought no one was looking. They were trying to be discreet. It wasn't obvious to the others.

Barnaby's mind was momentarily filled with the vision of the naked Astrud as he had last seen her on the bear rug in his lair on the Long Wharf. He tried to think of a vitally important reason to justify bringing her down to join the team. He knew she would come in a heartbeat, but her talents did not comport with the current expedition.

"Who wields the power here locally?" asked Macaulay.

"Nominally, it's the constabulary backed by the Royal Bahamas Defense Force," said McGandy. "Their job is to stop drug smuggling, illegal immigration, poaching, and violent crime. Up to a point, they perform those tasks."

"Up to a point," repeated Macaulay.

"In truth, one guy holds the reins here. His name is Juwan Brugg. He controls everything . . . drugs, prostitution, kidnapping, blackmail, extortion. He's got a big hammer . . . more like a sledgehammer. They're even afraid of him in New Providence."

"Juwan Brugg," said Chris Kimball. "There was an NBA player—"

"Same one," interrupted McGandy. "He grew up here and came back after he almost killed those referees. In public, he often wears an African ceremonial headdress that makes him more than eight feet tall. Some of the islanders revere him as a living god. Make no mistake . . . he's no clown. He's tough and he's ruthless."

"Where is his base of operations?" asked Lexy.

"You've probably passed his compound on Tollifer's Point on your way out to the Devil's Backbone," said McGandy. "It's that huge mansion house built like a fortress and surrounded by the ten-foot-high cement walls topped with broken glass. He has a palace guard to protect him and do his bidding."

"Like those regional warlords in Afghanistan," said Macaulay.

"Exactly," said McGandy before remembering something else. "I should correct one thing I said. Juwan Brugg isn't the only sledgehammer here. There's also his mother."

"His mother?" asked Barnaby.

"Yeah, she runs the day-to-day operation for him out of her beauty parlor on Revere Street," said McGandy. "She is called Black Mamba. I'm told she's more vicious than the snake."

"As a precaution going forward," said Macaulay, "I think we should begin standing watches after the harbor goes dark from around midnight until dawn. Chris, why don't you put together a watch schedule?"

"I volunteer for the four-to-six shift," said Barnaby. "I'm up anyway."

"It might make sense for whoever is standing watch to have some protection. I keep a .40-caliber Heckler and Koch compact semiautomatic in the pilothouse." Glancing at Lexy, he added, "It has a small frame for the hand and pretty fair stopping power."

"Very comforting indeed, Mr. Kimball," said Barnaby, "but all the stopping power I need is in my voice."

"He's probably right," said Macaulay. "That and the sight of him in his Churchillian boiler suit ought to frighten away most intruders."

After Chris Kimball took McGandy back to the town dock in the Zodiac, Macaulay went over the day's plans with the others.

"You be need me today, Genral Steef?" said Carlos, coming into the salon through the open glass doors from the stern deck after smoking his fourth cigarette.

He was dressed in an orange tank top and torn blue jeans and hadn't shaved in a week. His cadaverous face reminded Barnaby of the junkies he had often seen panhandling on Brattle Street in Cambridge.

Carlos had begun calling Macaulay General after learning about Steve's past air force career when they were last together in Belize. Pouring another mug of coffee, Carlos added four tablespoons of sugar to it. Lexy shook her head but didn't say anything.

"Yeah, I be need you," said Macaulay, ignoring Barnaby's mocking smile. "We're diving today."

In reviewing the data from the previous day's search, Barnaby had found an unusual reading in one of the side-scan sonar patterns. They had been crossing a deeper patch of water about a half mile off the Devil's Backbone when two virtual images were recorded that seemed to suggest a small ship broken in two on the seabed.

Macaulay and Lexy got up and went back to their staterooms to change into swimming attire. Barnaby remained at the table and watched as Carlos added another spoonful of sugar to his coffee mug.

"Can you be shave yourself one of these days?" asked Barnaby. "You be look more disreputable every day."

"Workin' on my look," said Carlos. "Chris she say they may be clean pussy over there and I be ready for him."

"Sounds like an admirable idea," agreed Barnaby. "Let me know if you find some."

Emptying his mug, Carlos went back out to the stern swim platform and untied the boat's dinghy. After rowing it over to the mooring that held the thirty-two-foot *Island Time*, he fired up its engines.

One of them was running a bit rough and he uncovered the engine compartment to adjust the fuel injectors. Leaving the mooring, he brought the boat alongside the Hatteras. Macaulay and Lexy jumped down to join him on the deck. Kimball handed Macaulay a cooler with their day's supplies.

As they cruised past Tollifer's Point, Lexy looked through binoculars at the massive walled compound owned by Juwan Brugg. She decided it didn't look all that menacing. A group of naked men were playing volleyball on the beach below the nearest wall.

Thirty minutes later, they were through the reef and out into the open sea. It was another stunning morning with a brilliant sun under a cloudless blue sky. There were minimal swells and Carlos kept the speed to around twenty knots as he fed the GPS coordinates into the navigation system that would take them straight to the position Macaulay had been sweeping the day before when the reading came through.

The navigation system began emitting a warning signal as they approached the target location and Carlos immediately slowed the engines until the signal became a solid keening whine. Macaulay was stationed on the bow. He fed out more than two hundred feet of anchor line before the Danforth bit into the seabed and held them in position.

"There are two separate parts to this thing down there," said Macaulay after they had donned their wet suits and strapped on scuba tanks, weight belts, and swim fins. "If it's the *Prins Willem*, it could be the bow section and the stern section lying fifty meters apart."

Both his and Carlos's diving masks were equipped with ultrasound voice communications equipment that attached to the masks' restraining straps. The technology relied on bone conduction from their heads and would allow them to communicate verbally underwater with each other and to Lexy aboard *Island Time*.

Macaulay had planned out the dive based on the recorded depth of one hundred thirty feet. Checking his dive tables, he figured they would have about fifteen minutes on the bottom before they had to slowly ascend again in staged cycles to avoid nitrogen narcosis. He picked up his small digital camera in the watertight casing and made sure it was sending signals back to the monitor mounted on the bulkhead of the wheelhouse.

Resting their buttocks on the port section of the stern, they dropped over backward into the slowly surging sea. After clearing his mask, Macaulay headed down hand over hand along the anchor line. Carlos followed behind him.

As they swam deeper, the water color slowly changed from pale green to darker green. Macaulay paused to clear his ears every thirty feet. When they finally came to the end of the anchor line, he swung around to look in every direction. The visibility was excellent, but all he saw was fine granular white sand, small schools of brightly colored fish, and sea vegetation.

Macaulay checked his wrist compass and pointed to Carlos to follow him. He began swimming north along the sandy bottom, rotating his head left and right to observe everything in their path. After he had gone one hundred feet, he turned right oblique, swam for another hundred feet, and then turned east. He and Carlos were swimming side by side on the easterly course when Macaulay saw something emerge from the green darkness ahead of them on the bottom.

"You see it, Steef?" asked Carlos through the ultrasound voice communicator.

Macaulay pointed his camera at the object as they swam closer. Aboard the *Island Time*, Lexy saw the first image as it registered on the television monitor. It looked like a gigantic shark fin arising from something cylindrical and glossy white sitting on the sandy bottom.

"It's a . . . catamaran," said Macaulay. "A big one . . . maybe sixty feet long and sitting straight up . . . no apparent damage that I can see."

Carlos swam over to the superstructure. The boat was configured for both sail and as a motor yacht. Its main mast was crowned with a small flag, but it was missing its sail. When he reached the stern, he dropped down to look at the name painted on the stern plate.

There was none. He came close enough to see that there had once been a name but it had been eradicated. He touched the area where the letters had been painted and felt the hard rough texture that suggested a heavy-duty sanding machine. He swam along the port side to the bow to look for the hull identification numbers. They had also been sanded off.

His eyes were drawn to another large object lying on the bottom maybe fifty meters away from the catamaran.

"I see another one, Steef," he said into the voice communicator. "Big boy . . . motor cruiser."

"Wait for me," said Macaulay as he finished taking photographs from every angle of the white-hulled catamaran.

One of the two foot-long rectangular portholes along the starboard side compartment appeared to be slid into the open position. As he watched, a red scarf floated out through it and disappeared in the slow current. He removed the Maglite from his weight belt and swam toward the dark porthole. Putting his face mask through the opening, he shone the Maglite into the compartment.

Macaulay's reaction was instinctive and unthinking as he reeled back away from the porthole. Calming himself for ten seconds, he swam back to the porthole and poked the light inside the stateroom again.

The woman's face was only inches away from his and her jellied eyes were staring straight back at him. Thick black hair floated around her bloated face like a coral fan. The woman's mouth was wide-open, the teeth bulging toward him as if locked in a permanent silent scream.

The gentle current had slowly carried her away from him. It was impossible to tell her age. Parts of her had already been eaten away. The swollen flesh that remained of her body had stretched the blue dress she was wearing to the ripping point.

Beyond her another figure floated into view. It was a man. He was naked and his genitals were missing. At one time, he had probably been strong and well built. Now he looked like a blown-up rubber mannequin. As Macaulay watched, they began what looked like a slow minuet together, their bloated hands touching for a moment and then drifting apart.

Macaulay swam free of the porthole and motioned Carlos to follow him to the second wreck. It was a motor yacht, at least sixty or seventy feet long and beautifully appointed with mahogany decks and an array of the latest electronics mounted above its bridge. Like the catamaran, it looked undamaged and was sitting straight up in the sand as if waiting to resume its journey.

Carlos swam around the stern and headed toward the bow. Like the catamaran's, the boat's name and hull identification numbers had been sanded off. Macaulay began taking pictures of it. As the images registered on the TV

monitor aboard *Island Time*, Lexy shuddered involun-
tarily.

"It looks like they were both deliberately scuttled,"
said Steve into the ultrasound communicator as he swam
into the cruiser's open wheelhouse. The compartment
doors that led into the main deck were fastened shut.

He wondered if there were more bodies floating inside
as Carlos swam toward him pointing at his wrist. Checking his dive watch, Macaulay saw that they had already
been at the bottom for twelve minutes. There was no
time to explore further.

He suddenly remembered something and headed back
to the catamaran. Beginning his ascent to the surface
alongside its mast, he paused at the top to examine the
little pennant hanging from the halyard. It was red and
white and he stretched the pennant to its full length before taking a picture of the tableau.

As they made their carefully timed stops on the path
to the surface, he wondered how the sunken boats had
gotten there and if there might be more. They were both
in superb condition. Together, they were easily worth a
million dollars or more. The catamaran could not have
been down there long. Small fish had already been feed-
ing on the bodies. It wouldn't take them much longer to
finish consuming them.

Macaulay broke the surface of the calm ocean into the
warmth of the sun.

TWENTY-ONE

28 May
Casa Grande Brugg
Harbour Island
North Eleuthera
Bahamas

The sound of the Muppets singing "Danny Boy" blasted through the sound system mounted on the wall of the mansion's formal dining room as Juwan sat alone at the head of the enormous damask-covered table and helped himself to the second of three roast chickens on the pewter platter.

Varna had placed him on a strict high-protein and raw-food diet and Juwan's weight was holding steady at three hundred ninety pounds. He was now limited to two meals a day, one after exercise in the morning and the second at five in the evening. Varna had told him that his previous late-night food binges were the principal cause of his serious eruption of intestinal gas. He was allowed to supplement the two meals with hand-pressed vegetable juice and raw tree nuts.

He preferred dining alone. It was hard to conceal his anger when a guest at the table would take something from a serving dish that he had been planning to eat. Juwan's mother, Black Mamba, supervised the preparation of both his meals every day. This morning's fare consisted of three barbecued chickens that had been marinated in rum and Rose's lime juice served with two pounds of broiled shrimp and lobster, followed by a platter of sliced pineapple, grapes, dates, mandarins, and pears. He sorely missed her sweet potato fries.

Emile Bardot, the head of his security guard and deputy to his mother, arrived at precisely ten thirty to deliver his morning update. His white uniform with formal ribbons and decorations was starched and pressed. He removed his gold-braided hat as he approached the table and stood at attention.

"I am pleased to report that all current activities are proceeding according to plan," he said. "Major Coelho wishes you to know that he sincerely regrets the imposition on your rest caused by his late monkey."

"Let it be a lesson to him," said Juwan in his deep, mellifluous voice. "I love all animals, but there are limitations."

Growing up, he had spent his last five years at St. Paul's Academy in Nassau studying diction under his Oxford-educated English master. When he got to the NBA, one ESPN commentator declared that Juwan was the only player in the league who "could foul like Bill Lambeer with a voice like Darth Vader."

"I have issued an order about future pets," said Bardot as the first Muppet song ended and another began.

Bardot was a lightly complexioned Haitian with dueling scars on both his cheeks. He had arrived in the Bahamas after being declared a fugitive from justice by the Haitian government following his indictment for running a million-dollar business that sold body parts from Haitians while they were still alive. Earlier, he had served as an officer in Jean Claude "Bebe Doc" Duvalier's TonTon Macoute.

The mansion dining room had twenty-foot ceilings and cross-arched oak beams that crowned the thick plaster walls. Juwan's diverse weapons collection was mounted on three of them. It began with ancient hand weapons along the first wall. The second went from swords to blunderbusses, and the third held a modern collection of rifles, shotguns, and assault rifles from virtually every nation in the world, along with movie prop weapons from *Star Wars* and the *Predator* series. The final wall contained many of Juwan's trophies. A gigantic billfish that had lost its last battle to Juwan's endurance and prowess adorned the prize spot over the fireplace.

"What is happening on battleship row?" asked Juwan, referring to the ever-changing array of superyachts anchored in the harbor beyond his compound.

"Typique," said Bardot, consulting his clipboard. "A Danish prince and his entourage, two British royals, three Soviet oligarchs and their guests, a Kuwaiti prince, a grotesque-looking Englishman with a fishing party, a minor Kennedy, an American sports team owner—"

"What kind of sport?" interrupted Juwan.

Bardot checked his list. "He owns a professional basketball team."

Juwan dropped the eviscerated chicken carcass on the plate and wiped his hands on a linen napkin.

"Which one?" he demanded.

"It does not say," said Bardot, knowing the familiar signs of a volcano about to erupt.

At that moment, Black Mamba came through the swinging door from the kitchen and approached the table. A six-foot version of Juwan with thick braids of black hair coiled above her head, she was wearing a loose-flowing purple muumuu.

"You didn't finish your chickens," she said. "You must keep up your strength."

"Find out which team," demanded Juwan, ignoring her. "What has the man been doing?"

"He hangs out at the bar of the Romora Bay Club after ten o'clock," said Bardot, checking his clipboard. "According to this report, he has asked a hostess by the name of Giselle to join him on his boat. So far she has refused."

"Why?" demanded Black Mamba. "I trained that girl since she was fourteen."

"The man is apparently somewhat unpleasant to look at," said Bardot. "She told him she would rather mate with a bull shark."

"Let me take care of it," said Black Mamba. "I'll have her bring him to Michaud's tonight."

It was a room over a seafood restaurant with mirrored ceilings and high-end digital video recording equipment. Potential blackmail victims were encouraged to participate in activities they would never want to share on You-Tube.

"Finish your chicken," demanded Black Mamba a second time, and Juwan meekly made short work of it.

When she had removed the platter, Bardot said, "I have made all the security arrangements for the charity event tomorrow night. We have been informed that the duke of Lancaster and his wife, the duchess, will be attending."

Each year the annual charity event in support of preserving Eleuthera's increasingly endangered rare bird habitats was hosted at one of the important estates on Harbour Island. For the first time, it would be held at Casa Grande Brugg. Varna had ordered liveried white uniforms for the Academy of Spiritual and Self-Healing students.

"I'm not sure if I will attend," said Juwan.

It was a tradition that the host and his spouse would inaugurate the festivities by dancing to the first waltz played by the local orchestra. He was imagining the reaction by the royal entourage to himself and Varna when Bardot interrupted his thoughts.

"There is one other piece of interesting news. It came through Sir Henry in New Providence."

Sir Henry Pindling was Juwan's lawyer and had been knighted by Queen Elizabeth after helping to curtail the investigation into a weekend tryst by Prince Andrew with potentially underage women near the royal compound on Eleuthera.

"What is it?" said Juwan as he thought about Varna doing his calisthenics upstairs wearing his spandex gymnastic tights.

"It is a reward, or you might call it a bounty," said Bardot, "offered by a Chinese humanitarian society seeking to find several Americans who they wish to honor with a lifetime achievement prize. It seems that they have sent a similar reward notice all over the Caribbean."

"Who runs this society?" asked Juwan.

"A Chinese industrialist named Zhou Shen Wui."

Juwan laughed.

"I can imagine the prize the three Americans will receive if he catches up to them," he said. "How much is the bounty?"

"Five hundred thousand American dollars," said Bardot.

"They are serious," said Juwan, leaning back from the table. "Are there descriptions of the so-called prize winners?"

"One of them is a retired American air force general," said Bardot.

"It might be some kind of underwater graveyard . . . a dumping ground for embarrassments," said Steve Macaulay to the others sitting around the lounge in *Trader's Bluff* as they looked at the succession of digital pictures on a television monitor.

"Should we report this to anyone?" asked Chris Kimball.

"If you do," said Mike McGandy, "it'll probably be reported back to Juwan Brugg or his mother before it ever reaches official channels, and they're probably the ones tending the graveyard."

"I say we continue our search right away," said Macaulay. "They're not going anywhere and we can notify the constabulary as soon as we are finished here in the next few days."

In the magnificent yacht moored near them, he could hear three young girls yipping and screaming as they leaped off the upper deck into the harbor and swam around to the stern to climb up and do it again.

"That makes sense," agreed Barnaby. "Based on all the readings we have so far, there are five prospective spots that have both the correct depth levels and unusual bottom characteristics from the sonar scanner that suggest a sunken wreck of substantial size."

"At a depth of one hundred thirty feet, we're going to have to be careful with decompression stages coming back up," said Macaulay. "To go faster, we'll use two teams. Carlos and Mike can dive the first site and while they're resting, Lexy and I can try the next one."

"To good fortune," said Barnaby, raising his mug of Courvoisier-laced coffee.

TWENTY-TWO

29 May
Aboard *Island Time*
Harbour Island
North Eleuthera
Bahamas

As they left the harbor, Macaulay decided to make a false run in an easterly direction on the lower side of the backbone. The same survival instinct that had served him well in combat and in a number of other dangerous situations was telling him they might be under observation from the island by men with binoculars.

When he had gone about three miles, he turned north and threaded his way across the reef through a cut he had found that morning on a chart in the *Bahamas Yachtsmen's Guide*. Once they were through, he put the boat back on the correct heading to reach the targeted search areas.

Carlos and Mike McGandy brought up the diving gear from the forward hold and began checking the regulators and tanks while Lexy organized the sets of masks, fins, weight belts, and wet suits for them. At one point, Macaulay asked Carlos to take the controls and motioned for Mike McGandy to join him in the cabin.

"You should know that we're not looking for a Russian cargo ship that dumped its cargo during the Cuban Missile Crisis," said Macaulay. "I can't tell you what we're really after aside from the fact that it's important."

"Above my pay grade," said McGandy with a smile. "I understand."

"You also need to know it could become very dangerous pretty quickly," said Macaulay. "I'll understand if it isn't something you want to take on."

"I grew up on the south side of Los Angeles on a block divided by the Street Saints and the Barrio Evil," said McGandy. "My father was Irish and my mother black. "I've known some danger."

Macaulay shook his hand. "We're looking for a freighter sunk by a U-boat at the beginning of the Second World War. Its cargo included a teakwood crate, about five feet square. It was supposedly well constructed."

"After eighty years, there's no telling if it would have retained its integrity," said McGandy.

"We can only look and hope," said Macaulay.

He heard the engine revolutions slow as Carlos cut back on the throttles. Glancing out the port window, Macaulay saw only open ocean. The sea was calm, with a light chop. It was perfect diving weather.

Blinding beams of dazzling sunlight danced across the surface of the water as Macaulay came back on deck. Checking the navigation system, he saw that they were

very close to the first target location. He killed the engines and as the boat drifted over it, Carlos hurled the
anchor over the side.

After a week on the open water, Steve had tanned to a
deep bronze. His hands had been toughened by the hard
daily physical work and he was back in the best shape he
had enjoyed since the ill-fated Greenland expedition. He
felt ready for whatever challenge awaited them below.

He decided that Mike and Carlos would do the first
exploratory dive to see what was down there. If it looked
promising, one of them would contact Macaulay through
the ultrasound voice equipment to join them below.

Lexy waited for her sixth sense to kick in, that inner
rush of exhilaration that might portend if Peking Man
was lying below them on the seabed. There was no hint
of it as the two divers went over the side.

Mike McGandy followed the anchor line down to the
bottom. Carlos stayed close behind him. When they
reached the half-buried flukes of the anchor, they began
their search using the rough grid Macaulay had written
on their underwater slate. He had suggested that the distance they searched in each direction should be determined by the visibility they found at the bottom.

McGandy estimated it to be about fifty meters. Two
abreast, they swam north for fifty meters and then turned
east for another fifty. The plan was that if they didn't spot
anything, they would end up back at the anchor line with
two more turns, and then move to the next location in
the grid.

They were on the southerly tack when Mike McGandy
saw what had to be the abnormality that Barnaby had
picked up from the side-scan sonar rig. It was a large

mound of coral outcroppings rising maybe twenty feet from the sandy bottom and a hundred feet along it. The cracks and fissures in its walls boasted a panorama of coral fans, sea grass, and exotic ferns.

They spent ten minutes swimming around the coral outcropping, but there was no evidence that it had ever been disturbed by anything man-made. Returning to the anchor line, they made their way slowly back to the surface, stopping for the required decompression stages along the way.

Bringing them back aboard, Macaulay punched the next set of GPS coordinates into the navigation system and gunned the engines. Twenty minutes later, he and Lexy were preparing for the next dive.

It was Lexy's first since she had arrived in the Bahamas and she was excited, wondering for a few moments if she was confusing this sense of anticipation with her occasionally prescient gift of knowing she was close to an important find.

After she put on her wet suit and slipped into her swim fins, Macaulay lifted the heavy gas tanks onto her back. She clinched the harness around her stomach, fastened her weight belt, then rinsed her mask with spit and put it on.

"Ready," she said.

Together, they dropped backward off the starboard side.

The water was as clear beneath the boat as a spring-fed stream. As the weight belt carried her down, she gazed back up at the surface. It looked like a sheet of polished silver. A distorted view of Carlos showed him gazing down to make sure she was all right.

Aiming their bodies downward, she and Macaulay peddled their swim fins in a steady rhythm and headed toward the bottom. Above them, the hull got smaller and smaller until it finally disappeared.

Lexy found herself feeling totally at home in the sea, breathing with the controlled easy rhythm she had been taught at a PADI diving school in Cambridge while she was still at Harvard. As they swam deeper, clouds of colorful fish began darting all around her.

At a depth of one hundred feet, Macaulay looked down and saw the outline of what appeared to be a wreck almost directly beneath them. It was about the size of a small freighter, but the configuration was different, and the man-made aspects of it seemed to be joined or fused to the natural elements. He led her toward the debris field and then over it.

Whatever it had once been, it wasn't the *Prins Willem*. Sections of a massive oak strut were embedded in the coral growth surrounding it. The ship's more ancient origins were confirmed when Lexy pointed out a cylindrical object about eight feet long buried in the coral.

"It's a cannon," said Macaulay through the ultrasound voice communicator, "maybe eighteenth century."

He took several digital pictures of it and was about to lead her back to the anchor line when she motioned to him to swim over to her. As he did, he saw that she was holding something in her right glove. Coming closer, he saw that it was standing on the tip of her forefinger.

No more than three inches tall, it was a sea horse, its color a bright Chinese red and exquisitely formed in miniature. He put his own index finger next to hers and it jumped over onto it.

"A good sign, I think," she said as he gently put it back on the coral outcropping.

They slowly began their ascent, rising with their air bubbles, careful not to get ahead of them as they paused for the required decompression stops along the way. Back aboard the *Island Time*, Mike McGandy was clearly fascinated with their discovery of the wreckage.

"It may not be the one you are looking for," said Mike, "but the cannon definitely looks Spanish and very old, possibly seventeenth century. It could even be one of those lost Spanish treasure galleons from 1715. Kip Wagner only found eight of the original eleven."

Macaulay laughed.

"You're welcome to come back and look it over more carefully when we're finished," he said as they headed for the third target site. "Treasure hunting isn't our line."

"A different kind of treasure," added Lexy with an enigmatic grin.

On their next dive, Carlos and Fred weren't on the bottom more than fifteen minutes when they found more sunken wreckage. Lexy and Steve watched the photographs of their find materialize on the television monitor in the wheelhouse.

"A ship all right," said Carlos. "A big one too."

"It's about the right size," said McGandy, looking up at the bridge deck, "but there are huge mounds of coal spilled out all over the bottom. I'd say it was a collier, a coal supply ship . . . maybe World War One vintage . . . definitely not ours."

As soon as Mike and Carlos had shrugged off their tanks after getting back on board, Carlos began charging the depleted air tanks with the portable compressor. While they headed to the next site, he smoked one cigarette after another and swilled several cups of sugar-laden coffee.

"They be ships all over this part of the sea," he said to Steve. "Like trying to find Jack in the Haystawk."

Lexy tried to keep their spirits up by pointing out there were still two good leads left to explore. It was late afternoon by the time they were anchored at the fourth site and Macaulay and Lexy were ready to go down again. In the distance he could see the islet where they had sheltered from the storm off North Eleuthera.

"We don't have a lot of daylight left," he said. "This will be the last one for today."

He didn't bother to mention that the amount of nitrogen gas in their bloodstream was accumulating with each dive and they would have much less time on the bottom to find the wreck if it was even there.

As Lexy tightened her tank harness, she suddenly felt a prickle of excitement at the nape of her neck. She didn't say anything to Steve about it as they went over the side and began to descend.

In the waning light, the visibility below fifty feet rapidly diminished. Both of them were carrying powerful Maglites on their weight belts that would hopefully cut through the murky darkness on the seabed floor.

Reaching the end of the anchor line, Macaulay employed the same plan for searching that he had earlier recommended to Mike McGandy. Turning on the Maglites, they swam north into the gloom. Macaulay had gone no more than a hundred feet when something on the bottom glinted up at him in the broad beam of light.

He finned down toward it. The small object was half-buried in the sand. Reaching down with his gloved fingers, he pulled it free and held it under the Maglite. About fourteen inches long, it was made of brass. Triangular shaped, it had a separate brass shaft attached to the top of the triangle, which hung free.

"It's a ship's clinometer," said Macaulay into the voice communicator.

He felt a quick surge of adrenaline as he read the words engraved on the base of it: OCTROOICENTRUM NEDERLAND 1923.

"It looks like a patent mark and it's Dutch," he said.

Laying it down on the sand, he swam farther ahead with Lexy beside him. She spotted the next, much larger object. It was a big farm tractor, sitting straight up on the iron rims of its four wheels, its round, concave metal seat awaiting the next rider.

Beyond the tractor, dozens more objects were scattered along the seabed, including freestanding engines, generator housings, a massive hay bailer, and other gasoline-powered farm equipment.

"It's a debris field from the cargo hold of a ship," said Macaulay, "and from what I remember in the manifest of the *Prins Willem*, she was carrying marine engines and agricultural equipment."

When he flashed the beam of the Maglite past the long trail of wreckage and debris, he saw the hull of part of a ship looming up out of the gloom. An explosion of some kind had broken its back. The forward section was canted over onto its port side. The stern section appeared to be resting straight up on the bottom.

Lexy swam toward it. The steel plates of the rusty

brown hull were covered with a thin coating of moss. When Lexy was only a foot away from the stern section, she used her right glove to rub off the marine growth that covered the ship's nameplate.

Prin materialized from the murk in dull, grayish-white-painted letters.

"We found her," said Macaulay, staring at the emerging name beyond her shoulder. "Come on down."

TWENTY-THREE

29 May
Aboard *Island Time*
Harbour Island
North Eleuthera
Bahamas

"From what I can see, the ship broke in two right after it took the torpedo," said Macaulay through the ultrasound voice communicator. "The cargo in the forward hold spilled out of her on the way down. It's scattered across the whole area."

While Mike and Carlos prepared for their descent, Macaulay and Lexy briefly explored the forward section of the ship. Its interior bulkheads were completely gone, carried away by the shifting mass of engines and machinery. The cargo hold was a hollow, cavernous hole, its steel ribs supporting only a bent and twisted deck. If the Peking Man crate had been stowed inside the forward hold, it was now part of the debris trail lying on the seabed.

Macaulay swam along the main deck in case the crate might have been lashed down there. There was nothing left on it but the ghostly remnants of a cargo boom, an electric winch with its steel cable extending over the side, two ventilation intakes, and scattered rigging, all of it coated with mossy green sea slime.

Macaulay called out on the voice communicator for the others to join him on the stern section of the *Prins Willem*. Unlike the forward hulk, it was sitting almost straight up in the sand. As he swam closer, he saw that one of the steel hatchway doors leading down below from the main deck was wide-open.

He waited for the others to join him near the hatchway. When they were assembled, he had them check the gas pressure in their tanks. Mike and Carlos had enough to stay down for another twenty minutes. He and Lexy had less than ten minutes left before they would have to begin making their ascent.

"There are only the two decks above the engine room and the bilge to explore," he said. "Some of the compartments were blown wide-open when the ship came apart. Carlos, you search the ones up forward. We'll try to get to the other compartments through this hatch. If you don't see the teak crate, look for objects that might be enclosed in airtight glass containers."

The ambient light at the bottom had gotten progressively darker as the sun faded above them on the surface. It was now an almost impenetrable black, but their powerful Maglites illuminated everything within twenty feet.

While Carlos headed off, Macaulay led Mike and Lexy into the open hatchway. Except for a drum of coiled hawser, the first passageway was entirely unobstructed, and he slowly followed it along. About thirty feet farther on, it intersected with the main passageway that ran along the ship's spine. In the glare of the Maglite, he could see a series of compartments heading back toward the stern.

The first compartment Macaulay came to had a wooden door with a brass plate affixed to it that read CAPTAIN. He motioned the others to move on to search the next two compartments as he tried the knob. It wouldn't budge. He shoved his gloved hand against the upper door panel. It came apart in a sodden mess.

Pushing halfway through the opening, he shone the Maglite into the cabin. It was an eight-foot-square steel cave. Whatever personal things the captain might have owned had all disintegrated. A steel bunk had been built into one wall and now held only the mattress springs. There were metal drawers underneath and above it. The empty wooden frame of an easy chair took up one corner. He saw the collapsed remains of a wooden desk along the far wall.

He moved back into the main passageway. From the glow of other Maglites, he could see that Lexy and Mike had already searched the next two compartments and were moving on to the last three. None of them yielded a teak crate or glass containers. Mike pointed to a steel gangway that was bolted against the far bulkhead and led down to the next deck below. He disappeared into the void and they followed him deeper into the bowels of the ship.

The first set of compartments along the passageway of the lower deck had no doors. They had been crew quarters. There had once been curtains across the openings to provide a measure of privacy, but only the metal rods that once held them in position were still in place.

The last compartment on the lower deck had another

steel door. Macaulay wondered if it might have been a storage room for important cargo. The door's metal handle was turned to the open position. Mike braced himself against the opposite bulkhead and tried to force the door open with his legs. It wouldn't budge.

Macaulay removed an iron pry bar from his utility belt and slid the end of it into the narrow space behind the metal handle. Pulling back on it with slow, steady force, he felt the door slowly give way under the pressure.

When it was opened far enough to slip past, he swam inside. His Maglite illuminated the murky darkness of what had once been the radio compartment. An array of moss-covered electronic equipment was bolted to the bulkhead wall.

A metal desk holding the radio operator's transmission keys sat underneath it, the operator's chair wedged under the desk. Still balanced in the chair was the upper half of a human skeleton. The lower half of it had fallen away. The man's skull rested alongside his transmission key. Like everything else in the ship, it was coated by green slime. Macaulay swung around and finned back into the passageway.

One more steel ladder led down to the engine room. He watched as Lexy followed Mike down the small black hole. There was no point in going down there, decided Macaulay. The captain would not have stored the teak crate in the engine room. He checked his watch and tank pressure.

"It's time to go," he called out, and took another breath of air.

There was no air. Nothing but the taste of rubber. It was as if the tank had been turned off at the source. He reached over his shoulder to check the air flow valve above the tanks. It was wide-open. Then it had to be the regulator. He remained calm. He had already expended precious air in talking. He was not about to panic.

"I'm in trouble," he said calmly into the voice communicator.

He sank back down along the side of the bulkhead until he was sitting on the slimy deck. He remembered once holding his breath for three minutes in a YMCA pool when he was fifteen. But he had filled his lungs with air before he went under. He glanced along the passageway toward the steel ladder leading down to the engine room. There was no sign of the Maglites.

Someone had once told him that drowning wasn't actually a bad way to go. Just remove the mouthpiece, open your mouth, and breathe in the water. It would all be over in a few seconds.

He felt his brain shutting down and knew there were only seconds before he lost consciousness. The radio operator's compartment across the passageway was still lit up in the glare of his Maglite. The radio operator's skull shone at his transmission desk.

Make the call, thought Macaulay as the light faded away.

TWENTY-FOUR

28 May
Aboard *Island Time*
North Eleuthera
Bahamas

Macaulay was floating free, breathing again, slowly and normally. The temperature of the seawater around him was definitely rising.

"You be okay, boss," came a disembodied voice at one point through the ultrasound communicator.

He opened his eyes to the gaunt face of Carlos peering at him from behind his face mask just a foot away. He was holding the mouthpiece of his regulator between Macaulay's lips while at the same time buddy-breathing off Mike McGandy's tank.

Macaulay regained full consciousness in the forward cabin of *Island Time* as they sped back toward Dunmore Town. Lexy was sitting on the edge of the berth, clasping his right hand in both of hers.

"It's about time," she said with a worried grin. "You can't sleep all day."

"It was almost the big sleep," he said.

"Carlos saved your life, Steve," she said, pouring two inches of sour mash whiskey into a plastic mug. "He found you in the passageway. For some reason, your voice communicator didn't reach us inside the engine room. We never heard you."

Macaulay tried to remember what had happened. "Was it my regulator?"

She nodded. "Mike took it apart . . . something to do with the O-ring, whatever that is."

Macaulay downed the whiskey. "I take it you're planning to get me drunk and ravish me on the way in."

"That's for later," she said. "Barnaby is waiting for us to brief him before he decides whether to bring in reinforcements from Ira Dusenberry."

It was dark when they got back to the harbor and slowly headed for the *Trader's Bluff*. Several of the superyachts were lit up like casinos. On one of them a full orchestra in formal dress was assembled on its deck and playing Gershwin's "Rhapsody in Blue."

Coming alongside *Trader's Bluff*, Carlos assisted Macaulay in climbing the gangway. The others went aboard behind them. Chris Kimball settled Steve in one of the deck chairs while Carlos ran *Island Time* over to its mooring before rowing back again in the dinghy.

The others were gathered in the dining salon when he got back. Macaulay was resting in one of the salon's overstuffed chairs with another drink in his hand. Lexy stood next to him taking his pulse.

Barnaby offered a toast with his wineglass.

"You do good, Mr. Lugo," he said as Carlos went to the coffee urn and poured himself a cup. "Thank you for bringing General Macaulay back to the land of the living."

Carlos saluted him with his mug and said, "We all be celebrate tonight."

"Not yet," said Barnaby. "So, where are we, Steve? Did you finish the search?"

Macaulay briefly described what they had seen on the last dive.

"It all comes down to where Captain DeVries would have stowed the crate," he concluded. "The stern section of the *Prins Willem* is relatively intact and we searched every compartment. The crate isn't there. If it was lashed somewhere on deck, it isn't there now. If it was stowed in the forward hold, it has been scattered all over the seabed. I suppose we could bring a full recovery team down here to organize a comprehensive search. Otherwise I doubt we could ever find a trace."

"He's right, sir," said Mike McGandy. "I've been diving on wrecks down here for the last ten years. It would require a huge undertaking to comb the marine bottom for small objects. You would also need the cooperation of the prime minister and the ministry of security."

"I'm not sure we have that mandate from Washington," said Barnaby.

Chris Kimball came in from the pilothouse to tell him that Tommy Somervell was calling on a secure line from Germany. Barnaby took the call at the wet bar.

"June and I are in Koblenz," said Tommy. "You wanted to know if that U-boat captain might have picked up survivors after torpedoing the ship."

"Have you located his log?" asked Barnaby, refilling his wineglass.

"Not yet," said Tommy, "but from what we have learned so far, the captain wasn't the type to pick up survivors. His name was Kaspar von Bulow and he was a true believer. He was tried and convicted in absentia after the war by the Russians for ordering that survivors from two torpedoed ships be machine-gunned."

"It doesn't sound like his logbook is worth pursuing," said Barnaby.

"June still thinks so," said Tommy. "Von Bulow was also accused of looting valuables off ships before sinking them. He died here in Koblenz in 1969, but June has found records here of a woman who may be von Bulow's daughter. She apparently inherited a fortune and moved to Uruguay."

"Montevideo is beautiful, they say," said Barnaby.

"I'm not sure she'll last that long," said Tommy, "but she thinks the log is worth going after."

When Barnaby returned to the dining salon, Chris Kimball was showing several pages of weather data to Mike McGandy.

"I don't mean to literally add any more rain to this parade," said Mike, "but it looks like a Cat-Three hurricane is brewing in the Lesser Antilles."

"Just what we needed," said Barnaby. "You'll have to monitor it, Chris. For now, it's time to honor Mr. Lugo. While you were down in the grip of Neptunus, I prepared a ten-pound standing rib roast that I discovered in the meat locker."

"What about some girls?" asked Carlos.

"No girls," said Barnaby. "Just prime rib."

*   *   *

Chris Kimball removed the Heckler & Koch .40-caliber semiautomatic pistol from the chart drawer in the pilothouse and fed a round into the chamber from the magazine. Gently depressing the trigger, he placed it in the hip holster behind his back under his loose-flowing shirt.

Before heading up to the foredeck to begin the first watch, he went to the array of switches in the captain's lounge, turning off all the exterior lights and then the wall sconces and overhead lamps in the lounges and dining salon. Heading to the stern, he checked to make sure that all the compartment hatches were locked and bolted. He checked his watch. It was a few minutes before midnight.

Two decks below, Carlos sat and waited in the engine room. He was familiar with the nightly routine. He knew Chris would now head to the tiny galley off the pilothouse to pick up his first mug of coffee before heading up to the foredeck.

Even if the others on the boat were too tired to celebrate, Carlos would do so on their behalf. He had spent a week in the Bahamas and hadn't even seen a pretty girl, much less talked to one.

Kneeling at the rear bulkhead of the engine room, he slid open the emergency escape hatch and crawled into the fiberglass storage locker built into the stern. Raising its cushioned cover, he climbed out onto the transom and untied the boat's dinghy.

Using two hand towels, he cushioned the oars before silently rowing beyond the nearest yacht and then turning back toward the public dock at Dunmore Town. By then, he was well outside Chris's visual range.

He tied up the dinghy alongside all the others at the

public wharf and headed into town. The two-lane macadam road was dark except for the lights from the small wooden-frame cottages along the way. Exotic plants and wildflowers filled the air with a fragrant smell.

He walked until he came to a crossroad that was lit by streetlamps. Several blocks down, he saw what looked like the beginning of a commercial district, with lit buildings and the distant sound of live music.

He passed the stores and offices and small restaurants that lined both sides of the street. They were all closed. In a couple of places, he saw cleaning people at work. Carlos couldn't read any of the names on the buildings. He had never learned to read and write, but he did know a bar when he saw one and figured at least one still had to be open.

He found one on the next block. It was set back from the street and had a wide veranda where people were smoking and enjoying their drinks. From inside he could hear loud music. He went inside.

The place reminded him a little of Lana's bar in Belize, where there was always a mix of local people and tourists of all different skin colors speaking all kinds of strange languages. Carlos loved all the colors as long as she was clean.

Inside, he passed through a crowd of young men and women all dressed the same. They had to be the crew of one of the big yachts out in the harbor. All of them wore the same starched blue short-sleeve shirts with white shorts and white socks that came up to their knees. The name of their boat was stitched over the breast pockets of their shirts along with what looked like little basketballs.

There was a long wooden bar with a mirror behind it

along one wall, but it was packed with people. The rest of the room was taken up by small pine tables and chairs, all of them filled. Ceiling fans stirred the air above them, carrying away the cigarette smoke.

Through the open glass doors at the back of the room, Carlos saw another section of the bar that extended outside. It had a thatched chikee hut and a lot of tables around it. He went outside and found the last remaining stool by the chikee hut.

"You be make a Goombay Smash?" he asked.

"Mon, we invented the goddamn things," said the old black bartender.

"I try one."

It tasted as good as any that Lana had mixed for him. It tasted as good as anything he had ever drunk. He cupped his big hand around the glass. It felt just right, frosty cold and smelling like the citrus grove behind his shack in Dangria.

He ordered another one and drank it down as quickly as the first. Opening a fresh pack of cigarettes, he lit one and exhaled the smoke. As it spiraled up into the darkness, he wondered how Lana was doing back in Dangria. And that new girl at the air charter service with the melonlike breasts.

He could hear a small band tuning up for another set after their break. When he turned around to look at the musicians, a girl was there standing behind him. She was maybe twenty-five with skin the color of butterscotch and a nice tight body.

She smiled up at him and said, "My name is Timaria. You buy me a drink?"

She was wearing a peach-colored dress that was fastened around her narrow waist with a white silk sash. Her black hair was tied with a red ribbon and her hair smelled of soap.

"Yeah, sure," he said, grinning down at her.

She ordered tequila and Carlos told the bartender to put it on his tab. She took one of the cigarettes from his pack and he lit it for her.

"Where you stayin'?" she asked with the Bahamian lilt of a local girl.

"On one of the boats out there," he said, pointing to the harbor.

"Big boat?"

"Not so big," he said, starting his third Goombay Smash. "We fish."

After the fourth one, he knew he wasn't speaking as clearly as usual. The words sort of ran together. He had been with far prettier girls. Her black eyes were a little too small and her face was too rounded, but she had a sweet smile and she was clean.

"I be celebrating," he said.

"Celebrating what?"

"I save my friend today. . . . We diving."

"I'll drink to that," said the girl, holding up her glass of tequila. "Here's to . . . What's his name?"

"She be Steef."

"That's a funny name for a girl."

"She a guy . . . a great guy," said Carlos.

The girl was looking at him as if she didn't know whether to believe him. Carlos thought she might be lacking in the brains department. He found himself telling her about his life in Belize and then Steve.

"He sounds like quite a guy," said the girl.

"Steef be a general," said Carlos.

"A general?" she said. "Like in the army?"

"The air army," said Carlos. "Steef a pilot."

"I have to go to the loo," she said, putting down her glass.

He lit another cigarette and thought of everything that had happened that afternoon. He had done good. The band began to play music he had never heard before, some kind of Caribbean hip-hop combined with calypso and reggae. He thought about dancing with the girl when she came back.

She didn't come back. Through the open glass doors that led into the other part of the bar, he saw her sitting at one of the tables, talking to an older man with scars on both of his cheeks. He was nodding as she talked into his face. Then she stopped talking to the man, got up from the table, and walked back to the chikee hut.

"I live very close," she said. "You want to come with me?"

Carlos checked his watch. It was almost two o'clock. Mike McGandy would be coming back to the boat soon to take over from Chris. He might see that the dinghy was missing. Somehow the girl didn't look as clean as she had seemed when he first met her.

"I be go," he said. "Maybe tomorrow night."

He staggered a little when he got up from the bar stool, but held himself steady as he walked through the rest of the bar. The crew people in their blue-and-white sailor suits with the basketballs on them were gone. The place was almost empty.

He walked through the veranda doors and out into the dark, cool night. He headed up the street that led back to the dock. At one point, his left sneaker got caught in a cleft in the sidewalk and he stumbled and fell. Laughing, he got back on his feet again. He could see the wharf in the cone of the dock lights.

Something slammed into the back of his head. He was on his hands and knees and tasted blood between his teeth. Two men grabbed his arms and hauled him to his feet. He opened his mouth to call out for help and felt the side of his head explode. He fell from the light.

TWENTY-FIVE

"Well, we found the *Prins Willem*," said Barnaby to Ira Dusenberry on the boat's encrypted satellite phone, "and the Peking Man crate is no longer aboard. It may have been scattered across the seabed when the ship broke up after it was torpedoed. If so, it'll require a major recovery effort and we will need the cooperation of the Bahamian government."

"There are new complications," said Dusenberry. "Apparently, the new prime minister shares certain offshore banking interests with one of the Mexican drug cartels. He may need to be spanked before we can deal with him on this."

"I don't care if you give him twenty lashes with a sjambok," said Barnaby. "Just don't leave us hanging here without support."

"It's not as simple as you think," said Dusenberry. "There are important diplomatic issues involved."

Dusenberry had just attended a meeting with the president in the Oval Office and had stayed behind for a few moments to savor the majesty of the setting when the call came through. It always gave him a rush to sit down in the throne chair. Glancing at the president's schedule, he decided to take the risk.

"I'm not asking you to invade Iraq again, Ira," said Barnaby calmly, "but you've put us at risk down here and one of our people is missing. We're probably going to need assistance very soon."

"All right . . . I'll activate a covert ops team to be on standby at Homestead Air Force Base," said Dusenberry, swiveling the chair around to enjoy the view of the Washington Monument. "They'll be ready if you need them and can deploy in less than an hour. In the meantime, just try to hold the fort."

"Do you save up all these clichés just for me?" asked Barnaby.

Dusenberry could hear the voice of the president's secretary saying he was on his way back.

"Just suck it up, goddammit, and lie low for a day or two," he growled before hanging up.

Barnaby passed the phone back to Chris Kimball and turned to the others in the dining salon.

"Well, you heard my end of it, said Barnaby. "He's putting a covert team on standby at Homestead, pending further developments."

"They've got Carlos," said Macaulay.

"Steve, he could just be sleeping off a drunk somewhere in town," added Kimball. "If he found a girl, there are plenty of places he could have spent the night with her."

Macaulay shook his head and said, "Carlos would have come back. I know him. He might have gone over there to have a few drinks and to check out the girls, but he never would have stayed over even if he picked one up. Somebody took him."

"We don't know anything for sure at this point," said Barnaby. "I asked Mike to do some quiet surveillance without alerting the local police."

They heard the sound of an outboard motor slowly approaching the boat. Chris Kimball stepped to the salon windows.

"Mike's coming back in the runabout," he said. "He's towing our dinghy behind him."

McGandy looked drawn and tired as he came into the salon and sat down.

"As you know, this is a small island. My wife is a doctor's assistant, so she has a pretty big network of friends. I had her make some calls this morning to ask if anything unusual happened last night. One of her friends lives across from the entrance to Brugg's compound. She said there was a disturbance at around two in the morning that woke her up. Someone was yelling blue murder."

"That might have been anyone," said Barnaby.

"She said that at night the compound is as quiet as a graveyard," said McGandy, "and the voice was in Spanish. She went to her bedroom window and saw two members of Brugg's palace guard dragging someone in through the gates."

"I'm going after him," said Macaulay. "Do you know anything about the layout inside the walls?"

"I've never been inside," said McGandy. "Under ordinary circumstances I would say that trying to get in there would be suicide, but here is one piece of luck. There's a charity event taking place tonight that is always hosted by one of the great houses on the island. This year it's at Brugg's mansion. My wife said the duke of Lancaster and his wife are supposed to be there with a lot of other dignitaries."

"That would give us a chance to find out if they might be holding him," said Lexy.

"And where," added Kimball.

"Is the public invited to these events?" asked Barnaby.

"It's invitation only to the money crowd," said McGandy. "No chance of getting a ticket, and security will be tight."

"Well, that complicates it," said Barnaby.

"Maybe not," added McGandy. "The caterer who is supplying all the food is one of my partners in the dive business. He's always looking for more help at these events."

Carlos awoke to feel the sickness inside his head. When he tried to turn over to vomit, he couldn't move his shoulders and the bile gushed out the side of his mouth. He was stretched out naked on his back on a long, thick slab of butcher block. His wrists were shackled above him at the head of the slab and his ankles at the foot of it.

The stone-walled room was dark and cavelike with no windows and a low stone ceiling. There was a rancid smell in the damp air. The only illumination came from a single lightbulb hanging over the slab.

The figure of a huge black woman loomed over him.

She removed a sponge from the bucket of cold water she was carrying and mopped his face clean.

"It looks to me like you haven't been taking good care of yourself, *querido*," said Black Mamba.

He remained silent as she pried open his mouth with her enormous fingers and probed around his teeth and gums.

"You're a heavy smoker, aren't you?" she said. "And your teeth show the sad results of your sugar craving. You should turn your life around before it is too late, *querido*."

He heard a hollow gagging noise from across the chamber. Carlos twisted his head to the left and looked into the gloom. Another man was sitting in what looked like one of the old wooden electric chairs he had seen in gangster movies. His wrists and ankles were shackled to the armrests and legs.

The other man was naked too. Maybe sixty, he had a pink beefy face and close-cropped iron-gray hair. A roll of flab hung at his midsection, and his glazed eyes were bulging. Someone had duct-taped his private parts to a basketball.

"Who be you?" called out Carlos.

The man looked back at him with his glassy eyes but didn't say anything.

"That is Mr. Dolan," said Black Mamba. "He is here to sell his sports team to my son."

Mr. Dolan began nodding his head up and down.

"And what is your name, *querido*?" she asked Carlos with a matronly smile.

When he didn't answer, she went across the room to what looked like a tool chest on the table next to the wall. She came back with a pair of needle-nose pliers, the type

Carlos had used almost every day working on the plane engines at the charter service.

"I only ask once," she said, gripping the fingers of his left hand. He felt the scrunch of the pliers on the nail of his index finger.

When he looked up at her, she was gazing down at him like a mother looking into her child's eyes. Several seconds went by and he felt her hand release his fingers. A moment later she ripped the nail of his index finger out by the roots. It sounded like the tearing of a sheet of paper. The pain was excruciating, but he gritted his teeth as she tore the rest of his nails out one by one.

"I'll ask you again when I come back," she said.

He watched as she headed up the stone steps at the end of the chamber.

"I be Bruce Willis, you fuckin' bitch," he shouted to her retreating back.

Juwan watched as Varna's academy students began clearing the Naugahyde couches out of the great hall of the mansion to make room for dancing. He grimaced at the thought of some of the reactions he might have to deal with during the inaugural dance that the annual hosts always conducted to lead off the festivities. Varna had begged to be part of it.

Emile Bardot approached him and saluted.

"The man hasn't said anything since we brought him in," said Bardot. "He's very tough, but Mamba says she will soon have him singing like Engelbert Humperdinck."

"What do we know at this point?" asked Juwan.

"He told the girl in the bar that he had saved the life of his friend while diving on a wreck off the backbone," said Bardot, "and that his friend was a general. We will soon learn which yacht he came from."

"Have Sir Henry notify the Chinese," said Juwan, "and request that the bounty should be paid in U.S. dollars."

"I'll call Sir Henry immediately."

"One more thing," said Juwan.

"Yes, sir?"

"Slow them down."

TWENTY-SIX

Chris Kimball stood on the foredeck of the Hatteras and pretended to be enjoying the view of the harbor as Mike McGandy's runabout headed toward the public wharf with Barnaby, Lexy, and Macaulay aboard.

Picking up his binoculars, Kimball slowly scanned the activity in the harbor. It looked just as it should, just as it usually did, with skiffs going back and forth between the yachts and the town, fishing boats heading out toward the backbone, and the ferry from the airport bringing new guests to Dunmore Town. If there was any indication that the *Trader's Bluff* was under surveillance, he couldn't find it.

He turned to do another sweep in the opposite direction and watched as two small local boys in a patched wooden skiff pulled up at the gangway of one of the superyachts anchored across the harbor. The stern section of their skiff was loaded with coconuts and low in the water.

They had become a familiar sight to Kimball over the previous few days. For a Bahamian dollar, they would majestically lop off the top of a coconut with a machete and serve the coconut milk with a straw to children and crewmen at the foot of a yacht's gangway.

Mike McGandy tied up his runabout at the finger pier of his dive club and led the others to his venerable Range Rover. The uninterrupted days of brilliant sun and blue sky had been replaced with a low leaden sky that portended rain.

McGandy drove them to his small cottage overlooking the ocean side of Dunmore Town. There, he introduced them to his friend and dive partner, Bob Littlefrost, who was catering the charity event at Brugg's mansion, and to Mike's Bahamian wife, Cora, a college-trained physician's assistant who managed a local medical clinic. To Lexy, she looked to be about six months pregnant.

Littlefrost was tall and blond with a hawkish nose, a sun-weathered face, and St. Bernard eyes. McGandy had assured Macaulay he could be trusted. In truth, they were running out of options. With Dusenberry putting any help on hold, he had to take the risk.

"Brugg's henchmen have tried to peddle drugs to some of my daughter's middle school classmates," said Littlefrost, shaking Macaulay's hand. "I'll help you in any way I can as long as it doesn't endanger my family."

"Our friend was forcibly taken into his compound last night," said Macaulay. "Is there any way to narrow down the possibilities of where they might have him?"

"I've been in there several times over the years," said Littlefrost. "The likeliest possibility is the cellar of the mansion. It was blasted out of the underlying coquina rock when they built the house. Local gossip has it that he keeps something incredible down there. It wouldn't surprise me if it's a torture chamber."

Lexy paled at the thought of Carlos subjected to terrible cruelty.

"They could also have your friend in the old barracks used by his palace guard. It predates the house and is located along the west wall of the compound. The only other possibility is the compound's utility building. It's built to withstand a hurricane and has a water desalinization plant and backup generators for when the power goes out."

"How do you propose to get us in there?" asked Barnaby.

"Between permanent and temporary catering staff, we'll have about twenty-five people working the events this evening," he said. "I've already had a team go over there to set up four different serving stations inside the house and on the terraces. We'll arrive there at about four o'clock in my two jitney buses followed by my refrigerated truck. There will be parking set aside for us near the outside entrance to the kitchen. My people all wear the same white uniforms, skirts for the women, twill trousers for the men. The food is already prepared and refrigerated. My kitchen staff will do the final prep work in the kitchen."

Littlefrost checked his printed schedule. "The guests will start arriving at five thirty for the cocktail party on the front esplanade, and then they'll eat a buffet dinner in the great hall. There is a charity auction followed by dancing and finally fireworks after it gets dark."

"How many people will be at the event?" asked Barnaby.

"I was asked to cater for at least a hundred guests."

"Is everyone in your company checked for identification?" asked Lexy.

Littlefrost shook his head. "They don't have the means. The one thing they will do is check for concealed weapons. I have to ask you not to bring any. That discovery would put both me and my family at great risk."

"Understood," said Macaulay, "and agreed."

"One more thing," added Littlefrost. "After the cocktail party is under way, there is also a personal tour of the house given by the host of the event. If your friend is being held somewhere else in the house, that might help to point the way. They will certainly avoid it."

"Who gets to go on the tour?" asked Macaulay.

"Special guests and major contributors to the effort to save the Bahamas endangered bird species," said Littlefrost. "This year they're expecting a number of royals, including the duke of Lancaster and his wife. She's the leader of the whole effort."

Littlefrost began sizing up Macaulay.

"You'll fit right in with the bartenders," he said. Turning to Lexy, he said, "Perhaps the waitstaff, maybe a hostess."

He turned to gaze up at Barnaby.

"And me?" demanded Barnaby.

"I'm afraid . . ."

"You're afraid?" demanded Barnaby.

"I just meant . . . it would be pretty difficult to disguise you," said Littlefrost.

"I'm going in," said Barnaby.

"You would blow our cover in five minutes," said Macaulay.

"I could cut his hair with my medical shears," said Cora. "I think that would help a lot."

"Sorry," said Barnaby. "No one has touched my hair since my second wife sliced it off with a Viking short sword when I was under the weather thirty years ago."

"You're lucky she didn't cut off something more important," said Macaulay. "Let her do it or stay behind."

Cora was able to shear his three feet of tangled hair surprisingly quickly. "Amazing," said Lexy when she was finished. "You look like Ichabod Crane."

"On steroids," added Macaulay.

"Prep chef," said Littlefrost to Barnaby. "The chef's hat will clinch it."

Lexy drew Cora aside as the others began to try on the uniforms Littlefrost had brought with him.

"Do you have a cocktail dress and some pumps I could borrow?" Lexy asked Cora. "I think we're about the same size . . . at least before you . . ."

Cora laughed and said, "I'll show you what I have."

Every breath was a silent sob. After the initial shock of having all his fingernails torn off at the roots, the agonizing pain began throbbing steadily behind Carlos's eyes like a mini jackhammer. He closed his eyes and willed himself to remain silent. He could smell cooking spices and the rank odor of sewage in the air.

He heard someone coming down the stone steps again and waited as the person approached the wooden slab. When he opened his eyes, she was smiling down at him with what looked like motherly concern.

"Where is the sunken ship?" she asked him.

He stared back up at her, saying nothing.

She walked back over to the toolbox and returned with a pair of handheld garden clippers, the type used to prune small branches. In her other hand she was holding what looked like a tube of ointment. She paused for a few moments as if waiting to see if he planned to say something.

Smiling again, she stepped to the end of the slab, grabbed his left foot, and snipped off his big toe. He watched as she squeezed the ointment on the wound. A moment later he felt a sea of pain rage like fire through his brain.

"Epoxy cement to stanch the bleeding," she said. "That pungent odor is formaldehyde. You don't want too much of it in your bloodstream."

She returned to his side and held his big toe close to his face. "You have only one more of those left. If you don't tell me what I need to know, you will no longer enjoy the use of fingers or toes. And that is only the start."

Carlos turned his head to look back at the man who had been strapped to the throne chair. The man was still sitting there, but his chin was now resting on his bare chest and his eyes were closed. He didn't appear to be breathing.

"Mr. Dolan suffered a fatal heart attack while I was attending to my rounds," she said with seeming sadness. "Like you, he was entirely too careless in worshipping the holy temple of his body. Now, where is the wreck of the ship you found?"

TWENTY-SEVEN

Light rain began to spatter the windows of the jitney buses as they arrived at the mansion entrance and were allowed through the immense bronze gates.

Mike McGandy was driving the first bus with Barnaby, Macaulay, and Lexy aboard. A slew of mansion security guards armed with semiautomatic pistols and wearing red-and-white uniforms flanked the open doors of the buses as the catering staff emerged. Each new arrival was carefully patted down and given a scan with a security wand.

Heading inside the kitchen, Littlefrost's small teams of professionals began to organize for the event. While one team brought in the provisions from the refrigerated truck, others began spreading out across the main floor of the mansion to stock the predesignated serving stations with wine, liquor, and mixers.

In the great hall, they began decorating the large plantation tables with flowers and serving pieces while the prep staff in the kitchen began warming the refrigerated dishes and the serving staff arranged the array of food selections on faux silver platters.

By the time the guests began arriving an hour later, Macaulay and Barnaby had found by process of elimination the only entrance door to the cellar. It was behind a massive oak door off the great hall. The door was locked.

Macaulay went outside with two of the bartenders at one point when they took a smoke break. Twenty yards away across the compound, Macaulay saw the steel door to the utility building. It was windowless aside from two large vents mounted on the second story of the concrete block wall. He wondered if Carlos was inside just steps away from him.

A security guard was deployed at each corner of the building and another two at the entrance door. He would have to wait until dark to make his try, he decided. As Macaulay watched, a white panel truck with the letters BEC stenciled on the sides drew up at the entrance. Two men in uniforms lettered with the BEC logo got out and approached the guards. They were allowed inside.

"Maintenance guys from the Bahamas Electric Corporation," said one of the bartenders to the other. "They must be having problems with the generators again."

"The mansion isn't on the local power grid?" asked Macaulay.

The bartender shook his head. "They wanted to be

completely independent. Even the fresh water in here comes from the big desalinization plant over there."

With all the required access to the utility building, Macaulay scratched it off the list of places they might be holding Carlos.

By five o'clock, guests were streaming through the entrance to the compound in the rain under brightly colored umbrellas, all of them gaily dressed, most of the men in ties and sports jackets and the women in a range of dresses and outfits tailored to their ages and figures.

The British royals arrived in a succession of four Bentley limousines. Juwan stood beside Varna to personally greet the duke and duchess of Lancaster as they came up the flagstone steps to the formal entrance.

"Welcome, Your Grace," said Varna with the flourish of a brief curtsy.

The old duchess looked to Juwan as if she hadn't eaten in a week and was carrying a dog the size of a big Gambian pouched rat under her right arm. She was wearing a yellow crinkled dress that reminded Juwan of the ones worn by the Southern belles in *Gone With the Wind*.

He stood impassively as the old lady extended her hand. He wasn't sure if he was supposed to kiss it. Instead he just took her thin fingers inside his own massive hand and gently shook them. They felt like dried twigs.

He wished that he had never allowed Varna to accept the invitation to host the event. There were too many things happening at once, including the imminent arrival of the Chinese. As he led them inside, he had an impending sense of doom that this wasn't going to turn out well.

Inside, the full orchestra that Lexy had seen playing on

the deck of the Danish yacht out in the harbor was now ensconced in the great hall and playing a medley of hits from Sir Elton John.

A white banner hung above the partiers that read SAVE OUR PRECIOUS BIRDS. The guests passed through a gauntlet of blown-up photographs of endangered Bahamian bird species before they reached the entertainment area, including the Bahama swallow, the red-bellied woodpecker, Kirtland's warbler, and the West Indian tree duck. Lexy moved about them with a tray of canapés, serving each new cluster of guests as they arrived.

Macaulay had asked Bob Littlefrost if he could man the serving station that had been located near the locked door that he already knew led down to the cellar. While setting up, he had stacked four wooden crates of mixers in front of it.

Now mixing drinks for a long line of customers, he watched as the hulking Brugg made his way around the great hall with his diminutive partner, shaking hands and welcoming the guests.

"I would like a gin martini, as dry as the Kalahari," said the next voice in line. "Straight up."

It was the duke of Lancaster. Macaulay recognized him from his entrance into the hall, which had been accompanied by applause from the other guests. In his late seventies with a silver ponytail, he was wearing flaming red Bermuda shorts under a safari jacket. A purple scarf was tied at his neck.

Macaulay reached for a martini glass. The duke shook his head.

"One of those," said the duke, pointing to the big glass tumblers that were used for mixed drinks.

"Yes, Your Grace," said Macaulay, filling a cocktail shaker with gin and ice and adding a dash of vermouth and bitters. After giving it several shakes, he served it in the tumbler with a cocktail napkin.

"Heavenly," said the duke, moving off.

Thirty minutes into the reception, Lexy saw Brugg approach the royal entourage. It was clear that he and his little friend were about to begin the tour of the house. Taking her tray, she walked quickly back to the kitchen. Laying the tray on the serving counter, she reached down to a lower shelf and retrieved the backpack she had brought with her on the bus.

In the servants' bathroom off the kitchen, she quickly changed into the cocktail dress that Cora had lent her and put on high-heeled black pumps. Unpinning her thick auburn hair, she ran a brush through it several times and then added a touch of lipstick.

Back in the great hall, she made her way to the group that had already formed up at the foot of the main staircase for the guided tour. Sidling next to the duke, she said, "You are really going to enjoy this, Your Grace."

His eyes came to the same level as her breasts.

Looking up into her violet eyes, he said, "Heavenly," and put his arm through hers.

As the group was about to begin ascending the staircase, the duchess put down her dog on the floor and led it on a silver-studded leash to the closest serving station where Macaulay was bartending.

"Could I entrust you with Winifred?" she asked him. "She is very dear to me and descended from the Yorkies raised by Queen Victoria."

"Of course, Your Grace," said Macaulay, taking the

silver-studded leash as he watched Lexy head up the stairs with the others. "I adore Yorkshire terriers."

A tall, light-complexioned black man with livid scars on both his cheeks was waiting for the tour group when it reached the second floor. He was wearing the red-and-white uniform of Juwan's security guard with a gold star on each collar. His shoes were two-toned, white and black.

"I am Colonel Emile Bardot," he said in French-accented English. "The first stop on your tour this evening will give you an opportunity to view the incomparable collection of marine life personally captured in the sea by Juwan Brugg."

What had once been an enormous parlor off the main staircase had been partially converted to a saltwater aquarium, the biggest one Lexy had ever seen outside a zoo. Its walls of brass-framed plate glass ran twenty feet square across the room, and rose to a height of ten feet above the stone floor. Behind the glass was a mass of large colorful fish swimming around live coral outcroppings and over a bed of white sand.

"That sound you hear is from a compressor that continually circulates fresh ocean water into this tank and provides a perfect living habitat for our friends from beneath the sea."

Juwan stepped to the side of the aquarium and turned to face them. "As you may know, the population of predatory fish in the ocean is down nearly two-thirds over the last twenty years. The species here include some of the most endangered ones, including the giant saw fish you see at the bottom. His saw-studded cutting blades are almost five feet long and he can turn a human intruder into hamburger in seconds."

"Those things look quite ferocious," said the duke, putting his arm protectively around Lexy's waist.

"These goosefish kill their prey differently," said Ju-wan, pointing to several fish about four feet long with hideously deformed jaws. They were all chocolate brown in color, mottled with white spots. "Both jaws are armed with inch-long teeth, all pointed inward toward its stom-ach. Once its prey is trapped inside the jaws, its teeth drive the meat of the victim down its gullet. The goose-fish can swallow a full-grown German shepherd in less than a minute."

The duchess of Lancaster visibly blanched.

"How would you know that?" she asked.

Emile Bardot watched the duchess's husband pawing the young woman and wondered if the old roué was sleeping with her. She was stunningly beautiful with a superb figure accentuated by the black silk cocktail dress. He assumed she was part of the royal entourage, since he hadn't seen her before on Harbour Island. He would have remembered.

Each time Macaulay went to replenish the bar mixers from the wooden crates by the cellar door, he studied its lock. The oak door was at least three inches thick, and the size of the keyhole suggested a key that was probably six inches long. That made the challenge of picking the lock a little easier.

When his first break came, he went to find Barnaby and found him standing behind one of the plantation tables where the buffet dinner would be served, arranging an empty silver tureen over an electric heating plate. He was wearing a white chef's hat that covered his ears.

"You look ridiculous," said Macaulay.

"Fuck you," said Barnaby. "I've been meaning to tell you that for a long time."

Macaulay grinned and quietly told him that there was no way they were holding Carlos in the utility building, which left the cellar and the guard barracks as the two likeliest possibilities.

"Meet me at my serving station in a couple minutes," he said. "I think I have a way to get you down there."

Heading back to the kitchen, Macaulay stopped long enough to brief Mike McGandy on their plan to search the cellar.

"When you're ready, we'll go after Carlos together," said Mike. "It'll probably be a two-man job."

Macaulay rummaged through several drawers before finding a thin, six-inch-long fillet knife. At the air force academy, he had once roomed with a cadet who could open just about any door with what he called a bump key. The ridges and valleys along its spine had been filed down so it would fit into most locks and usually engage enough pins inside it to turn the cylinder.

Two of the closets in the kitchen had lever lock-type keys that were smaller versions of the one that fit the cellar door. He removed one of them without attracting attention. Using a short length of tape to fasten the skeleton key to the end of the knife blade, he slipped it inside his shirt.

He was about to head back to his serving station when he saw one of the maintenance men from the Bahamas Electrical Company come in through the kitchen door and head to a room down a side passageway. Unlocking a door, he disappeared inside.

Macaulay followed down the passageway and paused by the open door. The maintenance man was down on his knees with his back to him in front of a green-painted steel compartment that covered most of the wall. Through its open sheet-steel cover panel, Macaulay saw that it housed the electrical system for the compound, including an inverter and several banks of electronic circuit breakers.

When he got back to his serving station near the great hall, Barnaby was standing near it holding the leash of the Yorkshire terrier.

"Good cover," said Macaulay before relieving the other bartender.

He waited until there was no one left on the drink line and then knelt behind Barnaby in front of the cellar door lock. Inserting the skeleton key on the end of the fillet knife, he tried to feel his way to a point where enough ridges on the key would engage the pins that turned the cylinder. Moving it in and out, he kept turning it in his hand.

"May I have a glass of red wine?" asked someone behind him. Leaving the key inside the lock behind the bulk of Barnaby, he poured the woman a glass of wine and then knelt again at the lock.

"I think the dog needs to urinate," said Barnaby as it nuzzled his pants leg. "Hurry up."

Macaulay felt the cylinder begin to move deep inside the lock. He heard a distinct set of clicks and watched the bolt recede.

"We're in," said Macaulay. "Wait for me to give you

the word and be careful. If he's down there, he's probably being guarded."

When everyone in sight around the serving station appeared to be occupied with other guests, he said, "Now."

When Macaulay turned to look back at the door a few seconds later, Barnaby and the dog were gone.

TWENTY-EIGHT

29 May
Casa Grande Brugg
Dunmore Town
North Eleuthera
Bahamas

The stone steps were cut out of sedimentary rock and led down in a rough circular pattern into the darkness. Barnaby had remembered to bring along a handheld fire stick used to ignite Sterno fuel under the chafing dishes.

The duchess's Yorkshire terrier seemed content to lead the way, and the tiny candle flame gave him enough light to see a few feet in front of him. The reverberating sound of the music from the orchestra slowly diminished to nothing as he reached a depth of twenty feet below the main floor of the mansion. He could hear water dripping from the rock ceiling as he found the bottom step. There was a dank smell in the air.

The dog seemed to know where it was going and it pulled him ahead into the gloom.

A solid steel door emerged in the flame of the fire stick. The door was embedded in the rock wall. There was no keyhole. If it was locked from the inside, there would be no way for him to open it. While he waited uncertainly, the dog went into a crouch and peed on the rock floor.

Come what may, there was no alternative but to find out what was behind it, he decided. He slowly turned the large brass knob and pulled on it. The door came open soundlessly on well-oiled hinges. Beyond the opening was only more blackness.

When he took a step forward, an automatic switch suddenly bathed the room in brilliant light, and Barnaby could only stand dumbstruck. The enormous chamber was as big as an NFL locker room and both clean and dry. He could feel fresh air flowing into his face from a source that apparently kept the chamber at a constant temperature with controlled humidity.

It wasn't a torture chamber as Bob Littlefrost had thought. It was a vast exhibition hall, and all the exhibits were exotic birds, each one mounted in situ in its own glass resting place. Some display cases held ten or more birds of the same species. Engraved brass nameplates identified not only the species, but the date of their capture and subsequent stuffing by Juwan Brugg.

It struck Barnaby as ludicrously ironic that many of them bore the same names as the ones he had seen in the photographs in the great hall, including the Kirtland's warbler, the West Indian tree duck, and the Bahama swallow. If the visual evidence was to be believed, Brugg was a one-man destruction squad for the cause they were celebrating upstairs.

Barnaby took the time to explore the rest of the chamber, looking for other passageways that might lead to where Carlos was confined. The one room was all there was. When he looked around for the Yorkshire terrier, he saw that it had lain down on the carpeted floor and was fast asleep. Barnaby left him there.

It was getting too dark for Chris Kimball to see any distance with his binoculars from the reclining chair on the foredeck of *Trader's Bluff*. Harbor activity had remained quiet through the afternoon and the evening.

At one point, a local police boat had slowly crisscrossed the harbor checking the hull numbers on each craft and doing random inspections aboard some of the vessels. They stopped briefly alongside the *Island Time* but ignored *Trader's Bluff*. Otherwise the only activity close by had consisted of the ten-year-old boys hawking coconut juice from their old skiff.

They were on their way back again. As he watched through the binoculars in the rapidly falling darkness, the boy manning the oars rowed it over to the *Island Time*. It was moored only thirty yards away from the Hatteras and Kimball thought about shouting to them that no one was aboard.

Then it struck him that the boys already knew there was no one aboard. They had been working the yachts all afternoon and their supply of coconuts was gone. Kimball had bought one himself.

When the skiff pulled alongside *Island Time*, one of the boys climbed onto the stern deck and raised the lid of the stern locker. A few moments later, he tossed something to the boy on the skiff.

The boy on the boat disappeared into the darkness under the roof of the wheelhouse. Kimball hoped that Carlos had secured the hatchway down to the cabin as he decided to use the boat's portable air horn for a few seconds to frighten them off.

Kimball was raising the air horn to issue a quick blast when *Island Time* disappeared in a blinding flash of brilliant light. A searing wave of heat hurled him backward into the front windshield of the Hatteras.

The explosion silenced any sound in his ruptured eardrums. He tried to sit up. A shard of metal, maybe six inches long, was embedded into his left arm. Still in shock, he glanced down at it, wondering how it had gotten there.

He could see small objects raining down from the sky and landing all over the deck. His arm began to pulse with pain, then his flash-burned face. As he sat immobilized against the cracked windshield, he looked back at the mooring where *Island Time* had been tethered.

There was nothing left of it or the boys' skiff.

Lexy stood in the bedroom shared by Varna and Juwan and stared at the photographic reproduction of a young Juwan on the cover of *Sports Illustrated* that filled one entire wall. Varna was explaining to the tour guests the manufacturing effort that had gone into constructing their ultra-king-size bed.

"Looks rather inviting, doesn't it?" whispered the duke of Lancaster in her ear.

Gently removing his hand from around her waist, she walked across the room and stepped out onto the balcony overlooking the compound. In the distance, she could hear what sounded like police sirens out in the harbor. The fourth-floor balcony ran ten feet in both directions, and she quickly moved away from the opening.

Emile Bardot watched her disappear into the dusky evening. It was clear to him now that she did not enjoy the inebriated groping of the old royal. What she probably needed was some French persuasion. He was about to follow her out when he felt his smartphone begin to silently vibrate in the breast pocket of his suit jacket.

Turning away from the tour guests, he looked down to see the text message from Sir Henry Pindling in Nassau. *Chinese arrive in thirty minutes—North Eleuthera airport—Private jet—Zhou's son plus twenty commandos—see data link.*

The data link consisted of descriptions of the three people being sought by the Chinese oligarch Zhou Shen Wui. There were grainy photographs of two of them. The retired air force general looked very young to have earned the rank. Bardot thought he bore a possible resemblance to one of the bartenders he had noticed downstairs. He wasn't sure about the second man, who was identified as an English archaeologist. The third photograph was crystal clear. The subject in it was standing thirty feet away from him.

Bardot pulled Juwan aside for a few moments.

"From Sir Henry . . . the Chinese will be here shortly," he whispered. "They are accompanied by a military team."

Juwan nodded and turned back to his guests.

From the bedroom balcony, Lexy looked down at the lushly landscaped compound. She had gone out there in the hope that the balcony would provide a vantage point for observing the guard barracks. None of the other rooms they had visited on the tour permitted a view of it through the dense foliage surrounding the house.

The balcony rose far above the trees and Bob Little- frost had told her where the guard barracks was located in relation to the house. She found it immediately. The brick building was two stories high and hidden from the mansion by the dense screen of banana trees, coconut palms, and eucalyptus trees.

Gazing down at it, she could see a small cone of light at the front entrance and a second at the rear. Three guards in shorts and T-shirts were standing outside the front entrance smoking marijuana. The distinctive smell of it wafted over the trees.

Behind her in the bedroom, she could hear the other tour guests leaving.

"Thank you for taking the time to join us on the tour of our modest home," she heard the little partner of Ju- wan Brugg say. "Dinner will now be served in the great hall."

She wondered if the duke would come out to retrieve her from the balcony and hoped that the duchess might have reined him in when she saw two figures at the rear of the guard barracks move into the cone of light.

The first person was enormous, almost as broad as tall. The second one was wearing one of the red-and-white security guard uniforms and he was carrying something over his shoulder.

It was covered by a sheet, but at one point the cloth dropped away and she saw that it was another man. He appeared to be naked and was clearly overweight. It couldn't be Carlos, she thought, as the two figures merged into the darkness for several moments, only to reemerge into the dim lights of the barracks parking lot.

While the first figure went on ahead, the guard carrying the body opened the rear hatch of a black panel van and dumped the man inside. After closing the hatch, he followed the first figure toward the mansion house.

"I could not allow you to miss the most exciting part of the tour, mademoiselle," said a voice behind her.

She turned and saw the man in the white suit with the scars on his cheeks.

"I was just admiring the lovely view," she said, smiling at him. "I lost track of time."

"I doubt that, Dr. Vaughan," he said.

"You must have me confused—"

"Hardly," he said, holding up his smartphone. "The photograph does not do you justice. Please know that I have no interest in harming you. I simply wish to know why you and your colleagues are so incredibly valuable to our Chinese friends."

Pulling out a slender object from his side pocket, he pressed down on it and a stiletto blade snapped into position.

"If you will follow me, Dr. Vaughan," he said.

They descended the staircase to the third floor with the knife held flat against her back and he led her down a side passageway. At the first door they came to, he stopped to unlock it with a key from his chain and nudged her inside. The fluorescent ceiling lights came on automatically. He locked the door behind him.

To Lexy, it looked like nothing more than a large storeroom. Aside from a table and chairs, it had shelves on two walls filled with canned goods and bottles. A stainless steel commercial refrigerator unit occupied most of the back wall.

"Please sit down and enjoy the view," said Bardot, motioning her toward one of the chairs.

Stepping to a circuit breaker panel behind him, he flipped one of the switches. A floor panel made of solid steel began to slide back to reveal a four-foot-square opening. She leaned forward to look down through it. The room was directly over the saltwater aquarium.

"A bit melodramatic, I will admit," said Bardot. "Juwan was inspired to build the aquarium after watching an early James Bond movie. No one thought about how the creatures were going to be fed until it was finished. This is their supply room. You would be quite amazed at the quantity and variety of the meals they consume every day."

TWENTY-NINE

29 May
Casa Grande Brugg
Dunmore Town
North Eleuthera
Bahamas

Macaulay watched as the tour group led by Brugg came back down the main staircase and began to disperse into the great hall. The duchess of Lancaster separated from her husband and came toward him.

"Where is Winifred?" she asked with a worried tone, looking around for her Yorkshire terrier.

"She needed to relieve herself," said Macaulay with a reassuring grin. "It's raining quite hard, so I asked one of the staff to take her for a walk on the covered terrace."

"Excellent," she said. "I'll be back to pick her up as soon as we finish dinner. I am certain that she will wish to repay your kindness with a special gratuity."

"Thank her for me, Your Grace," he said, glancing

back up the empty staircase and wondering why Lexy had not returned with the others.

As the orchestra began to play a Strauss waltz, Varna led Juwan by the hand into the center of the great hall. The crowd of guests parted to let them through. They had practiced the dance together for two weeks.

When they reached the dance floor, Juwan felt Varna's right arm reach around behind his back. Juwan shut his eyes. As the waltz music reached the precise moment, Varna began leading him in ever-widening circles across the open floor. Juwan kept his eyes closed, waiting for the inevitable laughter that would end the dance as well as the life of the man or woman who did it.

Macaulay suddenly heard the heavy splatter of rain on flagstone and glanced over to see the front door opening. Three men strode quickly into the foyer under wide umbrellas and stopped briefly to remove their raincoats.

From photographs Barnaby had shown him in New York, Macaulay recognized two of them as Zhou Shen Wui and his son, Li. Macaulay turned away from the bar toward the cases of mixer as they strode past his serving station to the entrance to the great hall. The Chinese stopped when they got to the edge of the dance floor and saw the two men dancing.

Li Shen Wui remembered being at a circus in Shanghai as a boy where he had seen a gigantic trained bear dancing with a midget. He was unable to stifle a laugh. Juwan's ears pricked up at the thin cackling sound and he opened his eyes to see the group of Chinese standing at the entrance. One of them was grinning at him like a spotted hyena.

Zhou Shen Wui issued a stern, one-word rebuke and

Li regained his composure as Juwan stopped dancing and came toward them. From the look on Brugg's face, Macaulay thought that the big man was going to murder the younger Chinese in front of the whole crowd. As he was about to reach him, his dancing partner sped ahead and began shaking the younger Chinese man's hand.

"I'm Varna. Welcome to Casa Grande Brugg," he said with an inviting smile.

Li found himself drawn to the younger man immediately. They were the same physical type, short, muscular, with swimmers' bodies, one of a piece, although Varna had a Latin flavor to his handsome pug-nosed face and Li a Chinese caste.

The rest of the couples began to dance and the tension at the edge of the floor slowly ebbed. The duke and duchess of Lancaster stopped on their way to the buffet and were introduced to Zhou and his son.

"I have always adored the Chinese," said the duchess. "When we lived in Hong Kong, our children's school had two Chinese cleaning people."

Macaulay took advantage of the lull to grab one of the metal serving trays filled with premixed drinks from a waitress. Stepping past the serving station, he headed up the main staircase alone.

There was no one in the broad hallway on the second floor and he put down the tray. Most of the doors of the rooms stood open. He poked his head into all of them, but the rooms were empty. Two doors were locked, but they yielded easily to his jury-rigged bump key. They were entertainment rooms and empty too.

The third floor reflected the same pattern, mostly open doorways and brightly lit parlors, along with a billiard room and a small movie theater. He was about to head up the staircase to the fourth floor when he noticed a small side corridor leading down a dark passageway. The first door he came to was closed. He stood outside it for a moment and listened.

In the distance, he thought he heard a police siren, nothing from inside the room. He turned the handle, but it was locked. He quietly inserted the bump key in the hole and was about to turn it when he heard a voice from beyond the door. The voice wasn't talking. The sound it made was more like a moaning wail followed by a low howl of outrage.

He turned the bump key, but this time it wouldn't engage. He kept twisting it against the locking pins to move the cylinder, but they didn't budge. When he turned it even harder, the blade of the fillet knife snapped off. From beyond the door, the first voice was replaced by a second one, this one deeper, issuing a snort of laughter.

Macaulay took three steps back to the opposite wall and then hurled his right shoulder into the spot where the door lock met the jamb. It splintered and gave way. A moment later he was in the room.

The space was filled with the vibration noise of a compressor. As he glanced down, his eyes registered the four-foot-square opening in the floor. Beyond it were standing shelves full of canned goods and a big commercial refrigerator along the far wall. In between them, a man was standing with his back to the door.

He had removed his uniform coat, and his trousers were down around his shoes. Taking a step forward, Macaulay saw there was a woman pinned to the table. She was bent forward and the man was behind her holding a stiletto to her throat. Lexy was still wearing her long black cocktail dress. The man was trying to raise the hem above her thighs with his free hand.

Hearing the door splinter, the man turned away from her and brought the stiletto around to face Macaulay in a smooth underhand motion. Macaulay was about to launch himself across the room when he saw Lexy slide free from the table. Still in a low crouch, she turned and drove her shoulder into the man's back.

The man stumbled toward him, his eyes staring down at the hole in the floor with abject terror, unable to free himself from the pants shackling his ankles above his two-toned black-and-white shoes. With short stutter steps, he lost his balance and scuttled to the opening, trying desperately to stop.

"Mère de Dieu," Bardot cried as he tiptoed over the edge and dropped straight down.

Macaulay stepped forward in time to see him land in a huge tank of standing water. It looked as though fish were swimming in it. A few moments later, the surface of the water was alive and churning from the man's thrashing arms and legs.

Lexy came into Macaulay's arms. They held each other as the man's single piercing scream died away and was replaced by the noise of the compressor.

"Sorry I couldn't get here sooner," said Macaulay as the water beneath them turned pink and then bright red.

"Allow me to introduce my son, Li Shen Wui, and Colonel Mu," said Zhou as the three Chinese settled into the couches flanking the fireplace in Juwan's first-floor study. "I understand that you have located the people we have been searching for."

Li looked up at the oil painting above the marble mantelpiece. It was a life-size rendering of a woman who looked like Juwan Brugg and appeared to be wearing a tent. He stifled another urge to laugh as Juwan stood beneath it.

"I only told Sir Henry to report to you that I believe the three people you are seeking are here in Dunmore Town," he said. "We expect them to be enjoying my hospitality quite soon. One of their friends is already providing some valuable information about their activities as we speak."

"I am very gratified by your efforts, Mr. Brugg," said Zhou. "Once you turn them over to me, you will be rewarded well beyond the terms of the original finder's fee."

"What makes them worth five hundred thousand dollars?" asked Juwan.

Zhou gazed up and said, "Two of them are archaeologists who we are hoping to honor with a lifetime achievement award."

Juwan smiled down at him benevolently. "And that is why you are accompanied by a commando team?"

"One can never be confident about one's safety in this dangerous world."

"You should know that the people you are seeking have been diving on an old shipwreck off the Devil's Backbone," he said. "I assume that this has nothing to do with your plans to honor them."

"Of course, we are interested in all their achievements."

It was Juwan's turn to laugh. "Then we will keep that

information to ourselves until you decide to share your real interest with me," he said, looking up to see Black Mamba silently enter the study through the French doors leading from the terrace.

He watched as she gave him a thumbs-down.

"Gentlemen, I would like to introduce my mother," said Juwan.

Bob Littlefrost stood guard outside the door after they gathered to plan their next moves in the servants' bathroom off the kitchen. While Lexy changed back into her catering uniform in one of the stalls, Macaulay told Barnaby and Mike McGandy about the confrontation with Brugg's guard commander and the fight leading to his death.

"We stopped on the second floor to look at the aquarium," said Macaulay. "The circulation system had already cleared the water of any trace of blood. If there was anything left of him, we didn't see it through the glass."

Lexy emerged from the stall to tell them what she had seen of the guard barracks from the balcony, including the body of the naked man being dumped in the back of one of the guard vehicles.

"You're sure it wasn't Carlos?" asked Barnaby.

"He was too big," she said. "But if he was imprisoned there, it probably means that Carlos is there too."

"You said the rear entrance is guarded?" asked McGandy.

"Two of them," said Lexy.

"We're going to need a diversion," said Macaulay.

"I have some thoughts on that," said Barnaby.

"Let's hear them."

"I need to find a way to lure all the bird saviors down to Brugg's mortuary in the cellar and to do it without leaving my fingerprints," said Barnaby. "We obviously need to get out of here without a trace so Mr. Littlefrost isn't implicated."

"To my knowledge, only Bardot discovered that we were here," said Lexy.

"Unless he has already shared that information with Brugg and his other lieutenants," said Macaulay.

"I don't think he had the time," said Lexy with an involuntary shudder.

"We have to go forward on that assumption," said Barnaby, heading for the door. "Make your preparations for getting across the compound to the guard barracks to release Carlos. I'll focus on the diversion. If I can make it work, how will I send a signal to you across the compound?"

Macaulay remembered the power utility room off the passageway from the kitchen. He told Barnaby what it contained and where to find it.

"I already unlocked the door," said Macaulay. "After you start the diversion, you'll need to disable it somehow."

"I know what to do," said Barnaby. "I'm off the grid with my own power system back in Cambridge."

Macaulay handed Bardot's uniform coat and hat to Mike McGandy.

"This might give you some protective coloring," he said.

"I already have the right coloring," said McGandy with a grin.

THIRTY

29 May
Casa Grande Brugg
Dunmore Town
North Eleuthera
Bahamas

A roaring sound woke him. It took Carlos a few seconds to realize it was the sound of rain pounding on a tin roof. The only light in the chamber came from the flickering candles she had set at the head and foot of the wooden slab.

He remembered where he was and what she had done to him. He could faintly hear what sounded like a live band or an orchestra carried on the rising wind. He turned his head to the side to release a mouthful of bile.

He knew he was done. When she returned to work on him again, he would tell her everything he knew and more. After watching them carry out the dead man with the basketball strapped to his scrotum, he had reached the breaking point. Dying would be a welcome release.

He felt a deep, agonizing ache inside from what she had accomplished with the mallet. It felt as if he had broken glass in his stomach. Each time he tried to move, he felt the grinding of his cracked ribs.

His hands were still on fire from the missing fingernails and he could no longer move his feet or his mouth. He wondered if he would even be able to speak well enough to tell her the location of the wreck and answer the other questions she had asked.

Inside his head, everything was twisted and distorted, images of memory combined with dazzling colors, purple and red and shimmering gold. Carlos heard a grating noise near the stone staircase and nearly cried out at the thought she was back to resume her work, all the while peering down at him as if he were her wayward child. Then he realized it was a shutter banging in the wind. He waited to die.

The rain was coming sideways as Macaulay and McGandy went out through the kitchen door onto the covered terrace. They were still in their catering clothes. McGandy was carrying Colonel Bardot's uniform coat and hat in an empty plastic food container.

Two uniformed security guards carrying light submachine guns stepped out of the rainy darkness and intercepted them as they began to move across the terrace to the parking lot. One of them poked a flashlight in their faces.

"You can't leave the house until the party is over," he said. "Go back inside."

"Fine," said Mike McGandy with irritation in his voice as he leaned closer to read the name tag on the guard's uniform coat. "I will tell Mr. Brugg that Corporal LePage denied us access to the catering truck to prepare more shrimp and scallops for him and his mother."

The guard stared down at the plastic food container and shrugged.

"You can go," he said, leading the other guard back under the protective roof of the terrace.

"We have to be in position to move when Barnaby springs the diversion," said Macaulay as they passed the catering truck.

Lexy had told them about the gravel path that connected the two buildings but that it was patrolled. They had to reach the guardhouse barracks without being spotted again. They would have no explanation if found on the other side of the compound.

The only option was to go straight across through the junglelike grounds. Macaulay had not anticipated the severity of the challenge. Once away from the manicured lawns, the way ahead was choked with a seemingly endless thicket of jacaranda, poinciana, and huge intertwined hibiscus plants.

The sweet scent of bougainvillea, jasmine, and citrus filled his nostrils as the dense undergrowth tore at his clothing and boots. McGandy followed right behind him, still carrying Bardot's uniform in the plastic container.

Five minutes later, Macaulay finally broke through the last line of shrubbery and came to the narrow strip of grass that surrounded the barracks. He and McGandy waited in the darkness while they surveyed the building.

Two guards with machine guns guarded the gravel path that led back to the mansion house. Another two were standing under the portico above the rear entrance.

A hundred feet past them Macaulay could see a small parking lot and a four-bay garage in a halo of misty light.

Motioning McGandy to wait inside the tree line, Macaulay crept forward in the darkness to one of the first-floor windows close to the back entrance to the barracks. Raising his eyes to the sill, he peered inside.

A fat brindle cat stared back at him impassively from the other side of the screen. Beyond the cat, one of the off-duty guards was making love to a skinny woman on a single bed, their bodies coated in sweat. A rotating electric fan snarled loudly above them, moving the humid air around the room.

The next window in line revealed a dimly lit bathroom. Inside one of the shower enclosures was the biggest cockroach Macaulay had ever seen. He crept along the edge of the building on his hands and knees until he reached the corner near the back entrance. Lying flat on the wet ground, he slid his head around the corner.

The two guards were huddled under the roof of the portico. Behind them, Macaulay saw that there were actually two entrances into the building. One was through a screen door behind them. The second was a set of steps heading downward. He saw the screen door open and then slap shut as another guard came outside. It was the one Macaulay had seen in the bedroom. He was now dressed in a pair of shorts.

"Big storm comin', mon," he said after lighting a cigarette. "This ain't nothing yet."

Macaulay crawled back to the tree line and told McGandy what he had seen. He briefly explained his plan while McGandy took off his catering shirt and put on Bardot's uniform coat and hat.

A minute later, McGandy emerged from the dense undergrowth near the parking lot and ran to the small garage beyond the guard barracks. Inside, he saw what looked like several expensive cars. He found a flashlight on the workbench and briefly trained it across the interior. One of the cars was covered with a shiny canvas tarpaulin. He pulled it off, revealing a red Ferrari. Taking the cover with him along with a length of cord, he turned off the flashlight and walked quickly to the parking lot.

There he found the black panel truck that Lexy had seen from the balcony. McGandy opened the rear door. A naked man lay sprawled on his back just inside the opening, his bulging eyes peering back at him. McGandy threw the canvas tarpaulin beyond the corpse into the bed of the truck.

Varna came into the study carrying a tray filled with a coffee service and a small platter of cookies. He had changed from his tuxedo into a formfitting jumpsuit. Putting it down on the coffee table in front of the matching couches, he served the new guests.

"Li Wui," said Juwan, pronouncing it Lee Wee as he stared at the younger Chinese. "You have any problems with that when you were a kid? You know . . . the other kids?"

Li had no idea what he was talking about. He already detested the mountain of blubber on the other couch. He wondered how a delicate young man like Varna could allow himself to be touched by this monster. He forced himself to keep his eyes rigid and unmoving.

Tā shuí cónglái bu zhǎyǎn. He does not blink.

Zhou turned to Brugg's mother, who had picked up

half the cookies on the platter with one sweep of her hand.

"May I offer you my assistance with your interrogation?" he said with a solicitous smile. "We Chinese have refined certain methods over the centuries that guarantee positive results."

Black Mamba remained quiet as she munched the cookies and thought about her answer. She did not want to offend this Chinese while Juwan was conducting a sensitive financial negotiation with him.

At the same time, she had almost reached climax while extracting the man's upper teeth with the needle-nose pliers. She was sure he had now reached the breaking point. When he next saw her descending the stairs, he would be ready. Once she had what he knew, she could go the rest of the way with him.

"I expect to have the answers we need shortly," she said.

Barnaby glanced at his watch as he stood behind the buffet line in the great hall. The first round of the dinner had been served to the guests. The catering staff was replenishing the serving platters and tureens as the orchestra played a medley of Tupac Shakur hits.

Barnaby wondered what had happened to Brugg and the Chinese, but was grateful for their absence. He was still anonymous for the time being, although as things stood that wouldn't be for long.

The only option he had left to create a diversion was to approach the bird saviors and inform them about the collection in the basement. Once they saw it for themselves, all hell would hopefully break loose. But there was no guarantee they would listen to him and everyone would then know of his involvement, which would implicate Bob Littlefrost.

Barnaby looked at his watch again. Hopefully, Macaulay was already waiting to undertake the rescue attempt at the guard barracks. He had to move. There was too much at stake, even if it meant betraying Littlefrost's trust.

He was heading around the buffet line when he looked up to see the duchess of Lancaster approaching a young server at the plantation table holding the dinner entrees.

"This ragout is quite divine," he heard the duchess say to the server. "Quite simple in its bouquet from the claret and the meat is simply sublime. Are you permitted to share the secret with me?"

Barnaby saw his diversionary plan materialize before his eyes. Stepping over to join the server behind the table, he raised his voice at least two octaves and said, "On behalf of my master, I can take the liberty of informing Your Grace."

As the server moved off, the duchess looked up at him expectantly. He ceremoniously stirred the concoction in the tureen and extracted a chunk of meat with the ladle, presenting it to her across the table.

"I prepared it myself," he said, preening. "It is a specialty of the house here at Casa Brugg . . . Yorkie fillet sautéed in dill butter with shallots and then lovingly stewed in a salsa cremosa with a Bordeaux claret."

The duchess's beaming smile gave way to an open-mouthed gape of confusion.

"What did you say the meat component is?" she asked hesitantly.

"Yorkies," said Barnaby solicitously. "Yorkshire terriers . . . only the breast meat, of course. . . . This recipe called for a dozen breasts."

She was staring at him with disbelief.

"You must be jesting," she said, her cheeks turning crimson. "And I hasten to say quite cruelly jesting."

"To the contrary," said Barnaby. "Thanks to Mr. Brugg's Chinese brokers, we have experimented with fox terriers, but there is precious little meat on them. You may have met his brokers when they arrived a little while ago."

The duchess's matronly demeanor disappeared, her face transformed into hard granite as she continued to stare at the chunk of meat in the ladle.

"My master keeps the birds and the dogs in the cellar through that door over there," went on Barnaby in a hurt tone. "I'm sure he would be thrilled to have Your Grace inspect them. I think I can hear one of the Yorkies barking down there right now."

The glower she bestowed on him went back to the ancient times when a duchess could have a servant drawn and quartered for failing to please her. She turned on her heel and began stalking toward the massive cellar door.

"Reginald," she commanded across the great hall with a voice that not only stopped the Tupac Shakur medley but would have sunk the Spanish Armada.

As Barnaby made his escape through the servants pantry, he glanced back to see the duke sprinting toward the cellar door followed by the royal entourage.

In the kitchen Barnaby gave a thumbs-up to Bob Littlefrost and picked up a full pitcher of ice water from the serving table. He carried it down the passageway to the electrical power room.

Macaulay had left the door unlocked. Inside, he walked to the sheet metal compartment containing the transformer and the panels full of circuit breakers and electrical lines. He hoped what he was about to do wouldn't electrocute him.

He remembered the electrical transformer that had exploded in the building across from his on Brattle Street in a thunderstorm and emitted a fireball three stories high. This was a tiny version of it, and contained in a watertight cover plate. He carefully removed the cover plate and set it on the floor.

He saw that the floor was carpeted. Good. His shoes were dry. Good. He could now hear muffled screams coming from the area of the great hall. It was time to go. Picking up a flashlight that was sitting on a shelf next to the compartment, he turned it on.

Stepping back a few feet, he held on to the pitcher while tossing its contents over the open transformer. A small sea of sparks and fire crackled across the compartment. The smell of ozone filled the air. The lights went out.

THIRTY-ONE

Macaulay watched the lights in the guardhouse barracks flicker and die.

If Barnaby had managed to disable the main power system, Macaulay figured it would take Brugg's people at least ten minutes to reconnect their power with the backup generators in the utility building. Ten minutes to find Carlos and for them all to get out.

Moving cautiously from his position inside the tree line to the side of the building again, he crept forward to the corner closest to the rear entrance. The two guards were standing under the portico out of the rain.

"I cawn't see nothin', mon," said one.

"Backup lights be on soon," said the second guard. "It happen all the time."

The beam of a flashlight suddenly lit up their faces.

"Why are you not at your posts?" barked an imperious voice from the path leading to the parking lot.

In the dim, hazy outline of its reflected light, Mike McGandy looked every inch the deputy commander. Both guards dashed down the portico steps and came to attention, holding their machine guns at port arms.

"Have you forgotten how to salute?" demanded McGandy in Bardot's imposing uniform cap.

Retaining their grip on the weapons with their left hands, they raised their right ones in a saluting gesture as McGandy strode toward them. Macaulay came up silently behind their backs and grabbed the machine gun from the left hand of the first guard.

"On your knees," Macaulay said, pulling back the bolt to cock the machine gun.

Without turning around, the second guard dropped his weapon. McGandy turned off the flashlight as he circled around them, picking up the second machine gun and quickly binding their wrists with the cord he had found in the garage.

Macaulay nudged them in the back with the barrel and said, "We're going down to the cellar. Call out and I'll kill you."

The stone steps leading down into the darkness were slippery with rain. As soon as they were out of sight, McGandy turned on the flashlight again. At the bottom of the staircase, Macaulay looked across the low-ceilinged chamber and saw flickering candlelight.

McGandy ordered the guards to lie facedown on the stone floor. While he bound them more securely, Macaulay headed toward what looked like a big slab of butcher

block with candles at each end. Looking down at the naked man lying on top of it, he wasn't sure he was alive.
The man's eyes were hidden in a mass of swollen purple
tissue.

"Carlos?" he said.

One of the masses above his nose slowly parted to reveal a sliver of eye.

"Steef?" came the ragged croak.

Macaulay gave him a reassuring pat on his shoulder. It
was one of the few places on his body that didn't show
visible signs of torture. Carlos began sobbing as Macaulay
unscrewed the two wrist shackles and released his arms.

"I be no tell nothing, Steef," he whispered through
broken and missing teeth.

"We're getting you out of here," said Macaulay. "We
have to move fast."

"No toes," he croaked.

"Sweet Jesus," said Macaulay as he reached the end of
the slab to remove the last two shackles.

The places where the toes had been appeared to be
cemented with airplane glue.

"You just enjoy the ride," said Macaulay.

McGandy had covered the guards' heads with two
feed sacks he had found after taping their mouths shut.
Carlos's clothes were on the table next to the toolbox and
McGandy brought them over.

"They never got a good look at me," whispered Mc-
Gandy. "Maybe they'll think I was Bardot."

Macaulay pointed to Carlos's feet.

"I wish I had a chance to spend five minutes with the
guy who did this," said McGandy as Macaulay helped
Carlos into his pants.

"Me too," agreed Macaulay.

"He be a woman," croaked Carlos, "a big woman."

"Black Mamba," said McGandy, "Brugg's mother. I told you about her."

"Let's go," said Macaulay, picking up Carlos and carrying him in his arms. McGandy carried the two light machine guns, their semiautomatic pistols, and two large pouches holding spare magazines.

At the top of the steps, McGandy paused long enough to make sure the area around the rear entrance was deserted. Over the noise of the wind and driving rain, he could hear laughter from inside the barracks.

"That's good. They're celebrating with rum," he said to Macaulay as they headed out into the driving rain.

In the garish light of battery-powered floodlights, the party guests flowed out of the house and headed to their cars. No one had bothered to wait for the fireworks display that traditionally capped the evening's festivities. Many had already witnessed the fireworks after the royal entourage viewed Juwan's collection in the catacombs under the house.

The mansion house staff had set up hurricane lanterns for people to navigate through the rooms on the main floor. By the time Juwan got back to the great hall, the duke and duchess of Lancaster were standing at the top of the cellar stairs with their black Yorkshire terrier in a shadowy pool of light.

"You are a monster," declared the duchess. "I will personally see to it that the authorities in New Providence learn of your atrocities."

When Juwan attempted to defend himself by declaring

that his birds were now protected forever from harm, she threatened to have the duke challenge him to a duel. The duke remained standing behind her and showed no indication of stepping into Juwan's orbit to slap his face.

They stormed out of the house with their entourage in tow a few minutes later. Varna stood on the terrace and watched them go with tears streaming down his face.

"Varna," said Juwan, tenderly encompassing his back in an affectionate hug. "This is nothing. Don't worry about it. I'll make it up to you."

"How can you do that?" said Varna. "You'll never understand me."

Pivoting on his heel, the little Panamanian made his way between the rows of departing guests and headed up the main staircase. Li watched as he mounted the stairs in his skintight pants.

"Where is Bardot?" demanded Juwan to one of the security staff.

"Lieutenant Mai said he saw him over near the guard barracks," said the young guard.

"Find him and bring him to me," said Juwan.

Zho Shen Wui stepped closer to Juwan and said, "It is highly probable that whoever did this may still be in your compound."

"Search every car as it goes out the gate," demanded Juwan before heading back inside the house.

When Black Mamba descended the steps underneath the guard barracks, she sensed that something was wrong. She could hear the noise from someone or something straining to be heard, but it was coming from the wrong side of the chamber.

Looking across toward her workstation, she saw that the heavy slab was empty. Someone had taken the man. There was no way he could have walked out by himself. Going to the source of the sounds, she found two men trussed like chickens lying on the stone floor.

Pulling the cloth sack off one of the heads, she saw it was one of the men she had left in place to guard the rear entrance. Several strips of duct tape encircled his lower head and jaw. She ripped it away.

"Where is my prisoner?" she shouted into his terrified face.

"Colonel Bardot took him," were the only words he could get out before she kicked him in the genitals.

"You're a liar," she said, heading for the toolbox.

Macaulay and McGandy waited for Barnaby and Lexy in the barracks' garage. Macaulay had told them to meet there as soon as they could after the diversion began. McGandy had found a first aid kit in the trunk of the Ferrari and dressed the wounds to Carlos's hands and feet. He gave him some water and Carlos was able to keep it down before he passed out again.

"I'm not sure if he is going to make it," said McGandy.

"Just a few more minutes," said Macaulay.

"Someone's coming," whispered McGandy as they heard heavy footfalls outside over the rain.

A few moments later, Barnaby staggered into the garage.

"I waited as long as I dared for Alexandra," he said. "We got separated by the crowd in the darkness. All proverbial hell is breaking loose over there."

The lights suddenly came on across the compound in

the mansion house, followed by the ones in the guard-house barracks.

"You two follow the plan," said Macaulay. "I'm going after her."

He was out of the garage and starting to run toward the mansion house when Lexy broke through the dense undergrowth near the parking lot. She was wearing her muddy catering uniform, her hair flattened by the rain.

They embraced for a moment before he led her toward the black panel truck.

Carlos was still unconscious and McGandy gently laid him down next to the naked dead man in the rear of the van. If a guard opened the door, he would hopefully assume they were both dead.

The black tarpaulin car cover that Mike McGandy had found in the garage was large enough to cover Macaulay, Lexy, and Barnaby in the space between the corpse and the front seats. McGandy put on Bardot's uniform cap over his gaudy uniform coat, started the engine, and headed toward the pillars of the compound gate.

A line of cars stretched ahead of them, and armed guards were demanding that everyone in each vehicle get out and open their trunks. McGandy could see several rain-soaked guests in the beams of their car's headlights angrily shouting at the guards to no avail.

"We have to go now," said Macaulay from under the tarp.

McGandy swung the truck out of the waiting line and onto the grass-covered strip that fringed the driveway. As he drove boldly toward the gate, one of the guards checking a car shouted for him to stop. He began chasing the truck as the two guards flanking the gate raised their machine guns and aimed at McGandy.

Stopping short at the gate, McGandy switched on the interior lights above the truck's dashboard. Seeing the uniform with its gold stars under the colonel's cap, the men at the gate immediately lowered their machine guns.

The guard who had chased the truck raced up to the rear door and yanked it open. He was about to vault into the freight bed when he saw the two bodies and recoiled backward.

Hidden as he was under the tarpaulin, Barnaby's head was propped directly behind the driver's seat and McGandy's shoulders.

"Hors du chemin," he shouted in French, his voice becoming dangerous. *"Hors de mon chemin vous imbéciles."*

From the way the guard in the rear slammed the door shut, it was obvious that Bardot's men were familiar with his tirades in French. The two guards flanking the gate immediately waved them forward. A few moments later, the truck disappeared into the rain.

THIRTY-TWO

30 May
Estancia da Fonseca
San Jose de Mayo
Uruguay

Tommy Somervell didn't think June Corcoran would last
out the day. She was visibly shrinking in front of him. The
only things that seemed to be keeping her alive and nour-
ished were cigarettes and coffee laced with apple brandy.
She had refused all food for the last two days along with
the painkillers she had occasionally taken over the previous few weeks.

They had arrived in Montevideo the previous night at
three in the morning on a military flight from Ramstein,
Germany. Tommy had gone straight to the American
consulate and arranged transportation for seven that same
morning. She had refused to stay behind at the hotel in
Montevideo when he told her that he would go after the
U-boat commander's logbook alone.

June was waiting for him in the hotel lobby when he

came down after shaving and taking a quick shower. She had on the same outfit she had been wearing when they left Berlin. But then he was wearing the same suit too.

He had slept a bit on the plane across the Atlantic, fueled by the bottle of Johnnie Walker Gold Label scotch he had purchased at the Ramstein PX. Every time he awoke during the flight, she had been sitting under the little cone of light from the upper console and scribbling in her notebook.

"I don't know how you managed to track down von Bulow's daughter so quickly," he had said.

She had ignored him and kept scribbling.

"What are you writing?" he had asked.

"*War and Peace*," she had said. "Part Two."

The American consul in Montevideo provided a car and driver and they drove south from the capital through the rolling, verdant countryside for almost two hours. It was a stunningly beautiful country, Tommy thought, even if it had harbored hundreds of Nazis after the Second World War. They had lived well.

He couldn't help noticing that she was dealing with an uncontrollable dribbling of saliva from the corner of her mouth. She stanched its flow by continually dabbing at her mouth with the small white hand towel she had taken from the plane.

Tommy felt deeply torn at allowing her to continue the journey. In Ramstein, he had almost decided to have her forcibly checked into the base hospital, and then changed his mind. Knowing her for as long as he had, he knew she would have it no other way.

At nine in the morning, they crossed the bridge over the Rio San Jose and entered the small city of San Jose de

Mayo. Their driver punched the address into his GPS that had been provided to them for the residence of Greta von Bulow da Fonseca, the daughter of U-boat Kapitan Kaspar von Bulow. It was in an enclave of imposing homes at the edge of a small lake.

The three-story brick mansion was surrounded by broad, manicured lawns. A clay tennis court flanked one side of the house and an Olympic-size swimming pool the other. Two tanned and beautiful young blond women were playing singles on the court as Tommy and June walked up the front path.

A butler met them at the door and led them to the rear of the house and up a set of stairs to a glass-walled solarium that faced onto the lake. A statuesque woman with a heart-shaped face stood in front of the windows. She was dressed in a white silk dress that emphasized her well-endowed chest and hourglass hips. Her long graying blond hair was crowned by a silver tiara laced with baby's breath.

"Please sit down," said the woman, beckoning Tommy and June into the Louis Quinze chairs that faced her own as a maid appeared with a coffee service on a silver tray.

"Thank you for agreeing to see us on such short notice, Madame da Fonseca," said Tommy in German.

She looked at his rumpled seersucker suit, stained white shirt, and blue-and-white polka-dot bow tie with a hint of distaste. Her eyes drifted over to June.

"I am receiving you this morning because the German consul in Montevideo is a personal friend and asked me to extend the courtesy," she said, responding in English. "I have little to do with the current regime in Bonn. When it comes to the current chaos in Europe, they are as passive as white mice."

Her voice was deep and husky, with an accent like Tommy remembered from Marlene Dietrich in *Destry Rides Again*. He looked up at the huge oil painting that dominated the interior wall of the room. Its subject was a balding old man with an impressive set of epaulets on his gold-bedecked military uniform. He was holding his hat to his chest and staring down at them with firm-jawed resolution.

"That is Field Marshal Manuel de Freitas da Fonseca," she said. "My husband is a direct descendant."

"Very impressive," said Tommy, responding again in German. "To come straight to the point, we are hoping to have a brief opportunity to review the logbook compiled by your father when he commanded German Kriegsmarine U-boat 113 in the early months of 1942."

Her face betrayed no sign of emotion or recognition. She sipped her coffee and put the demitasse cup back on its saucer.

"I have none of his logs," she said. "You have come a long way for nothing."

"The logbook in question was stolen from the Kriegsmarine naval archives in Freiburg im Breisgauin in June 2005," said June Corcoran in German. "I believe you were in the country at that time on a short visit."

"I do not wish to offend you, but you are drooling on my chair," responded Greta von Bulow in her accented English. "I want to know if it is contagious."

"Yes, it is," said June Corcoran. "I am going to die."

"I can see that," said von Bulow's daughter without feeling. "I saw so many die when I was a girl. In regard to your question, my travel back to Germany on that occasion was a family matter."

"I should tell you that at the behest of the United States government, the German war crimes prosecution office in Nuremburg is preparing to reopen the case of your father and his alleged atrocities against helpless allied prisoners," said Tommy Somervell. "If the case results in a guilty verdict, the heirs to those who were murdered will be entitled to full financial restitution for property that was commandeered by Kapitan von Bulow before sinking their ships. They will also be entitled to legally sue those to whom Kapitan von Bulow bestowed his assets upon his death."

"Did the Jews send you?" she hissed.

Ignoring the question, Tommy said, "In order to maintain continued good relations between Germany and the United States, we are prepared to help forestall this prosecution from taking place based on your cooperation with our request to see the logs."

"The Jews hounded my father into his early grave," said Madame da Fonseca. "He was falsely accused of these crimes. My father was a hero of the Third Reich."

Tommy stood up and helped June Corcoran to her feet.

"I gather that your answer is no," he said calmly. "I will report your answer back to the government in Bonn. You can expect to hear from the prosecutors within the next two weeks."

They had almost reached the door to the solarium when Marlene Dietrich's voice brought them up short.

"I will show you the logs," she said.

As they followed her back through the house, June turned to Tommy and whispered, "Was that all true?"

"What do you think?" he said, his arm encircled in hers.

The room in which Greta da Fonseca kept her father's logbooks was a windowless shrine to the past glory of Hitler's Third Reich. A bust of the Führer was spotlighted in a wall cubicle. The walls of the study were covered with photographs of her father in the glory days of the Battle of the North Atlantic. In one of them, he was receiving the Knight's Cross from Hitler in Berlin. A glass display case held all his medals.

Von Bulow's daughter unlocked a drawer in the Empire desk in the center of the room. She removed five bound books and laid them on top of the desk.

"You can read them here," she said. "You will not copy any of the contents. I will stay here until you are finished."

Tommy brought a second chair over to the desk. He and June sat side by side and began to examine the logs. Von Bulow had used an indelible marking pen to handwrite the year of operations for his U-boats on the canvas-backed covers. There were two of them for 1942. They put the others aside. The first logbook recounted the operations of U-boat 113 from January through March 1942.

"It has to be this one," said June Corcoran, opening it to the first page. Tommy couldn't help noticing that the small white hand towel was turning pink from each new dab at her mouth.

There were multiple entries for each day of the month. They included everything from ship sightings to disciplinary actions imposed on crew members. His log listed each radio communication to and from U-boat headquarters in Lorient, France.

They quickly scanned through the entries for January

and February that von Bulow had recorded in his cramped German writing style. Some of the pages had been stained with seawater, and the ink had become smeared. As they reached the entries at the end of February, June turned the page. At the top of the next one was the word SIEG.

Victory, he had written in large block letters.

The first line read *28 February 1942. 0427. Sank a freighter approximately seven thousand tons off Nord Eleuthra. Teufels Rückgrat.*

"Devil's Backbone," said June. "It's the one."

Tommy's eyes were focused on the next line. *Ship broke in half and exploded. Closed fifty meters to search wreckage. Secondary explosion schaukelte das boot. Suche uber Bord verloren.*

"Lookout lost overboard," Tommy heard June whisper before her head sagged slowly downward toward the desk until it came to rest on the open page of the log. Tommy gently placed his fingers on her carotid artery above the collar of her blouse.

"What is wrong with her?" demanded Greta da Fonseca.

"She is dead," said Tommy Somervell.

THIRTY-THREE

30 May
Dunmore Town
North Eleuthera
Bahamas

They had arrived at the deserted fish house an hour before dawn.

After escaping from Brugg's compound, McGandy had driven straight to his cottage. He helped Carlos and the others inside, and had then run the truck down to the far end of the island and parked it near the landfill. Using a moist towel, he had cleaned the door handles, steering wheel, and dashboard console and left it there with the body of the unknown man inside.

Chris Kimball had been waiting for the others in McGandy's living room when they arrived at the cottage. He had a splint on his left arm, and it was heavily wrapped in gauze bandages and tape. His face looked as if it had been exposed to a radiation blast and his eyebrows were singed off.

"Feels better than it looks," said Kimball.

"We don't have to worry about the Kingfish picking up any local women," said Macaulay, "unless they have a thing for Boris Karloff."

"We need to get back to the *Trader's Bluff* as quickly as possible," said Barnaby to Kimball. "I have to reach Dusenberry using secure communications to request our extraction."

"We can't go back to *Trader's Bluff*," said Kimball. "The local police made it part of the crime scene. When I got out of the clinic, I tried to get back aboard and they ordered me off at the point of a gun. I'm sure they are still there."

"Brugg is probably behind it," said Mike McGandy, arriving back at the cottage after getting rid of the truck. "If any of us are picked up by the police at this point, we'll be turned over to him. They have also closed the airport. Supposedly, it's for the duration of the storm. In truth, it'll be until they find you."

"How long for the storm?" asked Barnaby.

"It probably won't reach full strength until tomorrow afternoon," said McGandy. "Right now the wind is only gusting at about thirty miles an hour. I saw boats going in and out of the harbor on my way back."

Cora McGandy came down from the spare bedroom where Macaulay had carried Carlos and put him to bed. During the truck ride from the Brugg compound, Lexy had suggested taking him to Cora's medical clinic, but McGandy said it would be one of the first places they would search.

"He is lucky to be alive," said Cora, putting down the

tray containing her medical instruments. "I've dressed his wounds and given him a shot of morphine for the pain. His condition is stable, although he has several broken ribs and will need oral surgery. His feet should heal quickly once the infection from the glue is under control, but I doubt he will ever walk comfortably again without prosthetics."

"Should we try to contact Dusenberry at the White House by telephone?" asked Barnaby. "He might be able to send an extraction team in here before the storm reaches full strength."

"You might as well be calling him on a party line," said Macaulay. "It only increases the risk of our being caught in the meantime."

"Then I guess we'll have to wait it out," said Barnaby.

"Not here," blurted Mike McGandy, looking at Cora. "Brugg's men will come here for sure at some point. People will have seen us together in the past few days. This is a small place and they'll check out every possibility. There shouldn't be any trace that you were here when they go through our home."

"Where can we go?" asked Macaulay as the rain hammered down on the cottage's tin roof like a hundred bass drums. "We don't want to endanger you any longer than is necessary."

"What about my father's fish house?" asked Cora.

"That could work," agreed McGandy. "It's down at the commercial wharf. No one goes there at night. It'll be completely deserted right now. It'll also give you a good vantage point to see what's happening in the harbor area tomorrow morning."

"Would your father have a problem with it?" asked Macaulay.

"We believe he is dead. He disappeared a year ago," said Cora, "along with his charter boat and a party of Canadians he was taking on a weeklong cruise to the Abacos."

Macaulay thought about the sunken pleasure boats and bodies he and Carlos had found on their first dive. He decided not to mention it to Cora McGandy as the others began their preparations to leave.

Thirty minutes later, they had arrived in McGandy's Land Rover at the commercial wharf. It was dark and deserted when they pulled up on a side street lined with bougainvillea and coconut palms. The lush vegetation almost masked the back wooden stairs that led up to the second story of the old clapboard structure.

Inside, it was warm and dry. One big low-ceilinged room faced the harbor. The two rooms in back had been used as an office and crew quarters. Macaulay laid the unconscious Carlos down on one of the beds as Chris Kimball walked down the narrow set of stairs that led to the first floor. It was a storage room for boating and fishing equipment with two big doors that led onto the wharf. They were chained tight. The wind-driven surf had coated the concrete floor with seawater. Upstairs, McGandy was ready to leave.

"I'll be back in a few hours with some food and whatever information I can learn," he said.

Macaulay went downstairs to the storeroom and found some thick canvas boat curtains. He came back up to nail them over the upstairs windows. Going outside, he checked to make sure no lamplight leaked out.

Carlos suddenly began to moan loudly from the crew

quarters. It drew Lexy to the side of his bed. Kneeling down, she slid her right arm under his neck and gently pulled him toward her until his face was resting between her chest and shoulder. His body began to shudder uncontrollably.

"It's going to be all right," she said softly.

He seemed to relax as she stroked his ruined face.

"It's going to be all right," she repeated, not entirely sure whether to believe it.

"Let's all try to get some sleep while we can," said Macaulay.

Barnaby looked at the potential accommodations and grimaced. Between the barrels of gear, piles of canvas, and coils of rope, he finally found a place on the floor and stretched out on his back.

"I'm going to be seventy years old tomorrow," he grumbled as Macaulay turned off the lights.

"Happy birthday," said Macaulay. "I hope you get everything you wish for."

"Right now it's my lair back at the Long Wharf," said Barnaby. "And fuck you."

Dawn brought gray and murky skies still teeming with rain. Macaulay got up and began making coffee in Cora's father's old blue enamel pot. Parting the canvas covering on the window, he watched big ocean breakers slam into the beach and roll heavily toward the line of palm trees in a mass of white foam.

Juwan sat in the aquarium room with the two Chinese and a contingent from his guard unit. His mother came in to join them with a platter of freshly baked apple croissants and two pounds of maple-cured bacon.

"How is Varna?" he whispered to her as he helped himself.

"In your bedroom," she said quietly. "He has been sobbing most of the night."

"Where is Colonel Bardot?" demanded Juwan for the fourth time. "I told you to bring him to me."

Lieutenant Alvarez shrugged and said, "The guards at the gate said he left in the van with the body of the American millionaire and another man who they didn't recognize. They assumed—"

"They assumed?" shouted Juwan. "Bring those guards here now."

Black Mamba sidled close to him.

"Do not show your emotion, my son, in front of these people," she said. "Think of it as an important NBA game. . . . These Chinese are watching for any sign of weakness."

Juwan hated to be reminded of what he had once been in the NBA. His mind was reeling with images from his last All-Star game when the two guards who had been posted at the gate came into the room. One of them was visibly trembling. Juwan asked him to describe what had happened when the truck had arrived at the front gate.

"It was Colonel Bardot," he said. "He was in full uniform. He screamed at me in French as he often has done on the parade ground."

The guard who had opened the rear door of the truck supported him.

"Colonel Bardot was driving the truck," he said. "It had the body of the man we took at Michaud's in the back. Another man was lying next to him with his toes missing."

"I believe that someone may have impersonated your

Colonel Bardot," said Zhou Shen Wui, sampling one of the croissants.

A guard in a soaked white uniform coat entered the room, went to Alvarez, and whispered in his ear.

"We have found the truck," said Alvarez. "It was left at the landfill. Only one of the bodies was still inside."

"Which one?" asked Black Mamba.

"The American millionaire."

"My prisoner needed medical attention," said Black Mamba. "Have you searched the medical clinics?"

"Yes," said Alvarez, "and any other place he might have been taken for medical help."

"Keep searching," demanded Juwan Brugg. "They have to be here in town. Someone will have heard or seen something."

"Many of them are close-lipped," said Black Mamba.

"Post a reward," said Juwan.

"I have also made sure that all flights are canceled at the airport," said Alvarez.

Black Mamba's eyes were drawn to something at the base of the aquarium. Somehow it didn't seem to belong there. The object was long and pointed and sticking out of the sand. As she got closer, she saw that it was a shoe, a black-and-white two-toned shoe. Attached to it was a shred of white sock. There was something inside the sock that was drawing the attention of the tiny feeder fish.

"I believe it is time we became partners," said Zhou as he watched the big black woman staring at the hideous sea creatures.

He was certain the time was right to make a deal. Zhou never relied on a hunch or superstition. His actions were always planned and determined in advance, but never rigid in design. Flexibility was one of his brilliant hallmarks, the ability to make needed adjustments in any plan as it unfolded in real time. The huge black man was clearly out of his element, but necessary to fulfilling his mission.

"Complete honesty is the basis for any genuine partnership, Mr. Brugg," said Zhou. "This is your country. We are your humble guests. In that spirit, I will tell you exactly what we are seeking and why it is important us."

Juwan smiled and nodded as he finished the platter of bacon. Now they were finally getting down to it.

"We are attempting to recover fossils, ancient bones, that were excavated nearly a hundred years ago in China," said Zhou. "They are of the *Homo erectus*, the Peking Man. These bones do not have intrinsic value like gold or diamonds, but they are invaluable."

He paused for a few seconds to let the importance sink in.

"Homo erectus," repeated Juwan.

What did the Chinaman take him for to diss him this way, he wondered, with such an obvious lie?

"His bones are actually priceless and even worshipped by certain people in my country," said Zhou. "He is the first of his kind, the first man to stand erect and use tools. I am prepared to pay you five million dollars, if you will assist us in recovering the Peking Man."

"What if we don't find the homo?" asked Juwan, barely containing his derision.

"As a demonstration of good faith, we will pay you two million on top of your finder's fee regardless of whether we find him or not. You will benefit either way.

My son and I have a recovery vessel arriving here in an hour. It will be sufficient to meet our needs as soon as you locate the position of the wreck. We shall dive on it as soon as we know its location and my son's team can ensure that we have the proper security for our endeavors."

The first homo with an erection, thought Juwan, maintaining his composure in the face of the man's monumental bullshit, maintaining eye contact while nodding occasionally as the old Chinaman lied through his little rat's teeth. What could the treasure really be? he wondered. The old man had said it wasn't gold or diamonds, which probably meant it was. Whatever the treasure might be, Juwan and his own men would be there when they found it.

"Who are the others looking for homo man?" asked Juwan.

"A team of American archaeologists," said Zhou, deciding not to divulge the fact that the American government was behind their efforts. "Do we have an agreement?"

Juwan nodded and extended his hand. Zhou took it in his own, watching his fingers disappear, waiting to see if the giant would try to crush them. There was only ordinary pressure. He was not trying to prove anything.

"I am reminded of the ancient Chinese proverb," said Zhou. "*Yǎ ba chī jiǎo zi, xīn lǐ yǒu shù.* In English, it means when a mute person eats dumplings, he knows how many he has eaten, even though he cannot speak."

Juwan was trying to maintain eye contact with the old Chinese, at the same time trying to figure out what the fuck he had said. Zhou was smiling at Juwan as if the two had become blood brothers, clearly waiting for him to respond. Juwan remembered the rap slang used by a number of his former teammates in the NBA.

"All balls don't bounce," said Juwan. "Some balls hang. Ball don't lie."

THIRTY-FOUR

Li Shen Wui stood atop the wall facing the sea from the Brugg compound and watched as a violent wave of green water smashed into the beach with a savage boom. It almost matched the rage that was consuming him inside.

A few minutes earlier, he had watched from the terrace as a small caravan of Humvees formed up in the turning circle by the main entrance. His father and Brugg had gotten into the second Humvee and the caravan left the compound. They were on their way to meet the two-hundred-foot recovery vessel that had just arrived with Li's paramilitary team aboard. It was an outrage. They were Li's men, not his father's. He does not blink.

The rain had stopped for the first time since he and his father arrived. Li had overheard one of Brugg's house

328 ROBERT J. MRAZEK

staff say it was only the calm before the real storm. The low, brassy sky looked as if it was ready to unleash another torrent at any moment.

Two armed guards were standing by the iron-mesh gate cut into the base of the wall that separated the compound from the beach. When Li told them in English that he was going swimming, the first one looked at him as if he was crazy. The second one swung the gate open and allowed him to pass through.

On the beach, he quickly stripped off his clothes. As the wind-driven sand peppered his naked body, he watched as another huge roller came crashing into shore. Timing it perfectly, he dove into the receding wave and began to swim.

His body cut swiftly through the whitecaps that crowned the green slashing waves. Once again, his father had diminished him, this time in front of the gigantic simpleton. He was treating Brugg with a respect he never displayed toward his own son.

As always, Li found his release in the water. With an almost effortless crawl, he drove through the roiling sea, his mouth barely opening against his left shoulder with exquisite precision to take in air with a minimum of wasted effort.

Wǒ hèn tā . . . I hate him, he silently screamed with each stroke. *Wǒ hèn tā, Wǒ hèn tā, Wǒ hèn tā.*

When he stopped to look around, he saw that he was several hundred meters off the beach in front of the compound. It began raining again as he turned and began the journey back. Nearing the shoreline, he raised his head from the water and saw someone standing at the edge of the beach frantically waving his hands. When Li was close enough to body-surf the next wave into the shoreline, he saw it was the Panamanian Varna.

"I saw you from the window," said Varna. "I could not believe you were going to do it . . . I thought you were going to drown."

Over the Panamanian's shoulder, Li could see the two guards at the sea wall gate staring at them. Li put his clothes back on. Together, they walked to the mansion house. Inside, Li asked Varna if there was an exercise facility in the house.

"Of course," said the Panamanian. "I designed it myself."

"I would like to work out with you," said Li.

Varna's face lit up with pleasure. "I would be honored to join you."

Varna's training facility was located on the fourth floor near the bedroom he shared with Juwan. It was state-of-the-art, with Cybex treadmills, elliptical trainers, recumbent bikes, Stairmasters, rowing machines, and a Rogue Power Rack.

Varna was contentedly bench-pressing three hundred pounds to demonstrate his own fitness standard when he saw Li begin to take his clothes off again. Naked, the Chinese came over to the Power Rack and stared down at Varna as the Panamanian replaced the weight bar. Li was already aroused.

"I will take you back to China with me," he said, gazing into the Panamanian's brown foxlike eyes. "You will be safe and respected."

"No, I can't go with you," said Varna. "I love Juwan."

"You can't love him. The man is a monster," said Li.

"I am Juwan's," said Varna.

"Then what were you doing on the beach?" demanded Li.

"I was only worried that you would do harm to yourself," said Varna. "You are our guests."

"I'm more than a guest," said Li, forcing the Panamanian to his knees. "I think you're a despicable cock tease. I have had many."

When Varna continued to resist, Li slapped him hard in the face. He put all his hate into the blow. Varna seemed to shrink in front of his eyes. Li ordered him to take off his workout pants. He never heard the door to the workout facility swing open behind them.

"Varna," came the low voice of Black Mamba. "You bitch."

Mamba reached the Rogue Power Rack in two bear-like bounds. Varna was already scuttling backward when she clubbed the side of Li's head with her right fist. It felt like a sledgehammer blow and his head was already ringing as she grasped Li's left shoulder in a viselike grip.

Ducking downward, Li pivoted and grabbed her massive left wrist, using all his strength to force her fingers back from the palm. Although she clouted him in the head again with her right fist, he felt the familiar mist thickening in his eyes as he bore down on her fingers with relentless pressure. He heard the four bones break with a crunching sound followed by her loud grunt of pain.

Mamba's face was twisted into a frightening mask of agony as he put his right shoulder into her massive belly and drove her onto her back. When she opened her mouth to scream for help, he raised his leg and stomped her, driving the heel of his foot into her throat.

She let out a bleating whimper and then two loud

snorts as she desperately tried to breathe through her crushed larynx. Li continued to stand on her throat until she issued a last keening wail and her breathing stopped. Li stepped down from her body. He felt the mist in his eyes fade away as he looked into the stunned face of Varna.

"You will help me dispose of her or I will tell your giant imbecile you killed her after she found us together."

Macaulay's smartphone kept ringing until it finally switched over to his recorded answer.

"It's Tommy Somervell again," said Macaulay. "He wouldn't be calling if it wasn't something really important."

"Is your phone encrypted?" asked Barnaby.

"As well as one can be these days," said Macaulay.

"Take it," said Barnaby when the phone began ringing again a minute later.

Macaulay put it on the speaker attachment.

"I'll be brief, dear boy," said Tommy Somervell. "June Corcoran is dead, but she hopefully put us on the right trail. I have no idea how this fits into what you have already learned, but here it is. The butcher who commanded the U-113 that sank the *Prins Willem* was searching the floating wreckage after torpedoing the ship when there was a secondary explosion that rocked the U-boat. One of the lookouts was lost overboard, but no one noticed it until they were ready to dive. By then, he couldn't be found."

"Could von Bulow have picked up the crates?" asked Macaulay.

"There is nothing in his personal log," said Tommy,

"but I have a few more details about the lookout. He was only fifteen years old and was apparently a beloved mascot among the crew . . . an apprentice seaman named Dieter Jensen."

"Repeat that," said Macaulay.

"Dieter Jensen," said Somervell, his voice echoing across the room of the fish shack.

Mike McGandy grinned and nodded at Macaulay.

"Thanks, Tommy. I'm sorry about June," said Macaulay before ending the connection.

"Dieter Jensen is the old hermit you met out there," said McGandy. "That's why they call it Dieter's Island."

"If he's the same man, how could he have gotten there?" asked Macaulay. "It must be five miles or more from where the *Prins Willem* went down."

"Who knows?" said Barnaby. "As Conan Doyle wrote, if you eliminate all the other possibilities, it has to be the answer."

"He must have been the one who saved Morrissey's life," said Lexy. "You remember that Morrissey said he heard a strange voice while he was floating in the sea."

"And what were they floating on?" said Barnaby.

"A thousand-to-one shot," said Macaulay.

"Ten thousand," said Barnaby, "but we have to find out."

Turning to Mike McGandy, Macaulay said, "When did you say the storm was going to peak?"

"Sometime this afternoon," he said.

Macaulay checked his watch. "That gives us at least three hours to get out there and back. Is your dive boat seaworthy?"

McGandy nodded and said, "But you're going to get mighty wet."

"How long will it take to get out there?"

"The seas are running four to six feet right now with long, deep swells. I can probably make fifteen knots, so figure about thirty minutes each way."

Using his good hand, Chris Kimball punched their GPS coordinates into his cell phone and checked the latest forecast.

"Winds are now predicted to hit a hundred miles an hour by this afternoon," he said, "along with eighteen-foot seas."

"We'll be back well before then," said McGandy. "At least we'd better be. When Hurricane Andrew came through, Dieter's Island was underwater."

"When do we leave?" asked Kimball.

"You're not going with that shoulder," said Macaulay. Turning to Barnaby, he said, "And you're not either, old man."

"Try to stop me, General," said Barnaby. "I'm in charge of this party. If you don't like it, call the president."

THIRTY-FIVE

30 May
Casa Grande Brugg
Dunmore Town
North Eleuthera
Bahamas

Juwan returned to his compound with a feeling of new respect for the old Chinese after visiting Zhou's newly arrived ship in the harbor. Cleverly disguised as a fishing trawler, it was a lethal military platform, with a bank of cruise missile launchers, antiship missiles, and modern Gatling guns. It was also a deep-sea recovery vessel, with an internal diving platform and a submersible that could explore the ocean bottom and retrieve whatever it was they were searching for.

Zhou introduced Juwan to the Chinese military team that had also arrived aboard the vessel. Juwan was favorably impressed. There were only twenty of them, but they reminded him of his men, the type who would enjoy cutting a man's heart out, removing his tongue, or crush-

ing his groin with a well-placed kick. These men would
have to be reckoned with, he decided, after they located
the treasure.

He also noticed that everybody on the ship called the
old Chinese *lord*, as in *Yes, my lord. No, my lord*. They
were almost bowing and scraping to him at every turn.
Juwan thought he could get to like having a similar title.
Lord Juwan. It sounded good.

"Where is my mother?" he asked Alvarez upon returning home.

"I don't know," said Alvarez.

"Find her," demanded Juwan.

When he reached the fourth floor and walked into the
bedroom, he saw Varna disappearing into the bathroom,
and then the sound of the lock being turned from inside.
Juwan had already decided to give him more time to get
over his recent disappointments. He would make it up to
him, he decided, as he listened to Varna's choked sobs
through the door.

Deciding to take a nap while they waited for the search
for the archaeologists to produce results, he lay down on
the bed. Feeling a chill from the raging downpour outside, he reached down for the duvet that Varna always left
neatly folded at the foot of the bed. It wasn't there. He
lay back and thought about all the weird things that had
happened over the previous two days, finally falling asleep
as the rain slashed at the windows of the French doors.

The wipers on McGandy's Land Rover were losing the
battle to keep its windshield clear as he drove them across
the commercial wharf at the foot of Dunmore Town toward the finger pier where his dive boat was tied up.

Aside from an elderly man who was boarding up the downstairs windows of his store, the wharf area was deserted.

McGandy parked his Land Rover next to his boat slip. Wearing yellow rain slickers and hats, Barnaby and Lexy stepped aboard while Macaulay removed the large canvas duffel bag from the trunk of the vehicle and carried it behind them.

McGandy unlocked the steel cabin door to the wheelhouse and they stowed the gear against the side bulkhead of the almost-new Munson custom dive boat. It was thirty-four feet long with a ten-foot beam.

"Catamaran hull," said Macaulay admiringly.

"It'll give us additional stability in seas like the ones we're heading into," said McGandy, turning a switch on the steering console and firing up the two Yamaha outboard 250s. "In a calm sea, she'll do forty-five."

Lexy untied the bow and stern lines and McGandy nosed the boat away from the slip and along the pier toward the open sea. As they came out into the channel, Barnaby heard the sudden whine of a loud siren.

"Get down," ordered McGandy.

Across the harbor, the local police patrol boat was bearing down on one of the superyachts that had just slipped its mooring and was preparing to head out to sea. A Dunmore Town policeman with a loud hailer stood in the bow of the police boat.

"Return to your mooring," he demanded. "No one leaves the harbor."

"They're making sure you're not aboard one of the big yachts," said McGandy. "Just in case."

The Munson dive boat was painted dark gray and it

blended into the dark curtain of driving rain as they motored along the far side of the channel leading out to the Devil's Backbone.

"Even if they see us, there is no way they can catch us," said McGandy.

Within a minute, they were cloaked from view in the harbor by heavy mist and rain. McGandy swung the wheel to starboard toward the Devil's Backbone and gunned both engines. The bow rose and surged forward. Behind them a rooster tail of white foam arced high over the roiling green sea.

Once they were out on the open water, the waves quickly grew to ten feet, each one separated by a long roller. The bow of the Munson would breast one of the waves and then surge down into the following trough before rising back to meet the next one. Each time it smacked down on a cresting wave, two wings of sea spray would erupt from under the hull. McGandy stood braced at the wheel, his eyes trying to take in every shift in the direction of the sea.

Conflicting patterns of waves began hitting them broadside, driving the boat over at an alarming angle before regaining its stability. Hit by both at once, the boat would skid sideways before McGandy could bring it back on course.

The seas grew even more intimidating after they passed through the cut in the Devil's Backbone and were out into the true ocean. They began climbing mountainous slopes of water before careening down the following trough like an elevator in free fall.

Lexy felt her stomach churning as she sat wedged in the corner of the cushioned bench along the bulkhead.

Sea spray and rain lashed the windows with a loud drumming sound and the wind rose from a moaning whine to a full-throated howl.

"There is always a chance for a rogue wave," McGandy called out, searching the sea ahead of them.

Through the windshield, the clouds above them were almost pure black. McGandy could see occasional flashes of lightning deep inside them. The smell in the air was raw and primeval as if churned from great depths.

Macaulay had unzipped the canvas duffel bag and had begun cleaning the first of the two Steyr AUG machine guns he and McGandy had taken from the guards during the rescue of Carlos.

"Brugg chose his armory well," said Macaulay, soaking a clean cloth with solvent before cleaning the barrel.

"It's really light," said Lexy, picking up the second one.

"They're called bull pups," said Macaulay. "By placing the magazine back here in the stock behind the trigger group, they were able to shorten it to thirty inches. It weighs less than ten pounds."

He showed her how to operate the bolt action before fitting one of the thirty-round polymer box magazines into the chamber.

"Pulling the trigger all the way back gives you fully automatic fire," he said. "This button on the left exposes the red dot, which means it's ready to fire."

"I hope Alexandra does not need to play with any of your toys," said Barnaby, looking on from the bench. "We can assume that Jensen doesn't know we are coming, certainly not in this mess."

"He was armed the last time we were out there," said Lexy. "It only makes sense to take precautions."

The continued battering from the conflicting wave action had turned Barnaby's face almost lime green.

"Keep your eyes on the horizon, Dr. Finchem," said McGandy, taking in his condition.

"Where exactly is that?" said Barnaby tartly, and McGandy grinned.

Macaulay was looking toward the stern when he saw the fifteen-foot-high green wall of a rogue wave slam over the port side and fill the rear deck to the gunwales with seawater. It surged forward toward the wheelhouse and hammered against the sealed cabin door before the immensity of the weight drove the stern under.

With the outboard engines completely covered by the boiling sea, McGandy swung the wheel toward the next broadside wave. As the water drained out through the scuppers, the transom of the boat and its two smoking engines slowly emerged from the sea. Barnaby stared back at them and wondered what their fate would be if one or both failed in the face of the hammering they were taking.

McGandy seemed to divine his thoughts.

"Don't worry about the boat," he said. "I keep her at the top of the line."

"That is very reassuring, Mr. McGandy," he said as he leaned over an empty five-gallon cleaning bucket and heaved up the contents of his stomach. The sour odor immediately filled the cabin and almost induced Lexy to follow his example.

"We'll be there soon," said McGandy after checking

the color ten-inch LED on his Furuno navigation system. "Visibility is down to about two hundred feet. I'll be taking us in on instruments."

Fifteen minutes later Lexy saw the tall mangrove swamp at the end of Dieter's Island emerge from the curtain of rain and mist.

"The best place to land you is a footpath I saw the only time I came out here to bring him medical supplies when he got sick and radioed for help," said McGandy. "He wouldn't allow me to set foot on the island even though he could barely walk. I had to toss him the kit from the water. The path is off to the right of this mangrove swamp."

"Can you land the boat?" asked Macaulay.

McGandy shook his head. "It's too shallow for me to do more than get close and I don't want to anchor here in case the wind shifts direction."

Reaching under the steering console, he picked up a handheld electronic device. Turning it on, he handed it to Macaulay. It was a two-way radio.

"A Motorola weatherproof with a range of ten miles," said McGandy. "I'll be monitoring you on channel twelve if there is an emergency. You'll be in the clear, so just say the word *Keira* and I'll meet you back here at the head of the path."

"Why Keira?" asked Lexy.

"That'll be the name of our daughter."

"Just in case there are visitors, do you have any firepower aboard?" asked Macaulay.

"Yeah," said McGandy, "a souvenir from my days on the joint drug interdiction task force down here."

"Let's get going," said Lexy.

"Dr. Finchem," said McGandy, "I think it would be a good idea for you to wait here with me until they find out if it is even there."

"Thank you for your kind assessment," said Barnaby, "but if you think I'm going to wait here on this rocking horse after surviving that trip from hell, you're mistaken. Believe it or not, I am only seventy. That's the new forty. Besides, General Macaulay here is loaded with enough weapons to hold off the Cossacks."

Standing in her oilskins under the driving rain, Lexy couldn't help smiling as Macaulay lifted the canvas duffel bag and said to McGandy, "How do we get the intrepid Dr. Finchem over the side so he can unleash his investigative skills?"

McGandy walked to a locker built into the exterior bulkhead of the wheelhouse and unstrapped a small cylindrical container that was mounted above it. The container was constructed of molded white plastic and had a red handle connected to one end. He laid it on the deck. When he pulled the red handle, the container split open and the four-man rubber life raft that was inside quickly inflated itself with a loud hissing sound.

"Voilà," said McGandy.

THIRTY-SIX

30 May
Dieter's Island
Off Devil's Backbone
North Eleuthera
Bahamas

Macaulay dragged the raft up along the path from the edge of the brackish water in the lagoon and secured it to the trunk of a mangrove tree. Unzipping the canvas duffel bag, he handed Lexy one of the light machine guns.

After sliding a .45-caliber pistol into the hollow of his back inside his jeans, he picked up the second machine gun along with the backpack holding the spare ammunition magazines. He could hear McGandy reversing the engines on his dive boat and retreating across the lagoon to calmer waters. Macaulay motioned to Barnaby and Lexy to follow him up the narrow path that led through the swamp.

To Lexy, it looked like the mangrove trees were growing on stilts, with the aerial roots holding the trunks and branches above the water line and the root structures buried in the mud and briny water. Farther in, she stepped on what she thought was a rain-slick branch lying across the trail. The six-foot-long snake slithered across the mud and disappeared into the dense tangle of vegetation covering it.

A canopy of red and green leaves formed by the intertangled branches from both sides of the trail was thick enough to blot out most of the daylight and divert the rain from their heads. The wind was reduced to almost a whisper.

The smell inside the mangrove swamp was overpowering, a mixture of decay and rot and living and dead marine creatures. Someone, presumably Dieter Jensen, had spread a narrow bed of crab, oyster, clam, and snail shells along the path to provide better foot traction above its muddy surface.

Fifty yards farther along the path, the dense mangrove vines thinned out and gave way to a field of three-foot-tall saw grass. The boggy field bordered both sides of the path. Now that they were in the open, they were buffeted again by the rain and wind.

Off to their right, Lexy saw a stand of fan palms and Caribbean pines, the branches being whipped into a frenzy. Beneath the trees, she saw what looked like a clump of vertical poles sticking out of the ground. Wiping the rain from her eyes, she saw the poles had cross members too. They were crosses. A crudely made fence boxed them in.

Macaulay came to a secondary footpath that led off toward the pines.

"Mike told me he thought the old man's hut was on

the only piece of high ground near the middle of the islet," said Lexy.

"That's where this path is headed . . . toward the center," said Macaulay.

He held his machine gun at the ready as he led them forward again. Lexy carried the second one over her right shoulder. The trail took them through a grove of twenty-foot-high *Chrysophyllum* trees that screened the path ahead of them. On the other side of the grove, they came to successive rows of fruit trees and citrus plantings.

"He's cultivated a tropical fruit farm out here," said Barnaby admiringly as they passed ripening banana and orange trees, followed by crude wooden arbors as tall as a man that were choked with grapes. Barnaby plucked a handful and began to munch them as he walked behind the others.

His eyes were drawn upward to the top of the grape arbor. A gigantic frigate bird was perched on the upper frame. Barnaby recognized the familiar red pouch on the throat skin below the lower mandible of his beak. It silently gazed down at him as he went by.

"I think I can see his place," said Macaulay, peering ahead through the curtain of rain.

The hermit's home was no more than four or five feet high and appeared to be entirely constructed from cut coquina rock. Aside from a door, there was a small narrow window slit on one wall of the structure that Macaulay could make out. The slit was dark.

"Maybe only one of us should approach the house," said Lexy. "That might be less threatening."

"Put down your weapons," ordered a loud voice behind them.

She turned with the others. A man emerged from behind the grape arbor. Lexy saw it was the same one who had driven them off before. Drenched by rain, he now looked like the scarecrow from *The Wizard of Oz*.

Owl-like eyes bulged out of his face under a broad-brimmed, leaking straw hat. He was barefoot, his tattered white shirt and trousers plastered to his skin. His ancient Lee-Enfield .303 was pointed directly at Barnaby's chest. Barnaby slowly turned his head toward Macaulay.

"Please put down your toys, General, before he blows a hole the size of an armadillo in me," said Barnaby in an even tone.

Macaulay placed the gun down on the path. Lexy removed the one strapped behind her shoulder and placed it next to Macaulay's. Macaulay let his arms fall to his sides, his right hand inches from the .45 hidden in the hollow of his back.

"I've seen you before," said Dieter Jensen. "I told you what would happen if you came back and you did anyway . . . with guns."

"How did you know we were here?" asked Barnaby, trying to buy time.

"I heard your boat engine, mon," said Jensen in the Bahamian patois he had developed after living there for more than seventy years. "Is that McGandy's boat?"

"Yes, and he is waiting offshore for us now," said Lexy. "We are not here to harm you. We only want to talk."

"Nothin' to talk about," he said.

"We know you are Dieter Jensen and that you have lived out here since you fell from the U-boat 113 in 1942," said Lexy.

Jensen's owlish eyes suddenly looked crazed. A moment later, he swung the weapon toward Lexy. Macaulay was sure he was about to fire and was reaching for his .45 when Barnaby stepped between Lexy and the gun barrel and started walking toward Jensen.

Barnaby watched as the old man's index finger found the trigger. Reaching out with his right hand, he grabbed the barrel and shoved it upward. The explosion in his ear was deafening as he felt the shot sear the skin on top of his shoulder.

Still holding on to the barrel, Barnaby pulled the rifle out of the old man's hands. Jensen didn't appear to realize he had even fired the gun. His confused eyes went back to Lexy and he started to cry.

"How could you know that about me?" he said, his voice quavering.

"We don't want to hurt you, Mr. Jensen," said Lexy. "We came to ask you a few important questions. If you will answer them honestly, we will leave and not come back. You can return to your life."

"Let's get out of this rain first," said Macaulay.

He picked up the two guns as Lexy took the old man's hand and began leading him toward the coquina rock structure. Barnaby held out the Lee-Enfield rifle he was still holding by the barrel.

"What about this one?" he asked Macaulay.

Grinning, Macaulay said, "I think you're supposed to hold it from the other end. But you did just fine with it, old man. You saved her life. Maybe mine too."

"All in a day's work," said Barnaby, carrying it along. The frigate bird leaped down from his perch and followed behind him.

As they approached the rock house, Lexy saw that the stone roof cleverly concealed a cistern that caught and contained rainwater. There was only one window and it was a narrow slit like the kind in a fortified medieval castle keep. The walls were four inches thick.

The stout plank door into the structure was set at the bottom of three steps cut into the rock foundation. Although the walls of the house were only five feet above ground level, the excavated room below was high enough for her to stand.

Jensen's home consisted of a large room with a single window slit facing the path. The window opening had no glass. The thick wooden door was secured with a plank of wood fitted into two iron braces.

Inside, Jensen had constructed a crude table from raw lumber planks set on two stumps. A handmade chair with a soft cushion was tucked underneath it. An unlit kerosene lantern stood on the table.

After helping the old man into his chair, Lexy found matches next to the lamp and lit it. Macaulay and Barnaby came into the room and shut the driftwood door behind them. Neither could stand erect in the room. A narrow wooden bed platform supported a straw mattress along the far wall. Barnaby went over and sat down.

While Barnaby checked his grazed shoulder, Macaulay stood bent over and briefly explored the room. The old man might not have had much, but what he did have was organized efficiently and well.

A plastic water line was connected to the cistern on the roof, and a petcock at the end of it fed fresh water into a tin basin. A stone fire pit vented with a tin pipe provided warmth and a flat iron cooking surface. Dented pots and pans hung from racks above it. A homemade chemical toilet occupied a corner. It was also the perch of the frigate bird, Macaulay realized, as it hopped up on the seat and settled on it.

Two of the walls had floor-to-ceiling shelves that contained a variety of supplies. They reminded Macaulay of the fruit cellar in his grandmother's farmhouse. Neatly labeled glass jars of canned fruit and vegetables filled the spaces. An old CB radio powered by a hand-cranked generator provided him with communication to the outside world.

"We know you saved the life of a wounded man from the ship that your U-boat sank in 1942," said Lexy, looking into the old man's still-confused blue eyes. "Somehow you were able to get him to a place where he was picked up by a rescue ship that took him to Florida. You gave him the chance to live a long life. It was a very brave thing to do."

"Is he still alive?" asked Dieter Jensen.

As Lexy considered her response, the terrifying vision of what had been done to Sean Morrissey in the basement of his home burned through her mind.

"He died less than two weeks ago," she said. "He is the reason we're here to see you today."

The room was suddenly lit by a bolt of bluish white lightning. Through the window, Barnaby saw its jagged arc of crackling fire across the blackened sky followed by the loud slam of thunder.

"How did you reach this island from the sunken ship?" asked Lexy, her face only inches away from the old man's.

"We . . . floated on a piece of wreckage," said Dieter Jensen, his eyes starting to focus clearly on her for the first time.

"Alexandra," said Barnaby from Jensen's bed frame.

Her eyes followed Barnaby's to the wooden shelves holding the glass jars of fruits and vegetables. The vertical section of the built-in shelf facing her had once been painted red. Parts of it were still bright and glossy. What looked like a symbol of some kind was painted over the red section in black. She realized it was Chinese.

THIRTY-SEVEN

30 May
Casa Grande Brugg
Dunmore Town
North Eleuthera
Bahamas

"I ask you to judge this for yourself, Lord Wui," said Juwan Brugg, confusing Zhou's first name with his last.

They were sitting on the couches in Juwan's *Stargate Atlantis* replica movie theater on the mansion's third floor in front of its ten-foot-diagonal circuit screen. Zhou could hear the wind outside intensifying as he sat next to Li while waiting for news from the ongoing search.

Juwan had invited them to watch the original live coverage of the NBA All-Star game in which his basketball career had come to a sudden end. In response to Juwan's pleading, Varna had finally emerged from their bedroom to join them.

"Look at the way they kept fouling me," said Juwan. "I know now those refs were paid to look the other way."

To Zhou, he looked like Gulliver fighting off the Lilliputians. The other All-Stars kept flailing away at his arms and face. A hard elbow to his ribs brought a mighty bellow of pain, which reverberated through the theater's Klipsch THX speaker system.

In the darkened room, Li was able to keep his eyes averted from the grunting and sweaty bodies. On the ceiling above the screen, there was a fiber-optic star scape that offered the view of a new comet streaking across the sky every minute or so.

"I could have broken every record in the book, Lord Wui," said Juwan as the final minutes of the game played out.

Li wondered how long the imbecilic game would continue. He stared across the theater to Varna on the other couch. Varna refused to look back in his direction. The Panamanian was wearing loose-fitting workout clothes and sitting very close to Brugg.

Getting rid of his mother had not been easy. Together, he and Varna had managed to roll her inside the ultra-king-size duvet from the bedroom and then lift her into the laundry cart that Li had found in the fourth-floor service pantry.

They had wheeled her to the freight elevator at the end of the hallway and run her down to the first floor. Varna unlocked the armory, a cavernous room beneath the terrace where weapons for the guard unit were maintained and stored. There was a separate lock system for the airtight ammunition locker and Varna knew the code. After wheeling her inside and relocking the door, Varna broke down again.

The theater speaker system resounded with what

sounded like a bowling ball being dropped from a great height. Li looked up to see two men in striped shirts lying lifeless on a hardwood floor as people screamed and shouted.

The hallway door to the theater opened and Lieutenant Alvarez came in, followed by Colonel Mu. Alvarez looked at Juwan nervously before the big man hit the pause button on his remote device.

"You asked me to inform you of any developments," said Alvarez. "We just received this transmission."

Juwan opened the envelope and scanned the pages inside.

"This is in fucking Chinese," he barked at Alvarez.

Colonel Mu had another copy of the pages and handed them to Zhou, who put on his glasses and began to read. Li sat beside him, silently fuming. He was in command here, not his father. It was his right to read the document first. Zhou sat back and smiled up at Juwan.

"This could be enlightening, Mr. Brugg," he said. "My satellite telecommunications company in China has monitored and decrypted five unusual telephone transmissions that were sent and received from this area of the Bahamas since our arrival. These are the decrypted messages."

Juwan was still staring at the incompetent Alvarez. As soon as his mother returned, Juwan planned to ask her to find replacements for both Alvarez and the missing Bardot. Juwan had thought the Haitian had all the right talents, but he had obviously been wrong.

"Allow me to translate for you," went on Zhou.

"One moment," said Juwan. "Varna, please give us a few minutes alone."

Li watched as the Panamanian got up from the couch and obediently went to the door. It was clear that Juwan did not want Varna involved in his business activities. At the door, Varna turned and briefly glared at Li with a look of such hatred that Li thought the others might pick it up. Zhou waited until the door closed again.

"Four of the messages relate to desperate transmissions made to and from a pleasure yacht named *Hoops Heaven*. Apparently, the owner is a famous American sports millionaire who disappeared two nights ago. In one transmission, the owner's wife is asking someone at the White House to send troops to find him."

"That doesn't involve us," said Juwan firmly. "What about the other one?"

"It was an encrypted telephone call that originated in Montevideo and went to someone here in Dunmore Town," said Zhou. "Only the last part of the transcript is complete. It concerns a man named Dieter Jensen who was lost overboard from a boat when he was fifteen years old. He is referred to as a mascot of the crew. The last line reads 'June is dead.' "

"I don't know any June," said Juwan, "but there is a hermit named Dieter who lives on a small island beyond the Backbone near Spanish Wells." Turning to Alvarez, he said, "Call Ames at the police station and find out the last name of Crazy Dieter."

While Alvarez placed the call, Juwan said, "This hermit isn't fifteen years old. He was an old man when I was a little boy. He has to be pushing ninety."

"Ninety," repeated Zhou, thinking about the math for ten seconds. "That would suggest he might have been fifteen during the Second World War."

He looked up at Juwan.

"The ship we are looking for that carried the Peking Man was sunk in 1942," said Zhou. "You indicated to us last night that our rivals have been diving on a ship here. That suggests they already knew its location when the call about this man arrived this morning."

Alvarez ended his telephone connection and said, "His last name is Jensen."

"It cannot be a coincidence," said Zhou. "He may hold the key to finding the Peking Man on this island."

"Your homo," said Juwan, unwilling yet to challenge the lie.

"Yes," said Zhou. "We will need to question this hermit immediately."

"My lord," said Li after reading the transcription, "the message was recorded four hours ago. If it actually went to our enemies, then they are presumably on their way to this island or already there."

"A very good point, my son," agreed Zhou, sounding as if he actually meant it.

"Do we know if they are armed?" asked Li.

Alvarez leaned close to Juwan and whispered that whoever had rescued the man from under the guardhouse had taken at least two machine guns.

"Yes, they are armed," said Juwan.

Twenty minutes later, they were exiting the fleet of Humvees by the pier where Zhou's recovery vessel had been tethered for the duration of the storm. On the way there, Juwan had pressed to have seven of the elite members of his guard unit join in the assault on Dieter's Island.

"They know these islands like the backs of their asses," asserted Juwan, "and how to fight here under these conditions."

Before Li could pull his father aside long enough to say that he did not trust the hulking Bahamian any more than his dead mother, Zhou had already agreed to the idea. As they were going aboard the ship, Varna ran from one of the Humvees to join Juwan at the foot of the gangway.

Reaching up, he hugged the bigger man until Juwan was forced to gently push him away. From the top of the gangway, Li looked down and saw the Panamanian remove an envelope from his pocket and thrust it into Juwan's hands. In the pelting rain, Juwan just shoved it inside his coat before heading up the gangway.

He should have killed the Panamanian while he had the chance, thought Li, as he headed inside the passageway to the bridge. As the crew of the recovery vessel loosened the mooring lines and prepared to depart, the assault team leaders assembled on the bridge.

Colonel Mu had already used the ship's satellite scanner to project a virtual image of Dieter's Island on a flatscreen monitor mounted faceup beside the chart table.

"I would propose that we make separate landings with the ship's two assault boats," said Juwan. "Each one is big enough to carry eight fully equipped men."

He pointed down at the virtual image of the island on the monitor.

"Lee Wee here can land one of the boats with his seven men near the beach on the northern edge of the island," he said, pointing at the map. "I'll take the other boat with my seven and land on the opposite side near this mangrove swamp. It will make for harder going for us, but we can cut a path through it much faster than Lee Wee's men."

"That is generous," said Zhou, momentarily bowing his head.

"There is only one section of high ground on the island and it is somewhere in the middle," went on Juwan. "I remember that's where the hermit's shack used to be before Hurricane Andrew blew it away. We'll have whoever is there caught in a cross fire."

Juwan didn't tell the little Chinaman that the mangrove swamp where he would be landing was by far the easier assault point. From the one time he was on the island after the hurricane, he knew there was a path through it that would allow them a straight shot to the hermit. Beyond the beach on the north side where Lee Wee was going was a patchy network of bogs. From what the old Chinaman had said, getting to Crazy Dieter first might secure the treasure, whatever it was.

Li looked at the configuration of the island on the flat screen and said, "Yes. That could work."

Aside from what the ape had just said, the plan made sense to him. There would be no way for anyone on the island to escape from between the pincers of the attack. His eyes came to rest on the breast pocket of Juwan's military fatigues.

A corner of the white envelope was sticking up. Li could only assume that Varna had written out his confession and, based on the look he had given him in the theater, blamed him for the woman's death. In truth he had only been defending himself.

As soon as Brugg read the confession, Li knew, he would come after him. That was a given after what Li had seen him do to the basketball referees with twenty thousand people watching. Li had to somehow find a way to remove the letter from his pocket before Brugg read it or deal with him preemptively as soon as he had the chance on the island.

Li suddenly felt the ship cant over sharply to the left as it reached open sea, and he almost fell over onto the deck before he could brace his legs. At the same time, a full coffee mug slid straight off the chart table. Li watched as Brugg deftly plucked it out of the air without spilling a drop. For a big man, his reflexes were astonishingly quick.

"I will not be accompanying you," said Zhou. "As much as I would like to be there for the recovery of Peking Man, my participation would only be a hindrance to the success of your mission. I can tell you that your success will be rewarded in every way my grateful nation can provide."

Juwan showed no reaction as someone thrust open a hatch to the bridge deck and a burst of howling wind slashed through the compartment. The little Chinaman's words only confirmed that the story of the homo was a dodge. If they were paying him five million dollars to find it, then the real treasure had to be worth far more.

Zhou left the bridge to go to his private stateroom. Li followed him.

"This is the most important opportunity I have ever given you," said Zhou when they were alone, his eyes boring in on Li's.

"When we return to China with the fossil, I will see

that you are rewarded with a seat on the politburo. Your future as an independent oligarch will be assured."

"Thank you, my lord," said Li.

"If you do not return with the fossil, do not return," said Zhou.

THIRTY-EIGHT

30 May
Dieter's Island
Off Devil's Backbone
North Eleuthera
Bahamas

The wind outside the stone hut was easily gusting sixty miles an hour, thought Macaulay as he watched a huge palm frond sail past the window. He glanced at his watch. The storm would reach its peak in a couple of hours. They needed to find the fossil and get back to Mike McGandy's boat as quickly as possible.

"When we first came to this place, there was a half-burned shack built by whoever had once lived here," said Jensen. "The next morning I found an old skiff that had been left behind too. When I felt strong enough, I rowed the wounded man over to the mainland in the dark and left him there on the dock. I later learned the place was called Spanish Wells."

"What did you do with the glass containers that were inside the red crate?" asked Lexy gently.

"I opened the crate a few days later," said Dieter Jensen. "It contained the bones of a man. I knew from the way they had been carefully packed in the glass containers that he had been a person someone had loved and cared about in his life."

The old man's blue eyes were almost young again as he looked at her. A ghastly smile exposed his almost toothless mouth.

"My father was a Lutheran minister in Dortmund," he said. "I knew the words. I gave him a proper burial out of respect for his family. I said the words over his grave."

Lexy remembered the crosses she had seen across the field. "Did you bury him in the cemetery near the pine grove?"

"I buried a lot of things there over the last seventy years," he said. "I've had many friends, dogs, cats, birds . . . also a man whose body I found in the mangroves after the big hurricane. It's the only dry ground on the island to bury anything."

"Do you remember where you buried the man in the crate?"

Jensen nodded. "I erected a stout cross over the grave a few months after I got here."

"Can you take us to it?" asked Lexy.

The old man nodded.

"Do you know who the man was?" he asked, standing up from the chair. "The man in the crate?"

"Yes," said Lexy.

The old man started to open the driftwood door and turned to face them.

"You must follow in my footsteps," he said. "Do not stray off the path. There was a time when I was frightened they would try to take me away from here. I put . . . obstacles in their path if they came."

"What kind of obstacles?" asked Macaulay.

"Different things as they came to me," he said. "Once, I found a small barge beached in the lagoon. It was carrying outdated military stores from the naval base they closed down over there after the war. Before it freed itself and drifted off, I found some . . . good obstacles."

Taking in his words, Macaulay handed one of the machine guns to Lexy and strapped the second one over his shoulder. He found a box of bullets for the Lee-Enfield on one of the shelves and loaded the magazine before handing the rifle to Barnaby.

"Remember to use the right end if you need this," he said.

"I was once an Englishman and a Boy Scout," said Barnaby.

Two shovels were resting under a lean-to by the wall of the hut, and Macaulay slung them over his free shoulder as they headed out into the pelting rain. They were on the highest point of the island, and Macaulay could see a glimpse of ocean through the tree line.

Huge wind-driven rollers were pounding ashore near the northern end of the island, the foam-flecked green water surging deep inland before finally stopping to recede back. Jensen came to one of the side paths and led them down it.

Through the driving rain, the uneven row of wooden crosses that Lexy had seen on their approach to the old man's hut emerged out of the murky grayness. There were a dozen of them, several with little wooden boards carved with lettering. The graves were surrounded by a crude fence made of mangrove limbs.

Dieter stopped at a massive fan palm within the small grove of trees that ringed the old man's cemetery. Lexy saw a fluttering of wings above them and watched the man's pet frigate bird land nearby on the sand.

"Sometimes I forget who and what is buried around here," he said, "but I will always be thankful to this fan palm. I was tied to it when the big hurricane washed over the island. We survived together."

Macaulay quickly understood why Jensen had chosen this place for his cemetery. Unlike the boggy muck that coated most of the surface of the low-lying island, the soil was loamy and had good drainage.

"Keira here," barked a voice almost drowned out by the wind. It took Macaulay a moment to realize it was coming from the Motorola handheld radio attached to his belt.

"Back to Keira," said Macaulay after hitting the transmit button.

"Time to go," said McGandy while looking at the LED monitor of his Furuno radar system. "Large vessel approaching . . . definitely coming here . . . extraction now."

"Coming," said Macaulay, throwing down the shovel.

"We have to go," said Macaulay, picking up his machine gun.

"Who is coming?" demanded Dieter Jensen as Lexy hurried him along behind Macaulay and Barnaby. They had reached the main path again that led back to the life raft when Macaulay heard McGandy's voice again.

"Too late," he said. "Two small assault boats detached from ship. One going north round the island . . . the other south toward me."

"If you can see them, they can see you. Get out, Keira," ordered Macaulay.

"Soon," said McGandy, ending the call and pulling open one of the bulkhead lockers.

Macaulay gathered the others around him under the shelter of the grape arbor along the main trail.

"They obviously know we are here, and we can assume they know that Dieter's place is on the high ground. If we hole up there, they'll surround us right away. Our only chance is to have some mobility."

"Mobility?" muttered Barnaby, looking at their bedraggled crew.

"There is a natural chokepoint at the mangrove swamp," said Macaulay. "It would take hours to cut their way through it. They have to come along the path. One of us can stake out the trail where it opens up and can keep them bottled up there indefinitely."

"There is something else waiting for them along that path," said Jensen.

Based on the way he was shivering, Lexy thought he was coming down with fever. Barnaby saw it too.

"I'm a practiced hand now with this blunderbuss, General Macaulay," he said, still holding the Lee-Enfield. "Just show me where I need to be lurking in ambush when they emerge."

Macaulay quickly led him back from the grape arbor past the grove of *Chrysophyllum* trees. As they were about to clear the tree line, Macaulay saw a small declivity in the ground off to the right beneath the dense foliage. It was about fifty yards from where the path came out of the swamp.

Pushing through the ground vegetation, he said, "This is as good as we could hope to find. Aside from the muzzle flash of the rifle, they won't be able to see you. Your field of fire includes twenty yards on both sides of the path in case they try to flank you."

"How long should I try to hold?" asked Barnaby, abandoning any attempt at humor.

"The magazine is full," said Macaulay. "Ten shots. Just try to keep track of them and save a couple for when you have to pull back."

Barnaby unlocked the bolt to open the breech and smoothly shoved it home again to insert a round in the chamber. Macaulay extended his hand and Barnaby took it in his own.

"Don't wait too long," said Macaulay as they shook hands. "I'll see you back at the ranch."

"The good old ranch," said Barnaby, dropping to his belly and lying behind the declivity.

Lexy and the old man were waiting for Macaulay when he arrived back at the grape arbor.

"Where do you think I should meet the group coming in from the other side?" Macaulay asked Jensen.

"Behind the beach they will have to cross a boggy place," said the old man. "You want to move them toward the right of it after they come ashore. That row of boulders down there will give you a good firing position."

"Barnaby and I will fall back to the stone hut if we have to," said Macaulay to Lexy. "You stay safe until we get back."

Lexy reached out to embrace him for several seconds.

Macaulay suddenly heard what sounded like rapid fire from the south side of the island beyond the mangroves.

"That's Mike McGandy, I think," said Macaulay, "giving our friends down there an island welcome."

Yanking the bolt back to arm the Steyr AUG machine gun, he headed down the slope toward the row of boulders.

THIRTY-NINE

"I'm taking automatic fire from across the lagoon," said Juwan Brugg calmly and evenly into his radio. "Can you take it out?"

"Yes, we have it," came back the voice of Colonel Mu from the bridge of the recovery vessel.

Mu could see the position of the boat on the bridge repeater scan. It looked to be about thirty-five feet long and was stopped in the water on the opposite side of the lagoon from the planned landing spot.

"Arm a Dragonfly," ordered Mu into the bridge communicator as Zhou sat in the captain's elevated bridge chair and observed the progress of the mission.

The ship was violently pitching and rolling in the open sea, which made the Dragonfly a perfect choice. It was a cannon-launched guided projectile system, Chinese-designed, and the latest development in close-in weapon systems.

"Ready to fire," came the voice of the gunnery officer in the ship's fire control center.

"Lock on the target and fire when ready," ordered Mu.

Zhou felt the ship shudder momentarily as it yawed wildly in the heavy sea. Looking out the bridge window, he saw the fiery trail of what looked like a fireworks rocket disappearing into the gloom.

Ten seconds later, Colonel Mu looked up from the radar screen.

"The target has disappeared," he said.

Juwan stared in awe as the boat across the lagoon exploded before his eyes in a fiery ball of flame. There would be no more trouble from that quarter.

"Take us in," he ordered the helmsman.

A minute earlier, they had been about to run the assault boat up onto the path leading into the mangrove swamp when someone had cut loose at them with what sounded like a Browning Automatic Rifle.

It had raked the stern of the assault boat, nearly cutting in half one of the men deployed there and badly wounding a second one. When Lieutenant Alvarez said the wounded man would probably not survive, Juwan ordered them both jettisoned over the side.

He had already lost two of his seven men and they weren't even on the island yet. Maybe he should have had Lee Wee take this landing spot after all, he thought, as the assault boat came up out of the roiling water and lodged firmly on the path.

He had them over the side and forming up a few moments later. The point man in the guard unit called out to Juwan to join him farther up the path. When he got there, the guard pointed to an inflated four-man life raft tied bow and stern to the mangrove roots. Juwan gave it a three-second burst with his machine gun.

"Let them float on that," he said.

Li Shen Wui's assault boat raced out of control through the mountainous waves, the low turbulent pitch of the engines becoming an angry roar as they burst out of the sea and clawed through the air before dropping back down again and gaining purchase.

Through the curtain of rain ahead of them, he saw the landing beach suddenly materialize out of the gloom. It was a miracle that his helmsman had found the narrow section of beach they were aiming for instead of the coral outcroppings that bordered it in both directions.

He felt the assault boat surging up to take the next wave. It lifted them higher and higher until he saw that it would carry them straight across the beach and into the line of palm trees beyond it.

At the speed they were going, the boat would disintegrate if it collided with one of the trees. The wave descended toward the beach with a savage fury and the boat somehow slipped safely between two of the trees before coming to rest in a patch of ground vegetation.

He was out of the boat and ordering the men to form up alongside him a few seconds later. On the gentle upslope ahead of them, there were no other trees or vegetation. It looked more like marshland. To the left at the top of the slope were a few boulders, slick with rain.

Li ordered the men to keep at least five feet apart and to begin moving forward. The powerful wind kept pulling at him, peppering his face with sand and stinging his eyes. He should have remembered to bring goggles, he thought, as they pressed forward toward the marsh.

Li heard the stutter of machine-gun fire, a short burst. The man on the far left of the line dropped in his tracks and didn't move again. Two single shots rang out and the second man in line went down.

Li braced himself against the wind and fired back at the muzzle flashes near the boulders. When he looked up again, the rest of his men were running to the right away from the line of fire.

Li was following them when he heard another commando scream out in terror. He was only twenty feet ahead of him and appeared to be unwounded. As Li ran toward him, he saw that the man was standing in what looked like mud up to his thighs.

As Li watched, the mud rose quickly to his waist and then up to his chest, all in a few seconds. The man was extending his gun stock as far as he could, pleading with the man closest to him to pull him out.

"Don't go any closer," Li ordered as one of the others responded by stepping toward him.

A few seconds later the man's head disappeared.

"Keep moving to the right," yelled Li to the other three survivors.

More shots rang out from the top of the slope. They were no longer coming from the boulders. Either the man was moving with them or there was more than one. In a flash of lightning, Li saw the man outlined in the momentary glare of light. Li fired a long burst at him from his QBZ-95 assault rifle. He couldn't be sure, but it looked as though the man fell.

The remaining four men were strung out ahead of him as they attempted to get around the marsh. Li watched as one ran headlong into a tree. When Li came up on him, the man was lying on his back and gagging from the blood flowing into his mouth from his broken nose.

"Get moving," he demanded, kicking the man in the ribs, "or I'll kill you myself."

The man rolled over onto his knees, stood up, and saluted before following Li up the slope.

Barnaby stared across the field of saw grass that bordered the narrow path leading from the mangrove swamp. It had only been a minute since he had heard the explosion in the lagoon and seen the cone of fire erupt over the mangrove trees.

As he watched, a man stepped out of the cloaking murk of the dense trees. He was wearing a commando uniform with a Kevlar helmet and moving ahead slowly and cautiously, training his assault rifle first left and then right across the field ahead of him.

Barnaby sighted him through the aperture peep sight on top of the Lee-Enfield as another man emerged from the tree line, ten feet behind him. Like the man walking point, he swung the weapon to the left and right, looking for a potential ambush in the saw grass.

Barnaby waited until the first man was thirty feet out into the field. Aiming low at his legs, he gently squeezed the trigger. The harsh kick from the .303 cartridge slammed the stock backward into his right shoulder. He slid the bolt open and rammed it back home, inserting another round in the chamber.

The point man staggered forward several yards clutching his stomach before dropping facedown on the path. A third man had emerged from the trees, but he turned and ran back into the tree line.

The second one was caught in the open. Barnaby was about to fire again when the commando leaped off the trail into the saw grass. He had gone no more than five yards when he suddenly disappeared. A few moments later, Barnaby could hear his bellowing cries of pain.

He remembered the old man saying that there was something else waiting for them along the path. By the time the man stopped shouting, Barnaby could only assume it was a pit of some kind with sharpened stakes, the kind he had seen in the New Guinea jungles as a young archaeologist on his first expedition.

He could see no more movement inside the mangrove trees, and wondered how many commandos had landed on his side of the island. He knew there was at least one still across the field and probably more. He needed to be patient and conserve his ammunition. He still had nine rounds left.

Macaulay dragged himself away from the slope and back toward the stone hut. The last round fired by the Chinese commando had torn a hole through the fleshy part of his thigh. He knew it had grazed the bone because the pain was excruciating. A steady gout of blood was pouring from the exit hole and he knew he couldn't walk.

He quickly removed the arm strap from his machine

gun. After tightening it around his upper thigh and slowing the blood flow to a seeping ooze, he began crawling
back to Jensen's hut. In the distance, he heard the sound
of heavy rifle fire. It was the Lee-Enfield.

It was all going badly. While waiting for the Chinese
to land on the beach, he had heard the boom of an explosion and looked back to the south to see an eruption of
flames shooting high above the mangroves. It could only
have been Mike McGandy's dive boat. He had stayed behind too long. Macaulay tried not to think of his unborn
daughter, Keira, or how he would explain it to Mike's
wife, Cora. If he survived to see her again.

The last Macaulay had seen of the Chinese, they were
moving off to the right. It was only a matter of time before
they stopped and turned back toward the high ground and
Dieter's hut. He hoped he could get there first.

Juwan knelt on the path inside the mangroves and considered
his next step. He had seen the last muzzle flash from the trees
on the other side of the field. Whoever was out there had
been smart enough to recognize the natural ambush point and
had staked out the path. He had to deal with it before he
could get to the hermit.

"Crazy Dieter booby-trapped the field," he said to his
last three men.

He took two of them aside. Both were equipped with
machetes.

"I want you to cut your way through the vines for at
least twenty meters," said Juwan, pointing at the jungly
growth on both sides of the path inside the tree line.
"That should take you beyond his field of fire. The saw
grass in the field is three feet high. Stay low once you get

into it and get around behind him. Look out for more booby traps."

As the two commandos began hacking their way through the trees, Juwan crept forward and rested the barrel of his assault rifle in the crook of a tree where the trunk met a low branch. Setting it on single fire, he sighted it into the clump of trees where he had seen the last muzzle flash. He waited ten seconds and fired. And then again. And again.

Barnaby lay flat on his stomach in his muddy hole and waited. Whoever was firing at him from inside the mangroves knew where he was. The second round had slammed into the trunk of the tree right behind him. He thought about moving to a different position, but the declivity where he was lying was the only one in either direction. Getting up would only expose him to their fire.

Through the pelting rain, his eyes were drawn to something that appeared to move for a moment in the mangroves to the left of the path. Another brief movement followed it. After watching for several more seconds, he realized it was vines and branches dropping away to the ground. It had to be a man cutting his way through.

He raised the big Lee-Enfield to his shoulder and searched for the movement through the aperture peep sight. Finding it again, he tried to take into account the man's approximate height and position behind the cutting tool. He squeezed off a round. Nothing else moved. Return fire drove him back into the hole.

Li came out of the marsh area to find himself on a large path near a wooden grape arbor. One direction led up to higher ground off to the left. From that direction, he could hear only the shrieking wind. He heard gunfire from the direction leading to the south side of the island. Along with the reverberation of the light machine guns Brugg's men were carrying, he heard two shots close by from a heavier-caliber rifle.

Assembling the four remaining Chinese, he said, "Reconnoiter the trail heading up to the high ground. There should be a shack or a house up there. Kill anyone you find along the way unless it's an old man. Do not kill the old man."

"How will we know?" asked one of them.

"By getting close enough to see before you shoot," said Li. "I need the old man alive."

The four commandos saluted him before splitting up into pairs, spreading out, and moving slowly up along both sides of the path past the grape arbor. Li headed toward the sound of the firing.

FORTY

Juwan Brugg knelt behind the tree inside the perimeter of the mangrove trees and waited for the commando he had sent off to the left to get across the booby-trapped field behind the shooter.

After hearing the last two shots, he had ordered the only commando still with him to follow the trail of the one who had been hacking his way through the mangroves to the right. He had come back to report that the man was dead. Juwan ordered him to go back and finish cutting the path and circle around behind the ambusher from the right.

Juwan's fury was mounting uncontrollably. He had no more men on the recovery vessel and no way to bring more over from Dunmore Town in the middle of the storm. By now the little Chinaman Lee Wee was probably at the hermit's hut and torturing the secret out of Crazy Dieter. Meanwhile he was still pinned down in the mangroves with only two commandos left.

It was getting darker as the storm approached its full fury. Juwan was looking intently across the field in the direction of the ambusher when something emerged from the clump of trees. Through the rain and mist, he saw it was a man, a man almost as tall as himself.

Juwan raised the machine gun to his shoulder and was about to fire when he saw that the tall man was unarmed. Someone behind him was shoving him forward. The commando he had sent off to the left must have gotten around behind him and captured him, he decided.

He should have killed him, thought Juwan. Now he would enjoy the pleasure of doing it himself before moving on to the hermit. He stood up and headed out along the path across the field. He saw the ambusher stumble and almost fall as the commando behind him shoved his gun hard in the man's back.

Juwan heard a roaring sound. It seemed to come from a long way off. A brutal gust of wind nearly drove him sideways off the trail and a solid wall of rain swept over him like a silver impenetrable curtain.

Juwan couldn't see more than ten feet in any direction as he kept walking forward along the path. The figure of the tall man finally materialized out of the rain coming slowly toward him. He was old and his face was gaunt. Blood was running down his forehead from a wound on his scalp. His eyes seemed unfocused.

"Why didn't you kill him?" Juwan yelled to the obscured figure behind him as the tall man fell to his knees.

Li Shen Wui stepped from behind Barnaby. His eyes went straight to the breast pocket in Juwan's combat fatigues. The envelope was no longer visible. He could see the rage in Brugg's face.

"You read the note," shouted Li over the wind, glancing in both directions to make sure none of Brugg's men were in sight.

Juwan didn't hear what the little Chinaman said. He was intent on killing the ambusher and moving on to the hermit's hut. As Brugg raised his machine gun, Li brought his own assault rifle to bear.

"I killed your mother," he screamed, firing three rounds at point-blank range.

Li watched the three holes appear in a straight, even pattern across his massive chest. Confusion replaced rage in Juwan's face as he dropped his gun and stared down wonderingly at the wounds in his chest. Blackness began to boil up behind his eyes.

"I killed your mother," Li screamed again as Juwan fell backward onto the shell-covered path.

Barnaby remained on his knees gazing at the huge man lying next to him on the ground. His head was still ringing from the first blow he had received while lying inside the tree line. With the noise of the rain and wind, he had no idea someone was even behind him when he felt his head explode. He had been on his knees and getting up when the man slammed him again with the gun barrel.

When Barnaby looked up into the Chinese man's eyes, he saw there would be no clemency. There would be no way to reason with this one or to bargain for his life. He looked as merciless and primitive as an ax blade.

The driving rain slowly rinsed the blood from his face. As he waited for his execution, two more commandos appeared through the curtain of rain and slowly approached the big man's body.

"Your leader has been killed," said Li. "He died a noble death."

"What about him?" asked one of them, looking down at Barnaby.

"Bring him," said Li. "He may have value as a temporary hostage."

FORTY-ONE

A stabbing pain brought Macaulay out of his daze. He realized he had been unconscious. He didn't know for how long. He lay on the path leading to the hut.

Behind his eyes, something floated like an amoeba. The pain from the thigh wound was a blinding agony, shooting upward from the shattered bone in his leg to the nerve endings in his head and back again. He felt a rising nausea as he began dragging himself again on his belly toward the hut.

The storm must be close to reaching its peak, he thought. The wind was now a constant thunderous roar. He tasted salt on his lips, a combination of rain and sea spray. The feeble daylight was nothing more than shades of charcoal, from light to dark gray. He edged forward on the path, not daring to look around behind him.

A moment later, he felt two hands gently lifting his face. He looked up to see the frightened eyes of Lexy. Beyond her stood the old man. Together, they raised him by the shoulders and began dragging him toward the hut. Macaulay passed out again.

The Chinese commando closest to the hut watched as they dragged him toward the open door. He was still too far away to know for sure which one might be the old man. He was not about to kill the wrong one. He had once seen Li Shen Wui skin a man alive.

The commando turned around to see Li coming up the path together with the other three remaining Chinese. Behind them, two of the local black commandos were hustling along a tall prisoner. The man was bleeding from a head wound and looked worn-out.

"What do you have to report?" demanded Li.

"There are at least three people in the hut," said the commando, saluting.

"How do you know that?"

"One of them was wounded," he answered. "The other two dragged him into the hut."

"Why didn't you shoot the wounded man?" demanded Li.

"I was following your orders about not killing the old man."

"Why would the old man be wounded?" screamed Li.

The commando had no answer.

"I will deal with you later," said Li.

Macaulay regained consciousness to find himself lying on the old man's bunk. Lexy had lowered his trousers far enough to bandage his thigh wound with a gauze compress and tape from Jensen's medical kit.

"The bullet went through your leg, Steve," she said. "You've lost a lot of blood."

A shot rang out. A split second later the edge of the open window slit near the hut door exploded in a hail of stone splinters. A second shot found the same narrow opening. Lying on the bed, Macaulay heard the slug slam into the coquina rock wall behind him followed by the loud twang of the ricochet as it buried itself in the shelf across the hut, smashing two jars of fruit.

Lexy sat with her back to the wall facing the path. The old man stood near her dumbfounded, staring at the dripping juice. The next shot through the window slit ricocheted off the back wall and struck the rock ledge inches from Lexy, peppering her face with rock fragments.

"Someone is coming," said Dieter Jensen, looking through a crack in the stout door.

Lexy picked up the machine gun from the table and went to the edge of the window slit. Peering out, she saw Barnaby standing in the middle of the path fifty feet away from the hut. A black man in a commando uniform stood behind him pointing an assault rifle at his back.

Five more commandos were positioned behind trees and rocks farther away along the path. A Chinese man with gold stars on the collar of his uniform was approaching the hut carrying a sodden white towel. Unarmed, he stopped a few feet short of the door.

"I hope you appreciated my warning," shouted Li to make his voice heard over the wind. "Now please bring out the man Jensen or I will be forced to kill Dr. Finchem."

"He'll kill him anyway," said Macaulay from the bed, "and then us."

The old man shuffled toward the secured door.

"I cannot allow the man outside to die over the bones of a man long dead," he said.

"Once you show him where the bones are buried, he'll kill you too," said Macaulay.

"Why are the bones so important?" asked Dieter Jensen.

"They are much older than we led you to believe," said Lexy. "He may be one of the earliest of our human ancestors. Some people revere him as a god."

"If you come out now," shouted Li, "I give you my word of honor that you will not be harmed. I am only interested in Peking Man. After I have him, you will be free to go."

"He's lying," said Macaulay.

"Yes," agreed Lexy, "but what choice do we have?"

"Then let it be on your conscience," shouted Li as he turned around and slowly headed back up the path.

"I will not allow your friend to be murdered for the sake of a man's bones, no matter how valuable they might be," said Dieter.

Removing the timber beam securing the door, he swung it open and stepped outside into the rain.

"If you do not harm these people, I will show you the place where the bones are buried," Jensen called out to Li.

"It is agreed," yelled Li. "I am a man of my word."

Lexy helped Macaulay to his feet and put her arm under his shoulder to assist him to the open door.

"He needs help," called out Lexy.

Li ordered Brugg's two commandos to carry Macaulay. Stepping forward, they locked their wrists under his rump and carried him down the path through the driving rain. He lost consciousness again. Lexy joined Barnaby as they reached the side path that led toward Dieter's cemetery. She saw the open wound on Barnaby's head and put her arm around him.

"I deeply regret that my foolhardiness has led us to this end," he said.

"I'm an independent woman above all else," said Lexy. "I'm here because I wanted to be."

Closely followed by the armed men, Dieter Jensen didn't say a word as he led Li and the others into the crudely fenced graveyard. Lexy saw a familiar fluttering of wings above her head and watched as Dieter's frigate bird landed on top of one of the crosses marking a grave site.

As the bird sat adjusting its plumage, Lexy heard another shot and watched the bird drop to the ground in a bloody mess of feathers and bone. Jensen looked down at his friend's remains as Li holstered his semiautomatic pistol.

"No flying witnesses allowed," said Li, grinning at the other commandos.

The pistol shot brought Macaulay up out of his stupor again. The men carrying him had set him back down on the ground near the fenced graveyard with his back to the base of the huge fan palm tree. Barnaby and Lexy were standing alongside him. Two Chinese commandos stood guard with cocked weapons trained on them.

Fifty feet away, Dieter Jensen walked to a battered old wooden cross on the far edge of the cemetery.

"Here is where to dig," he said.

FORTY-TWO

Dieter picked up a short stick and marked off a five-foot-square section of ground beside the cross.

"The crate is quite large," shouted Jensen over the wind as he stepped back from the plot.

Hearing his words, Barnaby and Macaulay exchanged puzzled glances. They had both seen what remained of the red crate with Chinese lettering on it in the old man's hut. What crate was he talking about?

The two shovels that Macaulay had brought along earlier from the stone hut were still lying on the ground where he had left them. Li ordered Brugg's two surviving commandos to begin digging out the plot.

The soil was soft and easily dug. A mound of it grew higher as the hole went deeper. Li stood ten feet away with two of his commandos, a triumphant smile on his face. At one point, he looked over at his three captives at the base of the huge fan palm.

Macaulay caught the momentary unveiled expression in his eyes, the way a feral and hungry fox might look at the captive chickens in the henhouse. He knew Li would have them killed as soon as the Peking Man was safely aboveground.

The two diggers were down to a depth of three feet when Li heard a loud crunch as one of the shovels struck something hard.

"Be careful," he shouted as the men used the edges of the spades to clear the surface of what soon emerged from the loamy soil as the top section of a wooden crate.

"Come out of there," ordered Li.

As the two diggers were climbing out of the hole, Macaulay saw Li motion to the two Chinese standing nearby him. Brugg's men were walking toward them with satisfied smiles when the two Chinese raised their assault rifles and cut them down with two short bursts. Both were still moving. Li stepped close and shot each of them in the head with his pistol.

One of the Chinese commandos guarding Macaulay and the others looked down at him and said, "You kill my brother. You next."

"Let us see what we have," said Li, approaching the burial pit. "You had better have been telling the truth, old man."

Dieter Jensen was hunched over, leaning awkwardly for support against the nearest cross member. He had seemed to visibly weaken as the two men were digging the hole. Drenched by the pitiless rain, the old man was now shivering almost uncontrollably.

"You must be careful," said Jensen. "The glass containers are very fragile."

"Remove the top section," ordered Li.

The two closest commandos put their assault rifles down and dropped into the large hole. Carefully inserting the edges of the shovels under the cross-hatched wooden cover, they slowly pried it up. The men guarding the prisoners couldn't contain their curiosity and kept turning to look back at the discovery.

Macaulay suddenly remembered Dieter Jensen telling them about the things he had found on the barge carrying outdated military supplies. To make obstacles he had said.

As if in silent communion, Dieter Jensen stared over at Macaulay while continuing to lean on the wooden cross. Without attracting the attention of the commandos in the hole, he slowly waved his index finger in a circle, as if signaling it was time to go.

Barnaby was already screened from the burial hole by the broad stem of the palm. Macaulay was not. He waited for the guards to look back at the pit again and slid his legs farther around the base. Lexy was still standing fully exposed to the excavated plot, her eyes drawn in sympathy to the old man teetering on the cross at the edge of the hole.

The two commandos in the pit gently removed the crosshatched crate cover and laid it down next to the hole. Li saw that there were several inches of straw covering the next layer. He ordered the commandos to scoop it away.

Beneath the straw was a layer of heavy fiberboard. The

commandos removed the sheath knives from their belts and inserted them into the outer edges. After cutting around the entire length, they removed the fiberboard layer and tossed it over the wooden crate cover.

The contents of the crate lay exposed for the first time. Under the sheeting rain, it looked at first to Li like a bed of large orange mushrooms packed in individual wooden compartments. The painted metal crowns of the mushrooms were three inches in diameter. He wondered if the bones were individually packaged under the crowns.

Behind him, Dieter Jensen picked up one of the shovels and stepped to the edge of the pit. Jumping down on top of the open crate, he lifted the shovel in the air and then rammed the point of it down on one of the orange crowns. Li suddenly realized what they were, that the mushrooms were actually contact fuses on the nose tips of old artillery shells.

"Kill him," screamed Li as he pivoted away from the pit and began running.

One of the commandos in the pit raised the pistol from his belt and shot the old man in the head as he was bringing the shovel down on the contact fuse for a second time.

Macaulay grabbed Lexy by the knees and heaved her behind the massive base of the palm, enveloping her body under his. His guard turned back to see the movement and aimed his rifle at Macaulay's back.

Before he could pull the trigger, a man-made clap of thunder erupted from the burial pit, disintegrating the two commandos inside it along with the already dead Jensen. Seconds later, the shock wave of the blast obliterated everything in the surrounding graveyard as flames from the exploding ordnance erupted a hundred feet into the sky.

Barnaby watched as the two commandos guarding them were ripped off their feet and driven twenty feet in the air into the stand of pines that fringed the grove. Their bodies came to rest like broken rag dolls, one with his head missing and the other with his arms and legs flung out at impossible angles.

An unexploded shell landed with a loud thud a few feet away from Macaulay. Still protecting Lexy with his body, he saw the label on the side of the green cylinder. It read 4" NAVAL ILLUMINATING PROJECTILE.

A British naval star shell, thought Macaulay mechanically, probably military stores from the British naval base shut down at the end of the war. How many of them had detonated? he wondered. It couldn't have been the whole crate or they would have all been reduced to the bloody pulp that was all that was left of the men in the pit.

Barnaby gently pulled Macaulay off Lexy and helped her to her feet.

"We have to get Steve back to the stone hut," said Lexy, looking down at him.

Macaulay could barely hear her. He felt something warm running down his cheeks. A steady trickle of blood was streaming from both ears. The still-pounding rain quickly rinsed it away as Lexy and Barnaby began rigging a sling to carry him.

Barnaby looked for any sign that Li Shen Wui had survived the blast on the other side of the pit. There was nothing recognizable to be seen anymore. All traces of the cemetery and the vegetation beyond it were erased.

Macaulay passed out again when they were lifting him into the sling.

FORTY-THREE

30 May
Dieter's Island
Off Devil's Backbone
North Eleuthera
Bahamas

Zhou Shen Wui sat wedged into a chair in his stateroom aboard the recovery ship as it rocked and tossed in the brutal sea. He had been violently ill for the last two hours. The sour odor of his vomit filled the room as he waited for the sea to subside long enough to recover the assault boats and retrieve the Peking Man.

Spray was rattling against the portholes like hailstones as he heard a tap at the stateroom door.

"Enter," ordered Zhou.

It was Colonel Mu. His face was almost as green as Zhou's, although he had managed to control his stomach. His uniform was sopping wet. It was obvious that he had been outside on the deck and seen the conditions himself.

"The captain wishes me to respectfully give you his opinion that we can no longer stay here, my lord," said Mu.

"We cannot leave until the mission is completed," said Zhou firmly.

"My lord, the captain begs to inform you that he cannot hold his position in these seas," said Mu. "The barometer continues to fall and we are alarmingly close to the reef known locally as the Devil's Backbone. The captain says that if we do not navigate into safer waters, there is every possibility this ship will founder on the reef."

As if to confirm those conditions, the ship began to roll alarmingly over onto its left side. Colonel Mu lost his footing and fell sideways toward the bulkhead. Above his prone body, Zhou could see that the portholes were actually covered with seawater.

"What have you heard from my son?" demanded Zhou.

Regaining his footing, Mu held on to the table that was bolted to the deck and said, "We have lost communication with the penetration teams. Each one had a well-trained radioman equipped with a weatherproof transmitter. Both fell silent a short time after they landed on the island."

Zhou disentangled himself from his perch as the ship slowly righted itself again and went to the closest porthole. It was like no sea condition he had ever witnessed. The waves seemed as tall as the high-rise buildings in Shanghai. Even the cars of his supertrain would appear like toys against these monstrous and jagged mountains of water. For a moment, he wondered what it must be like for Li and his men on the little island.

"The captain recommends that we return to the protected anchorage at Dunmore Town until the storm subsides," said Mu.

The ship began another slow roll, this one more frightening than the last. Zhou returned to his perch and wedged himself in again. Beyond the stateroom door he could hear loud crashing noises as crockery and glasses broke loose from their cupboards in the dining compartment and smashed on the deck.

The ship began groaning loudly as it continued its roll. He could see how far the deck was slanted because it looked as if Mu were walking up a steep hill. It was so steep he could no longer stand on it and fell away toward the outer bulkhead. With horror, Zhou realized that the ship was not merely rolling. The deck remained slanted.

He waited breathlessly as the ship finally stopped rolling and began to come upright again. When it finally did, the motion did not stop, however. It kept rolling straight over to the other side, sending Mu tumbling through the air across the room again.

It is like living death, thought Zhou as he cracked his head against the corner of the metal cupboard by his chair and felt a jolt of dizzying pain.

"Tell the captain it is time to go," said Zhou.

"Yes, my lord," said Mu, dragging himself toward the stateroom door.

FORTY-FOUR

30 May
Dieter's Island
Off Devil's Backbone
North Eleuthera
Bahamas

Macaulay awoke to another clap of thunder and the gleam of a kerosene lamp in the shadowy light of the rock hut. He was lying on Dieter Jensen's bed. The wind was still shrieking like a demented chorus outside. Barnaby sat at the table eating peaches from a fruit jar. Lexy was trying to make the old man's decrepit radio work with the hand-crank generator.

"What time is it?" Macaulay asked.

Lexy's face lit up.

"You're back with us again," she said.

"You've only been out about thirty minutes," said Barnaby.

"I found an ampule of morphine in Dieter's medical

kit and a hypodermic needle," said Lexy. "Hopefully, it eased some of the pain."

Macaulay felt a deep ache inside him. His thigh was no longer on fire, the pain reduced to a dull throb unless he attempted to move it. He knew he couldn't walk. They would somehow have to carry him when it was time to go, or leave him and come back with more help.

"No lessening yet in the storm," said Barnaby, pointing down at the floor with his spoon. Macaulay glanced down. The stone outcropping was covered with six inches of water.

Barnaby had sealed the window slit opening with a block of coquina rock held in place by Jensen's heavy iron stove. The stout entrance door was secured with its length of timber inside its iron brackets.

"Are we expecting anyone?" asked Macaulay.

"No one has been invited for dinner, but it's better to be safe," said Barnaby, finishing the jar of peaches. "If you're hungry, I can offer you peaches and coconut milk."

His words were still in the air when they heard a loud rapping on the door. A shiver of fear crossed Lexy's face.

"If it was our friends from the ship, I doubt they would bother to knock," said Macaulay.

"It's me," came a voice over the wind. "Mike McGandy."

Lexy removed the brace and swung it open. McGandy swept in along with a rush of wind and driving rain. Lexy secured the door behind him.

"Sweet Jesus, I was sure you were done for," said Macaulay. "I thought your boat blew up."

"It did," said McGandy, shaking the rain off his poncho and sitting on a rock ledge. Barnaby handed him a fruit jar and he opened it, eating the Caribbean peaches greedily.

"I wrote off the boat when I decided there was no way I was going to get past that ship," he said, the juice running down his chin. "I figured if it had assault boats, the ship was equipped with smart weapons, and so I beached it across the lagoon at the closest island. When I opened fire on the assault boat with my BAR, it was from the shoreline. I think I put some hurt into them."

"How did you make it back over to Dieter's island?" asked Macaulay.

"I swam," he said.

"You swam back in this tempest?" asked Barnaby.

"You don't think black people know how to swim, Dr. Finchem?" he said in mock anger. "Actually I found one of the scuba rigs undamaged in the wreckage of my boat along with fins and a mask. Underwater it was easy."

"What are our chances of getting back across to Dunmore Town?" asked Barnaby. "We're going to need help from Washington to complete our mission."

"The storm should begin to lose power in an hour or so," said McGandy. "Between now and then, we ought to get Steve down to the mangroves. I found one of the assault boats there and it looks seaworthy. It also has secure radio communications gear aboard."

"We don't have any weapons," said Lexy. "Did you find any?"

McGandy shook his head.

"I don't think any of the Chinese are left," said Macaulay. "I dropped two of them near the beach and another went down in quicksand. Li and the other four were killed in the blast."

"I think I took care of at least two of Brugg's men in the boat," said McGandy. "I also found one dead in the mangroves and another along the path."

"One more was killed by an obstacle left by Mr. Jensen," added Barnaby.

"And two more were murdered by Li," said Lexy.

"That leaves one more," said Macaulay. "Probably Brugg."

"Wouldn't he have been at Dieter's cemetery with his two commandos if he was still alive?" asked Lexy.

No one answered.

"I think we'll just have to take the chance," said McGandy.

A few minutes later, he had rigged a crude litter for Macaulay with two lengths of two-by-fours inside one of Jensen's mattress covers. Barnaby and McGandy would carry him down to the mangroves. When they reached the assault boat, Barnaby would attempt to reach Ira Dusenberry at the White House.

They were on the main path and passing the grape arbor when a jagged spike of lightning lit up the purplish black sky. Lexy was following Barnaby, who was carrying the back end of the litter holding Macaulay. In the glare of the fire bolt, she turned to look over at the place where the cemetery had once existed. A few feet off the path, she saw something sticking out of the ground that glinted momentarily in the harsh light.

She walked over and bent down to pick it up. She was just starting to examine it when another flash of lightning revealed something so horrifying that it sent her reeling backward toward the path.

The man had been standing just a foot away from her.

All the hair had been burned off his scalp. His left eye was missing from its socket, and what had once been his face was now a fire-blistered horror.

Li Shen Wui was pointing his machine gun at her.

"Where is the Peking Man?" came the scream from his ruined mouth.

"We don't know where he's buried," said Lexy. "That's the truth."

"Then you are of no assistance to me," said Li, raising the barrel to her chest.

Macaulay saw it as an approaching monstrous shadow. Later, Barnaby said he thought it looked more like a moving basalt mountain. One moment, Li was about to fire the machine gun and the next he was enveloped face-to-face inside the massive arms of Juwan Brugg.

The Chinese dropped the machine gun and Lexy picked it up as Li was raised high in the air, furiously scissoring his legs. Fighting to release himself from Ju-wan's bear hug, he slashed down again and again with the heel of his hand at the bigger man's throat and face, all the while screaming something in Chinese.

Li tried to brace his legs against Juwan's knees to push away from him, but Juwan's strength seemed so massive there was no end to it. As the others watched silently, Li's efforts to break the hold slowly diminished as Juwan crushed the air out of his chest. The struggle ended with a loud crunching noise as Li's breastbone and ribs caved in.

When Juwan released him, Li crumpled in a heap to the ground.

"Sweet Jesus," said Macaulay.

Juwan Brugg stared down at the body for several seconds and then seemed to realize once more that he had three bullets in his chest. He looked toward the others and dropped to his knees.

"What was it you were all after?" he asked. "The treasure."

"*Homo erectus,*" said Barnaby before Brugg toppled over.

FORTY-FIVE

31 May
McGandy Clinic
Dunmore Town
North Eleuthera
Bahamas

Dazzling sunbeams splashed through the screened windows of the airy patient recovery room in Cora McGandy's medical clinic. The cobalt sea beyond the windows was calm and inviting.

Macaulay lay in a hospital bed with his elevated leg wrapped in pressure bandages. An X-ray had confirmed that the machine gun bullet had only grazed his fibula and Cora had assured him he would make a full recovery.

Lexy sat across the room from him in one of the two cushioned bamboo chairs examining a glass object. Barnaby was slumped in the second one, trying to stay awake. Since they had gotten back across the Devil's Backbone in the assault boat from Dieter's Island, he had wanted to do nothing but sleep.

That had been his plan for the entire day until he received word that the president's national security adviser was arriving by jet at the local airport in thirty minutes. Ira Dusenberry had come straight to the clinic.

"What happened to all your hair?" were Dusenberry's first words to the napping Barnaby when he stepped into the room. "You look like the loan officer at my bank."

"It was shorn for a good purpose," said Barnaby, waking up. "It may even have saved several lives."

"I'm glad to see you too, Dr. Vaughan, and of course General Macaulay, although it seems like whenever we meet, you're recovering from honorable wounds," said Dusenberry.

"Thanks to you," said Macaulay.

"Always in a good cause, I can assure you," said Dusenberry. "I gather you had a few challenges down here."

To Barnaby, it looked as if Dusenberry had grown exponentially since they last met in the situation room of the White House. He had abandoned his attempt to wear three-piece suits. His new tropical worsted suit jacket was bright orange and billowed away from his vast stomach like tent flaps.

"So, where are the Chinese?" asked Barnaby.

"Zhou Shen Wui left this morning after reporting the failure of his mission to his betters in China," said Dusenberry. "According to the transcript of the cable we just decrypted, he places the blame for failing to recover the Peking Man on his son, Li."

"It wasn't for lack of trying," said Lexy.

"Incidentally, where is the Peking Man?" asked Dusenberry. "Not that it's important anymore."

"He was on that island," said Barnaby. "He may still be there."

Barnaby described what led them to the old hermit's island, finding the remains of the red teak crate that had held the fossils, the ongoing gun battle in the storm, the massive blast of high explosives in the cemetery, and their survival at the hands of Juwan Brugg. By then, Dusenberry was checking his latest text messages on his smartphone.

"It sounds like one of those lurid thrillers I hate," he said, texting back to someone in Washington. "Anyway, I'll take it from here."

"We owe Mike McGandy a new dive boat," said Macaulay.

"That and any other losses he or the people you worked with here sustained," said Dusenberry. "By the way, I checked on your friend Carlos Lugo. He is at Bethesda Naval Hospital and doing well. They have plenty of experience treating battle casualties that lost toes and fingers."

"You said a little while ago that finding the Peking Man was no longer important," said Macaulay, his voice rising in anger. "Why not?"

"The important thing is that the Chinese now believe we have the Peking Man," said Dusenberry with an indulgent smile. "You found him. That's the message that is going to Beijing through back channels. The Peking Man was on the *Prins Willem* when you dove on it. The whole recovery is documented now thanks to you, Tommy Somervell, and June Corcoran. By the time Zhou Shen Wui gets home, he'll be facing a firing squad for letting Peking Man fall into the hands of the Americans."

"What about the religious movement . . . all those people who are getting slaughtered for their beliefs?" asked Barnaby.

"The word will continue to spread as it does with all these religious movements. They will believe that hope is on the way. Someday we'll deliver it."

"Yeah . . . that's great," said Macaulay.

"And you have earned the gratitude of the president," said Dusenberry. "He wanted me to tell you that you're all welcome in the White House for an overnight in the Lincoln Bedroom. For now, feel free to stay down here to recharge the batteries at the nation's expense."

"I'm flying back with you," snapped Barnaby. "There is someone I need to see in Cambridge."

The image of his natural blond goddess Astrud lying naked and waiting on his bear rug in the Viking bed was already recharging his own batteries.

Dusenberry's phone began to bleat like an angry gerbil.

"I have to take this. . . . Be back in a minute," he said, heading for the corridor outside.

When he was gone, Lexy brought the object she had been examining over to Barnaby.

"I found this last night," she said, putting it in his hand. "It was lying near the trail about fifty meters from the blast site."

The object was a jagged shard of glass, about two by three inches. One of the edges was straight and held a narrow wooden frame. In a corner of the frame were four tiny letters. Dusenberry put on his reading glasses to see them clearly.

"P . . . U . . . M . . . C," he said aloud.

"Peking Union Medical College," said Lexy. "You may recall that was where the Peking Man was packed in glass containers before the marine convoy picked up the red crate."

"Some of those containers might still be intact where the cemetery was," said Barnaby. "As soon as you get the general here on his feet and put the roses back in his cheeks, it might be worth another trip out there."

Lexy glanced out the window into a morning bathed in sunlight. Beyond the grounds of the clinic, the beach was littered with storm debris. As she watched, a spotted sandpiper landed near one of the fallen palm fronds.

The brown-and-white bird walked stealthily along the beach, occasionally stopping to stab its needle bill into the sand and extract its tiny unseen prey. She wondered how the sandpiper always knew it was there.

ACKNOWLEDGMENTS

I took substantial artistic license with this remarkable story. The mystery surrounding the disappearance of the Peking Man fossils on December 8, 1941, will almost certainly never be solved.

The fossils were probably lost forever near a railhead in Chinwangtao in northern China after the U.S. Marine detachment escorted them there from the Peking Union Medical College in the first tumultuous hours after the war began, only to discover that the ship they were planning to meet at the port city had been sunk. In all likelihood, Japanese soldiers captured and ransacked the crates containing the fossils and, failing to recognize their priceless value, trampled the bones into the dust.

I would like to thank my old friend, the fine historian Robert K. Krick, for tracking down a trove of illuminating military records concerning the disappearance of Peking Man at the Marine Corps Records Center in Quantico, Virginia.

The trove includes the most enlightening information I have yet read on the subject of the disappearance, including affidavits and letters from the commanding officer of the marine detachment at Peking in December 1941, his executive officer, and the American woman who packed the Peking Man fossils in glass containers before they were handed over to the marine detachment. The Quantico material comes closer to revealing the answer than anything else I have yet read.

I am also grateful to my friend Tom Hurd, who generously gave me valuable advice and suggestions on the plot and characters from inception to conclusion. I hope he writes his own book soon. He is a talented storyteller.

Finally, I wish to thank Brent Howard, my gifted editor at Penguin Random House, and David Halpern, my longtime wonderful literary agent. I benefit greatly from his guidance and support.

Readers who wish to contact the author are invited to do so at rjmrazek1942@gmail.com.

Also available from

Robert J. Mrazek

VALHALLA

Along the Greenland ice cap, an expedition team makes an astounding discovery. Buried five hundred feet below the ice cap is the wreckage of an ancient ship—and nine perfectly preserved Vikings. Rune markings indicate it went missing in 1016 BC.

Energized by the find, retired Air Force general Steven Macaulay assembles the foremost scholars of Norse archaeology, including Harvard academic and master decoder Lexy Vaughan. But the mission is violently sabotaged—because this discovery holds the key to a mystery that will change the human race.

To put together the pieces of the puzzle, Macaulay and Lexy plunge headlong into a web of chaos and betrayal—all the while hunted by a covert primeval society that will stop at nothing to protect their secrets.